# Lord of Midnight

ROMANCE

# Jo Beverley

# Lord of Midnight

WHEELER
PUBLISHING, INC.
ROCKLAND, MA

★ AN AMERICAN COMPANY ★

Published in Large Print by arrangement with Topaz, an imprint of
Dutton Signet, a member of Penguin Putnam, Inc.
in the United States and Canada

Wheeler Large Print Book Series.

Set in 16 pt Plantin.

·

*Library of Congress Cataloging-in-Publication Data*

Beverley, Jo.
   Lord of midnight / Jo Beverley.
     p. (large print)  cm.(Wheeler large print book series)
   ISBN 1-56895-662-2 (softcover)
   1. Large type books. I. Title. II. Series
[PR9199.3B424L66  1998]
813'.54—dc21                          98-34893
                                      CIP

*This book is dedicated with appreciation to*
*Jennifer Sawyer Fisher,*
*editor extraordinaire.*

*And to romance readers everywhere,*
*because they read for pleasure.*
*Every novel deserves to be closed*
*with a smile.*

# Chapter 1

With the rhythm of a tolling bell, men pounded stake after stake into the dry summer ground. Others trailed behind, tying ropes to mark off a grassy circle. A court battle, a battle to the death, would draw a fair crowd, and a crowd must be controlled.

On the dais, the carpenters' hammers beat a more urgent rhythm. The platform must be ready soon, ready for the king and his officers. It was a plain structure, without canopy or trimming for no ladies would attend. Today, this field would become a court of law, where men defended their right with their bodies.

It would also be a field of execution.

Shadowing the grassy circle loomed the White Tower, reminding all that the Norman kings were mighty, and not to be opposed. As proof of it, the recent rebellion had led here, led to this court of death.

Even before the pounding stopped, the first spectators trickled out from nearby streets and lanes, flowing around the ropes to seek the best viewpoints. Many still munched their breakfast bread, or swigged from pots of ale.

Vendors came too, crying ale! pies! and fruits! Entertainers tumbled to pipe and drum. Fortune-tellers read palms. Mountebanks offered nostrums and charms against all ills.

1

Though no noble ladies would attend, there were women among these common folk, both gawkers and money-makers, for courtly rules did not apply to them. Some had brought stitchery or spinning to do as they waited. Many had brought children.

"Morning, Truda," one woman said to another, distaff deftly feeding her spun thread. "Not be much of a fight, they say."

"Older against younger, aye. But you never know, Nan. Older ones are canny."

"Heard he wasn't much of a fighter, this Clarence of Summerbourne."

"Nah," Truda scoffed, shoving the last of some honeyed bread into her mouth then wiping her hands on her apron. "Why'd he be here if he weren't a fighter? But he probably didn't look to face the king's champion."

"Then he shouldn't have challenged the king's right, should he? Still"—and Nan piously crossed herself—"God will speak. If he has the right, he'll win, even against a stronger man. Of course, he hasn't the right," she hastily added, glancing around.

"'Course not!" Truda crossed herself too, as much for protection from earthy powers as hellish ones. Quietly she added, "Don't know about this business of God speaking, though. My Edwin lays out any man he thinks insults him, and I wouldn't say he was always right. He's just bigger and stronger."

"Ah, but do they both call on God first?" Nan waved her distaff to make the point. "*That's* the trick, Truda. God can't be attend-

2

ing to every little thing, now can He? But when He's *called* upon..."

"Oh, I see. It's the calling—"Truda broke off to step aside and rain slaps upon a bunch of writhing boys. She separated her own towheaded urchin. "I told you, Willy. No fighting or you go straight home!"

"But he called me a—"

She boxed his ear. "*No fighting,* or I'll toss you in the ring and *you* can take on the king's champion."

The lad pulled a face, but he sat down at his mother's feet and began pulling grass out of the dusty soil.

"Need rain," said Truda. "Cisterns are getting low."

"Hard to get decent water," agreed Nan. "There's clouds over to the east, though. Look promising, but I hope they hold off a while..."

They contentedly discussed the summer weather until Truda's son pulled on her skirt and asked, "Mam, is that the king?"

By then, all the spaces along the rope were taken two or more deep, and people nearby, caught by the lad's words, looked over. The men climbing onto the dais were only bringing benches, however, and one big heavy chair.

"No, lad,"Truda said, "but that's his chair, see. He'll be here soon."

"And when'll the fight begin?"

"When they're good and ready. Shut up."

But the lad tugged on her skirt again. "*Why* are they fighting, Mam?"

"I told you. One of them says the king has no right to be king. That the king's brother should be king."

"So why isn't the king fighting him instead of watching?"

"Because kings don't fight these sorts of battles, love. They have men to fight for 'em."

The lad pulled up another clump of grass. "Don't seem fair," he muttered. "I 'as to fight me own fights."

Truda slapped his head. "Don't be so cheeky. As if there'd be anything in common between your affairs and those of the king's!"

A sudden hush settled as the first noblemen strolled out of the Tower. In tunics and braies, they could be any men except for the rich colors, and the gold and jewels twinkling in the dull sun.

"Mam, is that—"

"No, Willy. The king'll be wearing his crown. And if you're not good," Truda added, "he'll have your head chopped off."

The lad scuttled back an inch or two, and pressed closer against his mother's skirts.

Now, men-at-arms in chain mail and conical helmets marched out of the Tower and spread to take their places all around the rope, long spears rooted in the ground. No one could be permitted to interfere in a court battle.

"Not long now," Truda said.

The nobles began to gather along a section of rope that had been kept for them, but a few split off to mount the dais and sit on the benches to either side of the chair.

"The ones up there will all be important men," Truda said softly to Willy. "Earls and such. A bishop or two. They'll see that everything's done right." She turned to Nan. "Can't say as they look any too happy about it."

"Heard tell this Clarence is a popular man. Perhaps they don't want to see him die."

"But he has to."

Nan nodded. But then she leaned close. "What I heard—from my sister's husband's cousin, who's a guard up there—is that they left his door unlocked this past week, hoping he'd hop it."

Truda's eyes opened wide. She whispered back, "You mean, they think he might *win*?"

Nan shook her head. "No. They just don't want to see him die."

A blare of trumpets silenced them. Truda pulled her son up by his collar. "There, lad. There's the king!"

Henry Beauclerk, youngest son of the Great Conqueror, now King of England himself, walked out of the White Tower, gold crown upon his curly dark hair, rich purple cloak brushing the ground. He strode toward his chair on the dais, followed by four men who took position standing behind him.

"Isn't that FitzRoger?" Nan muttered. "The tall one in green. He's the king's High Champion. But unless he's fighting in wool, he's not fighting today."

"They're not going to have the fight?" Truda said—too loud, so a nearby man-at-arms turned his head.

"Oh, they're fighting, mistress. Don't worry."

"So who's fighting for the king?" Nan asked him.

"New champion," the man answered, eyes forward, speaking out of the corner of his mouth. "Renald de Lisle's the name."

"Oh." Nan sorted out a tangle in her thread, a tangle caused by a distracted moment. "Shame that. I hear he's the best—FitzRoger. I'd have liked to see him fighting for blood."

"Newly married," said the guard, even turning a bit to wink. "Likely worn out."

Both women chuckled, but stopped as the trumpets blared again. The king was in his seat, his cloak pooled about him.

Summoned by the trumpets, a man walked out of the Tower—a man of metal, clothed all in chain mail. A wide leather belt was the only break, and from it hung a scabbard.

An empty scabbard.

"Why don't he have a sword, Mam?" Willy asked. "Aren't they going to fight with swords like you said?"

" 'Course they are. His squire'll have it." Truda squinted at the attendant who bore shield and helmet, but no sword. "What do you think, Nan?"

Nan turned her distaff, frowning. "Dunno, Truda, and that's the truth. I've only seen one other court battle like this, and they both wore their swords."

"Oh, yes. Went on all day, that one did, and he surrendered in the end... What was his name?"

"Can't remember. Don't matter now, does it? Lost his eyes and balls. He'd have been better off dead."

Willy stared up. "Why'd they do that to him, Mam?"

She ruffled his hair for comfort. "He lost, see. So he was proved to be a traitor. But he didn't die like he was supposed to, so they had to punish him. That's what happens to traitors."

"Not to most of this last lot," muttered Nan, moving her lips close to Truda's ear again. "They say there were so many mighty men rode out to support Duke Robert that the king couldn't be harsh to them all. He's thrown a couple out, but most, he just fined and sent home."

"Aye," breathed Truda. "I heard. So why..."

But they both fell silent to watch the other man come out. He was dressed as the first except that his scabbard contained a sword. He stood nearly as tall as the champion, but even with mail, lacked his breadth. In fact, Truda thought, he looked as if the armor weighed him down.

The two men stood facing the dais. The trumpets sounded a last time, commanding silence.

The king leaned forward. He did not shout, but Truda could catch his words. "Clarence of Summerbourne, will you renounce your error, swear fealty, and accept my mercy?"

The slender man stood straighter. "I cannot, Henry. You do not have the right."

The king jerked so sharply it was as if he

7

were hit. Then he raised a sharp hand and his crier stepped forward.

"Hear ye, hear ye! Lord Clarence of Summerbourne, having taken up arms against the king, and proclaimed to all that our just King Henry has no right to the Crown of England, stands here accused of treason. Clarence of Summerbourne, how plead you?"

"Not guilty!"

"Who stands to support this accusation?"

"I, Renald de Lisle." The voice rang clear around the area, strong and firm. "I claim the right as champion of Henry, rightful King of England."

Even as the crier opened his mouth to recite the next part of the procedure, Lord Clarence cried, "I protest! I demand that the king himself defend his cause!"

Whispering astonishment ran around the circle and the men on the dais turned to speak to one another. Then the king beckoned the crier and spoke to him, and silence fell.

The crier straightened and bellowed, "Lord Clarence of Summerbourne stands here today as representative of the king's brother, Duke Robert of Normandy, supporting Duke Robert's false claim to the throne. It is right and proper, therefore, that the king, too, have a representative. However, King Henry here declares that if ever his brother Robert comes to challenge him in person, he will stand against him right willingly and prove his cause on his body."

At this, a great cheer rang up from all present.

"Now that'd be a fight!" said Truda.

Nan chuckled. "But one that'll never happen. Duke Robert landed, but as soon as he saw his troops were outnumbered, he took a sackful of money and scuttled back home."

The trumpets sounded again to command order and silence from the crowd.

The crier unrolled another scroll. "This being the first occasion upon which Renald de Lisle will act as champion, the king gives him this sword." A servant stepped forward, bearing a naked blade. "A sword of finest German steel, gift of the emperor, the hilt set not with a jewel, but with a stone from the tomb of Christ in Jerusalem. May it fight always with honor."

The champion walked forward to kneel before the king and accept the sword.

"If the champion loses," Truda asked, very quietly indeed, "what happens then?"

Nan's eyes shifted all around and she leaned very close. "As I understand it, God will have said that the king can't be king."

Truda blessed herself. "Lord a'mercy!"

The champion returned to face his opponent and both men put on conical helmets, lacing them under the chin, and took up their long shields.

"Do you call upon God," the crier demanded, "to use your bodies to prove justice and right?"

"I do!"

"I do!"

A priest stepped forward. No, not a priest but a bishop in his glittering robes and tall miter. He presented a golden crucifix for each man to kiss. Then he sprinkled holy water on each man's bowed head. Finally, he dipped a thumb in holy oil and anointed them, so whichever died would have received the Last Rites.

When he stepped back, the crier announced, "May God show the truth of your cause!" and the king raised his hand.

As Lord Clarence of Summerbourne drew his gleaming sword, a cloud skittered across the sun, stealing any touch of brightness from the moment.

It was slow at first. The men swung and blocked with shield or sword, but despite thud and clang, they were just testing each other. As they worked their way across the circle kicking up dust, the rhythm became almost monotonous.

In a show fight the crowd would be jeering by now, calling for more action, but nothing here was for show. One of these men would die today, and if they wanted to tread the path warily, that was their right. A battle like this could take all day, and be decided in the end more by exhaustion than warlike skill.

Truda didn't think Lord Clarence would last all day. Something in the way he moved already suggested weary muscles.

Then, as if contradicting her thought, he surged forward. His blows rang harder, striking sparks from that German blade and from the iron around the champion's shield.

Sir Renald held his own but no more, retreating steadily. Then he changed the rhythm and began to drive Lord Clarence back.

The accused man stumbled. The crowd gasped and the champion swung backward against the edge of his shield. Instead of beating it aside, however, the sword bit deep, right through the metal band and into wood.

And stuck.

As the crowd gasped again, Lord Clarence seized his moment. He aimed a swinging blow at his unbalanced opponent, a blow designed at the very least to crack ribs. At the last moment, Sir Renald's shield turned it away, but awkwardly, leaving him wide open to a thrust.

But in the same movement he kicked Lord Clarence's shield to free his sword, and leaped back out of danger.

Like one body, the crowd let out a breath. The two men paused to gather themselves.

"Oooh," said Nan. "That was a nasty moment."

"I've never seen a sword cut through a shield like that," said Truda. "German steel? Lord Clarence had best watch out. That sword could cut through mail."

"He's got the right idea, though. Break some bones and it won't matter if the champion's bigger and stronger and has a German sword. He'll be a dead man."

Truda stole a look at the king, whose fate apparently hung in the balance here. He sat still as a statue, hands relaxed on the arms of his chair, face almost contemplative. She liked that. A king should have dignity even in the face of disaster.

Especially in the face of disaster.

A clang told her it had started again and she turned back.

Lord Clarence must have been encouraged. Now he swung mightily, pushing the champion back under a torrent of blows. Truda found she had her knuckle between her teeth.

Trouble for kings always meant trouble for lesser folk.

But then Lord Clarence's furious swinging turned wild. Now he looked like Willy and his friends, playing with sticks and swinging without much plan or skill. The champion still had his strength. In a move that even she could see was graceful, Sir Renald turned the fight. Steadily he forced Lord Clarence to retreat.

The accused man staggered, as if his legs were failing, and his sword drooped on a weary arm. Instead of surging for the kill, the champion checked his swing. Truda thought his lips were moving. What could there be to say at this point?

Perhaps it was a taunt, for with a hoarse, defiant cry Lord Clarence revived and swung.

Sir Renald blocked that wild blade with his shield, beating aside his opponent's shield with his fist. Then he impaled Lord Clarence through chain mail right to the heart.

"*Oooooooh*." The sound wove around the circle even as the traitor crumpled, dead before he hit the ground.

The champion collapsed to his knees, and for a moment Truda thought he'd been injured as well. What would that say about the right of the king to the throne? But then the man blessed himself and started to pray.

Chatter rose from the field like a flock of starlings.

"Bit short," said Nan, tucking her spinning into a bag.

"Is he dead, Mam?" asked Willy.

"Yes, love. And the king is proved to be the good and just man we know him to be."

"Didn't last long."

"Long enough, Willy. Long enough to kill a man."

Truth to tell, it had been a strange sort of fight. Even as she steered her son to follow the crowd back to market stalls and houses, to breweries and smithies, she glanced back at the tableau in the dust.

"Mam?"

"Yes, love?"

"I thought mail was suppose to stop a sword."

"It is, love. It is. I've never heard of someone being killed that way before. Normally it's bash, bash, bash until one's too bruised and broken to keep going. Neater this way, though..."

Something about the scene around the body made her pause.

Lord Clarence's attendant was on the ground, his master in his arms. He'd taken off his lord's helmet and pushed back his mailed hood so he could stroke the sandy hair. During the fight, clouds had gathered, weighting the scene with shadow, but now a chance beam of sunlight picked out the group.

Picked out Sir Renald, still kneeling in prayer. Picked out jewels on the clothes of the three standing nobles who'd gathered, forming a backdrop to the men on the ground.

Why, it looked just like the picture on the wall of St. Mark's, the picture of Christ taken down from the cross! Truda hastily blessed herself in case she'd thought a sacrilege.

The champion must have dropped his sword, for one of the other men picked it up. It was the High Champion—the one called FitzRoger—with his dark hair and rich, somber clothing.

He cleaned the blade on a cloth which turned scarlet, then presented it to the kneeling man. The blade looked strangely shadowed, as if it ate the dull light. Everything froze, becoming like a painting, but then the victor pushed wearily to his feet and took the sword. After a moment, he kissed the hilt and pushed it into his scabbard. Then he turned and walked over to the dais where the king awaited.

"Well of course," said Truda, half to herself. "It's that stone from Jerusalem. It was a miracle him being able to kill that way, that's what it was."

"Mam!"

She looked down. "Stop pulling my sleeve like that!"

Willy let go, but jiggled around. "There's a pie-man over there. Can I have a pie on the way home? Can I?"

"No, you can't!" But then she shook her head. "We'll buy a few and take them home for all to share. Come on. Let's hurry."

14

The rain had started, plopping heavily to make dark circles in the dusty ground. In one spot, it began to form a crimson pool.

## *Chapter 2*

Claire of Summerbourne bent over her desk, trying to wipe the smile off the face of a cow. The ink had soaked into the parchment, however, so she picked up her knife and scraped down to a clean surface. She couldn't do that often, or she'd scrape a hole in the page.

Drat the weather. It had rained for more than a day, and still it pelted down, gusted by winds. She didn't dare open the shutters more than a crack, and no one could do fine work by candlelight.

It was madness, she knew, to be trying to draw, but the rain showed no sign of letting up and she needed to do it. This work had been her solace ever since her father had ridden off to join the rebels. Against her dread of disaster, she had placed an act of faith. If she finished this work, finished writing and illustrating his favorite story, he would come home to see it.

He would come home safe.

She raised her head, chewing the bone hilt of the knife. He should be home by now. It was weeks since Duke Robert—the coward— had fled back to Normandy. Other local men had returned, and rumor said it was the same all over. A few of the leaders like Robert de

Bellême had been exiled, but most of the rebels had merely been fined and sent home.

A neighbor, Lambert of Vayne, had ridden over not long ago, his mood a curdled mix of bitterness at his penalties and relief to be pardoned. According to him, her father had survived the one brief skirmish. Lambert hadn't known where Lord Clarence was now, however, or what punishment was likely.

Surely no worse than Lambert's. After all, her father and the king were old friends. She was in her father's study, where she always worked, and she looked at the shelf holding a precious goblet set with jewels. It had been sent by the king a year ago, shortly after he seized the throne of England. Sent to his friend.

*Ad dominum paradisi de rege angelorum* it said around the rim. *To the lord of paradise from the king of angels.* That was because Henry had loved to visit Summerbourne and had called it a little bit of paradise. The king of angels bit referred to an old joke between the two men.

Claire had heard Henry Beauclerk say that her father's stories and riddles were worth the whole treasury of England. Surely they were worth a pardon.

"It's too dark to read."

Claire grimaced at her young brother Thomas, who was sprawled on a bench, a precious book almost sliding out of his hands. He was supposed to be reading to her, but she'd become so absorbed, she'd not noticed when he stopped. It was hard to get an active twelve-year-old to study, even one mired in rainy-day boredom.

"Come a little closer to the window," she said.

"I'll get water on it and you'll nag me." He closed the book and put it carefully away in its chest. At least he was thoroughly trained to that. Then he came to lean against her desk. "I'll read some more later. Honest."

She gave him a look. "Later, the rain will stop and you'll be out with your friends."

"I like those kittens. What story's this?"

"Read it for yourself," she said as she leaned closer to redraw the cow's mouth.

Haltingly, tracing the words with his fingers, he did so. " 'And so the Brave Child Sebastian set out from his home, leaving behind his cat, his hound, and his favorite cow...' I don't think anyone has a favorite cow, Claire."

"I do. The one with the white horns."

"Oh, that's the one you've drawn! It looks just like her. You're good at this."

Claire laughed at his astonishment. "Thank you, kind sir."

"I wish you'd draw me."

Claire leaned down to find the sheet she'd been working on the day before. She'd not shown her brother yet because she wasn't sure how he'd react. "I have," she said, laying the sheet out on a clear surface. "You're the Brave Child Sebastian."

He looked at the picture of the sturdy youth with the curly blond mop, staff in hand as he marched off to face the enemy. "Do I look like that? He looks brave."

"You are just like that. Upright and brave."

"I'd rather have a sword than a staff."

"You will in the later ones."

"Oh yes, when I face the evil Count Tancred and strike him to the heart." He swung an imaginary blade, almost sweeping her ink pot to the ground.

"Thomas!"

"Sorry." His cheerful face didn't show much repentance, but then sank into a scowl. "I wish I had a *real* sword now."

"Why?"

"'Someone has to be able to fight if we're attacked."

"No one ever attacks Summerbourne."

He gave her a look that suggested he wasn't as blind to the situation as he sometimes appeared. But then he leaned over to study the picture of himself again. "It is a grand tale, isn't it? One of Father's best. I love it when Sebastian challenges the evil count to a court battle, and everyone laughs. Not that they laugh, but that they're *so* wrong. Have you kept that part?"

"Of course. It's just as Father tells it."

"And when Sebastian kills Lord Tancred, and the warrior looks so surprised as he dies! That's the best bit. And Sebastian being proclaimed a hero, of course."

"And everyone being able to practice their Christian faith."

But he ignored the inner meaning. "If an enemy comes here, God might strengthen my arm as he strengthened the Brave Child's. Then I'll smite them all."

Claire bit back a protest. It would never happen. She prayed daily that it would never happen.

But her father had turned traitor. Or at least, he had opposed the king. Who therefore must be wrong, because her father must be right. So it wasn't treason. Not really. But sometimes people suffered for being right. Like the holy martyrs.

What was right? What was wrong? Last year, the old king, William Rufus, had died of an arrow while hunting. An accident, they said. A very convenient accident, with his younger brother there ready to seize the throne.

That younger brother was Claire's father's friend, Henry Beauclerk. Rufus's older brother, the Duke of Normandy, had invaded to assert his right to England, and many lords had ridden to support him. Not enough, however. Duke Robert had assessed his chances and let his brother buy him off, then run back home leaving his supporters to their fate.

Supporters like Lord Clarence of Summerbourne.

King Henry was a clever man, however, and had made peace with most of the rebels. He'd merely demanded their oath, fined them, and sent them home.

Her brother wandered over to the chess board to slide the stone figures around like toy soldiers. "I wish Father would come home."

"So do we all."

"Lord Lambert's home. Why not Father?"

Claire wished she knew. "Perhaps the fine Father has to pay hasn't been settled yet."

"I heard Mother talking to Gran." Thomas looked up, unusually somber. "She'd heard Father was in a tower because he wouldn't swear the oath to the king."

Claire cleaned her brush. She'd hoped Thomas hadn't heard that. "In *the* Tower," she corrected. "It's a great keep the Conqueror built in London."

"But how long's the king going to keep Father there? It's not fair!"

"We don't know it's true. It was only a tinker's tale."

"Tinkers are usually right. So how long?"

"Until Father swears the oath, I suspect." She turned on her stool to face him. "You know Father. He's the gentlest, kindest, sweetest man on earth, but once he decides something is right or wrong he's like a rock."

"The king's going to keep him there *forever*?"

"Of course not. Father will have to give in. He won't want to sit in prison for years."

Thomas, however, threw her own words back at her. "You know Father!"

"Yes. And I know Father's clever. He'll think of a way around the problem." She resolutely turned back to her work. "When he does come home, I want this ready for him. Without a smiling cow!"

As she'd hoped, Thomas shrugged off his bleak mood and came back to study the picture. "But you know, I think that white-horned cow *does* smile."

Claire leaned back. "By the angels, you're

right. Why does it look so silly on parchment?" Thomas poked at her gold leaf. She slapped his hand and answered herself. "Because the parchment world isn't real, so it has to be more real than real."

"That's silly."

" 'Tis not." She hunched over the writing desk to add the slightest touch of a smile to the cow's face. She had it finally as she wanted when the watchman's horn blared, and she dripped a blob of ink.

"Jesu!" At least it hadn't fallen on words or pictures.

"Someone's coming!" Thomas shouted, turning toward the door. "Bet it's Father!"

Claire threw down her cloth and chased after him into the great hall of Summerbourne, with its mighty wooden posts and warm central hearth. "Who comes?"

They were all there in the smoky hall, shutters closed tight against the weather, busy with tasks that didn't need much light. Her mother was spinning, her aunt Amice plucked flower petals for a perfume, and her aunt Felice played her harp. Her grandmother sat hunched close to the fire, her swollen joints probably agony in this damp weather.

"Comes?" her mother asked, catching her thread.

Claire flung one set of shutters open to the rain-pounded bailey. "The horn. I heard the horn!" Surely she hadn't imagined it. No, the dogs were barking. She ran over to the big doors.

"Is it Clarence?" asked Amice behind them.

"Of course not," replied Felice, continuing to riffle a tune. "In this weather? Our brother likes his comforts."

Claire halted by the closed doors, hope shriveling. How true. Her father wouldn't struggle home in this weather when in a day or so it would clear into summer. Even so, she pushed open one of the doors and stepped outside, where the overhang of the thatched roof still sheltered her from most of the rain. Thomas came up beside her.

"It *could* be Father."

She shivered in the damp chill. "Certainly someone's out there. See, the guards are going onto the walkway to check."

As she spoke, one guard turned and climbed down the steep wooden steps to wade through the bailey toward them.

Not her father, then. They'd have opened to him immediately.

Disappointment was chased by foreboding. Who *would* travel in such weather?

"A party of armed men, lady," the guard said to her mother, who had come out swathed in a cloak. "Can't make out the pennant or banner in this weather."

"And they wish to enter here?" Lady Murielle asked.

" 'Pears so, lady. Do we open?"

"Not without knowing who they are! Return, and have someone inform me as soon as we know."

As the man waded back to the palisade, she said, "We can't let strange men in without your father here, can we Claire?"

"I don't know. It's so horrible out there. Can we refuse?"

"We *can*, I suppose. Oh, I don't know. I wish Clarence..." She covered her mouth with her hand, and Claire wrapped an arm around her.

"If someone travels in this weather, it's their own fault," she said, though deep in her bones she felt that someone traveling in this weather had a dire purpose.

"You're shivering, dearest!" Her mother drew Claire under her own cloak and called for more coverings. Servants hurried out and soon Claire was physically warm. It didn't really help the shivers.

She looked at her mother. "What if it's something to do with Father?"

"Oh, don't think that Claire!"

Claire returned to watching the wooden gates, wondering how someone was supposed to block thought.

"Why?" asked Thomas. "I *want* news of Father."

Lady Murielle looked at him helplessly. "How can it be good news, Thomas? It's been weeks since we heard that your father was in the Tower, and he's not returned home. I can't think why..."

Claire hated putting things into words, but she hated avoiding the truth more. "He's doubtless refusing to take the oath."

Her mother sighed. "I do fear that. He can be so stubborn."

"Is it stubborn to stand for what he believes is right?"

"Don't lecture me, Claire. You're as bad as he is sometimes!" She gestured at the gate. "Someone is out there, and I know it is some consequence of your father's stubborn folly. I *told* him not to go!"

Claire sighed, remembering her mother arguing with her father, pointing out the dangers, weeping over the consequences. She remembered him cheerfully assuring his wife—assuring them all—that right would prevail, that God would support the just.

How could anyone argue against that?

Her mother could. She'd lost her temper. "It's not a *game*, Clarence! What are you going to do? Take arms against men who live for war? The blooded swords, as you call them? Your sword is blunt, and your armor rusty from decades of neglect!"

"Murielle, my love," her father had answered mildly. "God does not require that all His tools be perfect. But see, I will have Ulric clean my mail and have my sword honed."

Claire had fled to weep out of sight, even though there'd been some laughter in the tears. Her mother was haranguing because she loved her gentle husband and was terrified. Her father probably truly thought he could appease her by having his weaponry and armor put in order.

"He's refused to take the oath," her mother said, hand over mouth again. "I know it."

The guard was scrambling back down the ladder, almost slipping in the mire at the bottom in his haste.

"The king!" he gasped as he staggered

toward them, sliding again and having to use his spear to stay upright.

"The king?" Lady Murielle exclaimed "*Here?*"

"Nay, lady!" the man panted. "But 'tis his banner held before those outside the gates. What are we to do, lady? What are we to do?"

Panic rang in his voice, the same panic that shot through Claire. Why would men come with the king's banner except to execute the king's justice on a traitor's home? Would King Henry take direct revenge on the family? It had been the way of things in the past. Killing and maiming to teach others to be more cautious.

And raping. The traditional male revenge.

Claire hugged herself. The king was her father's friend. He'd held Claire and Thomas on his knee—

Abruptly, making her jump, a horn blared beyond the gates. It answered a lot of questions, for it was the demand of a lord to enter his property. It was almost a relief. A usurper wouldn't destroy, would he?

"So," said her mother dully. "We are lost."

Amice and Felice appeared behind them, huddling under one cloak. "What is it?" Felice demanded.

"The new Lord of Summerbourne," said Lady Murielle in a shaking voice. "Admit him, Niall."

Face grim, the man trudged back to the gates, his steps dragged down by more than rain and mud.

Her aunts were exclaiming, protesting,

complaining. Amice, as was her way, had started to weep.

"Are you just going to stand here and do nothing?" Felice demanded.

"What can we do?" Lady Murielle said. "We'll have to seek refuge at St. Frideswide's. Will we be allowed to take our clothes? And what of Thomas? Thomas?"

Claire realized then that her brother had run off. Her brother, who had just lost his heritage here. She looked around, but knew she wouldn't find him, and she couldn't try now. She only prayed he wouldn't do anything foolish.

Thank heaven he didn't have a sword.

A cracked voice split the air. "What's going on out there? Have pity on an old woman, you thankless creatures!"

Claire turned to see her grandmother struggling out of her chair supported by her stick, looking like a hunched gargoyle backed by the fire.

"Claire! Come tell me what's happening!"

Lady Agnes of Summerbourne, mother to ten children including Lord Clarence, was a difficult woman made worse by crippling pain, but it wasn't right that she be left alone at such a moment. Claire went back into the hall, dropping the damp cloak once she was beyond the doors.

"Well, girl?" Lady Agnes demanded. She had to scowl up for she was bent almost double and needed her solid stick to even move. "What's happening?"

Claire helped her back to her padded chair by the fire. "A troop of soldiers are before the gates, Gran. We don't know who they are, but they carry the king's standard and have demanded entry as of right."

"Ah." Lady Agnes slumped down, gnarled hands tight on the bent top of her stick.

"It seems the king has given Summerbourne to someone else. We'll have to leave." On a day drenched with rain and sunk deep in mud, they would have to leave their home. "Mother speaks of going to St. Frideswide's—"

She broke off, remembering that Lady Agnes and Mother Winifred of St. Frideswide's had been at war for years over ownership of coppice rights in Sydling Wood.

"Foolishness," grunted her grandmother.

"You think we can deny them entry?"

She received a withering stare. " 'Course not! But I've no mind to run away, especially to that woman's cold charity. Wait and see. That's the best course. Wait and see." But then she stared into the glowing logs and muttered, "I did think I'd live my last days in peace though. Foolish boy."

Claire saw a tear in the creviced face.

It stirred the dread in her heart. Lady Agnes, too, feared the worst, the unspoken worst. That's somehow—how? how?—her father was dead.

A sudden rumble spun her to face the hall doors. She knew that sound. The mighty bar was being winched up so that the double gates of Summerbourne could be opened. The king's men were about to enter.

The new lord was about to take possession.

Servants were gathering around the doors,

quiet in their muttered concerns. Claire went over, commanding her way back to the front. They pelted her with questions as she passed.

"Who be it, lady?"

"Are they come to throw us all out?"

"Is Lord Clarence returned?"

"Will we keep our places?"

"Will we all be killed?"

"What should we *do*?"

She tried to give honest answers. "A troop of men. I don't know. Perhaps. I don't know. Probably they won't hurt you unless you anger them. Stay calm. Be sensible..."

Then she, like her mother, was staring at the opening gates as if she could see through them. In her present mood, she wouldn't be surprised to see Lucifer himself there, with a horde of horned devils at his back.

But as the gates swung wide, they only revealed more rain, rivers of mud, and a troop of weary men at the far side of the wooden bridge. At the front ranked a handful of horses whose riders were hidden by long hooded cloaks. Behind she could just make out some packhorses, and a half-dozen foot soldiers armed with long spears. Hardly force enough to take Summerbourne if they resisted.

What point in that, however, with the weight of the king's authority on the invader's side?

One rider bore a sodden pennant that she couldn't make out, but at the front another held the king's standard. The square of cloth hung straight on its frame, still able to catch the dull light with threads of gold.

Strangely, the mounted men showed no sign of moving forward.

She grew desperate enough to think of running out into the rain, of wading through the ankle-deep mud to get up on the palisade walk. But then, finally, finally, something happened.

A foot soldier led a horse slowly through the deep puddle that always formed at the far side of the bridge during heavy rain.

A riderless horse.

A packhorse? There was something on its back.

What had the king sent?

Hooves beat an ominous drum roll on the wooden bridge.

Then, alerted by their own mysterious instinct, her father's hounds ran forward, already howling their dirge, and Claire's tears started. Swelling, trickling, bouncing down onto her damp tunic, they almost seemed part of the relentless rain.

The whole world wept, as well it should.

Her father, Lord Clarence of Summerbourne, had returned to his home.

Amid the mournful chorus, the cloaked man led the horse up to the hall, to within a foot of where Claire stood.

"This be the remains of Clarence of Summerbourne," said the foot soldier, stolidly reciting his piece. "Lord Renald of Summerbourne has conveyed him here with all speed, and grants his family till vespers to mourn before he will enter."

With a bow, he turned and slogged back out of the manor.

Claire watched him go, able to do nothing but stand frozen. She didn't want to touch the bundle. She didn't want to cut ropes and unwrap it. She didn't want to see the final brutal truth.

Then her mother wailed and embraced the bundle, calling for servants to come help take care of Lord Clarence. The servants wept, too, as they eased the leather bundle off the horse and carried it gently into the hall.

The world wept.

Claire trailed after numbly, and watched as they laid the bundle on the table and began to cut the ropes that bound it.

She turned away, not ready to face the truth, then started when she heard a mighty thud.

What was happening?

What were they destroying?

Then she realized it was only the bar settling back to seal the closed gates. Ah, yes. The invader would stay outside until vespers, but then he would enter to seize her home.

Because her father was dead.

Claire made herself turn back.

The servants were gently peeling back the sodden, hooded cloak. She'd seen death. She'd helped to lay out the dead, including her grandfather, an uncle, an aunt, and a baby brother and sister.

She didn't want to lay out her father.

As the last part of the wrapping was peeled back, she stared. This wasn't her father! This mailed man wasn't Clarence of Summerbourne.

But it was, though she could scare believe the picture before her eyes. After all, he'd ridden out in ordinary clothes. She'd never actually seen her father in armor before.

Now a mail coif covered his soft, pale hair, and he'd shaved off the mustache and beard he'd always worn in the old English manner. A sword and battered shield lay neatly on top of him, his hands clasped around the hilt.

No, she wanted to say. No. This is all wrong. He should be in his favorite blue wool gown with his rabbit-fur blanket over his legs to keep them warm. Instead of a sword, one of his books should lie open under his gentle hands as if he had just paused in reading it.

She stepped forward over the hounds that lay slumped down now, sad heads on paws. Looking at her father's pale face, she could almost believe he was sleeping.

No. That wasn't true either.

He looked dead, and rather older. Only thirty-five years old, with roundish cheeks often rounder with smiles, he'd been her friend as well as father. Now his cheeks had sunk, and gray death had stolen the merry man. She fell to her knees.

People spoke in hushed voices, moving around her. She knew she should be doing something—caring for her brother, or supporting her mother. For now she could do nothing but kneel here, wet cheek to hard, cold iron, saying farewell. How wrong this harsh, violent stuff must have felt against his skin. If only he had never felt called to put it on.

In the end people moved her and lifted him to a long board so as to carry him to the chapel. She watched the cortege leave, knowing she should go too, with her mother and brother.

But she couldn't. Not yet.

She needed to know *why*.

She needed to know *how*.

She needed to know who to blame.

According to Lord Lambert, her father had survived the fighting. So why was he sent home in his mail, his bloody mail?

According to the tinker, he'd been imprisoned in the Tower. How could he have died in chain mail in the Tower?

And where was the God who was supposed to fight on the side of justice?

## Chapter 3

Claire turned to where her aunts sat huddled near the fire. Amice wept steadily as the rain. Felice had an arm around her but stared forward, beautiful face cold with resentment. "Clarence was such a fool."

Amice sniffed. "Oh don't, Felice... Not now..."

"I only speak the truth. He has brought us all to ruin. At vespers we will be thrown out naked into the storm!"

With a wail, Amice fell back into tears.

They were late-born twins, only two years older than Claire herself. Both were beautiful, with the blond hair and fair skin of their mother's English heritage, and fine bones given them by their Norman father. In temperament, however, they were two sides of a coin. Felice was haughty as a falcon, and just as sharp in beak and claw. Amice more closely resembled a terrified rabbit, constantly atwitch over something.

Unlike falcon and rabbit, however, they were inseparable, each seeming to need the other. Amice needed Felice's fierce strength; perhaps Felice needed someone to dote on her.

Whatever the case, Claire needed neither tears nor complaints at the moment. She went over to where her grandmother sat hunched in her chair by the hearth, staring into the flames.

"Did"—Claire had to swallow to clear her throat—"did anyone say exactly how he died?"

"By a sword," said Lady Agnes, bitterly. "In the chest."

"But how? In battle?"

"How else?"

"But there haven't been any recent—"

"What does it matter?" Lady Agnes looked up, face grim. "Pay attention!"

Claire jumped. "What?"

"We had no choice, either." Her grandmother glared between the three of them. "We had to let them in. We hoped it was our own men returning victorious—my father, my brothers. We knew in our hearts it wasn't. We knew strangers had come to seize Summerbourne."

Oh, sweet Mary mild. Clearly her son's death had turned Lady Agnes's wits. She was back nearly forty years to the time when the Normans came to England. Claire gestured a servant over, intending to order a soothing tisane.

"Stranger to us than these are to you," Lady Agnes said. "Pay attention, Claire!"

Claire waved the servant back again.

"Foreign devils on their big horses with no hair on their faces. Armor different. Weapons different. Language different." She thumped her stick on the floor to emphasize each fact. "Strangers, they were. Invaders who'd killed our men at Hastings. Come to take our home."

Lady Agnes had never said much about those days, but there were daunting similarities. Claire sank to a bench by her side. "Did you resist?"

The old woman turned to speak to her alone. "We had more sense than that. Our walls can keep sheep in and wolves out. Two-legged, or four. But not the Norman kind of wolf."

"What happened?"

"Do rabbits fight wolves? All our able-bodied men had gone with my father and brothers to stand against the Normans. Only women, children, and ancients were left. We all hated him—Thomas of Argentan, arriving here still stained with the blood of slaughter. We cursed him behind his back, and gave

34

poor service, but my Thomas was wise enough not to use the mailed fist. Of course, the first thing he did was marry me." She turned away to look into the flames. "I was given no say in it, so I lay under him in the bed and gave poor service there, too."

Claire frowned. She'd never thought of how her grandparents had married. Her early memories, however, were of a happy couple. "But you came to love him?" she prompted.

"Oh, aye." A smile flickered, giving a brief illusion of youth. "He didn't add fat to the fire, see." She turned to look at Claire. "My Thomas was a good man. He didn't bring in his own ways all at once. He listened. He respected the people's traditions. He helped bring back prosperity."

"Then I wish he'd spent some of the money on stone walls!"

Her grandmother shook her head. "Stone walls are a mountebank's trick, girl. They'll not keep out a fierce enemy. The secret is not to make fierce enemies. Thomas had no enemies, so we never needed stone walls."

Perhaps grief had addled her after all. "They'd be useful now, though, wouldn't they? Since Father has made enemies."

Lady Agnes actually growled. "The shock's turned you silly, girl. *What* use? Henry Beauclerk is his father's son, the Conqueror's son. He's taken a tight grip on his kingdom. If we so much as blink at this man he's sent, he'll swoop with an army to scourge the area. If we had stone walls he'd tear them down and use them to crush our bones!"

"So what are we do to? Why are you telling us all this?"

"Heaven help us all, girl. You do as I did!" She glared at the three of them. "There's three young maids in Summerbourne. One of you marries the man, and we all live here as before."

"Just as before!" Claire leaped to her feet in outrage. "Have you forgotten Father is *dead*?"

Her grandmother looked up at her, and Claire saw the tears. "I birthed him and fed him from my breast. I guided his steps and birched him to teach him sense." Then she scowled again. "I obviously didn't birch him hard enough. So now one of you must marry this new lord."

"It certainly won't be me!" said Claire.

"Nor I!" yelped Amice, pale eyes huge.

"Nor I," snapped Felice. "Come, sister, we must go and change into somber clothing."

However, Claire had detected a hint of hesitation in Felice's response and it stirred hope. As her aunt steered her twin toward the wooden stairs, Claire told herself that if a marriage was necessary, Felice would come to like the idea.

Despite a notable degree of beauty, at twenty Felice had not yet found a husband. She wanted one, but only one she considered worthy of her. She wanted to marry a great man, or one destined for greatness. Surely a man given a rich estate...

"Felice won't do," Lady Agnes said.

Claire turned to her. "Why not? As the

bride's mother, you'll be able to live here."

"Live in hell. She could eat honey morn till night, that one, and it wouldn't sweeten her tongue."

"She'll be better tempered when she has what she wants—a man of importance in her bed."

"And why doesn't she have one, fair of face as she is?"

Claire tried to be tactful. "The nearby families are not of great estate. And Father was more inclined to invite scholars to Summerbourne than nobles. You know Felice complained of it."

"Half the county knows she complained of it! But what makes you think a visiting noble would have fallen prey to her charms?"

"She is very beautiful."

"Beautiful as glass, and just as hard. True enough that none of the local men were good enough for her, but did you ever see any of them try to court her?"

"She made it clear that she had no interest—"

"A man can spot a shard of glass when it glints at him."

Claire turned to look into her grandmother's eyes. "Well, if Felice is cold, hard, and sharp, she's exactly the bride this usurper deserves! Anyway, the man's probably married with a family of his own."

"Landless men don't marry, and this is probably his first estate. It's the usual way. Seal ownership by marrying into the family. Happened to me. It'll happen to one of you."

"Not to me. I'd rather leave."

"Has to be you."

Claire tried to turn the conversation. "Shall I help you to the chapel, Gran?"

"I'm not moving," the old woman grumped, seeming much like a peevish child. "I suffered enough bringing him into the world. I'm not suffering to see him out." But she knuckled away some tears and Claire knew how deeply she must be suffering.

Claire could cry too, but if she started, she might never stop.

She knelt by her grandmother's chair. "I'll order one of your herb drinks to help with the pain so you can get there."

Lady Agnes turned watery eyes to her and patted her cheek. "You're a good child, Claire. A good child. You remind me of myself back when my Thomas rode up. You've got to marry this man."

"No!"

"Yes. You've the strength for it, and the looks. I was a bonny lass, just like you, and it helped."

"Bonny? Felice is the beauty."

Lady Agnes shook her head. "It's you who's got what men like. Curves and big titties. Your hair's as gold as hers, your skin as good, but it's the curves and titties that count. You can use those to rule a man."

"Felice—"

"A man wants something soft in the night. And what's inside shines through. Why do all the local men come courting you?"

"Courting? They're just friends, or friends of Father's—"

"Friends who light candles at your altar."
Lady Agnes shook her head again. "You've been
so bound up in reading and writing and such,
that you've hardly noticed what's around
you. You have a power over men. Now's the
time to use it."

"I wouldn't marry this man to save my
immortal soul!"

"Then marry him to save your family! Do
you want us all thrown out? You may not
care about me, or about my foolish daughters.
But what about your brother?"

Claire scrambled to her feet. "Thomas will
be all right. It's clear this man won't be
harsh."

"There's harsh and harsh, girl. What do you
think's going to happen?"

"We'll all go to St. Frideswide's—"

"I won't, so there!" Lady Agnes stated.
"That woman's not lording it over me. And
Thomas can't go there."

Claire turned away to hide her sudden terror. "One of Father's friends will take him in."

"Take in a traitor's son? But this man, this
Lord Renald—if wed to a winsome wife—he
might make sure her brother gets a start in life."

Claire swung back. "Never, never, never!
I could *never* marry the man who's stolen
Summerbourne."

"No one's asking you to marry the king, girl."

"The king?"

Lady Agnes thumped her cane. "Whose
fault is all this? Why couldn't the fool kill his
brother right, so other fools like my son
wouldn't get stirred up over it?"

"That's treason, Gran!"

Lady Agnes scowled. "To say Henry Beauclerk killed his brother? Or to say he should have done it better? I'm past caring. But if you care, you do the right thing to patch it all together."

Claire rubbed her hands over her face. It broke her heart to think of all the suffering, the suffering now and the suffering to come. But she couldn't. Even if it would patch it all together, she couldn't.

"It won't be too bad, Gran. Truly. I'm sure we can all find a comfortable spot."

Lady Agnes's bottom lip came up, and her grizzled brows came down. "I haven't been comfortable in ten years, and I'll never be comfortable again until I'm in my grave. But I was born in Summerbourne Hall, and I intend to die here."

The old woman's need beat at Claire, but she resisted. "I can't do it, Gran."

Lady Agnes sat there, as fixed as a weatherworn rock. "You will. I've buried parents, brothers, and five children. I've learned that people do what they have to do. And in time, the horror fades, like the pain in my joints fades under the herbs."

Claire seized the chance. "I'll go and order your potion."

She almost ran from the room, but wasn't fast enough to escape her grandmother's shout. "You can't flee this, Claire!"

She paused before the covered walk that led to the kitchens. "Oh yes I can," she whispered.

Marry the invader?

She'd rather tramp the roads of England!

When she'd ordered the tisane, she knew she should go to pray at her father's bier. Her feet didn't want to make the journey, however. She didn't want to face the confirmation of the end.

Vespers. It couldn't be long until Vespers when they'd all be cast out. Should she start to gather their belongings?

What would they be allowed to take? Everything must now belong to the invader.

Her father's precious books! The thought of leaving such treasures in barbaric hands was almost worse than the reality of his body lying cold in the chapel.

What of the work of her own hands—her notes on local customs, her leech book, her writings of his stories, so carefully illustrated? Must she leave those, too?

She stood frozen there, trying to make decisions.

"Lady Claire!" Her maidservant, Maria, gathered her into her arms. "Come along, do. The other ladies are clean and dry and here you are all soggy. You'll catch your death, and that'll do no one any good. And your hair's a mess..."

Claire allowed herself to be herded away from tangled problems, upstairs to the room she shared with her aunts. At least they'd gone down again so she was spared Amice's weeping and Felice's complaints. Standing like a child, she let Maria and her other maid, Prissy, strip off her damp, muddy clothes.

Now, however, her grandmother's words

drowned out practical worries in her mind. It was true—landless men rarely married. Henry Beauclerk had himself been single and landless before seizing the throne. He had a household of similar men waiting for rewards.

But she couldn't... She *couldn't* marry the man who had stolen her father's land and place.

If this Renald planned to marry into the family, how would he go about it? What if he lined them up and took his pick! Claire didn't believe that she was more attractive than Felice, but she had to be sure not to be chosen. When Maria brought forward rich, somber clothing, Claire pushed it away. "Find me something dull. Something ugly."

"Ugly? Why?"

"Don't ask why. Do it!"

The startled maid backed away. "There's that old brown kirtle, lady. The one where the dye faded. I don't know what kind of tunic, though—"

"The gray," said Claire. "It's only trimmed with a bit of blue braid."

When Maria gave her the garment, she pulled out her sharp knife and began frantically ripping out the stitches holding the braid in place. Yes, streaked and faded brown with dull gray on top should keep her safe.

"You'll look like a scullion," Prissy protested. Where Maria was plump and gentle, Prissy was lively and never slow to speak her mind. "At least we'll have you a bonnie one." She started unraveling Claire's long blond plaits.

*You've got what men like. Curves and big tit-*

*ties. And your hair's as gold, your skin as good...*

Suddenly terrified, Claire seized one long plait and sawed it off as close to her head as she could.

"Lady!" Prissy shrieked.

Claire hacked off the other. She couldn't do anything about her curves and titties, but what was a woman without her "crowning glory"?

She tossed both plaits on the floor where they lay like thick golden snakes. "Find me a dull head cloth."

The wide-eyed maid dug in a chest and finally found a length of gray cloth. With this wrapped around her strangely-light head, Claire felt safe enough to leave the maidens' room and go to the church to kneel by her father's body.

By the time she knelt at the foot of his bier, she was already feeling a little foolish, and very guilty. She could imagine him shaking his head and saying, "Claire, Claire. Was this a wise act? Was it a fair one?"

When she bowed her head, it was as much with shame as grief. She could pretend she'd cut off her hair in mourning, but she'd done it out of fear. She'd done it to avoid an unpleasant fate. She'd done it hoping one of her aunts would have to suffer in her place.

She covered her face and prayed harder. It hardly seemed necessary to pray for her father's soul, good as he'd been, so she prayed for her own. She begged God's pardon for her selfishness, and she asked for the courage to do what needed to be done to save her family.

But she couldn't say the holiest words—Thy will be done. Instead, she begged God that her cup not be the ultimate sacrifice.

Marriage to the man who had stolen Summerbourne.

Too soon, in the distance, the convent bell tolled vespers. Again the horn sounded, demanding entry for the manor's new lord and master. The family hurried back to the hall, gathering in the doorway to watch as the great gates swung slowly open once again.

Beyond, a camp had been set up. Tents hunched against shielded fires, stuck among rivulets and mud. Men hunched too, surely deeply uncomfortable. Claire was fiercely glad, but she wondered at it.

Why set up camp out there when they'd come to claim Summerbourne? Why did men stand at the far end of the bridge, but make no move to enter?

One called something.

"What now?" Claire muttered. Was this some strange form of torture, all these delays and negotiations?

After a brief exchange, Niall trotted toward the hall. "Hostages!" he gasped. "He demands hostages!"

"*What?*" Lady Murielle exclaimed.

"Clever man," said a cracked voice from behind.

Claire whirled to face her grandmother. "You sound as if you're on his side."

"If we have to have a new lord, I'd rather a clever one. Like my Thomas."

"Grandfather was a different type of man altogether!"

"I had no way to know that. Nor do you."

Claire turned away, but she acknowledged that demanding hostages *was* clever. Throughout the vigil by her father's corpse, she'd thought of revenge. In the Bible, Judith had killed her enemy Holofernes by driving a spike through his head...

If Renald de Lisle didn't feel entirely secure, it was not surprising.

"What kind of hostages?" her mother was demanding of the man, her hand gripping Thomas's shoulder. He was the most likely.

Niall looked warily between them. "He says there are three young maids in this hall. Two are to go out as hostages."

"What?" Despite the exclamation, her mother looked weak with relief. She continued strongly, however. "The monster wants two gently bred young women to live in his muddy camp with his men?"

"They'll be safe enough, Murielle," said Lady Agnes. "Or as safe as they'll be anywhere at such a time. Either he's a man of honor, or he isn't. If he isn't, he'll have 'em here on the hall floor then pass 'em to his men."

With a wail, Amice fainted.

Claire and Felice dropped to their knees beside her, raising her up as she recovered, and chafing her hands.

"Oh, now look what you've done!" Lady Murielle cried. "You know how sensitive she is!"

"And is being sensitive going to help? He wants two hostages, does he? What about the third?"

They all looked to the uneasy messenger. "He says the third is to be his bride."

"Told you so," said Lady Agnes.

Amice fainted again.

Claire and Felice shared wary, assessing glances.

"Bride?" Lady Murielle declared. "No, this is all too much. Claire, get Amice up off the floor. Spiced mead for the ladies!" she demanded of the hovering servants, waving a hand. "I won't permit this. I will protest. Someone fetch my cloak. I'm going out to speak to this man. He cannot force such a thing."

Felice and Claire pulled Amice to her feet and helped her to a bench by the fire. Lady Murielle pulled on her cloak and hurried out of the hall. She looked determined, but Claire had a sinking feeling that a man carrying the king's standard could force anything he wanted.

Felice was silent and her face was deliberately blank, but surely, now she'd had time to think, she would see this as an opportunity. A man given such a rich estate must be high in the king's favor. Exactly what Felice wanted.

Amice would be allowed to stay here with her twin sister. As Felice's mother, Lady Agnes would keep her place by the fire. If they were all amenable, perhaps the usurper would even make suitable arrangements for Thomas.

That just left Claire and her mother to settle.

Claire suspected that her mother would be happy to move to St. Frideswide's. As for herself, much though she loved Summerbourne, she wanted to leave. She might take the veil. Or perhaps she'd look at her local friends with a new eye and find a husband.

As she sipped the spiced mead and listened to Amice weeping, she ran over the local swains in her mind. Lambert of Vayne was probably a suitor, though he'd done little enough about it but visit often. He was somewhat of a silly fellow, much given to boasting.

It was possible that Eudo the Sheriff had some interest. His first marriage had been childless, and since his wife died he'd talked about remarrying. The post of sheriff had passed down his family for generations and he wanted a son. Was she imagining that he'd looked at her with some interest? He certainly liked Summerbourne and could well seek a connection.

He was close to her father's age, however, and she blamed him in part for her father's folly.

Robert of Pulham? Amiable, but so dull-witted.

John de Courtney? She suspected he had a cruel streak—

Her mother came back in, wet and defeated. "He's an unfeeling monster. He says it's no choice of his. The king commands that he wed one of Lord Clarence's unmarried women."

"And the rest of us?" Claire asked, then bit her lip at the keen look Felice flashed her way.

"*If* he marries here—he stressed the if—then he is to take care of the rest of your father's family. Except Thomas." She looked sadly at her son. "He is to go to court."

"Oh, that's kind," gulped Amice.

"Don't be a ninny," snapped Felice. " 'Care for.' What does that mean? And poor Thomas will be nothing but a hostage to be maimed or blinded at his whim."

Thomas swallowed a cry and began to tremble. Claire ran over to gather him into her arms. "Felice. Mind what you say!"

"I say the truth."

Lady Agnes broke in. "Then the truth is, no one will get hurt if everyone behaves themselves. Not even hostages."

"I don't trust it," Claire said. "Why would the king want to take such care of a traitor's family?"

"To keep order." Lady Agnes sighed with weary patience. "By the cross, you lot are enfeebled by years of comfort. This is the way it always goes! Men fight and die, and women are passed on as chattels. Does the king want to stir more unrest by casting us out? No. He wants the appearance of an orderly transfer."

"Then we must not give it to him!"

Lady Agnes thumped her cane on the wooden floor. "And what comfort will that be, girl, as you beg for bread?"

"*Think.* If we defy the king in this, we'll be lucky if anyone even tosses us a crust."

Amice was wailing now, and even Felice looked shaken.

Claire's mother sighed and came over to

gather her son and daughter into her arms. "Lady Agnes is right. We are helpless. Heaven knows, I would give myself to this man if I could, but he would have no interest in a woman so far past her prime."

"So," said Lady Agnes, "which of you is to be the bride, and which the hostages?"

Amice abruptly stopped crying.

"None of us!" cried Felice, her color high. "It is brutal. We'll all take the veil. Not even the king can stop a woman becoming a bride of Christ."

"Perhaps not," said Lady Agnes, "but will the Church take you? You don't own anything anymore. None of us do. Not our clothes, not the food on the table. Certainly not our property. Even brides of Christ are supposed to bring something with them to the cloister."

"This is impossible," said Felice, but even she sounded shaken. Amice seemed too shocked even to weep.

Claire saw her mother smile, and was surprised, but then Lady Murielle said, in her best persuading voice, "He doesn't seem so terrible a man, Felice. He's shown consideration. And whichever of you ends up as his bride will have high rank. She'll be Lady of Summerbourne."

Her mother was tempting Felice, and Claire prayed it would work.

"Of course," interrupted her grandmother, "Felice would have to curb her tongue. A man like that, he'll take his belt to a contrary wife. Still, as long as she's sweet and meek..."

Felice was as sweet as rhubarb.

Lady Murielle flashed a ferocious look at Lady Agnes then smiled at her sister-in-law again. "You have beauty enough to keep any man content, Felice. And he'll likely hardly be here, being a *favorite of the king.*"

Claire appreciated the neat way her mother slid in that telling point. Felice desperately wanted to marry a great man, or one headed for greatness.

"Who says he's a favorite of the king?" Lady Agnes demanded.

"He's been given Summerbourne, hasn't he?" That clearly was a telling point, and Lady Agnes fell silent, scowling.

"He must be a very busy man," Lady Murielle continued. "His wife will doubtless have to run his estates and raise the children alone while he's at war, and at the king's court."

"Court?" Felice straightened with interest.

Lady Agnes rallied. "Court. Where he'll be, while his wife stays here to count pigs."

"I'm sure he would take a wife to court sometimes," said Claire's mother.

"Hardly. After all, if Felice was his wife, she'd be known to all as a traitor's sister. He'd want her hidden away."

"Then his wife would have even more independence here."

"You think he'd trust a traitor's sister with his affairs without check?"

Lady Murielle's smile widened. "Your husband trusted you."

Lady Agnes smiled back, showing the gaps

50

between her remaining teeth. "Only after a year or two—tricky years at that—and only because I took care to please him."

Felice glared at her mother. "Are you saying I can't please this man?"

"You haven't managed to please one yet, have you? Amice might do better if she'd stop crying."

That, of course, set Amice off again. Lady Agnes had been at odds with her late-born daughters since the hour of their birth.

"Stop it!" cried Claire, rising to her feet. "Father would hate to hear such dissension in the family."

"This is all Clarence's fault," snapped Felice, surging up to face her. "His folly has brought us to this, and his daughter should pay the price."

"She's the youngest," Lady Murielle protested.

Felice's elegant face set into the hawklike harshness they knew too well. "Only by a few years. She's eighteen. Old enough to be a bride."

But then Amice surprised them all. "No," she whispered, tears still leaking. "I... I'll do it. To save Claire. I'll d-do it." She was visibly shaking, her pale face a collection of damp, quivering angles.

Claire met her grandmother's demanding eyes. She knew quite well what the old woman was up to—trying to get her own way as usual.

Claire would let Felice do it. Even if he did take his belt to her now and then, she thought

Felice would get enough out of the bargain—marriage to a powerful man, and control of Summerbourne. But Lady Agnes thought Felice would be a harsh mistress here, and that she'd anger her husband rather than sweetening his moods.

She might be right.

Amice would never do. She'd quite likely make herself ill over it. Even if she survived, she'd never be able to manipulate such a man.

Claire went over to hug her aunt. "I don't think we need to make firm decisions yet, Amice. He can't expect any of us to marry him today." Remembering her grandmother's story, she shivered and hoped she was right. "But I know you'll feel safer with Felice, so why don't you and she go as the hostages? I'll stay here, and if he chooses to assume I'm the bride, let him. Once we've met him, we'll know better what to do."

Yes, that was it. If he turned out to be a tolerable sort of man, he'd suit Felice and all would be well.

Of course, that meant if he was completely intolerable, she might have to marry him herself. She'd face that when they came to it.

Amice looked up, tears drying. "Oh, Claire. Are you sure? Are you sure you can face him?"

How on earth had her aunt thought to marry the man, if facing him was beyond her? Claire patted Amice's trembling hand. "I'll have Mother and Lady Agnes to support me. Don't worry."

Amice began to weep again, but this time with relief, and Felice led her off to collect some belongings.

"Claire, why did you do that?" her mother wailed. "You'll end up married to him. Marriage is for life, you know, and a cruel husband is a terrible thing."

"Then we should hardly wish him on Felice, should we?"

"*Don't* lecture me!"

"I'm not—"

"You're as bad as Clarence. You never listen. You always think you're right."

Claire pressed her hands to her aching head. "Mother, it's just an early move. We have to give him hostages. How else could it be arranged?"

Her mother stared at her. "You're not planning anything, are you?"

"No." Claire wished she did have a plan. She couldn't imagine marrying this man, but if Felice remained set against it, she might have to. How could she let her whole family suffer?

"Oh," said Lady Murielle, dabbing at her eyes, "I could *strangle* Clarence!" But then she covered her mouth with a trembling hand. "I didn't mean that! Anyway, he's already dead—"

"Murielle," snapped Lady Agnes, "stop twittering!"

Claire's mother glared, but she did steady. She looked at Claire with a watery smile. "Thank heavens, at least, that you are pretty and have a sweet nature. You'll make sure we're all taken care of."

Claire had to stop herself touching the gray cloth hiding her ruined hair.

What if she had to marry this man and it angered him?

What if he took out his anger on everyone here?

Her mother went on: "I've been telling you for years that if you'd only pay attention to the young men—"

"What young men?"

"You have had suitors, you know. You just never noticed! All Clarence's fault, of course. He never encouraged any of them."

"He knew I wasn't interested."

"He wanted you home to read and sing with him."

Her mother's tone shocked Claire. Had she been *jealous*? Lady Murielle could have spent more time with her husband. But, Claire realized, she'd never had much interest in study and books.

She turned away to hide her trembling lips. Everything was breaking apart. Everything!

Her grandparents' marriage had seemed happy, but it had come about by conquest, and perhaps by rape.

She'd thought her parents loved each other, but now she doubted. Perhaps it had only ever been a comfortable arrangement between two people of an accepting nature.

Her home and everything she believed about it was being ripped out from under her!

At a touch, she whirled, and found her mother there, studying her anxiously. Anxious for her feelings, or anxious as to whether she would play the part of sacrificial maiden?

She'd always felt sure of her mother's love, but now even that was eaten by cankers of doubt.

"Why not go and put on something prettier, Claire?"

"On Father's burial day?"

Lady Agnes thumped her stick. "Put death behind you, girl. Look to life."

Claire whirled to confront her. "Could you, that first day?"

"I don't remember." It was clearly a lie. She, too, wanted Claire to submit so she could keep her place here.

Claire looked over to her brother, who seemed mainly numb, but who surely needed her sacrifice if he was to make anything of his life. Hers or her aunt's.

Amice and Felice came back into the room, swathed in cloaks, servants behind bearing their chests. Amice seemed to be largely held up by Felice, but at least she was walking. Felice was frowning.

Hoping the frown was one of indecision, Claire said, "Are you sure, Felice?"

The frown disappeared. "Completely! Better a night or two in the damp than a life shackled to a monster."

Claire gave up for now, and went to kiss Amice. "Do you have your herbs?"

Amice nodded. "Claire, I wish—"

"Hush. This is better. You know me." She even found a smile. "Things just bounce off me."

55

Felice was frowning again. From years of experience, Claire knew her aunt was trying to decide if she'd achieved a clever escape or been cheated out of something. In the end, no matter what the truth, she always decided she'd been cheated.

Perhaps this time Claire had misjudged her and the frown was genuine concern, for as they exchanged kisses Felice said, "God go with you, Claire. If we're allowed to return, I'll try to protect you from the worst."

"What if he turns out to be a veritable Roland, worthy to be a hero?"

Felice's eyes slid away. "Then I suppose you'll keep him."

"No, I promise. No matter how noble in mind and body, I do not want him."

Felice looked back, picking at the statement to find the catch. "We'll see."

Unfortunately at that moment, Claire's head cloth began to slip. Claire put up a hand to hold it, but Felice lunged forward and pushed it all the way back.

*"Claire!"*

It seemed to come from all voices at once, but Felice overrode it shrilly. "Now I see it. You pretend to be willing, but you plan to make yourself so unappealing that he'll reject you. Well, it won't work. He'll have to take you, shorn or not!"

With that, she hustled the wide-eyed Amice on her way.

Lady Agnes cackled. "Your hair won't make a farthing's worth of difference in the dark."

Lady Murielle was staring. "Oh, Claire...

56

Don't you know your looks could have been a weapon?"

Red-faced, Claire declared, "Not one I'd want to use."

"You foolish girl! But now you must certainly put on some becoming clothes."

"For a vicious upstart? Why?"

"To wrap a vicious upstart round your fingers. Have some thought to the fate of all here. Think of your brother!"

Claire winced.

"Or," asked her mother, "are you truly pretending to be willing while planning to be rejected?"

"No!" But then Claire realized that *had* been her plan. Her selfish, selfish plan. Oh, but she deserved a vicious monster for a husband.

"It can't matter, Mother," she said. "He clearly doesn't care what sort of woman becomes his bride. I will do what I must. I cannot, however, pretend to be willing. This is a house of mourning, and this usurper cannot make us pretend otherwise."

Claire dipped her fingers in the ash at the hearth's edge, then smeared it on her face and down her clothes. Thus marked, she went to stand by the open doors, ready to face the monster she might have to marry.

## Chapter 4

Brother Nils, clerk to Renald de Lisle, new lord of Summerbourne, stood shivering in the drenching rain despite a good cloak, feeling true sympathy for the ladies having to leave their home. He'd only been with Lord Renald for a few days, having been recommended to him by the king, but his first impression had been of a compassionate man. Cold, perhaps, but not cruel. Now this.

The people of Summerbourne had opened their gates without resistance. Why demand hostages, and gentle ladies at that? When he'd ventured a question, Lord Renald had merely said, "I'll have no more foolishness from this family. One death is enough."

Now, when the ladies' servants had to carry them through what was clearly a muddy mire, he tried again. "My lord, surely this is not necessary."

"Brother Nils," said the big man by his side, "you are neither my conscience, nor my tactical adviser. However, you can store in your memory that drainage work needs to be done here. And the ditch is so shallow it hardly needs a bridge. And the wooden walls need outward spikes at the top at least. Find the nearest source of stone for walls."

The man turned to him, though he could almost be a headless monster for all that could be seen under his hood. "You have all that?"

"Yes, my lord."

"I'm not going to harm them," he added, and a touch of humor warmed his voice. Nils had found there was humor in Lord Renald, like a gold thread running through dark granite.

"But you will leave them here with your men."

58

"You think my men will harm them?"

Nils didn't bother to answer, for none was needed. Lord Renald had built his troop around a core of men belonging to his friend FitzRoger of Cleeve. As he'd been the Lord of Cleeve's lieutenant for many years, these men knew him well. The rest were as new as Nils was, however. It had been... interesting to watch them being turned, in a matter of days, during a grueling storm-battered journey, into a household.

These men would do exactly as their lord wished, as he would himself, though for different reasons.

He returned to watching the servants carry the women through the small pond that had formed at the end of the bridge. Certainly, drainage was a priority, and Nils wondered at the previous lord who'd let such a matter go unattended. From what he'd heard, Lord Clarence had been a charming man with a gift for storytelling and riddles. But clearly, as a landholder he had been somewhat lacking.

"Who do you think's coming?" asked Josce, Lord Renald's squire. Also new. "Or rather, who do you think's staying?"

Josce of Gillingford thought this business of marrying a fair damsel romantic. Nils had at first but now, as they waited to find out who would be the bride, he was imagining all the women in the world he wouldn't want to be tied to. He wondered how Lord Renald could appear so unconcerned. Marriage was for life, after all. He could have lined them up and taken his pick. It might have been wiser.

But as Lord Renald had pointed out, Nils was neither his conscience nor his adviser, except perhaps on matters to do with estate management and administration.

Since Lord Renald hadn't answered, Josce went on: "I'll bet it's the aunts. They'd want to stick together."

"The Ladies Felice and Amice," supplied Nils, since it was his business to keep track of such details. "The daughter is called Claire."

"Happiness, Love, and Light." Lord Renald gave a dry laugh. "All rather unlikely brides in the circumstances. Well, let's find out."

The servants had reached the rocky ground where the tents were set, and had put their burdens on their feet. Huddled in their cloaks, raising their skirts, the two ladies picked their way toward the big tent outside which the men stood waiting.

"My ladies," said Lord Renald, "here is my tent. I think you will find it has the essentials for comfort."

At a command, a man by the test flap raised it and the women hurried into shelter and pushed back their hoods. Both were revealed to be fine-boned beauties, with damp, golden hair.

"Mmmm," said Josce to Nils. "Not bad."

"Don't forget, lad, these are the ones who *won't* be Lord Renald's bride."

They were very alike, though one looked haughty, the other terrified. Almost certainly the twins.

"I am Renald de Lisle, my ladies. And you are?"

"The Ladies Felice and Amice of Summerbourne." The haughty one glared down a long, straight nose. "It is intolerable that you drag us out here to live like pigs in a sty."

"We will make you as comfortable—"

"Comfortable! Only beasts could be comfortable here."

"It is—"

"It is evidence of lowly birth, sirrah!"

Nils winced. It was a true accusation in a way. Lord Renald came only from the petty nobility of France, and from a family dispossessed into poverty. This sudden rise in fortune was unexpected.

The woman was continuing her harangue. "What arrogance makes you think you are *worthy* to marry into our family?"

"Oh, Felice, take care!" The other had eyes swollen and red with weeping and she flinched as if expecting a blow. As well she might.

"Don't let him cow you, Amice. I insist that—"

Lord Renald turned and walked away, gesturing for Nils and Josce to follow. They headed for the horses, pursued by screamed complaints.

"If that was Happiness and Love," said Nils's lord, taking the reins of his horse, "light should prove to be a suitably dark and dismal lady."

Claire had planned to face the usurper with courage and defiance, but nerves began to shake her.

If only she had some idea what to expect!

In the drumming of rain, she had watched Felice and Amice being carried out, watched as they picked their way toward the tent. One of the cloaked and hooded men had accompanied her aunts there. Presumably Lord Renald.

She'd peered through the rain, desperate for any hint of the foe she must face. He looked big.

Of course he'd be big. He was surely one of the men who lived by the sword. Blooded swords, her father had called them. Wolves of war. He'd not welcomed them here. That had been another of Felice's complaints, for where else was she to find a great man except among the ambitious wolf packs?

So, if he was that type, he'd appeal to Felice.

What if he wasn't? What if he was too big for her taste? Or badly scarred. Or deformed. Or foul-smelling. Or had the manners of a pig.

Then Claire would have to marry him.

She tried to persuade herself that it wouldn't be so terrible. Her grandmother had married in worse circumstances and made a good life out of it.

She went over her mother's words to Felice, telling them to herself. If she was meek, he'd not be brutal. He'd rarely be here, so most of the time she'd be left in charge of Summerbourne. She could see her home kept as it had always been, a prosperous place of arts and learning, full of laughter and music.

But when he was here he'd share her bed and use her body.

Claire had known some men she would rather die than lie with. Baldwin of Biggin sprang to mind. Sir Baldwin had claimed hospitality here some months back and proved to be a revolting man.

He had the big, strong body of a fighting man, but padded out with fat. His belly overlapped his belt and his cheeks bulged up, making his eyes like those of a pig. He ate like a pig, too, spilling food and drink down himself. His hands were enormous, each finger like a fat red sausage stuck with dark hairs, and he'd liked to use those fingers to pinch bottoms and squeeze breasts.

Claire had tipped a bowl of soup over him when he'd tried it with her. He'd just laughed and said he liked spirit in a woman, looking at her as if she were another dish at the table. Her father had got rid of him, of course, but she shuddered at the memory. Now, she had no one to protect her from men such as that.

She started when her mother clasped her hands around a warm goblet of mead. "Drink, dear. It will steady your nerves."

The heat was welcome, and the spicy steam soothed, but Claire swallowed tears as she sipped. Her mother couldn't rescue her, and now she wasn't even trying. She wanted Claire steady to face the sacrifice. Didn't they give condemned men a drink before execution?

She suddenly felt terribly alone, exposed like a felon in the marketplace, every nerve vulnerable to the harsh winds of grief, and the hail of fear, with none daring to protect her from her fate.

She looked out at the camp again and saw her fate turn from the tent and walk toward the horses. She drained the mead in one gulp.

Soon four cloaked men approached the gates, but to her surprise, they led their mounts. They waded the muddy pool and crossed the wooden bridge, their horses' hooves rapping on the wood like ominous hammers.

Thomas moved up beside her. She couldn't hug him, nor would he want to be hugged. It would mark him as a child he could no longer be. But she rested her hand upon his shoulder hoping he couldn't feel her fear. Her mother was right. Right. Thomas was the one most vulnerable here. If marriage was the price of his safety, she'd do it, no matter how revolting the man turned out to be.

As soon as the men were through the gates, one took all four sets of reins and led the horses to the stables. Claire swung her attention back to the other three. Which was the new lord? They all looked the same, tall, broad, and cloaked.

And hard-pressed.

She almost giggled at the incongruous sight. They were struggling through the ankle-deep mud toward the hall, their long riders' cloaks dragging them back like lead weights. Surely the mighty warrior wished he were stalking majestically over his conquered land.

She whipped her mind back into order. Nothing about this was funny. Her father lay dead in the chapel, and muddy ground didn't make these men any the less dangerous. They were doubtless used to muddy slaughter.

With a whispered command, she sent Thomas away, to their mother. To safety.

The long, water-dark, leather cloaks concealed the men's bodies, and hoods sheltered their faces. She caught a glimpse of mail around chins, however, and the metal nasals that must extend down from helmets. Why were they so heavily armed? Didn't they know they were wolves among rabbits?

Doubtless the middle wolf was her enemy.

Broad, broad shoulders. Probably a big-bellied swaggerer with thick, hairy fingers. It would hurt to see such a man in her father's place, but perhaps he would appeal to Felice.

She began to pray that he not have a deforming scar, or warts, or bad teeth. Felice disliked disfigurement.

As the three men drew close to the hall doors the sheer size of de Lisle caused a swirl of fear in Claire's belly. She tried to remember that he was just a man, but the dark cloaked mass of him began to block out the world. She realized she was retreating instead of standing her ground, but couldn't stop herself.

Despite her will, she was trembling now, a faint yet violent tremor that ran through her whole body and set her teeth to chattering.

"Go any farther, girl," snapped Lady Agnes, "and your skirts'll be in the fire."

Claire started, looked down, and hastily moved to the side out of danger.

By the time she looked back, de Lisle was

by the hearth too. Head and shoulders taller than she and twice as broad, he pushed back his hood with bare hands.

Big, strong hands.

But not sausage-like.

She looked at his face. As she'd thought, he was armored, but she could see a square chin and firm lips. Not thick. Not at all slack.

The formidable set of those lips made her heart thump like a warning bell.

Slowly, he scanned the room, assessing the family by the central hearth and the servants huddled against wooden walls. She could tell he was ready for danger, ready to draw his sword and kill. The simple power of his readiness to kill filled the room like a fierce, hot wind.

In her peaceful life, Claire had never experienced such a thing.

Then he relaxed and unlaced his helmet. He pushed it off and tossed it to the man on his left. That man had pushed back his hood, too, pulling a face as if it was a huge relief to be rid of it. He was quite young, with reddish hair and freckles. Big and strong, though. Another fighting man. Probably de Lisle's squire.

Claire jerked her attention back to her enemy, desperately squashing fear. She must watch him and study him if they were all to survive.

Chain mail still hid his hair, but his face was rather square, with strong bones and dark brows. She preferred a man with more delicacy in his features, but she had to admit that he was comely for his sort. No obvious flaw.

Hope stirred. Surely Felice would find him pleasing.

His eyes were dark, too, but seemed worn. Bloodshot, perhaps. Probably the result of constant debauchery.

He unclasped his cloak and tossed it to the squire. The casual movement showed his strength, for a cloak like that, sodden with days of rain, was not an easy thing to handle.

*Of course he's strong, Claire! He's a warrior to the last, iron inch.*

Chain mail covered him to the knee, blousing over the wide, studded belt clasped around his hips. That drape of the mail was the only soft touch about him. No bulging belly here, no puffy cheeks. She suspected he'd be as hard to the touch without the armor as with it.

And as cold?

She dismissed that fanciful notion. He was flesh and blood like any man. Like any animal. Not an ox, though, despite the massive chest. He was more like a war stallion, fluid and powerful in his muscles.

Oh, Father, poor Father. Did you have to face men like this?

He scanned the room again, then looked back at her. She guessed he had been seeking out the other maid of Summerbourne, and because of her dull clothing had taken her for a servant. Since neither her mother nor grandmother could be his wife, he now knew it was she.

Her grandmother had been right.

He was no fool.

He frowned slightly as he pushed back his

chain hood to reveal wavy brown hair falling down to his shoulders, and onto his brow. Then he shook himself like a dog coming in from the rain and moved closer to the warmth of the hearth, holding out his hands.

The very ease of the action, the possession it implied, offended her in a more direct way than her deeper hurts. He'd assessed them all, decided they were rabbits, and was sure he was safe.

It would be immensely satisfying to kill him simply to wipe the smugness off his face!

He bowed to her mother. "Lady Murielle. I assure you I am sincerely sorry for the events that have led up to this moment."

*Oh certainly,* sneered Claire silently. *Events that have led to you seizing a handsome property.*

Her mother twittered nervously and introduced him to Lady Agnes. He'd probably taken her for an ancient servant, too. Corrected, he gave her a courtly bow and his sorrow over the death of her son.

Claire gritted her teeth and waited for Lady Agnes to ingratiate herself with the conqueror.

Her grandmother, however, stared up with cold, weary eyes. "You just watch yourself, young man. I've no quarrel with you. But hurt my chicks and I'll fix you. There's not much you or your king can do to make my life more miserable."

"I have no intention of hurting anyone, Lady Agnes. But if anyone here attempts to hurt me or mine, not only will the hostages suffer, the king will doubtless visit his own revenge. It is always best to have these matters clear."

On the last words, he turned to Claire. "Would you not agree, my lady?"

It was a direct challenge that took her breath away.

She made herself look him in the eye, frightened by how hard it was. "Certainly, Sir Renald." She deliberately did not give him his rightful title of Lord. "I wish to make it clear that you are not welcome here."

He didn't so much as blink. Without looking away, he snapped his fingers. "Ale."

Claire didn't let the flurry distract her, but in seconds a tankard was in his hand. His strong, warrior's hand...

She jerked her eyes back to his face where she'd intended them to stay.

"Since Ladies Felice and Amice are in my camp, you must be Lady Claire."

For answer, she just dropped a curtsy.

"A still tongue. Virtue as well as comeliness." He drank deeply of the ale. "When you're cleaned up a bit, that is."

As he took another draft of the ale, he frowned at her hair. "My lady, neither of us has been permitted our choice in this. It would be foolish to set out to be miserable."

"Since I am completely miserable, Sir Renald, the question doesn't arise. Must I remind you that we are mourning my father, whom I loved deeply?"

For a brief moment, his lids shielded his eyes and she was fiercely glad of it. At least she'd managed to jab him in some way.

But then he looked at her again. "This is certainly not the time to discuss our future. It can at least wait until he is laid to rest." He turned back to her mother. "I assume you have a solar here?"

"Of course—"

"I and my men will sleep there. My possessions will be brought over soon."

"That is my parents' room!"

They both turned to her, and her mother flapped her hands. "Hush, Claire. All here is now Lord Renald's to do with as he wishes. Of course that room will be his!"

"And yours too when we are wed, Lady Claire."

She did her best to suppress the shudder. Thank the saints and angels that she wasn't going to have to marry this man. Felice would snap him up. For a wolf, he was good-looking and though cold, he didn't seem to be vicious.

Claire could even, with the logical part of her mind, accept that her mother and grandmother were right. This situation was not his fault. He was merely the beneficiary of it.

Still, she had meant what she had said. He was unwelcome.

And she meant what she hadn't said. She wanted him married to her aunt so that she could leave Summerbourne. So she wouldn't have to see the defilement of the place she loved.

They buried Lord Clarence of Summerbourne that evening, the mourners all cloaked

70

against the never-ending rain. Sir Renald and his men had the tact to stay out of sight.

Claire wept to see her father's body settled into inches of cold muddy water, but at least she'd persuaded them to bury him in his favorite blue gown beneath the winding sheet.

She turned from the grave and looked up instead at the heavy sky, letting rain mingle with tears. Presumably somewhere beyond the clouds was the golden light of Paradise. She hoped there were books there, and furs, and good music. She hoped the angels liked his wonderful stories, and clever riddles.

*Be happy, Father. But watch over us, too.*

As the men began to fill the grave, laboring to lift shovels of sodden earth, the family returned to the hall, each going to their own room to mourn.

Claire found her bedchamber strange, for she'd shared it all her life with her aunts. The too-empty room reminded her of how her life had been shattered. Could she have done anything to prevent disaster? Could she have persuaded her father not to go? Though they were close, she didn't think so. As she'd said to Thomas, once her father made up his mind on something, he was like a rock.

She turned bitter thoughts toward Eudo the Sheriff. He'd been the one to stir her father up about the king's right to the throne. Working quietly on her illustrations in her father's study, she'd often heard their talk. She'd heard Eudo going on and on about regicide and duties, debating the matter endlessly on every visit.

Then, in the end, Eudo's courage had failed him and he hadn't joined the rebellion at all. Last she'd heard he, like so many others, had slunk off to London to pay homage to the man he believed to be a murderer. He'd certainly been confirmed in his position as sheriff of the county.

But the damage had been done. Her father had come to his decision and after that, the Archangel Gabriel complete with fiery sword couldn't have deflected him.

So he'd kissed her and told her to take care of everyone at Summerbourne until he returned. Then he'd ridden away as if off to market except for the weapons and armor on the packhorse trailing behind.

Take care of everyone.

That memory froze her in her steps. Would her father want her to take care of Summerbourne by marrying his successor?

*Yes,* said an inner voice.

"No!" she said out loud. He'd want her to find a way out of it.

Trying to escape her conscience, she seized her needlework and sat by the window to embroider more flowers along a long linen band. Then she realized it had been meant for a new shirt for her father.

Almost she tore it in two, but then she forced her fingers to keep working. Waste was evil, and someone would make use of it. But could she bear to see someone dressed in clothes intended for her father? No, no more than she could bear to see that dark, cold man in her father's place.

Sweet Mary, it was all so impossible.

Felice. Felice would be willing.

Her needle froze. What if the usurper wanted to drag her to altar and bed today, as her conquering grandfather had done?

When Maria came to say she was wanted in the hall, wanted by her mother and Lord Renald, Claire gulped and wanted to hide under the bed. Did he have the priest ready?

Well, she'd refuse. Folding her work, she told herself even the king couldn't blame her for not taking a husband on the day she buried her father. With that thought like a talisman before her, she headed down the stairs.

It was only as she walked into the hall that she realized that the setting sun was shining through breaks in the clouds. The rain had stopped.

The usurper entered the hall from the solar, dressed now in a blue linen tunic so dark as to be little brighter than his iron armor, but now he wore heavy gold bracelets at his wrists and a belt with a buckle set with colored stones. A tonsured monk walked behind him, carrying documents.

Claire realized with surprise that this must have been the third "monster" who had entered Summerbourne— de Lisle's clerk! And he was not particularly warlike, having a softness to him, and merry eyes.

Had all her reactions been so disordered? She glanced again at de Lisle—big, hard, and somber—and decided they had not.

Claire's mother was already in her own chair, and with an anxious smile, she patted the bench by her side, calling Claire over. Lady Agnes sat fixed in her usual place, glaring at the world in general.

De Lisle sank into her father's chair and she hated him.

"My ladies." His voice was deep and steady. "We must settle the matter of this marriage without delay."

Claire made herself look him in the eye. "None of us wish to marry you, Sir Renald." When her mother reached to control her, she twitched free and stood.

"And what do wishes have to do with it, Lady Claire?"

"We need time. None of us can be a merry bride on my father's burial day."

His brows rose. "But I can expect a merry bride one day? I confess, it's more than I'd hoped for."

Heat rose in her cheeks. She must remember that he was no fool. "If you give us time, my lord. Perhaps a month—"

"But the king commands that the ceremony be immediate, Lady Claire."

## Chapter 5

"Immediate!"
The lady went pale, and Brother Nils was not surprised. Was Lord Renald truly intending to drag the poor woman to altar and bed within hours of her father's burial? There was no need for such haste.

"Brother Nils, the documents."

The crisp words snapped Nils out of his worry, and swung the Lady Claire's attention to him. Though not as beautiful as her aunts, she was a woman he could imagine marrying. If he wasn't in Holy Orders, of course. Nils opened his pouch and pulled out the scrolls.

"Do you read, demoiselle?" Lord Renald asked.

Lady Claire turned back to face him. She had courage, Nils was pleased to see, and without her aunt's foolish pride. "Yes."

"English or Latin?"

"Both."

Lord Renald raised his brows in that way he had. "Nils, give the documents to Lady Claire. She can read everything for herself."

Nils went over to present them. "Lady, you have here the king's commands for you and for this place, Lord Renald's right of possession, and the betrothal agreement. The latter requires only the bride's signature and that of witnesses."

"How presumptuous."

Lord Renald answered that. "The king has a right to presume obedience, Lady Claire. Do you deny it?"

From the tightening of her lips, Nils suspected that Claire of Summerbourne would deny King Henry anything she could, and he knew his lord was right to fear folly from these people. But at least she lowered her eyes and guarded her tongue for now.

Nils saw her hands tremble as she unrolled the soft parchment, and felt true pity for her. What would it be like for a lady to have to marry a stranger, and such a stranger? And she did not know the worst of it yet.

She read the documents aloud for her mother and grandmother, and in a clear, steady voice. A remarkable woman, Claire of Summerbourne. It was a shame, really.

Claire fought back tears as she read the first document, the one that declared her father traitor, and all his property attaindered. Had it been written before or after his death? She hoped he had never heard the words.

In the second, Summerbourne and all attached estates, rights, and duties were given to "the king's right trusty servant, Renald de Lisle, knight and champion."

Champion. She glanced up to find Renald de Lisle watching her. If stone had eyes, they would look like that.

Hastily, she looked down again, but the word jangled in her head like an alarm bell. Champion meant that he could be called upon to fight in the king's name in single combat. It told of his quality as a fighter, but it also told her that he was a true blooded sword. She could see for herself that he was soulless.

Her whole body began to tremble at the thought of such a man owning Summerbourne. It was almost sacrilege.

Though her eyes blurred, she sucked in a deep breath and continued. "Because of past kindness between Lord Clarence of Summerbourne and Henry, now King of England…"—*as well to call it past, foul friend.*

"…the king in his mercy commands Lord

Renald of Summerbourne to take the said Clarence's dependents under his care as if they were his own. For this purpose, Lord Renald is permitted and commanded to choose one of the three maids of Summerbourne and take her to wife without delay."

That was the end. Claire looked up at him. "Permitted to choose, my lord? Why pretend that we have the choice?"

"Summerbourne may choose the bride."

"Not by this document. This gives *you* the choice."

"And I pass it on. It matters not to me."

Claire rolled the parchments, trying to find a hint of untruth in that flat statement. There was none. He truly didn't care which maiden was his bride.

Ludicrous to feel insulted, but she did. Her sacrifice, or the sacrifice of one of her aunts, meant nothing to the man.

The king's will was clear, however. De Lisle must marry one of them, and "without delay." What did that mean? She doubted a month or even a week would fit.

But a day? Surely they had at least a day.

It shouldn't take even that long to persuade Felice.

Though cold, Renald de Lisle wasn't a brute of a man, and he must stand high in the king's favor. Yes, thought Claire, aware of persuading herself, he was a gift from heaven for Felice. She would only have to get a good look at him to appreciate it.

But a jolt of alarm shot through her.

Felice was out in the camp and Claire and

de Lisle were here in the castle! What if he wanted the ceremony before he'd let the hostages back in? *Keep a calm head, Claire.*

She looked up, hoping her panic didn't show. "I do see that the king expects speedy action, my lord. But surely we are allowed a little time to grieve."

What was he thinking? She had no idea. She longed for a spontaneous word or gesture by which to judge him, but he was as incomprehensible as a text she'd once seen written in the Arabic script.

Those dark eyes studied her, shielded and quiet. "A little time, yes, Lady Claire. But do not try to avoid this."

She started. It was as if *he* could read *her.*

Then let him. She would not pretend. Claire rose and stalked over to thrust the documents back into the clerk's hands. Only his startled look alerted her to the fact that she'd crushed them in her anger.

She fought to stay calm, to keep her goal clear. She must, to delay any vows and get Felice back into Summerbourne. The best route to that goal was to sweeten him.

Though she hated to do it, she spoke meekly and gave him his correct title. "You must see, Lord Renald, that we are offering no resistance—"

"Must I?"

She swallowed. "No *effective* resistance. I pray you, my lord, bring my aunts back into Summerbourne. You have no need of hostages, and they must be in danger of an ague out there."

His steady eyes never left hers. "The sooner we're wed, Lady Claire, the sooner they can sleep in a dry bed. We can have the ceremony now, if you wish."

"No!" She found she'd taken a step back.

"You prefer your aunts to suffer an ague?"

"I prefer them safe and dry in here."

"Then marry me. What point in delay?"

"I need time to come to terms with—"

"Claire!" snapped her grandmother. "The man has a point. Get it over with."

Claire whirled on her. "He has *stolen* my father's property—your son's property!"

"Whose father stole it from my father. Don't forget that."

"It's not the same!"

"Seems the same to me."

Then Claire realized she'd not been able to stay meek for a moment.

Lady Agnes poked her with her stick. "If you'll take the advice of an old woman whose been through this before, you'll either marry this instant, or stir people into producing a decent meal. They're probably all standing around letting the stew burn, and there's nothing like good food to mellow a man. Or at least"—she winked—"only one thing."

Claire knew her cheeks had turned bright red. She wanted to scream that she'd rather poison this invader than feed him. But she'd much rather feed him than bed him. She glared at him, hoping he would read the message.

He simply stared back with that implacable, unreadable, complex expression. He planned to marry his bride-in-the-hand and secure his claim to Summerbourne. He didn't care which bride. He didn't care about the bride's feelings. He didn't care about looks or temperament, either. She'd sacrificed her hair for nothing. She and her aunts were pieces in a game, not people at all.

"Felice," she said in desperation, "the Lady Felice might be more comfortable with this marriage than I, my lord."

"Then she should have stayed behind."

"If you would just bring her in—"

"I have already explained why that is impossible."

"The Lady Amice could remain as hostage..." Oh, poor Amice. She'd faint with terror. "Or my mother could perhaps go out—"

"The choice has been made, Lady Claire."

She heard a sob and realized it was her own. She sucked in a deep breath. Time. Perhaps he'd think better of it with time.

Felice was beautiful. If she could only stand side by side with Felice, he'd surely see reason, especially now Claire was in ash-stained drab and with ruined hair.

She needed time so she could do something about Felice.

Time.

*Food!*

Suddenly her grandmother's words hit her. Food would soothe him and pass time, and arranging it would give her an excuse to leave the hall. To escape.

"I must go and see to the meal, my lord."

She expected objection, but he nodded.

As she turned to leave the room, Lady Agnes said, "Take the boy with you."

Claire saw Thomas standing in a shadowy corner, glaring at the usurper with bitter hate. Sweet Jesu, no. The last thing they needed was her brother doing something rash.

She went over to him. "Come with me to the kitchens, love."

"I want to stay here."

"Why?"

"To watch him."

"Why?"

He looked up then, so at least she'd broken the spell of fear and anger. "I *hate* him. That's Father's chair. We should—"

She squeezed his shoulder hard. "Don't, love. Don't. There's nothing you can do."

"Felice said I'm the man, now. That I have to protect you all. And I am, aren't I?"

Claire wished Felice an extra century or two in purgatory. "Thomas, there's nothing any of us can do now. And it's not really his fault."

"But you're going to marry him, aren't you? Then you'll take his side. Like Gran."

"Gran doesn't take his side. She just doesn't see any point in opposing him."

He shook his head, his blond curls bouncing with his frustration. "I mean after Hastings, when Grandfather came! Do you know Sigfrith in the stables?"

What on earth was he talking about? "Yes."

"He's Gran's cousin. He was part of the family

here, but now he works in the stables, and Gran doesn't care! That'll happen to me, won't it?"

Claire pulled him to her, smothering his rising voice with her body. "No, love. No, I'll make sure it won't." She pushed him back and looked into his wild eyes. "But, Thomas, the only way we'll make anything out of this is to step carefully. Come."

She pushed him before her out of the room, but couldn't resist one glance back. Renald de Lisle was watching her. A raised finger brought his squire to his side. A moment later, the young man followed her.

"I'm only going to the kitchens to check on the food. Presumably you want to eat."

"I'll be no trouble, lady."

No, she thought. You'll just stop us from running away. In such a short time Summerbourne had changed from home to prison.

To her surprise, the kitchens weren't in disorder. The mood was somber and some women dabbed at their eyes with their aprons, but work was going ahead. There would be a decent meal shortly.

The servants all clustered around her, of course, seeking information and reassurance. She gave the best she could.

"Is it true you're to marry him, lady?" asked the cook.

"One of us will marry him, yes."

"Better you, lady. Better you."

With that he turned away, but he'd placed another burden on her shoulders. Of course the people here wouldn't want Felice as mistress. She had a quick temper and a sharp hand

82

with punishment. Her way of always thinking the worst curdled the air.

"I can't take everyone's cares on myself."

It was only when she saw sympathy in the squire's blue eyes that she realized she'd spoken aloud.

She turned her mind firmly to efficiency and food.

As Claire was discussing a problem about the beer casks, laughter startled her. She glanced over and saw her guard relaxed at the long table and amusing the curious servants. Whether by accident or design, his youth, freckles, and cheerful grin were lightening the atmosphere in the kitchen by the moment.

She pushed away the hurt of that. She couldn't stay to take care of the people here, but she didn't want them miserable. If the squire and the master brought happiness, she must approve of that. It hurt, though, to see Thomas by his side, looking calmer as he listened to a story about London.

Oh, mercy, wasn't that what she'd wanted—that he put his anger and fear aside and accept the situation? Claire didn't know what she wanted anymore other than escape.

Why couldn't she slip out to the camp now? She would persuade Felice of the advantages of the match, and her aunt could come back in to prepare for her wedding. Claire would stay with Amice in her place.

First, she tried the obvious thing and strolled out of the kitchen.

Immediately, she heard the young man behind her.

She stopped to face him. "Are you going to creep around after me everywhere?"

"I'll stomp around after you if it'll make you feel better, lady."

"What point is there? Where would I go?"

He had an honest, open face, and seemed genuinely concerned. "Now that, I don't know, lady. But Lord Renald said to stay with you, so stay with you I will."

"Is he such a fearsome lord?"

"He expects his orders to be obeyed, lady. Doubtless you are the same."

He had her there. She must remember that the squire was no more a fool than the master. So, how to escape him? "I'm going to the maidens' chamber. Do you plan to follow me in there?"

"Is that upstairs, lady?"

"Yes."

"Then I reckon I'll make do with waiting outside. I don't suppose you can fly."

Claire puffed out a breath in annoyance and stalked off, but inwardly she was satisfied. So, he thought being on the upper floor would make escape impossible, did he?

The lower floor of the wooden manor house was mainly taken up by the great hall, her parents' solar, and her father's office. The upper floor held storage rooms, and sleeping chambers for the sons and daughters of the house. The windows were high off the ground. No wonder he thought her secure.

Claire went into the maidens' chamber and shut the door in his face. Then she dug in a chest, looking for the coiled rope.

This had been her father's idea after some people in a nearby town had been burned to death on the upper floor of a house. He'd ordered knotted ropes stored in each room and iron rings set into the wall to hold them.

Claire carried the rope to a window and assessed the area.

She immediately saw that it wasn't going to work.

Both windows overlooked open spaces, and now that the rain had stopped servants were hurrying about anxious to get on with long-neglected tasks. They could hardly miss her, scrambling down a rope. Perhaps the castle people wouldn't give her away, but she couldn't be sure.

Impatient though she was, she'd have to wait till dark. She could afford to. No wedding was planned for today. She tucked the rope back in the chest and left the room, ignoring the squire who followed her down to the ground floor like a patient hound.

The hall was deserted except for her grandmother in her usual spot, and the servants beginning to set up for the meal.

"Where is everyone?" she asked Lady Agnes.

"In the study. Lord Renald and his clerk are going over the records with your mother and some others. He has matters well in hand."

"Seized in a firm grasp, you mean."

"If you want. What *do* you want?"

Yesterday, thought Claire. Or rather, months ago, before madness, before death. "Choice," she said.

"Choice? That's a luxury indeed! But you have choice. Choices, in fact. You can marry the man and keep Summerbourne as it should be. Or you can talk Felice into it, and we'll all suffer under her bile. Or you can insist we all go out to be poor but honorable."

Claire faced her. "There's nothing wrong with honor."

"There's plenty wrong with starving to death." Then her grandmother shook her head. "Claire, Claire. Accept reality. I'll confess I was worried, urging you to marry a man sight-unseen. But not now. He'll make a fair husband for a woman of sense."

"I could never forget how he came here."

"You'll be surprised what you can forget. I forget my children's saint's days, which I never thought I would as I struggled to give them birth." Her lips twisted into a smile. "But I remember, too. I remember my mother talking to me much as I'm talking to you, and I remember thinking she was a heartless monster to be going on so when her husband and sons lay dead in a pit somewhere. Like it or not, Claire, I know what you're going through, and it doesn't seem so long ago, either. I tell you, in twenty, thirty years it won't seem much of anything. So don't do anything foolish. It's not worth it."

Claire turned away. Persuading Felice to marry the man wasn't foolish. True, Felice could have a sharp edge to her tongue, but she'd be gentler when contendedly married.

The question was, would she be content when married to Renald de Lisle?

Of course she would. They'd match like two

icicles under the eaves.

When a servant hurried over to tell her the dairy roof was leaking, Claire thanked heaven for escape from her tangled thoughts.

It wasn't an emergency, but she went outside anyway, raising her skirts and picking her way carefully over the logs laid down between the buildings. She still got her feet wet. It was another folly, and she knew it, but it was a relief to be outside and doing something.

A glance back showed her the squire following, grimacing as he tried to find footing in the slime. With a flicker of mischief, she thought that perhaps she'd go and check the waste-pits next.

However, by the time she'd arranged for the benches in the dairy to be moved out of harm's way, and for the thatcher to work on the roof the next day, any inclination to drag de Lisle's watchdog through the stinking middens had faded. The poor young man was only doing his duty.

It was only as she headed back toward the hall that she realized that taking care of Summerbourne wasn't really her job anymore, hers or her mother's. She could have sent the servant to de Lisle with his problems.

Ha! A war-wolf wouldn't know thatch from farrowing.

Thinking of farrowing reminded her that a new litter had been born just before the storm. She picked and slithered her way over to the sties to find the piglets virtually swimming in mud and loving it. She even found herself smiling at their antics.

It was true. Life went on.

"Fine healthy animals."

She swiveled and found that the squire had been replaced by his dark master.

Her smile died. "Why shouldn't they be?"

He leaned against one of the fence posts, making it look like a stick of kindling. "I don't know a great deal about husbandry, Lady Claire, but I suppose healthy stock doesn't come by accident."

It was the first time they'd been so close, and she found herself staring at his chest, estimating the amount of cloth needed to cover it. She made herself look up and meet his eyes instead. "What *do* you know a lot about?"

He did have true dark eyes, a deep dark brown, and large enough to be pleasing. But they looked bloodshot and weary. She realized he must have traveled long and hard, perhaps through the night, and wondered why. Even bearing her father's body, a halt for sleep, particularly in a storm, wouldn't have been unreasonable. Haste to see his property, she supposed.

And his bride.

"What do I know?" he echoed. "Weapons, defenses, armor, fighting."

"Killing matters?"

"Yes. I'm very efficient at killing."

*"Efficient!"*

"If it comes your time, my lady, would you rather be killed clumsily?"

Claire clutched onto a rail. Was he threatening to kill her?

He straightened. "I beg pardon, I did not

mean to frighten you. It is mere truth. If a person faces death by a sword, he hopes to face a tidy killer. If death by an ax, he hopes the ax bites true. If death by sickness, he hopes it strikes swiftly."

She stared, wondering if he had any human feelings at all. Then the horn blared for the meal and she seized the chance to escape. She turned too fast, however, and slipped in the mud. A strong hand caught her arm, steadying her. The next she knew, she was being carried in his arms.

"Put me down!" She felt helpless as a tiny child, and heaven knows she was not tiny. But her panic came from a startling jolt at being touched by him.

He stopped. "In the mud?"

"Yes!"

His face was so close she could see dark stubble, and that his lashes were long and thick.

"Lady Claire," he said, "no one of sense would choose to wade through this mire. If you could carry me, I'd gladly let you."

A giggle tempted her and she hastily looked away, surprised and unbalanced to discover that he wasn't many years older than herself, and that he could make a joke.

Perhaps it hadn't been a joke.

Navigating the muddy logs wasn't easy, even for him, but it was clear her weight was as nothing. She wasn't used to feeling so helpless.

Felice.

Definitely.

It must be Felice.

All the same, she couldn't deny the effect of his body against hers. She could feel that her cheeks were flushed, and could almost count her own rapid heartbeats. And it wasn't fear. It was, she knew, a woman's primitive reaction to a man.

She recognized danger.

Women did foolish things under that spell.

Once on solid ground, he eased her gracefully to her feet, but it seemed to involve a moment in his arms, a moment held close against his alarming body, looking into his rather handsome face. He touched the ends of her hair. "It seems a shame."

She fought against weakness, against this perilous attraction, and used the crudest weapon. "My father's death is a shame."

"True." But it was as if he wore armor against such things.

Fingers moved in her hair, setting up a tingle on her wanton scalp. She pushed back against his arm—slightly, but enough to tell her that her whole strength wouldn't break her free. Against her will, she began to tremble.

Abruptly, he let her go. "Your father's death was definitely a shame, Lady Claire. He was a good and gentle man." With that, he went to his place at the head table.

She wished she could take some insignificant seat, far away from him, from his disturbing body, but she had to go to the head table and sit at his right hand.

# Chapter 6

One of the household began to play music, and the squire brought water and bowl for hand washing. Ale came around and Lord Renald served Claire and her grandmother before taking any for himself. Claire noted his excellent manners with relief. She didn't need to feel guilty about foisting him off on her aunt. She really didn't.

So, how soon could she make her escape from Summerbourne... ?

"Lady Claire," he said, "do not seek to thwart the king's plans."

She stared at him. Could he read minds? "I'm still considering—"

"It is settled. When shall we be wed?"

Claire looked around, as if help might suddenly appear. Heavenly angels, perhaps? "My lord, my aunts must have the chance to meet you!"

"We have met."

She laughed shakily. "In the rain. At a difficult time. They should—"

"You are my bride, Lady Claire."

Lady Agnes was the only one close enough to be following the conversation, and if anything, she was grinning.

Claire tried a smile. "That was not quite what we had in mind, my lord."

"It was the arrangement made."

Perhaps there were angels around. The first platters interrupted. She served him soup, then took some herself, and concentrated on eating, hoping that would be the end of it.

As her nerves settled, she observed him out of the corner of her eye, counting up virtues to list to Felice.

He was the king's champion—that must mean he was high in Henry's favor.

He was quite handsome, if a lady liked a square face and big bones.

He spooned his soup neatly, without spilling any down himself.

Her perilous time in his arms had told her he didn't stink. Something of an aroma of horse and leather, but nothing foul.

He caught her looking at him, and his brows went up.

She spoke quickly before he started talking about weddings again. "Where do you come from, Lord Renald?"

Perhaps there was a hint of amusement in the tired eyes. "France, my lady. An area called Sauveterre."

"The savage land?" To Claire, it seemed all too suitable.

"It is harsh and craggy."

Like him. But not craggy. No...

"Do you miss the place?" she asked hastily, realizing she'd been studying him. This time his lips twitched with definite humor, but she shivered to think that he found her amusing.

"Perhaps we all miss our childhood homes a little. But England is my home now, and has been good to me."

A mouthful of bread threatened to stick in Claire's throat. Indeed it had. England had provided a rich and comfortable estate. She was grateful when he refilled her cup, and gulped down the ale.

A glance showed de Lisle watching her, one brow raised.

"When did you come to England?" she asked quickly.

"We visited now and then, but only settled here after Henry's coronation."

"We?"

He smiled more fully then, and she lost the suffocating sense of being a predator's plaything. "I speak of my friend FitzRoger and myself. We have been confreres for many years."

Confreres. Like brothers.

Brothers in arms.

The panic returned.

She'd heard of the man called FitzRoger— all England had. Bastard FitzRoger, he was usually called, from his irregular birth, and probably from his nature. He was apparently undefeated in the barbaric tourneys they held abroad, and had been appointed King Henry's High Champion. He was doubtless a man like Baldwin of Biggin.

"My friend married not long ago," he continued, breaking the end off a loaf and sharing it with her. "A lady of lands north of here, a place called Carrisford. Perhaps you have heard of it."

"I've visited there," she said in surprise. "It is a mighty stone castle and contains many works of art. Lord Bernard, like my father, is a scholar and appreciates beautiful things."

"Alas, lady, Lord Bernard is dead."

Her memory coincided with his words. "Ah, yes. We heard. A sad event."

But then another mouthful threatened to choke her. The news had come that Lord Bernard had died of wound fever after a quite minor hunting injury. They had all been saddened, for he'd been a good man. No one had suspected foul play.

Now Claire wondered. A great man dead and his daughter, poor gentle Imogen, given to another of the king's favorites. Had she, too, been told to marry immediately, forced to the altar to wed a man even bigger and more brutal than this one?

She pushed aside her bowl.

"The pottage does not agree with you, Lady Claire?"

"I have little appetite today."

She thought he'd press her to eat, but he didn't. He didn't press her to talk, either, but turned to converse with her grandmother. Claire turned to his clerk, who sat at her other side.

"Have you served Lord Renald long, Brother?"

He had an amiable, undistinguished face and mousy hair, but his eyes were keen and intelligent. "Not long at all, lady."

Now she couldn't think what to say next, especially as her mind was buzzing with thoughts about Carrisford. "What do you think of Summerbourne?" she tried.

"A very pleasant spot, and prosperous, it

94

would seem." He smiled at her. "I come from the north, lady, which is a harsher land."

They managed a desultory conversation until the meal was over. Then she could escape up to her room to worry about Lord Bernard of Carrisford's convenient death.

First Lord Bernard. Now her father. Two estates tossed into the hands of the king's favorites.

Was there more to her father's death than an accident of battle? She hated to even think it, but had her father been *murdered*?

Her father had believed that God defended the just, but did God protect against murder? Too many examples said no. Simply riding the roads it was possible to be attacked by unruly soldiers or outlaws. One of her uncles had died that way, and he'd surely been a better man than his murderer.

No, God did not tamper with ordinary life, keeping everything fair. Crops failed and people starved. Fires burned down houses. A few days ago, the cooper's sweet, young daughter had drowned.

But if it was murder, what should they do? What *could* they do?

Claire slipped downstairs to her mother's room—her new room, the small chamber next to the solar, used in the past for babies.

"Imogen is married to this FitzRoger?" said her mother, who was already in her loose night robe. "Well, for all we know he's an honorable man."

"*Bastard* FitzRoger? Mother, Lord Bernard's

death was so unexpected! And now Father—"

"Clarence's death was not at all unexpected, Claire. What nonsense are you following, now?"

Claire twisted her hands together, wondering if this all was driving her mad. "Do you know exactly how Father died?"

Her mother put her hand to her throat. "How can you ask—"

"I need to know! Whether it was... righteous."

Her mother sighed deeply. "It was a sword wound to the heart, Claire. From the front. With him in mail. It could only have come about in battle. Now please, cease all this wild thinking!"

"What battle? Perhaps we should ask where and when—"

Lady Murielle flung up her hands. "Claire, I don't want to know where and when! What will it change?"

Claire looked around as if someone might have sneaked into the room to overhear. Then she whispered, "What if the king somehow arranged Father's death..."

Her shoulders were seized in a desperate grip. "Claire, Claire! Are you chasing treason too? It doesn't matter if Henry Beauclerk killed your father with his own hands! Clarence supported a treasonous invasion. The invasion failed and all was lost. The only thing now is for you to marry Lord Renald."

"But—"

"Claire, *think*! Think of your brother's plight. Do you want to see him a beggar?"

Claire bit her unsteady lips. She loved her brother, but she wished her mother would consider her own feelings. "It's my life, Mother. My whole life."

Lady Murielle gentled her grip and patted Claire's cheek. "You should have been married years ago, dearest, and here's a fine, handsome young man for you. I know it's hard, coming so fast after your father's death, but in all other respects he is an excellent match. I'm sure he will make you a good husband."

Claire stared at her mother. "He's made of granite and has a soul of lead. He talks about death as you and I would talk of needlework."

Her mother's smile became rather fixed, but still she smiled. "You are fanciful. This day has been no easier for him than for us. Give him time to show you his gentler side."

What gentler side? Claire asked, but silently. There was no point. Her mother would see virtues in Satan if he offered security to her vulnerable son.

She returned to her room, swallowing tears that came of abandonment, holding on to the thought that darkness was falling and she soon would be able to escape. To get to Felice and persuade her to marry Renald de Lisle.

She called for Prissy and Maria and let them prepare her for bed. Naked, she slipped between the sheets as her women settled on the pallets on the floor. Now she had only to wait for them, for all of Summerbourne, to be deep asleep.

It took a while to get used to being alone in the big bed. When she thought of how her world has changed in one day, tears started, turning into a private, healing flood of them. She drifted into sleep and awoke later with a start in the dark.

In the distance, the convent bell was ringing matins. Midnight. It was time and past time! She slipped out of bed and into her clothes, then eased up the chest lid and took out her rope. Trying to be silent, she tied it firmly to the hook by the window.

Looking out at the dark night, her heart raced. Midnight was the dark hour—the time of monsters and dark magic, when evil lurked. She'd never been out of Summerbourne in the night. But then she realized that the manor was no longer safe, even if she huddled by the hearth fire. Midnight had invaded in the form of the new lord.

Everyone but the guards was asleep. By the light of the half-moon, she watched two of them walking the palisade. They'd be Summerbourne men, but still might call the alarm. She waited until they were as far away as possible, then eased over the sill and quickly down the rope.

The ground was a little firmer, so it wasn't too hard to pick her way toward the postern gate. She was glad that she knew the place, however, for the moonlight did little to ease the shadows and played tricks on the eyes. She kept imagining de Lisle in his long dark cloak, lurking in dark corners.

She crossed herself. *Sweet Virgin protect me from the evils of the night.*

The postern lay behind the stables on the opposite side of Summerbourne from the main gate. It was a waist-high hatch, firmly barred on the inside, but providing an emergency escape. She supposed it could be used in attack, too, but not easily since a person had to go through it on hands and knees.

She eased up the bar, opened the door, and crawled through.

After carefully closing it again, she slithered down the muddy side of the ditch, praying that no guard glanced her way. She didn't expect them to be alert. Armed men were camped outside as extra defense, and if the enemy wanted to get in, they had only to knock.

The smell hit her, and she realized—too late—that the rain would have filled the ditch with foul drainage. She sank in it up to her knees and had to choke back a cry of disgust. Holding her breath and her nose, she waded through. By the time she scrambled up the other slippery bank, the stench was part of her.

She collapsed on the grass, realizing then that she hadn't thought how she was going to approach an armed camp and get into one of the tents.

Impulsive yet again. Tears stung her eyes, and she wasn't sure if it was misery or just the fumes rising off her.

Resolutely, she pulled herself together. It was her life at issue here. She was out. That was an achievement. Now she had to make her way around to the front of the manor enclave to where her aunts were held. As she pushed to her feet she decided that the most likely thing his men would do with her would be to put her in with her aunts and send for their master.

There, see. It would be easy. By the time he arrived, Felice would be a blushing, eager bride.

She soon found that it wouldn't be easy.

For a start, she couldn't just walk. Her father might not have been warlike, but he'd kept Summerbourne secure. No one could sneak up on the manor because the ground all around was kept clear by the sheep that grazed there.

She tried scuttling along bent double, but that only gave her a great deal more sympathy for her grandmother. She settled in the end to crawling over the muddy grass, her skirts dreadfully in the way. She prayed that if the guards saw her, they'd think she was a sheep.

She bit her lip. She'd thought that they were all sheep to de Lisle's wolf. She'd thought that midnight was his hour. Now she prayed she was entirely wrong and that Summerbourne's wolf was fast asleep.

She reached the corner of the palisade with only a few encounters with sheep droppings to add to her disastrous state. Just this side to go along and she'd be almost there. Then she heard voices behind her. Someone had found the unbarred postern!

She rose to run, but then realized that would give her away entirely. Already the guards on the palisade were answering faint questions. She went flat on the soggy ground and lay still. Perhaps they didn't know she'd escaped and would think the gate had been left unbarred.

Then she realized that she'd left the rope hanging down the wall.

Fool!

Impulsive, silly fool.

Silence fell, as if the world held its breath.

What was happening? Had they given up and gone back to bed?

Dare she move yet?

She heard a rustling nearby. Her imagination.

No, there it was again. Sheep.

Or a rabbit from the warren.

Would a rabbit squelch?

Hobgoblin? Or worse...

She couldn't bear it. Slowly, she eased her head to the side to peer. A huge, dark shape blocked the sky, leaned down—

At the first touch, she tried madly to scramble away. A hand grasped the back of her clothes and stopped her. Before she could scream, she was lifted straight out of the mud and tossed over a massive shoulder like a bundle of old rags.

The wolf!

In terror, she kicked and pounded at his back.

A hard, stinging slap to her behind made her go still, but terror still choked her. What would he do to her?

At the portal gate, he virtually dropped her. "Through."

This was no time to argue. Claire scuttled through then turned to watch him crawl through after her. The tight squeeze didn't ease her fear. Two of the castle servants stood nearby bearing torches, but they wouldn't help her. They were staring at her as if she were a monster at a fair.

His squire—her guard—came through after de Lisle and gave her a disgusted look. Would he be beaten, too?

Claire straightened her spine and tried to pretend that she wasn't mud-covered, stinking, and terrified.

De Lisle seized her arm and dragged her toward the hall. She didn't protest. She was potently aware that he could crush her flesh down to the bone. It was dawning on her, moreover, that she'd failed. She might have to *marry* this man, the one with midnight in his soul.

He stopped, and they weren't at the hall yet.

Looking around wildly, Claire saw that they were by the well. Was he going to drown her?

"Josce, pull up some water."

She stared at him, nearly beyond rational thought. "What are you going to do?"

"Clean you up, you stupid woman."

"I'll bathe—"

"You're too filthy for a bath. And after chasing you, so am I." He took the bucket from his squire and poured water over her.

She cried out in the icy deluge, but when she tried to run, he grabbed her hair. In moments another bucketful sluiced over her and her teeth started to chatter.

"No more," she gasped. "I'm sorry."

"This isn't punishment." He turned her roughly, shaking his head. "Go on, then. Your women should be ready by now. Don't touch anything until you're stripped and washed."

Claire was almost too dazed to make sense of his words, but she grasped that she had a reprieve. She fled for the safety of the hall.

Prissy was waiting for her, still half asleep, but awake enough to shriek at the sight. "Lady Claire! What now?"

She was hustled to the kitchen and a tub. Claire had to accept that stripping off her ruined clothes and sinking into the warm, herb-scented water was not the most terrible thing that had happened to her in her life.

But as she scrubbed she cried.

She cried because she'd failed and she knew he'd never give her another chance to escape.

She also cried from fear because he'd implied that punishment was still to come. In her gentle father's house, punishment was rare and mild. She'd heard stories, though, and the thought of that blow to her behind combined with his wide leather belt set her to trembling.

It was fear that kept her in the water long after it had cooled. In the end, Prissy held out a towel. "Come on, Lady Claire. You'll wrinkle like a summer apple if you stay in there much longer!"

Claire had to stand into the large, warm

drying cloth. Too soon, she was in a clean shift. "I only need a blanket to wrap round me while I go to my room, Prissy."

The maid gave her a strange look. "If you want, lady. But he's waiting to speak to you."

"Now?" It came out as a squeak, so she cleared her throat and repeated it. "Now?"

"Yes, now. And if you ask me, he's the patience of a saint. You running out like that. I don't know what you were thinking of…"

Claire let the lecture wash over her.

Now.

He was waiting for her now, doubtless growing angrier by the moment.

"Hurry up, Prissy!"

The maid had brought some of her best garments—a fine, cream linen kirtle and a pale green tunic worked in cream and pink flowers. Claire was too weary and frightened to protest. And in truth perhaps a bit of prettiness might be wise. It might weaken his rage.

She was seriously regretting her hair.

It took all Claire's courage to enter the passageway to the hall. She hoped he couldn't hear her teeth chattering.

He waited in the shadows, mighty arms folded across massive chest, frowning darkly into nothingness. At some sound she made, he straightened, instantly lethal. A squeak of panic escaped and Claire stepped back.

He relaxed and his eyes traveled over her once quickly, then again a great deal more slowly. "I was right. You do improve with cleaning."

*All the tastier for my big, white teeth.* **She** decided silence was safer, especially since she wasn't sure she could be coherent.

With a slight jerk of his head, he said, "The office," clearly ordering her to lead the way.

Claire was glad to obey. If she could keep her back straight, he might not know about her fear. She would not give him the satisfaction of seeing her tremble.

She hadn't counted, however, on how her father's special room would affect her. She and he had spent so much time here.

Someone had lit the tall standard candle. Despite the fact that this man had used the room, claimed it as his own, in the warm glow it looked as if her father had just stepped out.

His rabbit fur still lay draped across a bench, waiting for his hand. Claire remembered snuggling under that fur with him on winter days as he taught her to read.

Most of his books were out of sight, locked in the chests which were themselves works of art. One book, however, lay open on his lectern. He'd risen from reading it and ridden off to rebellion, and she'd left it that way, waiting for his return.

The rich hangings stirred under a breeze from the open shutters as if the room sighed.

Claire covered her mouth with her hand, trying to hold back the pain that swelled from her chest, burned around her eyes...

She didn't want...

She couldn't...

It burst free.

There was something big and strong to cry into, to beat against, to fight as she spilled out her agony of loss. She raged against fate, against heaven, and against the usurping King of England who'd proved to be such a false friend.

When she realized it was Renald de Lisle she cried into, she pushed away, backed away, scrubbing her face free of the betraying tears. Ah, Jesu, he was the last man she wanted to see her like this!

Turning away, she squeezed her hands together, sucking in deep breaths, fighting the battle for control. When she thought she could speak, she faced him. "So..." It came out hoarsely and she cleared her throat. "So, what are you going to do with me?"

He studied her thoughtfully, all burnished angles and dark shadows. "It seems that I'm going to marry you, Lady Claire."

She shook her head. "Not that. How are you going to punish me?"

The silence stretched. Her teeth started chattering again and she couldn't stop them.

He suddenly shook his head. "I don't care for minor thrashings, Lady Claire. I'll keep a tally of your crimes until I think you deserve a really good one." He looked around the room. "Your father had many books. Do you, too, enjoy reading?"

Bewildered, but beginning to think she'd keep a whole skin, she said, "Yes."

"I'll have them moved to the solar for your use when we are wed."

"But you—"

"I am scarce able to pick out words, my lady. They are no use to me. But if you've read them," he added, a sudden edge to his voice, "I'd expect a little more wisdom. What, by the cross, did you think you were doing?"

She scrabbled for a story, but in the end could only tell the truth. "I wanted to speak to Felice."

His brows rose. "And for that you crawled through the ditch?"

"I was desperate."

"*Why?*"

Nerves jumping again, she gabbled, "I hoped to persuade my aunt to marry you, Lord Renald. She's desperate enough..."

She dried up, hearing how insulting she sounded.

She should have known not to be concerned about sensitive feelings. It bounced right off him. In fact, she thought she saw a flicker of light in his eyes. "An enthusiastic wife is certainly an attraction. She'll be more willing than you?"

She hadn't considered persuading *him* of the advantages. "I'm sure of it! She's keen to marry, and she'd like such a one as you—a man high in the king's favor." It was an excellent time to give him some hints of how to please Felice. "She was fearful, my lord, and at first impression, you are a little daunting. But I'm sure you could assure her..."

His brows rose. "Perhaps I really am daunting, Lady Claire."

"Oh no, I'm sure that—" Claire broke off,

for she was not sure of any such thing. "I'm sure you can't be as bad as—" That was even worse. His brows were up again, but that predatory humor twitched his lips.

Just like a wolf eyeing a trapped rabbit.

Claire sucked in a breath. "If you can show Felice how kind and gentle you can be, my lord, she will be willing, I'm sure."

"Kind and gentle." He raised a hand and rubbed those troubling lips with a knuckle. "I see. But why should I want the Lady Felice as wife?"

"She is very beautiful. Perhaps you couldn't quite see that in the rain." Claire dug in her mind. "And gifted at music. She's also an excellent manager. Very frugal."

A true smile flickered, and Claire was astonished to feel a tiny flare of regret, a suspicion that there might be something about this man worth discovering.

The smile touched his dark eyes. "Are you reconsidering, Lady Claire?"

"No!" She stamped on the folly.

Despite the smile, he lived his life in midnight shades, stained with blood. He had chosen violence as his life. He was a killer with no interest in arts and beauty. He had come here to seize all her father's possessions, the most valuable of which he couldn't appreciate at all.

The smile disappeared. "Lady Felice seems prideful and sharp of tongue. I may be slow to anger, but I will not take insolence."

"Felice would not be *insolent* exactly. She just... just likes to express her opinions."

"And you do not?"

Even on short acquaintance, he must know that wasn't true. "My opinions are more moderate, Lord Renald."

"Are they, indeed? But if we marry, you would be meek and dutiful?"

Claire didn't like the direction of the conversation. "*Felice* is much better suited to be your wife, my lord. She's the oldest, you know."

"Lady Felice, however, does not want to be my wife. In the few words we exchanged, she was even less flattering than you. I seem to remember something about low birth and manners."

"She was frightened, my lord, that's all. We all were. Now she's had time to think, when she really meets you..."

His brows rose again. "But you have truly met me, demoiselle, and seem desperate to escape."

Cheeks that showed every touch of embarrassment were a great nuisance. Claire tried pure honesty. "I have a particular feeling about violence, my lord. About men who make violence their life. If I marry, I will choose a man of peace."

"It's rather hard to marry a monk."

"My father was not a monk!"

"Your father was unique," he said flatly, "and died too young."

"He would not have died young if—"

"If he'd taken the trouble to train for war?" de Lisle offered, but the look in his eyes told her he knew that wasn't what she'd been about to say. That he'd have been safe if Henry Beauclerk hadn't stolen the crown.

Claire turned away from the tormenting man. "Please, my lord, let me at least write to Felice. I'm sure I can persuade her that there are many advantages to being your wife."

"Why not list them for me? They sound like pleasant hearing."

She ignored that frivolity, and waited for a reply.

"Very well."

She turned back to study him warily.

"Write it now." He indicated the parchment and inks on her desk. "I will have it sent to the camp and your aunt awoken so she can read it." He moved the tall standard candle to provide light.

In a strange way, that little thing settled it. Claire could hardly move the heavy iron object, yet he lifted it one-handed and set it down by the desk with perfect control. That proof of what he was entirely wiped out an intriguing smile and a sense of mystery.

She sat at the desk and chose a scrap of vellum, considering her words. Then she wrote the arguments she'd prepared in her mind. She read it over and didn't find it very persuasive. It seemed to be largely negatives. What positives would Felice want in her "great man"?

Claire wrote that he was handsome and seemed healthy. Desperate to snare her aunt's interest, she expanded upon that a bit. She even mentioned his smile.

It still didn't seem enough.

She knew Felice was very interested in bed

matters but had a fear of big men. Big in certain parts. Some story or other had convinced her that slim-hipped women risked being torn in the marriage bed. She'd often embarrassed Claire by eyeing men's crotches and trying to assess their size, and her desire for a "great" man who was not also "big" had made her search for a husband even more difficult. Though she hated to, Claire speculated on such matters.

Thanks be to God that he couldn't read!

She went over what she'd wrote, guiltily aware of having gone beyond strict accuracy. She had no idea about his intimate size or bed skills. Her pen hovered as she struggled with whether to cross it out or not.

But then she put down the pen and gave it to him. Felice's fears were nonsense anyway. Women were built to take men, and apart from the hymen, no damage occurred.

He rolled the vellum and tucked it under his belt. "Now, Lady Claire, what am I do to with you for the rest of the night?"

She was sliding off the seat, but at that she froze. "What do you mean? I intend to return to my bed."

"But will you stay there?"

"I have no reason to wander."

"You had no reason before."

She stood and faced him. "You are going to have to trust me, Lord Renald."

"Why?" He walked over and opened the door. His squire—Josce—stood outside, caught in mid-yawn.

"My lord!" He snapped to alertness.

"Go find the lad—Thomas." De Lisle turned back to Claire. "Where does he sleep?"

"With some male servants on the upper floor. But you can't—"

"A hostage will ensure that you are here come morning."

"You have my aunts out in your camp!"

"I suspect your brother means more to you." He turned back to his squire.

"No. Please!"

When he turned slowly back, she said, "He'll be so frightened."

"I'm not going to hang him up by his thumbs—unless you run away, that is. He should sleep with me and my men. It's more suitable."

"More suitable!"

"He must start his training as a page."

"But..." Claire couldn't think of a rational argument. She could only imagine her brother's terror at being awoken at midnight and dragged off to share a room with these rough men. "No, please. I promise. I'll be here in the morning."

He studied her long enough to make her want to fiddle with something. She caught herself licking her lips.

"Josce needs his sleep," he said abruptly, "as do I. So I'll trust you. But I give you fair warning, my lady. Play me false and I'll find you, and your tally will definitely be complete."

Brother Nils struggled out of deep sleep to find the devil had him by the shoulder. But then he realized it was just Lord Renald looming in the dark room. His lord beckoned him out of the solar, and with a groan, Nils had to go. They'd ridden through the previous night without rest. Was the man human?

Rubbing his eyes, he staggered after him to the study, where a letter was thrust at him. "Read that to me."

At this time of night? But Renald de Lisle, though a good lord, was not the type one argued with. Nils unrolled what was clearly a scrap from the edge of a skin. The writing was fine, however, worthy of the best documents. *"To Felice of Summerbourne from her affectionate niece, Claire."* Nils looks up in surprise, both that the lady could write so well, and that he was being asked to read a private document.

"Go on."

Nils shrugged. The lady was soon to be his lord's wife. *"My dear Felice, I write to you about Lord Renald de Lisle, and his request to marry one of the maidens of Summerbourne..."*

Nils read through what was clearly a review of a discussion held earlier. It placed great emphasis on the fact that the unwanted husband would mostly be absent.

"Like a wild animal," Lord Renald commented, "best viewed from a distance." Nils had to suppress a smile, for it sounded exactly like that.

"Does she have anything more positive to say?"

"Oh, yes, my lord. She writes, *I do not think his wife will find him intolerable in the times when he is at Summerbourne. He has not shouted, or bellowed, and has not yet struck anyone. He has*

113

*not broken anything through clumsiness or rage, and he eats neatly and with clean hands.*"

As he read, Nils flickered glances at Lord Renald, wondering just what he was making of this. Not many men get to read such a frank analysis of their virtues and flaws.

Renald just said, "Is that the best she can do?"

"Er... no, my lord. *In those brief moments in his camp, Felice, and all being cloaked, you may not have seen that Lord Renald is a handsome man—*"

"Ah."

Nils looked over and completed the sentence. *"of the heavy sort."*

After a moment, Lord Renald said, "She should meet Luc le Gros."

Nils laughed at that, but he carried on, keen to read more of this extraordinary document. *"He seems in excellent health and still has all his teeth, at least at the front. His skin suggests a healthy man, and is free of scar or blemish. There is no foul smell to him that would indicate internal problems or a lack of cleanliness..."*

He couldn't resist looking up to check the reaction.

"A positive hymn of praise."

As often was the case, Nils couldn't tell if Lord Renald was amused or not. He himself was close to losing control of his voice. *"...though he does smell rather strongly of horse, leather, and such. It is only to be expected of a man of his sort, and I'm sure he can be encouraged to strip before intimacy, if that be your will."*

"The Lady Claire is clearly an excellent judge of character."

Nils gave in to laughter, dabbing at his eyes with his sleeve.

"Is there more?" Renald asked.

"Oh, yes, my lord."

"In a similar vein?"

"I suppose…" Nils ran his eye ahead a bit, then looked up, rather alarmed.

"Go on."

Nils did begin to feel guilty at reading this, which the lady clearly would not ever want Lord Renald to hear. *"What is more, Felice, I feel sure that Lord Renald would be a lusty and satisfying lover. From the way he eyes the pretty maids, he is clearly interested in such matters. From the fact that he does not bother them, I judge him to use restraint and courtesy in his loving, which must surely make for a good bed partner. And though he is a big man, I'm sure his personal endowments must be…"*—Nils thought about changing it, but couldn't see how—*"modest…"*

"Modest? As in shrinking violet?"

*"And I think he would be able to use his…* She's scribbled over and scratched out here, my lord. I'm not sure what she means."

"I am, but I'm very curious as to what she actually wrote."

Nils put the parchment closer to the candle and squinted. "Ah… *able to use his genitalia*—"

Lord Renald was shaking his head, but his lips were definitely unsteady.

"—*with consideration,*" Nils continued, *"out of…"*

115

"Yes?"

Nils looked at him. *"Out of long practice."*

"Well, that's one thing right. Is that it?"

Nils was a little surprised. Lord Renald hadn't shown much interest in women in the few days he'd known him. He hadn't talked about them, or told a dirty joke. But then, circumstances hadn't been favorable.

"Just the ending, my lord. *So I ask if you wish to reconsider. If you decide that you want to be the bride, Lord Renald will arrange for you to come into Summerbourne and for me to join Amice in the camp. As oldest you have first right to take him as husband, and I would not deprive you of that, him being so close to your ideal man."*

Lord Renald nodded. "Clever girl. She is clever, Nils, even if remarkably stupid about some things."

Having been given a glimpse into her secrets, Nils felt rather protective of poor Lady Claire. "She's young, my lord."

"Little younger than you."

"But I'm not being forced to marry a stranger."

The dark brows rose. "The mere thought of you in such a situation could tangle my mind." Renald rose to pace the small room. "I wonder if that letter will sway the aunt."

There was a question in it, and Nils couldn't resist saying, "I thought I wasn't your adviser."

"Don't be impudent."

The tone carried no threat, however, and Nils laughed. "There's no way to say, my lord. You do not plan to send the letter?"

"I keep my word. But I don't want the

116

Lady Felice tempted, even for a moment." He stood in thought for a moment, then nodded. "The delicious Lady Claire, however, has just told me how to make sure her aunt doesn't change her mind."

## Chapter 7

Grief and anxiety are not good pillows. After a restless night, Claire was relieved to see sunrise, especially as it brought the hope that today Felice would offer to be the invader's bride. The next step, however, would be to leave Summerbourne. She lay, watching sun play on the beams of her bedchamber, storing up the lifelong sounds of her home.

She was realizing that her grandmother was right. She'd had suitors, and could have married. However, none of the men had been tempting enough to outweigh the love of her home. Her mother had warned that one day she'd have to leave, but Claire had imagined that life could drift on forever as it was.

Folly.

When her maids stirred, she slipped out of bed, only remembering her plaits when she reached out of habit to move them. The ends felt strange, like rough floss, and the breeze chilled her naked nape.

She couldn't exactly regret the act. It had been one of anger and rebellion, yes, but also one of deep grief. Her father, however, was doubtless shaking his head in heaven over her impulsive act.

Was it any better, she thought rebelliously, that he had considered for nearly a year before becoming a rebel? It had still led to disaster.

She pushed away such disloyal thoughts and chose the clothes she had worn the night before. Since Felice would be de Lisle's bride, there was no longer any need to try to appear unattractive.

Her hair was beyond hope, however. All she could do was hide it, which wouldn't be easy now that it was developing a wild independence. Stray tendrils had always curled around her face, but now it was springing out in all directions. She must look like a dandelion puff!

Refusing to moan over what couldn't be changed, she simply draped a long veil over it all and secured it with an embroidered circlet, well pulled down. Then she ventured out to attend to her usual duties in the house.

First she visited her mother. Lady Murielle seemed composed, but had no interest in taking care of Summerbourne. It was someone else's property. Let him do the work.

Claire, however, wasn't sure he would or could, and she wasn't the sort to stand by and watch things spoil. She sighed and went off to do the work of four. Five, if de Lisle was included. As she rushed from hall to kitchens to pantry to stores, she kept an eye open for Thomas. She hated to imagine what he could be up to. Had he given up his anger? Even if he had, she wasn't sure he would obey commands from de Lisle. If he didn't, what would that man do to him?

In view of her mood, Summerbourne was distressingly normal. The servants attended to their usual tasks. The busy kitchens wafted the comforts of baking bread and roasting meat. When the cook complained again about the beer, Claire headed for the brewhouse, hoping there'd be less good cheer there.

The fresh morning sun was out, however, the dismal rain only a memory in muddy corners. She couldn't resist stopping to turn her face up, eyes closed, to drink in the light and warmth. Sounds became clearer—the comforting background of everyday activity with the curlicues of birdsong frolicking on top.

Today it was easier to imagine a golden heaven, to picture her father up there in perpetual sunshine, surrounded by angel song, smiling down like the sun on his home. Tears welled, but they were gentle ones. She couldn't doubt that he was in paradise, so he must be happy now, happy as he never could have been if he had shirked the call of his conscience.

Abandoning the brewhouse for the moment, she slipped into the fenced garden to gather flowers, then scattered them on the raw earth of her father's grave. In time the wound in the earth would heal, as would the wound in her heart.

Grass would grow here, and she would plant flowers in his memory and—

But she wouldn't be here to tend his grave.

That thought shocked her to stillness. She couldn't stay, and once Felice was Lady of

Summerbourne, she wouldn't want to, but she wished she could tend her father's grave.

If she married de Lisle...

She shook her head. The price was too high—marriage to the wrong sort of man, and having to live in Summerbourne under such unworthy ownership.

Grasping the comfort of duty, she hurried off on an errand to the stone brewhouse. Perhaps in discussing the problems there, she could forget other things.

When she emerged, however, a movement caught her eye. Renald de Lisle had come out of the hall and stood watching her. In a dark red tunic and gray braies, he was like a bloody cloud on the lovely day, and his gaze, even from a distance, brushed like a chill breeze.

She hurried on, tugging her circlet down to try to keep her veil decorously in place. Soon however, he came up beside her, ominously preceded by his shadow.

"Where is your brother, Lady Claire?"

Oh no. She stopped to face him. "I don't know. I'm sure—"

"Did you sneak him out of Summerbourne last night? Was that the purpose of your mad folly?"

Claire gaped. "No! Of course not. He must be around somewhere." She searched the courtyard desperately. How could Thomas be so foolish?

"It is time, past time, for him to learn discipline."

"Discipline!" She immediately thought of the rod.

"He must work. He must prepare for his future."

"I know that. I'm sorry. But please don't beat him. He's not used—"

She saw his jaw tighten. "He should be. Nothing grows well growing wild." But then he took a deep breath, pulling a strangely disarming face. "I won't beat him, Lady Claire. This time. For your sake. But persuade him to obey."

That *for your sake* ran along her nerves like a rasp. Like a threat. "I'll go find him," she said and moved away.

He grasped her arm, not with the strength she knew he possessed, but firmly enough. "Why not show me around? We might spot him as we go."

She had no escape from this man yet, and perhaps this way she could distract him from Thomas's rebellion. "If you wish, my lord."

He released her, and they walked on side by side. Meek and pleasant, she thought. That's the key. "I think you'll find all in order, my lord, except that the last batch of barrels seems to have been poorly made. I'm about to discuss the matter with Rolf the Cooper."

"Summerbourne seems a thriving place."

"I think so."

"Due largely to your work?"

"Not at all. My mother and aunts do their part. When they are able and present," she added before realizing that wasn't exactly meek.

"I can do nothing to ease your mother's grief,

121

but you and your aunts will be back together as soon as I am betrothed to one of you."

"I'm sure *Felice* will be eager, my lord." Claire plunged with relief into the cooper's shop.

She spoke to the man and de Lisle didn't interfere, but he still made her nervous. As a result, she spoke to the cooper more strongly than she'd intended, and as they left, she sighed.

"Correcting the peasantry upsets you?"

"I am upset with myself because I was harsher than I meant to be."

She half turned to go back, to moderate her words, but he stayed her with a touch. "His work was not shoddy?"

She edged away from his hand, his disturbing hand. "His young daughter drowned in the river last week. It's not surprising—"

"What if his poor work endangered others?"

"I know. I know. But I spoke so sharply to impress you, my lord. For no other reason." Oh dear. That wasn't wise.

The brows rose. "Have you decided you want to be my bride after all?"

"No!" At his look, she confessed. "I just didn't want you to think of me as a child or a fool. After last night."

Something flickered in his eyes. "I assure you, my lady, after last night I do not think of you as a child."

She would have run from him then if dignity had allowed. Instead, she turned away. "Come to the dairy, my lord."

The cool of the stone building was welcome to her panicked cheeks. She must stop letting him fluster her like this! Soon she'd be free of him. Very soon.

"The milking shed is through there." She indicated a wooden door. "But the milch cows and goats will be out in the pasture now. Do you understand how a dairy works, my lord?"

He looked around, big and dark in this woman's place. "I see maids hard at work." The maids brushed and dimpled at him, and Claire knew some of them would be happy to warm the new lord's bed. Well, that would be Felice's problem, not hers.

"The herdsmen milk the animals," she said, "then bring the milk here for the maids to sieve. Now it's had time to settle—"

"They are skimming the cream."

He strolled over to where one maid deftly scooped the cream off the top of the milk then poured it into a stone jug. Joan was one of the best dairymaids, and didn't spill a drop, but at that moment Claire could have tossed her out to work in the fields for the way she was eyeing Renald de Lisle.

He smiled back at the dairymaid as he slid a fingertip along the top of her milk so it gathered a yellow cap. Then he raised it to his lips, but turned to Claire. "Fine cream."

Claire knew she had turned bright red—partly with anger, partly with some other emotion. "Fine cream makes fine butter—if it is not guzzled by passing rogues!" Her cursed veil slipped, and she pushed it straight and tugged the circlet fiercely down. Almost immediately it started to ride up again. Oh, if only she had the dignity of her long hair back!

She marched over to the churn, which was operated by sensible, middle-aged Freda, but even Freda grinned at de Lisle as if she'd like a chance in his bed.

Claire directed his attention to a large vat. "Cheese. Not today's milk. The curds are setting." She held out a wooden cup to him. "Buttermilk?"

He took it and drank. "Yesterday's, of course."

She stared. "How did you know?"

"I know it takes time to make butter, and besides, the contents of that churn are still liquid. The sound says it."

She drained her cup and put it down with a slap. "I'm not surprised that you're familiar with dairies, my lord. After all, the maids rarely are."

"True enough," he said as he followed her out, and she heard humor. He didn't even have the shame to deny her implication that dairymaids were often wanton.

"Where next?" he asked.

"The weavers." Her veil slid backward this time. With a huff, she salvaged dignity by snatching it off and carrying it wadded into a ball. She must look a figure of fun, but at least she wouldn't be distracted by trying to manage it. She was having a hard enough time managing her wits. She knew she'd never be able to manage this man.

They entered the wooden weaving sheds, promptly surrounded by the clack of shuttles and the thump of weaving bars. Tufts of

124

fibers danced in the air.

Claire led him toward one loom, batting a tuft out of her face. She felt something and whirled. He was rolling some wool fibers between his strong fingers. "Is the local wool good?"

He must have plucked it off her hair. She hadn't known hair could be so sensitive. "Some of the best, my lord."

"And is much sold, or is it all kept for Summerbourne use?"

"We sell some as fleece, yes, and some as cloth. It is one of our—" She cut off her words, remembrance of the true situation hitting her. "One of *your* best sources of coin."

He dropped the lump of wool. "It could be 'our' if you wish, Lady Claire."

It was suddenly tempting. This was, after all, her home and this journey through it only made it the more precious. These were her people, known since birth.

But no, she would be in this man's power. Completely in his power.

"I do *not* wish, my lord. Come and meet Elf-gyth, *your* head weaver. She can make these patterns, you see, and work in fine thread." She went on to praise the cloth growing under the woman's busy hands—a warm blend of dyed yarns in shades of brown and gold.

"It is indeed a lovely cloth, Mistress Elfgyth," he said.

The older woman didn't so much as look up. " 'Twas to be the lord's winter tunic."

Her shuttle flew, her bar banged, and the cloth rippled to the ground, mute accusation.

"What did you expect?" Claire asked, surprised by the expression on his face. "I'm sorry if my father casts a shadow on your triumph, my lord, but his presence here will never fade."

If there'd been a flicker of sensitivity there, it had gone. "Memories do fade, demoiselle, and sometimes we are grateful for it. That cloth can make a winter tunic for the lady of Summerbourne."

"Felice does not like those shades," Claire countered as she led the way into the sunshine.

"They would suit you as well as they would have suited your father."

Her breath caught at memory and implication, but she plowed on. "Where next, my lord?"

"Perhaps that is enough for now."

"But this is all yours!" Claire said, facing him, searching for one hint of discomfort, any sense that he knew he was a usurper. "You should know your property, my lord. *Down to the last midden.*"

He merely smiled. "Then later, the Lady Felice can show me around the domain we will share. For now, the bell calls us to breakfast."

As Claire went with him to the hall, she felt as churned as the cream in the dairy. His words stung, she couldn't deny it. Felice did her duty, but she was careless about many parts of Summerbourne. What would become of it all in her hands?

And she'd been jealous in the dairy. She was

too honest to deny it. She couldn't understand how she could be jealous over a man she despised, a man she didn't want.

She was bothered, too, by the way her father was fading from his home. Certainly Elfgyth had recalled Lord Clarence, but none of the other workers had. The dairymaids had been too busy simpering and winking at the new lord!

They entered the hall, and talk and laughter surrounded them. It could be any day, not the day after her father's burial. And it wasn't only the servants who were leaving her father behind.

Her mother had come out to breakfast and looked much as she had over the past few weeks. She was not the happy woman she had been months ago, but nor was she deep in grief. The grieving had started the day her husband had ridden away, and now was coming to an end.

Lady Agnes was her grumpy self. It was always hard to tell what she felt.

Thomas was the only one who seemed truly unhappy, but that was probably because he'd been caught and was having to serve at table. She hoped the frequent splashes and dropped food were clumsiness not rebellion.

When Thomas presented a platter of bread to her, his lower lip was definitely rebellious. She smiled at him, trying to lighten his mood. He just scowled more.

Oh, Jesu. De Lisle was right. He was spoiled. He should have been trained to such duties years ago.

She'd loved her father dearly, but he'd liked peace and smiles. He'd not thought of training Thomas to be a warrior, and as for learning, with Lady Murielle wanting Thomas happy, it had been easier for her father not to insist on study. Claire had been the one who'd dragged her brother into reading, or considering customs and talleys.

Now her brother had no estate, but lacked the learning to be a cleric, or the skills to be a fighting man. What would become of him if cast out into the world?

"So"—Lady Agnes poked her head forward—"have you decided which to marry, young man?"

"It is for the ladies to decide."

Thomas was back, this time with a platter of bacon. De Lisle took some to place on Lady Agnes's trencher. "Isn't there a story of three goddesses fighting for the favor of a man?"

"Fighting for favor?" Lady Agnes cackled. "These three are fighting to escape the ogre."

De Lisle turned to Claire. "Ogre?"

Claire wished her grandmother would suffer a temporary loss of voice. "Her word, my lord, not mine."

"But you are indeed all fighting not to wed me."

She picked up the piece of meat he'd served to her, glad of an excuse to look away from his perceptive eyes. "Is it surprising? You come here a stranger..."

She reached to take some meat for de Lisle, but with a smirk Thomas tilted the platter so much of it slid off, to the delight of the hounds. De Lisle reached across the table, covering both the boy's hands, and straightened the wooden board. "I know many interesting exercises to help correct clumsiness, Thomas. Let me know if you need them."

Whether it was touch, voice, words, or simply a look in the eyes, all trace of scowl disappeared and her brother gulped. "No, my lord. I mean, yes, my lord..."

De Lisle let him go and turned back to her, politely calm. "You were saying?"

As nervous as Thomas, she chose a piece of meat, trying to remember what she'd been saying. Something about who should wed him, of course. "Felice will find you pleasing, my lord."

"But you don't."

She picked up her own food, but she couldn't face putting it in her dry mouth. Desperately, she asked, "Is it not time to send for my aunt, my lord, or to go and talk to her?"

He swallowed, looking at her thoughtfully as if the question were a mighty one. Then he tossed the remains of his breakfast to the hounds, wiped his hands, and rose. "Very well. Let us go out and put the matter to the test."

As they left the table, Claire heard her grandmother mutter, "Foolish child."

De Lisle held out his hand, and Claire felt obliged to take it as they left the hall. He kept possession of her hand all the way across the courtyard and over the wooden bridge. At least he had no excuse to lift her into his arms today, for the big puddle at the end of the bridge had drained to mud and she only had to pick her way carefully around the edge.

His camp looked more cheerful, too, in the dry and sunshine. His men were clearing up after their own breakfast, or mending clothing, armor, or harness. They seemed orderly for rough soldiers. A guard stood outside the large tent that held her aunts, but he was relaxed and chatting to friends nearby. He snapped to attention at the sight of his lord.

Claire let de Lisle lead her toward the tent, handsome in its bright colors, but she wavered as if suddenly at the brink of something perilous, as if she should stop and beg for time to think.

The guard stepped aside, and de Lisle looked at her as if he could read her mind. "Are you sure?"

For answer, she pulled back the flap of the tent and walked into the dimness. "Felice? Amice... ?"

It was a large tent, luxuriously appointed, but it wasn't large enough to hide two people. "Felice... ?"

After a frozen moment he stalked by her to the back wall of the tent. He wrenched wide a cut right down it and stepped through.

Claire hurried after, numb with astonishment. "They've *gone*? Where? How?"

"The how is clear enough. *To me!*" His bellow brought men running and he glared at them. "Just because we're in peaceful countryside, you didn't think to keep watch all around?" Two-handed, he seized the heavy cloth and tore it yet more. "You thought this was a stone wall, perhaps? *Where are the women?*"

His seething rage made Claire's heart race with panic. She wasn't surprised to see the hardened soldiers backing away.

Sweet Jesu, the man must be a terror when roused!

"My lord!" She made herself step between. "Have pity! I'm sure my aunts seemed docile enough. I can't imagine why they felt driven to flee. They must not have received my letter."

He put her out of his way. "You!" He pointed to one man. "Was the letter delivered?"

"Aye, my lord. Exactly as ordered, my lord!"

"And when were the ladies last seen?"

The man swallowed as if he was about to confess to a mortal sin. "Last night, my lord, when the letter was given to them, my lord! They said they didn't want to be disturbed until they called. They had their own servants there with them..."

Claire waited, trembling, for repercussions—for floggings, perhaps even slaughter—wondering what she could do to prevent it. But suddenly de Lisle grimaced with exasperation. "Fooled by pretty faces, were you?"

Claire blew out a breath. For a while there, she'd been truly frightened.

Then she became aware of the men eyeing her. She touched her hair, thinking that must be causing them to stare, but they weren't those kind of stares. A glance showed her clothes were all in order.

Then she realized. They must know that one

131

of the maids of Summerbourne had to marry their lord, and now she was the only one left. They thought they were looking at the bride!

She seized his sleeve. "My lord! We must go after them. They cannot have thought..."

He turned on her. "Your letter doesn't seem to have been very persuasive, Lady Claire. I wonder what you wrote."

She snatched her hand back. "You can't think... I assure you, I do *not* want to marry you! I wrote only good things."

One brow rose. "I should warn you, my lady, that I consider lying a very serious offense."

Neatly caught, Claire felt her cheeks turn red. "I didn't exactly lie."

"So you think me a paragon, but choose not to marry me. 'Tis almost a riddle, my lady, but we can unravel it another time. For now, let's find the other candidates. Where will they have gone?"

Claire considered the matter seriously. Sweet Jesu, they had to get Felice back! "St. Frideswide's. It's the only place."

"How far?"

"No more than a league."

"And they are on foot. Or at least"—he spoke caustically to his men—"I assume you didn't let them steal horses as well."

"No, my lord!" It was almost a chorus of terror.

"Then saddle four."

Claire teetered on a dilemma. If he was such a terrifying master, could she push Felice into the marriage? She told herself that he was only harsh with his men. After all, despite his veiled threats, he'd not raised hand or voice with her.

Yes, that must be it. He was gentle with women. Some men were like that. But she dared not let him ride out after her aunts in this mood, or not without her.

"My lord Renald, I beg you. Let me come with you."

His look could raise blisters. "I think not. Your interference seems to have a contrary effect."

"Me? Probably your men did something to frighten them."

"And why would they do that?"

At the end of her nerves, Claire put her hands on her hips and glared. "Because they're rough and uncouth, just like their master!"

He raised his brows. "Lady Claire, am I paragon or ogre?" Without waiting for an answer, he shook his head and stalked off to interrogate his poor men. She noted that he commanded them over to the far side of the camp where she couldn't hear or see what took place.

Claire wrapped her arms around herself and shivered despite the lovely day. He *was* an ogre. She now had the evidence of her own eyes and ears. He had a terrible temper and his men feared him. The trouble was, if de Lisle really was a brute, she'd have to marry him. She couldn't foist him off on Felice.

And if he *wasn't*?

Then she would work to give him to her aunt.

She shook her head. He was right. It was

a riddle worthy of her father's inventive mind.

## Chapter 8

Claire was relieved to hear no more shouting, no sound of blows, no screams. Perhaps his rages were brief and soon over. That wouldn't be too bad. A wife would only have to learn how to keep out of his way at the worst moments.

Could Felice do that, however?

Of course she could. She wasn't stupid.

He came striding back just as Josce trotted out of Summerbourne with his sword and shield. Other men led up four lively horses.

De Lisle looked her over. "Do you want to go pillion?"

She wouldn't normally sit astride in her finest clothes, but she didn't want to be up behind him. "I can ride."

He called for the smallest horse and she mounted without help. She caught what looked like approval in his eyes and it soothed a part of her. She wasn't used to being seen as helpless and silly.

Also, she noted, he didn't look the same man as the angry one. He was a veritable Janus, with two faces to show the world. How would a person ever know which was the truth?

He chose two other men to accompany them, and in moments they were riding toward St. Frideswide's. In fact, the convent bells sounded terce, as if to summon them.

Claire analyzed the situation. "There are two ways."

He reined in, signaling for his men to halt. "Two ways?"

"To the convent. This road and a path through the woods. I don't know which they'd take. The road is easier, but if they wanted to hide, they'd go through the woods."

"Michael, Gerard, follow the road. Lady Claire," he said, turning to her, "lead me through the woods. But this had best not be a trick."

The thought hadn't occurred to her and she looked him in the eye to prove it. "I merely want to find my aunt, Lord Renald, so you can have the most suitable bride."

"Then we have the same goal. Lead on."

Claire obeyed, praying that they would overtake her aunts, but fearing they must already be inside the convent. What if they wouldn't come out?

On the narrow path, they had to go in single file, so when he spoke, he was behind her. "When I marry your aunt, Lady Claire, what will you do?"

"I might marry. Or take the veil."

"Will you enter this nunnery?"

"No, my lord. Summerbourne is too painful for me now. I intend to go far away. Perhaps to France."

He said no more and Claire was glad of it, for his questions upset her. She'd never thought of going so far, and putting it into words was frightening. But what else could she do?

As they rode, she found herself studying each tree, each boll, each glade, and storing it in her memory. She didn't want to leave her home. She certainly didn't want to cross the sea to a foreign land.

She could stay. She thought of the man riding behind...

No, no she could not. She could not marry a cold wolf like de Lisle.

In the green shade of the summer woods, Claire felt a prickling, as if enemies were all around.

But this was her land, where she'd never suffered any attack, and she had an armed man at her back. Then she realized the prickling was caused by that armed man. Renald de Lisle made her nervous, and not just because he was big and a blooded sword.

She shivered with relief to see a break in the trees framing the convent. Set comfortably by the river, and bathed in warm sunshine, it looked like a safe haven. In moments, she too was in the blessed sun.

Tall wooden walls surrounded the thatched-roof buildings of St. Frideswide's, making it very like Summerbourne itself except that it lacked the watchtower. As usual, the gates were closed, but the place clearly wasn't in any state of alarm.

As they approached the convent, the two men cantered up without prisoners. Felice and Amice must be inside with Mother Winifred, who was notoriously jealous of her domain.

De Lisle leaned from his saddle to ring the bell. Claire dismounted and went to the peep-door in the gate to be ready.

It slid back. "Yes? Oh, Lady Claire!"

"I'm looking for my aunts, Sister. Ladies Felice and Amice."

"They're here right enough, but I'm not sure they'll want to see you." The nun's eyes were wide. "Especially with armed men at your back."

"These men mean my aunts no harm. I would like to come in and speak to them."

"I'll ask Reverend Mother." The door slid back with a loud *smack*.

Claire swung around and glared at her escort. "You could try to look less frightening!"

"But it's what we do best, my lady." His men smirked, and perhaps humor glinted in his eyes. It could be disarming except that he was right. It was their trade to be frightening, and it wasn't just for show.

She heard the convent gate unlatch and turned back to face Mother Winifred.

The gate swung open—the smaller portal within the larger—and the reverend mother filled the opening with black robe, white headdress, and square pale face. Round as a barrel, there was nothing soft about her or her stern eyes.

"Lady Claire. Why are you bringing warwolves down upon us?"

Claire dropped a curtsy. "This is Lord Renald, the new lord of Summerbourne, Reverend Mother. My aunts have disappeared and we hope they are here."

"Disappeared is not quite the word, is it,

young lady? Escaped, more likely. Escaped a murdering brute." She glared up. "Which of you is Renald de Lisle?"

Claire turned a little so as to be able to see both sides of this confrontation. She expected it to be a fiery one, but was shocked by the look of cold menace that suddenly settled on de Lisle's face.

"And whom have I murdered, Reverend Mother?"

Dear Savior, *had* he murdered someone?

"Doubtless hundreds," snapped the nun. "You're a mercenary and a tourney fighter, a man who lives by blood. Can you deny it?"

"No." He smiled coolly, totally unrepentant.

Claire shivered. Mercenaries could be excommunicated. Tourney fighting was considered a sin.

Mother Winifred just glared. "We are not used to your type in these parts, my lord. Lord Clarence was not a man of violence."

"Which only shows that avoiding violence offers no security."

"Prayer and good living does."

"Only in the next life, Reverend Mother. In this one, it needs to be surrounded by efficient blades."

Claire remembered their purpose. "Reverend Mother"—she interjected—"Lord Renald has behaved like a good and just lord since arriving at Summerbourne."

Mother Winifred's sharp eyes turned to her. "Indeed. Then you'll be happy to marry him, won't you?"

"Reverend Mother—"

"You made an arrangement with your aunts, did you not, Lady Claire? If this man is so meek and mild, why are you trying to change your mind?"

"I didn't say... I just felt..." Claire pulled herself together. "Felice and Amice were nervous, Reverend Mother. We all were. Before it is too late, they should know that Lord Renald is not the ogre we thought."

"Sweet words," murmured a voice behind her.

Claire plowed on, knowing her face was turning red. "I know Felice would like to marry—"

"And you don't think she can find a husband any other way?"

Claire felt her cheeks flare even more. "I never said that."

"Why else are you here?"

Claire silently cursed herself. She should have thought more about Reverend Mother Winifred's role in this. The woman had always wanted one or more daughters of Summerbourne in her community. Now, she must think she had two birds in the hand.

The nun smiled, a tight, triumphant little smile. "Or perhaps," she suggested, "you are convinced this man will be a monstrous husband and wish to put another victim in your place."

"No!" Claire insisted, though she wasn't sure she was innocent. "Reverend Mother, I must insist on speaking to my aunts about this." Suspecting that Felice would have found a way to listen to this exchange, she added, "Amice

139

and Felice are both older and have a prior claim. I must be sure that they haven't changed their minds before I agree to marry Lord Renald."

She deliberately made it sound as if she wanted to marry the wolf, and Mother Winifred's eyes might have glinted with appreciation of the move. She simply turned and went back through the door. "Come."

Claire hurried after, but as one foot went over the threshold a hand seized her girdle, stopping her in her tracks. De Lisle must have almost thrown himself off his horse to have reached her so fast.

"What's the matter? I just want to—"

His strong left arm cinched her to him, drawing her back. "I'm not letting my only bride-in-the-hand disappear through those gates." He looked to where the Reverend Mother glared at them. "Bring Lady Felice to the door to speak to her niece."

Mother Winifred turned away and the door slammed shut, leaving Claire crushed to his body. "I would have returned."

"Forgive me, but I couldn't be sure of it."

She wasn't sure either. Mother Winifred would have delighted to have all three maids of Summerbourne within her walls. And once safe inside, Claire wasn't sure she would have had the honor and courage to come out again.

Being pressed against his body like this, however, only reminded her of all the reasons she must escape. It was like being squashed against a wall—a tall, wide, hard wall. She, on the other hand, felt very squashable—soft, weak, unformed almost. But not entirely from fear.

"It's a good thing I'm not of a sensitive disposition," he said, voice low and rumbling through her back as well as into her ears. "This battle to escape could be hurting my feelings."

"If you had any."

"Everyone has feelings, Lady Claire. It would be foolish to forget that." He'd moved his head slightly, and she felt his breath riffle against her cheek. She twitched, turning breathless and even dizzy.

The portal swung open and Felice stood in it, arms crossed, face set. "I'm not coming out, Claire. You made your choice."

Claire forced a smile and hoped her frantic nerves looked like desire. "Felice, I'm only trying to be fair. As I said in my note, Lord Renald will make a fine husband."

"Indeed?" he whispered into her ear.

Feeling her smile waver, Claire tried to look lascivious by raising a hand and curling it around the strong forearm that confined her.

Immediately she knew it wasn't wise. He wore a short-sleeved tunic, so she touched his hot, hard flesh. Knowing she'd turned bright red, she made herself stroke it. "I will be completely happy to marry him, Felice."

At least the effect was right. Felice was looking between Claire's hand and face, frowning slightly, clearly wavering.

Claire made herself keep stroking the arm despite an awareness, like pepper on the tongue, of power there, burning power such as she'd never known, leashed beneath her fingertips. She licked her lips. "My conscience couldn't rest, Felice, for thinking that I had stolen such a husband from you."

Felice looked up at him, and licked her lips, too. Claire wished she could see his face. *Smile,* she silently begged him. *Don't scowl. She's beautiful. You want her.*

Then she turned her wishes on her aunt. *Come on, Felice. He's no monster. He's handsome and powerful, and he's making my knees shake. You want him. You know you do.*

Knowing that everything hung by a thread of doubt, she leaned back, moving her body sensuously against his.

"Lady Claire," he whispered, "be careful what fires you start on a dry day." And he pressed against her moving body, pressed with a distinctly hard piece of his anatomy.

Claire instinctively stiffened and pushed away from him.

Perhaps it was that, or perhaps her act hadn't been good enough, but Felice's indecision fled. She scowled even more firmly than before. "You're welcome to him. Just you wait until you discover what he's really like, Claire. You won't be so pleased with yourself then!"

*"Felice!"*

But the door slammed shut.

Claire stared at the solid oak that marked her fate.

She was going to have to marry Renald de Lisle, and the sizzling sensation around them just made her all the more terrified. Here in the open, fully clothed, he made her feel naked.

Dazed, she let him turn her in his arms. "Completely happy," he murmured, taking possession of her with his dark eyes. "Lady Claire, you give me hope of heaven."

He meant bed. She pulled back. Uselessly. "I said that to try to persuade her!"

"Lies?"

"Lies!" she threw at him. "Beat me for it if you want. I couldn't hate you more." And yet she still shivered with the effects of being held so tightly in his arms.

He smiled. "I think first I'll try to save your soul by making your words true."

"What?"

He let her go. "By making you completely happy."

Claire gave a laugh that sounded wild, and brushed off her clothes, wishing she could brush his effect away like creases and dust.

"We will be happy, my lady, when you accept your fate."

"*Accept* you? You're a mercenary and a tourney fighter. You just admitted it without a hint of conscience!"

"Perhaps I have done my penance."

She frowned at him, balked. True. Penance wiped out sins. "Have you?"

"That, my lady, is between me, my confessor, and God. Come," he said, directing her toward the horses, "let us return to our home."

*Our* home.

With her aunts secure in the convent, there was no one else left to marry the invading wolf. Claire went as if in a dream, not yet ready to accept that there was no escape.

That she was shortly going to be entirely in this man's power.

In fact, when Summerbourne came into sight, for the briefest moment, Claire saw it as a refuge. It was her familiar home in all its pleasantness, wooden walls and thatched roofs blending in with the summer countryside all around, all humming with the activity of growth and prosperity.

It seemed so normal that she could almost imagine her parents there, ready to advise and protect. Then tears stung. Her father was gone, and her mother was willing to throw her daughter to the wolves.

The wolf riding beside her hadn't troubled her with words until now. "It is a fine place, Lady Claire, and together we can keep it so."

There was no escape, not without sacrificing her family. "Will you do that? Will you promise that at least you will cherish Summerbourne?"

His jaw tightened. "I intend to cherish both my wife and Summerbourne, and my children in time. For a man like me, such things are doubly precious."

He kneed his horse on, and Claire followed, trying to take some comfort from his words. But what would such a land-hungry man do to gain his dream? What had he done?

War. Tourney. Bloodshed.

He'd admitted it.

He gave orders to break the camp, then led the way between the gates. Claire's mother was waiting and hurried forward. "I heard that Felice and Amice had disappeared! Are they safe?"

Claire slid off her horse before he could help her. "They're at St. Frideswide's. I tried to—" She halted, unwilling to be cruel about him or Felice. "I tried to make Felice see that Lord Renald would be a comfortable husband, but she wouldn't listen."

"So it is settled?" Lady Murielle looked anxiously between them and gave him a placating smile. Claire wished she wouldn't do that. They might all be in his power. They didn't have to grovel. She made a sudden, firm decision. She would never grovel to him.

"It is for the best," said Lady Murielle, putting her arm around Claire and leading her into the manor house. "We'll all still be in our home, and—"

"My ladies."

His voice halted them and made them turn. "It is the king's will that this be dealt with speedily. Please give my clerk a list of those you would want at the betrothal, but only people who can be here by tomorrow."

"Tomorrow!" her mother gasped.

"It's too soon," Claire stated, chin high.

He brushed aside her pitiful rebellion. "We have already delayed, my lady. We plight our troth tomorrow. Whether you have guests here or not is entirely up to you."

Claire might have argued further, but her mother pulled her into the hall. "Claire! You heard. It's the king's order. Don't anger him now. Especially if he's to be your husband."

"He's a tyrant!"

"All the more reason to be meek. Humor him, dear, and he'll come around." Her mother patted her hand. "He seems a reasonable man. After all, he could insist on the betrothal now, without any guests or celebration."

"I might prefer it. It would be more fitting so soon after Father's death. The documents are ready."

"No!" Lady Murielle wailed. "Claire, I will *not* have my only daughter betrothed without a single neighbor to stand as witness."

Claire stared at her. "But Father—"

"Don't lecture me, Claire! Clarence would have wanted your bridals to be joyous, you know he would."

It was true, but to Claire this all felt wrong. "Perhaps a quiet affair, then."

"No." She'd never known her mother could be so stubborn. "We will do it properly. Come. Let's send out messages, and then we'll start to work on the feast. Such a lot of work, and Amice and Felice locked away..."

She was towing Claire past Lady Agnes, and Claire forced a halt to ask, "Gran, is there no way out?"

"Where's Felice?"

Claire explained the situation.

"Then no," said her grandmother. "There's no way out. He has to marry one of you."

"Which is what you wanted."

Lady Agnes seemed as impervious as de Lisle

to her attacks. "Aye. And it'll be for the best."

Her mother put an arm around her. "Come along, dear. Your grandmother is right. It will all be for the best. Felice would not take care of everyone as you will."

But her mother's gaze was on Thomas, sprawled on the floor, sulking. Claire wished he'd at least look grateful for her sacrifice. "You should be about your duties," she said, ashamed of the tartness in her voice.

He shrugged. "No one's told me what to do."

"What about earlier? They were looking for you."

"I don't have to be at their beck and call day and night."

"That's exactly what you have to be!"

He sat up, jaw set. "Well, I won't!"

"Of course he won't," said Lady Murielle. "Really, Claire. He's a lord's son, not a serf."

Claire looked at her brother. "If I marry de Lisle, it will be for my family, especially for you. But you will have to do your part. You'll have to prepare to make your own way in the world."

"It's not fair."

"It's not fair that I have to marry the man. I'll be stuck with him forever while you'll be able to make a new life for yourself."

He did look a bit guilty at that. "I'll learn about swords and things."

"You'll learn what you're told to learn. And that includes service and the law."

"That dull stuff."

"Thomas, they'll *beat* you if you don't do as you're told, and don't think I'll be able to

147

stop them. You've already taxed Lord Renald's patience."

"And this is only for a little while, dearest," Claire's mother said to her son. "Once Claire is married to Lord Renald, I'm sure she will persuade him to make more suitable provision for you."

Claire wanted to throw up her hands in exasperation. Everyone seemed to think that if she just married this man, the world would go on as before.

"If he mistreats either of you," said Lady Agnes, "we'll deal with him."

"Deal with him?" Claire whirled on her grandmother, sure everyone was going mad. "You'll bring the king down on us!"

Lady Agnes chuckled. "You've all gone soft in the head living under Clarence, dear sweet boy that he was. Women have always had ways of handling men as long as they stick together." Her eyes shifted to behind Claire. "Fair warning, lad."

Claire turned to see that de Lisle had entered the hall.

"I have no intention of mistreating anyone," he said shortly. "Lady Murielle, do you have that list of names? No? Please provide it. Thomas."

Claire jumped almost as much as her brother did, bouncing to his feet.

"Attend me." With that brusque command, de Lisle walked into her father's office. Lady Murielle put out a hand as if to stop her son leaving, but then let it fall.

After looking around in hope of help,

Thomas slouched after de Lisle.

"Sweet Mary protect him," Lady Murielle whispered.

"Mother! Thomas puts on that oppressed manner when asked to do anything he does-n't like!"

"At least my child is still here. I can stand between him and cruelty."

Claire wished her mother would remember that she had another child here.

"It's a cruel world, Murielle," Lady Agnes snapped. "It's time the boy learned to deal with it."

Lady Murielle glared at her mother-in-law. "I suppose you want the poor boy beaten five times a day."

"Only if he deserves it." Lady Agnes turned on Claire. "You need a good whipping too, girl, making such a fuss about nothing. Stop putting on a mourning face."

"But I *am* mourning," Claire almost screamed. "Have you forgotten?"

"No. But Clarence's death isn't this man's fault. He's comely and courteous—what more do you want?"

"Warmth. Honor. Sensitivity!" Claire cov-ered her face with her hands. "I just don't want to marry him." She turned to Lady Murielle. "Mother, you understand, don't you?"

Her mother wrapped an arm around her, patting her shoulder. "Of course, dear. This has been a terrible few weeks, and the pain of your father's death is still sharp for all of us. But life must go on. I agree with your grand-mother. If a husband had to be imposed upon you, fate could have thrown you a far worse one than this."

And, added Claire to herself, if the price of Thomas's future is to throw you to a hungry wolf, so be it.

She reminded herself that this merely proved how desperate the situation was. De Lisle was being so moderate that it was easy to forget that the world had changed. None of them had a place here by right anymore. None of them had a possession by right, either—not a garment or a morsel of food. Certainly no ornaments, instruments, and books.

Unless she married him.

She had to do it, and it wasn't her way to play the martyr.

She took a moment to steady herself, then found a smile. "Certainly he does not seem to be a bad man. So, what do we do?"

"Good girl." Her mother smiled with relief. "First we must give him those names. We can't have a betrothal without all our good neighbors."

"I have writing materials in the maidens' chamber."

"Excellent." As they climbed the stairs, her mother said, "We must decide what you will wear for the ceremonies, too."

Claire thought briefly, longingly, of dull clothes and ashes, but it would be pointless. She was fiercely glad, however, about her hair. Nothing could mend that and traditionally a bride wore her hair uncovered.

At least all the hastily assembled guests would know she did not go lightly to her dire fate.

# Chapter 9

"Capon," said Lady Murielle later, surveying the bailey like a storehouse. "No time to roast an ox... Suckling pigs!"

Claire felt a pang for those piglets, who'd been wallowing so cheerfully in the mud two days before. She ordered the slaughter, however, then hurried after her mother to the brewhouse and wine stores. They didn't drink much wine at Summerbourne, but in addition to plentiful ale they had mead, and two small casks of Bordeaux. They were ordered rolled into the hall so they'd settle before the feast.

Feast.

Claire rubbed her temples, not feeling at all festive.

Her mother's voice broke into her sad mood. "Are there any cherries left? I wonder if there are blackberries still in the woods. Send some children to see, Claire. Even if this is all done in a hurry, we must do it right."

Claire looked at her mother who seemed to have drowned grief in hard work. Perhaps that was the secret. She stuck her mind to the strictly practical and relayed the orders. Then she bustled around with her mother making sure that the hens were laying well and the dairy animals were giving plenty of milk. The beekeeper assured them that the hives flowed with honey.

"Provide enough rich cakes," said Lady Murielle, "and everyone will be happy."

"Until their stomachs rebel," Claire remarked, and they even shared a wry smile.

They were walking back into the manor from the beekeeper's hut when Claire saw de Lisle on the wall, watching.

Her mother followed her gaze. "I'm surprised he's not out hunting with his men. His type enjoy the sport."

"He's sent his men out?" Claire asked.

"Yes. Any deer or small game they bring will be useful. Strange he didn't go, though."

"He's making sure his one remaining bride doesn't sneak off to St. Frideswide's."

Her mother flashed her a look. "Claire—"

"Don't worry, Mother. I'm a willing sacrifice."

Willing didn't seem quite the right word, but what other word applied when she was not going to fight? At least tomorrow would only be the betrothal. She'd have time to try to steel herself for the marriage bed.

Having ensured that they had enough provisions, they now settled to supervising the preparations, and even baking themselves. Claire claimed a space in the bakehouse and started making her specialty, honey-almond cakes.

How many would come to the hasty betrothal? she wondered as she ground the nuts. She'd be surprised if every family of substance within the half-day's ride didn't send someone. With the recent rebellion, there'd be plenty to talk about, and everyone would be curious about the new lord, and the whole situation.

She paused in kneading her dough. The invitations had included news of her father's death, so they'd come in a sense to mourn, too. She went back to pounding her fists into the sweet, sticky mass. This was going to be the strangest betrothal ever known.

She hoped people wouldn't want to talk about her father's death, but they probably would. That made her think about how little they knew. She couldn't tell anyone where he had died, or how, except that it was by a sword through mail to the heart.

Frowning, she wondered again what had happened to Ulric.

She wrapped her dough in a damp cloth and began to make the pastry. Her father had considered his rebellion a personal act so he'd not taken any men-at-arms. However, Ulric, his manservant since birth, had refused to be left behind. He must be dead, poor man, doubtless in the same skirmish, for he'd never leave her father's side.

"Lady Claire!" One of the women snapped her out of her thoughts, stamping in red-faced to complain. "I'll swear those men aren't doing the hens right. Such a mess as they're making of it. Been at the drink, if you ask me."

Claire sighed. "I'll be there in a moment, Heddy." She tossed a cloth over her pastry and reluctantly went outside. She liked to keep as far away from slaughter as she could. Felice had always supervised such matters. It seemed a sign of the miserable changes in her life that she now had to go and watch hens having their necks wrung.

It was mayhem, but that was normal. Hens

and chickens high-stepped in all panicked directions, squawking the alarm. Laughing men caught whatever bird was passing and swung it by the neck to its death. The corpses were tossed carelessly to waiting maids who chopped off the heads and plucked them. The plucked hens were plunged into tubs of cold water. Other women were pulling out the cool ones to clean them.

The stink of gut and gore was everywhere.

Claire saw one man kick a passing hen for sport and called, "Alby, stop that!"

Suddenly aware that the mistress was present, the men sobered and set to catching the victims with less play. The hens still died.

Carefully stony-faced, Claire watched, thinking about death. Necessary death. Pointless death.

Which sort of death had come for her father?

Someone at the betrothal might know, but she realized that she'd come around to her mother's way of thinking. She didn't want to know. She didn't want to talk about it. She wanted to remember her father as the peaceful man he truly had been, not as a creature of iron and blood.

She should be less grim at this moment, in fact. No one else here thought slaughter a cause for sadness. Already, despite her presence, some of the joking and laughter was returning.

She turned away, but couldn't escape the squawking, the shouting, the regular thunk of the hatchets severing necks.

The sounds of death.

Suddenly she heard the high-pitched squeals of piglets.

Dear heaven, what sort of joyousness was this?

Aware of being foolish—for did she not eat meat every day?—Claire inched farther away.

"My lady?"

She started at de Lisle's voice, and turned to face him.

"Are you unwell?" he asked.

"No, of course not."

His eyes studied her. "You do not look as hearty as you usually do."

"It's just that there's so much work."

He glanced behind her. "Or work you do not like."

She sighed and gave up trying to conceal the truth. "How did you know?"

"You have the look of a lad after his first battle. Without," he added with the hint of a smile, "the delirium of having survived." He glanced behind her again. "You must have seen chickens killed before."

Claire wished he wasn't always coming across her when she was being foolish. "I— It is not my task. Felice or Mother always does this."

"Animals must die if we are to eat."

She met his cool eyes. "I know that! I know it is a silly thing. But I do not like it."

"What would you rather be doing?"

"Making honey cakes."

This time the smile was more than a hint.

"I'd far rather eat honey cakes than roast fowl. I will do duty here."

"*You?*"

His brows rose. "I am, after all, eminently suited to supervise slaughter."

She gulped at that cool reminder of what he was, but she grasped the main point. He was willing to take on the job she abhorred. "There's the piglets, too—"

"Who so recently were enjoying the mud." He raised her hand and kissed it. "I do understand, demoiselle." The delicate, courteous brush against her knuckles made the world tilt.

Then, almost contemplatively, he kissed her hand again. "Ginger. Honey. Spicy and sweet." Eyes holding hers, he ran his tongue across her captive fingertips. "Don't think about death at all, my lady. Leave that to me, whose proper domain it is, and return to the land of milk and honey."

Claire stared into eyes that seemed terrifyingly deep. With a gasp, she snatched her hand free and fled back to the bakehouse.

She paused in the doorway, however, and looked back. What was this effect he had on her? Good, or evil? What was he?

She stood there contemplating death and the man who dealt in death, and her own inner mysteries, for she could not deny a secret, wicked response to the invading wolf. Perhaps, just perhaps, if Felice changed her mind and stormed into Summerbourne demanding her husband, Claire might feel a small sense of loss.

She turned sharply and plunged back into the crowded heat of the bakehouse. Only a very, very small one.

She did *not* want to marry Renald de Lisle.

Her mother was in the bakehouse now, checking the growing stacks of cakes and pastries, still quite happy amid all the work. She was red-faced, however, her brown hair sticking to her sweaty forehead, and Claire feared she looked much the same. She was reminded why Felice preferred to supervise the slaughtering. It was cooler outside and a lady didn't become such a mess.

"Oh, Claire, there you are!" said her mother. "We found some cherries, and the children have brought back plenty of blackberries and some raspberries as well."

"I could put some in my tarts."

"Yes, do that."

Claire toiled on, creating sweet delicacies the guests would love. Her mind, however, wandered philosophical ways. These sweet delicacies would not sustain life, whereas the coarser product of slaughtering would.

She remembered de Lisle saying as much to Mother Winifred.

Her work, the writing and illustrating she loved so much, was really of no use, whereas the violence the warriors embraced was necessary in this harsh world. It was not so long since parts of England had been subject to Viking raids. At such times, the peaceful people like herself and her father—or the inhabitants of convents and monasteries—had died. Their work had been stolen or destroyed unless a war-wolf stood between them and other predators.

Perhaps men like de Lisle were not so bad...

Her thoughts were shattered by a maid bearing a pail full of blood. "The livers, lady!" she announced to Claire's mother.

"Oh, yes, thank you, Ilsa. Claire, why don't you make that special dish. The one with the spices."

Claire sighed, but went into the main kitchen. She didn't like handling the still-warm organs of the victims, but it wasn't as bad as watching the slaughter.

She organized the chopping of the delicate piglet livers, then mixed them with eggs, cream, and spices. She ended up with just one earthenware pot of it to place in the side of the scorching oven, but it was only for the most honored guests anyway. The Earl of Salisbury might accept his invitation if he wasn't at court. After all, though she saw little of him, he was her godfather.

A cook was preparing the piglet carcasses for roasting whole tomorrow. Determined not to be stupidly squeamish anymore, Claire made a special cherry sauce to serve with them.

She was pleased enough, however, to wash her hands and escape back into the "land of milk and honey." As she mixed nuts and fruit she considered the man who'd said that, playing with the idea that a blooded sword, a wolf of war, could perhaps be a tolerable man.

He had, after all, taken over a task that

upset her, even though as Lord of Summer-bourne it was beneath his dignity.

Despite his rage with his men when her aunts escaped, he hadn't actually done anything vicious. She'd told Felice the truth when she'd said he'd not raised his fist to anyone here.

She put her tray of tarts by the oven to wait its turn, and straightened to rub her aching back, finding that her head was beginning to ache too, doubtless with all the tangled thoughts. Guiltily, she glanced around the crowded bustle of the hot room and decided to steal a moment to catch some fresh air.

Just a moment.

The long day was fading, and a blessed breeze danced over her sweaty skin. She sighed at the surprisingly pleasant feel of it playing in the short hair at the back of her neck, and raised her hair a little more, rolling head and shoulders to relieve the ache.

"Life in the land of milk and honey must be as hard as in the crueler world."

Of course. He would still be on guard. She turned to look at him. "You are enviably cool, my lord."

"There must be a moral there, somewhere. That death is easier than other ways, like the primrose path?"

"Certainly Felice always manages to stay neat by witnessing the slaughter."

His brows rose. "You still think your aunt and I well suited?"

"Perhaps, but someone has to get hot and sweaty in the kitchens."

"You see. Ours is clearly a match made by destiny."

"Made by force, you mean." Then she wondered why she felt so calm about rebuffing him. Perhaps it was just the sheer exhaustion of a long day.

"Destiny or force," he said, undisturbed, "I have no complaint. About bride or property. My bride makes honey cakes, and Summerbourne is in excellent state apart from its defenses."

"Defenses?" she queried, trying not to be offended by the way he was assessing his ill-gotten gains.

"Don't be alarmed. You're safe enough in these times, but we need stone walls."

"No!" He'd caught her alarm but completely misunderstood it. "Stone walls are cold."

"Cold and strong. Give me a very small army and I could take this place in hours."

She raised her chin and glared at him. "You didn't even need an army, did you? A bit of trickery, a bit of killing, and we are yours without a blow struck!"

"What about that bit of killing?" Though he scarcely moved, a sudden anger in him dried her mouth. She took a step back, but only let it be one. "What are you accusing me of, my lady?"

She'd meant the king's murder of his brother, but she had wit enough not to spit that out. The only counter she could think of, however, was to ask, "What are you ashamed of?"

His thumb tucked into his wide leather belt, and the anger still simmered. "I am ashamed of many things. Do you have an unsullied conscience?"

"At least I haven't killed hundreds!"

"Nor have I." He studied her for a dark moment, then shrugged. "I have no plans to change the fortifications here yet. We can fight over this later."

"But you expect to win."

That dark humor returned. "What would you, lady? I am a warrior. I fight to win."

"And I'm a sheep with no recourse from the wolves."

He smiled. "Except me."

She could point out that he was the wolf in question, but he knew that. "I must go back."

She turned away, but he stopped her with a word. "Lady. I think you've worked enough."

"Not if there's work still to be done."

"Do we not have adequate servants?"

"They must be supervised. I can't leave my mother to cope alone."

He considered her a moment. "I'll send Nils and Josce to act as her lieutenants."

"In the *kitchens*?"

"Thomas can help, too. The busier we keep him, the less trouble he'll get into." He snagged a passing servant and sent him off with the messages.

"My lord," she protested, "they can know little of kitchens! I really should go back—"

He captured her arm. He didn't hurt her, but she was shiveringly aware that he could. "And leave me alone?"

161

She tugged against his hold. "Don't think I don't know what you're doing! You're guarding me. You're afraid I'll slip away to St. Frideswide's."

"Not afraid, no. But I have put extra guards on the gates and the postern. My men, of course."

She stared, wondering if it was a joke. But wolves don't joke. "Very well, my lord, if you must watch over me, come do it in the kitchens. You can even be useful. You have strong hands," she added, glancing down at the one that restrained her, "and there's always bread to be kneaded."

The hand relaxed just a little, and moved, rubbing her sleeve disturbingly against her skin. "How pleasant to be bread," he murmured, "and to be kneaded by you."

Or had he said, needed?

Claire swallowed and tried again to get away. "I really should—"

He drew her closer and captured her other hand.

"My lord!"

He wound his fingers between hers. "Walk in the gardens with me, Lady Claire. After all, tomorrow we say our vows." He gave it the tone of a request, but his touch made it a command.

Then his thumb rubbed gently over the back of her hand and she looked at him, startled—startled by the action and by a response in herself. Rough though his hand might be, that gentle friction was sweet.

He smiled.

He had rather a nice smile. For a wolf.

The next she knew, she was walking down a path between the tall frames that supported peas and beans, impelled by his arm around her. There was nothing brutal about his touch and yet she shivered just as she'd shivered before the convent.

She didn't like the fact that he could turn her giddy with a touch and a smile.

What would happen to her if he kissed her? She knew he'd brought her here to kiss her.

But when they stopped, he went behind her. "Speaking of kneading..." His big hands began to massage her tight and aching shoulders.

She stiffened. "You shouldn't—"

"Is it a sin?"

After the first shock, Claire was finding it sinfully pleasant. "No. But—"

"But?" His hands moved lower, finding a particular point between her shoulder blades, and she groaned with pleasure.

"But?" he reminded her.

"But it's the kind of service a lady might give to her lord," she said in a whisper. Her voice seemed to have melted like the rest of her. "Not the other way around."

"Is there a rule about it?" She thought she heard humor in his voice, which relaxed her as much as his big, strong hands. "It should depend on who's been doing the hardest work."

"And I've been fighting almonds and cherries. Not to mention piglet livers."

"Ah, poor maiden..."

His thumbs pressed just hard enough to ease, but not hard enough to hurt. She remembered writing to Felice something about him knowing how to control his size and strength.

How right she had been. "You're good at this."

"A squire learns to work the knots out of his lord's muscles," he said. "Or men do it for each other." He began pressing along the tight tops of her shoulders. "I'm glad I have at least one war-born skill that will please you."

His thumbs made circles up the back of her neck, sending fire down her spine. She let her head fall forward to give him better access, but didn't respond to his words for he was right. His primary skills, his fighting skills, could never really please her. But this one did. Oh, indeed it did.

A new touch startled her—his lips, brushing gently over her exposed nape. At that, she tried to move away, but his hands gripped her shoulders, keeping her close.

"A naked neck presents such irresistible opportunities." She felt teeth then, gently pressing on her flesh. Even as she shivered and resisted his hold, her legs shook, and her belly ached with a mysterious longing.

Even her toes curled.

It was too much. She pulled free and turned to face him. "Thank you, my lord, but that is enough."

His brows rose in that manner he had, but he merely inclined his head. "It will always be my pleasure to serve you, my lady." Seeming completely at ease and unmoved, he looked around the nearby garden, then frowned. "This place doesn't seem very productive."

"What?" She gathered her wits and looked around, seeing healthy plants.

"The peas and beans. They bear no fruit."

"Oh, we've stripped everything edible for the feast."

"Is that wise?"

She walked to a frame of peas and lifted a leaf to reveal small pea pods, still flat. "And there are still blossoms. In days, the good earth will produce more."

"I'm relieved. I don't care for a diet of roots."

She looked over. "I see the old adage is correct. A man's main concern is his stomach."

"No. I wouldn't say my main concern is my *stomach*."

She remembered the way he'd been hard against her out by the convent, and suddenly, despite birdsong and insect hum, despite the distant noises of the manor, the garden seemed very isolated, the leafy shadows deep.

Claire edged a little farther from him. "Your *stomach*, at least, will not be deprived, my lord. Tomorrow we feast, and then we live on the remains of the feast for days. You'll soon be very tired of cherried pork and saffron chicken."

He seemed to be watching her lips. "I'll bear even that, sweet lady, if it's fed to me by your own hand."

Though he didn't move, it was as if he circled her, trapping her. She knew she could never outrun him. "My lord…"

He stepped closer. "Yes?"

Like a rabbit, she froze and soon his hands settled on her shoulders. She just stared as his lips came down to hers.

She expected a crude assault, but he merely brushed his firm lips against hers, a butterfly touch, no more, though lingering. When he stepped back she felt strangely dissatisfied but disarmed.

A moment later, she knew that was his intent.

"Do you play chess?" she asked, frowning.

"Yes. Why?"

"I thought so."

He laughed, and she thought there was a glint of admiration in it, which eased her pride. He was playing her like a hawk being trained to the hood, or a horse being coaxed to the bridle, and in the end she would have to submit. She was a woman, however, not an animal, and though she must marry him, she would not be easily mastered.

He did not try to touch her again. "Claire, I have two requests to make."

"Yes?" She eyed him suspiciously.

"Nothing too onerous, I assure you. First, I would have you cease your labors now and rest for tomorrow."

"You wish me to be a sluggard, my lord? You'll regret that one day."

A slight smile curled his lips. "Not if your laziness inclines you to loll around in our bed."

"And your second request?" she asked hastily.

"I wish you to follow a custom of my own

land. Once the first guests arrive, I ask that you keep to your chamber and see only your family and your women until the betrothal is about to begin."

"Not even my friends?"

"Just until the ceremony. There will be time enough later for gossip."

She gritted her teeth at the indulgent tone. "There will be too much work to be done."

"It will be done without you."

"My lord, you clearly have no idea of the amount of work necessary to put on a feast! Do you forget that Felice and Amice are absent?"

He ignored her forceful words. "It is not such a great thing to ask."

She shook her head. In a way it was not, and yet it would feel so strange to hide away in idleness while others drowned in work. "I will do it, my lord, but I assume you want a wife who is fat and lazy."

"I just want you for wife, my lady Claire. That is all."

It seemed an odd thing to say at that moment, especially in such a flat tone. Had he lied about the king's orders? Had he been ordered specifically to wed *her* so as to seal his possession of Summerbourne?

Had her father perhaps made a will that stated that?

But no. She had read for herself the documents taking away all the possessions of Clarence of Summerbourne. Any will would carry no weight.

She could make no sense of his words or

manner, and shied from any thought of her father. The sun was sinking rapidly now, drowning red with blues and grays, and plunging all around into misty darkness.

Dangerous darkness.

He gestured. "Come, my lady, let me escort you back to the hall."

She set off by herself. "I won't slip away between here and there, you know." He escorted her anyway, as she knew he would. At least he didn't touch her again.

Until they arrived at the door to the hall. It was a mere brush of a finger along the edge of her jaw. "I hunger for tomorrow," he said softly. "When you become mine."

Hunger, indeed! Claire longed for the coherence to say something cool, something that would cut through the net he wove around her. Instead, helplessly, she flashed him a frantic smile and ran, memory of his touch still tingling on her skin.

She fled to her room to change before the evening meal. But she knew she was really running from a hungry wolf.

## Chapter 10

Nils, flustered from kitchen duty on top of other things, ran Lord Renald to earth at the base of the stairs, and caught sight of Lady Claire fleeing up them as if she had the devil at her back. Nils was somewhat anxious about his lord's handling of his bride.

"My lord?"

Lord Renald turned, and grimaced at the parchment in Nil's hand. "More documents?"

"Managing an estate is mostly documents, my lord."

"As I am finding. Come then."

"The Lady Claire angers you?" Nils asked, following into the office.

"Not at all."

Nils knew a rebuff when he heard one, but he persisted. The lady seemed a truly good woman, kindhearted and dutiful, much loved by her people. And Lord Renald was... shadowed. "You seemed to frown, my lord. Because the lady still resists?"

"Because the lady does not resist. Come, Brother"—he flung himself into the big chair—"what business plagues you now?"

The fact that the chair belonged to the father of your bride, the man you killed. Nils knew better than to speak of that even here. Their orders were clear. What was going to happen, however, when Lady Claire discovered the truth? He'd been tempted now and then to tell her, despite the consequences, but he knew that knowing wouldn't help. The marriage must go ahead.

"Nils?" Lord Renald prompted, brows high. "Estate matters?"

"Salt pan rentals on the coast." But Nils couldn't leave it. "You think her wanton?"

"Who? Claire? Of course not. You and Josce fuss as if you think I'll hurt her."

"Won't you?"

To his surprise, his lord flinched. "Yes.

But there's nothing you or I can do to prevent it. Explain salt pans."

At the terse tone, Nils knew he had trespassed as far as he dared. He hastily got back to business.

Claire would rather have stayed in her room, but duty drove her down to the hall for the evening meal—duty to supervise the servants, and duty to play her unwelcome bridal role. She felt as if everyone, even her maids, was watching her, assessing how successful she was being at placating the threatening wolf.

She entered the room cautiously, braced for another encounter with de Lisle, but instead bumped right into her brother.

"I hear you've been out in the gardens, rolling around with *him*."

"Thomas!"

"You're falling in love with him, aren't you?" His voice was shrill, and people were staring. "The man who's stolen *my* home."

"No!" She pulled him into a quiet corner. "Thomas, I don't *want* to marry him. I'm doing it for you. For you, and Gran, and Mother, and everyone. I have no choice."

He glared up at her and she knew the first numbness had worn off, bringing him sharp pain. She wished she could hug him, but he was too old for that. "Be obedient," she told him. "I will take care of you as soon as I'm able. But in the meantime, you must not anger him."

"He's come here and ruined everything—"

"No," she said firmly. "Lord Renald was

given Father's property. None of this is really his fault, and we could have fallen into the hands of someone much worse. You must admit that. Remember Baldwin of Biggin?"

He grimaced, and she ruffled his hair. "Go on. Get on with what you are supposed to be doing."

He went, but at a slouch.

"Claire!"

She turned to find her mother positively glowing as she reached to pat Claire's hand. "I hear you were out in the gardens with him. Good girl."

Claire wanted to groan. Renald de Lisle could stop guarding her. She clearly couldn't take a step without the whole manor knowing. "We talked, that was all," she lied. It was almost true.

"If you talked, I'm sure you've realized that he is not a fearsome man."

"I'm resigned, Mother. Isn't that enough?"

Lady Murielle paled and her mouth trembled. "Why must you be so difficult? I only want both my children to be happy."

With a sigh, Claire put her arm around her mother and hugged her. "Mother, I'm sorry! I know I have to do this. You're right. It won't be so bad. But please don't try to make us into lovebirds yet."

Eyes damp, Lady Murielle touched Claire's cheek. "But I *want* you to be lovebirds. I want happiness for you."

Her mother's needs dropped on Claire's shoulders like a yoke. She concentrated on looking at ease. "I'm sure I will be happy in time. As you say, he is not a bad man. But it is too soon for love yet, Mother. You must see that."

De Lisle entered the hall from the study then, still talking to his clerk. His eyes scanned the room in that way he had, checking for danger, then rested thoughtfully on Claire and her mother.

It seemed to Claire that everyone in the hall watched them watch each other. With a sigh she prepared to play her part—the part of the uncomplaining bride. She went over to take her seat at the high table.

Lady Agnes was already there, and looked up to say, "Hear you've settled to it. About time."

"Does no one in Summerbourne have anything better to do than watch me?"

"You hold our fate in your hands, girl. Of course we watch you."

From across the room, where he stood with bowl and cloth, ready to serve, Thomas was back to scowling. The trouble was, the happier she appeared, the more miserable he would likely be. She was like to be torn apart by all this!

De Lisle strolled over and took his seat beside her. Claire saw Josce push her brother toward the high table and prayed that he'd behave. Thomas did perform his duties adequately, but his eyes stayed fixed on the bowl, and his mouth was set with discontent.

Claire picked at the simple meal, grateful that at least de Lisle only bothered her with necessary comments. When the meal ended and she rose, however, he caught her hand. "Stay, Claire." His tone was light, but his hold on her hand was firm. "See, some entertainers have already arrived and wish to give us a taste of tomorrow's fare."

Claire looked to where man and woman were preparing to juggle goblets. "I don't feel very merry, my lord."

"Our people deserve their pleasure. They've worked hard through a long day and will work as hard again tomorrow."

She knew that *our* was a weapon, deftly used. "But do we have to stay? I long for peace and quiet."

"For a while at least. Yes."

Another dutiful burden. Claire sat for the sake of her anxious people, and even smiled.

He smiled, too, and applauded the clever tricks, but she suspected he gained as little pleasure from the entertainment as she. In fact, at one point, his fingers rapped an uneasy message on the table in counterpoint to a merry melody.

He turned abruptly to her. "I know this is not easy for you, Claire. But by the king's will this betrothal must be soon."

She reminded herself that in some ways, he was as much a victim in this as she. After all—new thought, this—he might have favored another lady before the king gave him Summerbourne, and instruction to wed here. And he had given the maids of Summerbourne free choice. It wasn't his fault that two of the three had bolted.

"I understand, my lord. I am resigned."

They watched some dancers, but the silence began to press on her. What could they talk about that wouldn't lead into uncomfortable paths? When the dancers had finished and been applauded, she said, "Tell me more about the harsh land where you grew up, my lord."

He looked at her as if he was searching her question for traps, but then he said, "My father was not a noble. A knight, yes, in that he had a warhorse. But his property was little more than a farm with walls, stuck to the hillside."

So the lordship of Summerbourne was a great rise for him, and clearly he felt prickly about it. It was not, however, something Claire would hold against him.

"I've never been to a really hilly place," she said. "Would I like it?"

"Probably not. It's a harsh land, breeding harsh people."

"I don't find you harsh." It was instinctive courtesy, but she realized a moment later that she meant it. Hard, yes. Cold, a little. Dark in some way she did not understand. But harsh? No.

Dark eyes met hers. "Perhaps you just don't know me very well."

And she felt she should deny that, which was ridiculous. They'd known each other for a day, and spoken together just a few times. Why should she feel she knew him at all?

Perhaps because of the communication that came from body pressed to body. She shivered. "You sound as if you are pretending to be what you are not, my lord."

He glanced at her as if startled, then she saw him shield himself. "We are all both more and less than we seem at first."

Claire turned to watch a conjurer, trying to hide her own expression from him. He *was* pretending about something.

What?

Her stressed mind took flight, imagining that perhaps he was an imposter. Not Renald de Lisle at all. Or that the documents giving him Summerbourne were forgeries. Or that he already had a wife—

She made herself stop. Those were all ridiculous. Life was difficult enough without letting her vivid imagination run wild.

She returned grimly to the relatively safe matter of his home. "Were you a younger son, then? You clearly didn't inherit."

He picked up his goblet and sipped from it, looking away at a female tumbler who performed with manly braies beneath her skirts. "None of us inherited. My father lost favor with his lord and we were exiled."

"Like us," she breathed, feeling a sudden, sharp connection. "How old were you?"

"Ten."

"Is that why you're being patient with Thomas?"

"In part." He glanced at her. "Mostly it is to please my bride."

Could she believe such a cool statement? She thanked him anyway as she must, and added, "I will try to make sure that Thomas sees reason once all this is a less raw wound." She looked over to her brother, who was watching the performers, but with a scowl. "He still hopes the world will turn again and put him back where he was."

"I remember that feeling." He took another moody sip of his ale.

Claire watched the tumbler do cartwheels up and down the room. "The affairs of man do seem to roll in circles," she said.

"But unlike acrobats, never backward." He looked at her. "The past is dead, Claire, and cannot be undone, no matter how much we might wish it so. The great wheel of fate can only run into the future, and the future is ours to shape."

She didn't feel at all in control of her future, but essentially he was right. Her father was dead. Summerbourne was lost. In a way, she was as bad as Thomas, still hoping deep inside that something would make all this disappear and put her back where she had been, happy with her father in Summerbourne. Free of this marriage.

He put his hand gently over hers. "Claire, with God's will and good hearts, we can make something of this. Work for the future, and persuade your brother to do the same."

Aware of his warm skin against hers, she looked over to where Thomas sat glowering. "He can be horribly stubborn."

"Then he must change before he joins the king's household."

Claire bit her lip at the thought of the consequences of rebellion there. "He'd be safer here."

"In my tender mercies?" His hand tightened

slightly. "Or do you think to control me?"

She looked at him, realizing that was exactly what she'd thought. "Surely a wife has the right to plead—"

"Not for the impossible or disastrous."

"It wouldn't be *disastrous* to keep Thomas here for a while."

"It would be disastrous to thwart the king's will."

"But—"

"No."

It was an absolute, lordly, commanding *no*.

She snatched her hand away. "I am not good at blind obedience, my lord!"

"Then I suggest you learn."

"Or you'll beat me into submission?"

Brows rose, as if the question astonished him. "If necessary, yes."

Claire realized her own hands were fisted, pathetic little fists on the table. He captured one in his big, dark hand, and there was nothing tender in it at all. "We obey the king's commands. At all times."

"What if the commands are *wrong*?"

"That is for God to judge."

She tried to pull free again, and couldn't. "Some of us have consciences to serve as guides, my lord."

"Like your father? See where his conscience led him."

She leaned closer to hiss, "To heaven at least!"

"Whereas I am destined for hell?"

She bit back agreement. That would be

wickedly unchristian. "You said you'd done penance."

"I said that I could have."

"If you haven't, you should. Any sin can be forgiven if repentance is true. Even yours."

"You give me great solace, my lady," he said in a tone so dry it should burst into flames.

A tubby, middle-aged man stepped into the open area and held up a hand for silence. Claire seized with relief an escape from such a flammable conversation. But what if he hadn't confessed? What if he didn't feel sorry for all the lives he had taken?

What did that say of their future together?

Her relief at the interruption soured when she realized the performer was not a story-teller but a riddler. She wasn't ready to hear riddles here, in the hall of the man who had been master of the art. She made herself keep her seat and her smile, but took a deep drink to steady herself.

The ruddy-faced man was quite good. Though Claire had learned riddles from the cradle and guessed every one, she began to enjoy his clever way of telling them. It helped that his style was different from her father's. He used more gestures, and roamed the hall, playing to his audience. He liked risqué twists, too, something her father had tended to avoid.

"One for you, my young sir!" he cried, halting before Josce, who was bracketed by Claire's attentive maids. The squire sat straighter, blinking. His mind clearly hadn't been on riddles at all and people chuckled.

"I rise up straight and tall in the bed, young sir," said the riddler, grinning. "Erect and proud, I am, but hairy underneath in shadowy places."

Josce's freckled face turned deep red, and laughter rippled around the room. Claire could see the squire had never heard this one, and she murmured, "Lord Renald, do you think—?"

He shook his head. "One of life's many lessons."

"Women relish me," the riddler continued. "Some even say life has little savor without me. The bold ones, young sir, they seize me to put me in a special dark place for their pleasure. But I have my revenge when I make young maidens weep. So, young sir, what am I?"

Josce gaped and looked, appalled, at the two young maidens by his sides. Prissy, who must have recognized the riddle, was giggling. Maria was as red-faced as the squire.

"Well, Josce?" asked Lord Renald. "A good warrior never sees only the obvious way. And what you're thinking should not, with care, make maidens weep."

Brought back to his wits by his lord's calm voice, Josce's high color ebbed and he frowned slightly. Then he laughed. "Very good, Sir Riddler! It is an onion, I think."

The riddler led a round of applause. "And good for you, young sir! As your wise lord says, no one should always look to the obvious. And that is the riddle master's art, to teach people to look beyond." He bowed, then returned to his seat so that a minstrel could perform.

Wise lord. Claire had not thought of Renald de Lisle as wise. She glanced at him. "Had you heard it before, my lord, or are you just good at finding the less obvious ways?"

"Both." He stood and held out a hand. "I think we can retire now." De Lisle led her toward the back of the hall, to the stairs leading up to her chamber, pausing by the door to her father's study.

"There are many books here. Do you wish to take any of them up to your room?"

The kindness startled her. "I thank you, my lord, but it's too dark now for comfortable reading, and I am weary."

He leaned against the wall, looking somewhat tired himself. "Brother Nils tells me there is some unbound writing of your father's here. Stories and illustrations. Would you like me to have them bound for you?"

Claire had hoped not to have to tackle this problem quite so soon. "The work is mine," she admitted. "My father wove magic with words, but he had little patience with fine writing, and no talent for illustration. We were working together on a collection of his stories and riddles."

"I see."

She tried to read his shadowed face. "Will you want me to stop?"

He straightened. "No. Of course not. Brother Nils showed me the illustrations. They are cleverly done. You must finish it."

She was about to thank him with warm

honesty, when he added, "We'll have it bound, and a copy made as a gift for the king."

"By no means! Henry Beauclerk does not deserve—"

He slammed her back against the wall, hand over her mouth. "Guard your tongue."

She stared up, shaken, but when he took his hand away she hissed, "So, even you fear him!"

"Anyone of sense fears a king, and you have no reason to feel ungrateful."

*"Have I not?"* Still pressed by his body, hard wood bruising her back, she snapped, "The king claimed to be my father's friend, but he did *nothing* to save him. Nothing. And then he stole Summerbourne from my brother to give to you."

"A traitor's property is always lost."

She pushed at his rocklike chest. "My father was *not* a traitor!"

He snared her struggling hands. "Claire, he joined an open rebellion."

Pinned almost to immobility, she still met his eyes. "Then perhaps the rebellion was just."

He looked down at her, and she knew she'd gone too far. She'd spoken treason.

Suddenly, abruptly, he stepped back. "Go to your room and cease such folly."

Dismissed like a child, Claire fled, grateful to escape. But treason still ran fiercely through her. Her father had been *right*. Henry Beauclerk had killed his brother and thus should not be king.

How dare Renald de Lisle try to praise the king to her? How dare he suggest sending her father's precious stories to the man who had caused his death? She'd rather burn every last sheet!

Instead of letting her wide-eyed maids prepare her for the night, she paced the chamber, scrubbing away tears.

What a weak fool she was.

How could she have begun to accept the usurper, forgetting that he was a king's man? Her father had paid with his life to say that Henry Beauclerk had no right to the throne and here she was, turning limp as a plucked daisy over the usurper's champion!

Of course women were not supposed to bother with such matters. They did not have to take oaths—except to their husband. But by doing so, they accepted their husband's bonds.

Tomorrow, she was going to have to swear fidelity through de Lisle to Henry Beauclerk!

She stopped dead. What choice did she have?

She clutched her spinning head.

If she refused, her family would be cast out and her brother would in truth be a menial servant. But how could she speak her vows with honor?

She grabbed her cloak. "I'm going to pray by my father's grave."

She slipped down the stairs and out of the hall, constantly wary of another meeting with her enemy, her husband-to-be.

Her offering of blossoms was already limp, and new tears escaped as she brushed them away. So foolish to leave flowers without water. It was wanton killing, and did not plants deserve as much respect as animals? Men deserved respect, too. If they must die, their death should not be a waste.

By the uncertain moonlight, she dug up some small flowering plants and carefully reset them in the raw earth of the grave, watering them well then patting the soil gently back into place. "Was your death a waste, Father?" she murmured. "Henry Beauclerk is still on the throne, and Duke Robert has run back to Normandy. So, was it all for nothing?"

No answer came. She knew from history that not every rebellion succeeded, and that martyrs were sometimes stepping stones to a distant victory. Any struggle created losers as well as winners. Success or failure was not the crucial point. Honor was.

Doing the right thing.

"Am I doing the right thing, Father?" she whispered. "I'm marrying him to save the family, and to be able to care for Summerbourne. But he's a king's man and you thought Henry Beauclerk had no right to the throne." She slumped cross-legged by the grave. "I don't seem to have any choice. You wouldn't want us all martyred in the cause, would you?"

As expected, the grave gave no answer.

Wind rustled through nearby leaves, and on the far side of the bailey someone shouted a message, but not an urgent one. A door slammed. A dog barked. The light breeze ruffled the few remaining petals on the mound, but the grave stayed silent.

She gathered up a few lingering dead blossoms, poor wilted violets, and breathed in the last of their perfume. "He implied that you'd met. I wonder where, and what you made of him."

Leaning back, she looked up at the glowing half-moon, wondering where heaven was, where her father was.

A star caught her eye, a bright one that twinkled. She chose to imagine it was her father, dancing through the night sky, exploring the universe. He'd like that. He'd wondered what the moon was like, and often studied the stars and constellations, saying that there was a great deal more to them than lights in the sky.

Like balm to her wounds, she remembered that he'd believed death to be a liberation for good souls, that heaven was freedom to explore beyond the limits of the human state. So, he was free now, unlike her.

Put simply, she had no acceptable choice other than this marriage. She pushed to her feet and dusted herself off.

Walking back to the manor house, she thought of all the rebels who presumably had thought like her father, but who had sworn to Henry and slunk home, grateful to be alive and to still hold their property. How could it be wrong to do as they had done?

A large shadow moved.

She choked back most of her cry, instantly recognizing Renald de Lisle. "You frightened me!"

"Why did you leave the hall?"

At his tone anger drowned fear. "You can't still think I'll run from you!"

"I guard against it."

"Guard. Guard." He was little more than a big shadow in the dark. Perhaps that's why she felt bold enough to challenge him. "I'd rather you trusted my word, my lord."

"You haven't given your word, my lady, except to promise last night that you would be here this morning."

She realized that was true. It bothered her that he seemed so untrusting, but she could see that he must worry about her running off to St. Frideswide's.

Would she do that if she could?

No. If he was pinned by duty to the king, she was similarly trapped by duty to her family. "You have my word," she said. "I will be here to plight my troth to you tomorrow."

"Thank you." He caught her hand and raised it. Soft lips brushed her knuckles again, his warm breath teased her skin. She could come to like that kind of kissing.

"My lord..." She felt that in some way she should resist.

He turned her hand to kiss the very heart of her palm.

She tried to pull back then, but he held her captive and nuzzled her. She heard and felt him take a deep breath.

"Violets," he murmured. "First spices, now flowers. You wield mighty weapons, my lady Claire."

"I was just tending my father's grave."

His hand tightened on hers, but so little she really shouldn't have been able to sense it. It must be the darkness that helped her detect such things—things like a slight tension in his hand, and a sudden stillness in his body.

"I know my father lies between us…"

"A very uncomfortable image, that."

She dragged her hand out of his. "You are lewd! I mean that the way you have come here lies between us. My father's recent death steals joy. Your allegiance to Henry Beauclerk distresses me. But I can forget and forgive all that. I will not, however, forget my father. I will tend his grave. I will love him all my days!"

The silence lasted a breath too long, and her nerves jangled. But she would not wilt anymore.

"Of course you will," he said at last, sounding so unmoved it was almost an insult. "Perhaps one day you will feel a matching regard for me. I hope you've not forgotten your promise for tomorrow."

He didn't care. She must remember that. He played the suitor out of courtesy, but all he cared about was securing a bride according to the king's orders. She should be grateful. She *was* grateful. She didn't want stormy emotions swirling around her. With cool heads, everyone would be safe.

"I've not forgotten, my lord. When the first guests arrive, I will retreat to my room and be like a cloistered nun until the ceremony."

"You sound aggrieved."

She thought of explaining—that the work still had to be done so she'd have to rise earlier—but it didn't seem worth the effort. "I'm sure it will be pleasant to have some time to myself. Good night, my lord."

With that, Claire hurried on into the hall and went up to her room.

Renald de Lisle listened to her footsteps, to the closing of her door, then slowly raised his hands to his face seeking the memory of violets, the memory of Claire. In two short days, the bride delivered to him by fate had wrapped around him like a perfumed vine, stealing his senses, nearly stealing his reason. Her courage, her devotion to her family, even her occasional impulsive folly, were all like jewels in a crown on her absurd, charming, tempting froth of curls.

How long before the truth arrived, the truth of how her beloved father had died? Pray not until she was bound to him.

He was constantly aware, like a man reaching to grasp a naked blade, of excruciating pain soon to come. He'd avoid it, if he could. To shield Claire of Summerbourne from it, he would pay almost any price.

But not the price of losing her.

To keep her, he would grasp the blade, and force her to seize it too.

# Chapter 11

By the time horns announced the arrival of the first guests, Claire was heartily glad of de Lisle's custom. Rumpled, hot, and with a touch of the headache, she was pleased to head for her room. However, when she saw her grandmother in her chair by the window enjoying the sun, she went over. "It is turning out as you wished, Gran."

Lady Agnes looked up. "Don't scowl at me as if it's my fault."

"Whose fault is it, then?"

Lady Agnes's mouth worked for a moment. "Clarence's."

Claire stepped back. "It was not! It was"— she dropped her voice to a whisper—"it was the *king's*!"

"If it helps you to think that, do. Just don't try to revenge yourself on him. And take care of your brother. He was here not long ago, whining."

"He's not whining. He has reason to be upset."

"Being upset butters no beans. Just get on with it."

"I am, aren't I?"

Lady Agnes looked up. "Yes. You're a strong one. Like me. I had a sister, you know. Dead of a fever long ago. She got upset. I married the man because it had to be done."

"I wish Thomas would understand that."

"I told him, and sharply. Perhaps it'll help."

Harness bells and voices in the bailey

warned of the first guests. "Did you have any younger brothers?"

"Me? No."

"What about Sigfrith?"

Lady Agnes stared. "Sigfrith in the stables? He was a cousin's son, raised by my father."

"Could you not have done more for him?"

"What? He refused to take the oath, so he couldn't be a fighting man. He's had a place here all these years."

Claire's headache bloomed. What would happen if Thomas refused to take the oath when he was older?

"Where are you off to now?" Lady Agnes asked. "Work all done?"

"I'm vowed to seclusion until the ceremony. Some custom of the Franks."

"Not one I've heard of, but considerate. Off you go, then."

Claire took two steps, but then turned back. "Was it like this? For you?" She realized that was the question she'd wanted to ask all along.

Her grandmother pulled her lips together, considering. "Rougher. Times were chancier, it being within days of Hastings. Your grandfather had the priest out and the deed done before we'd stopped crying over the news. No betrothal. No witnesses other than the hall people."

"How awful."

Lady Agnes shrugged. "I don't remember much of it if the truth be told. I was mostly numb. But once it was done he was gentle with me. Wooed me. It came right in time. It could for you, too."

Her grandmother's eyes fixed on something behind Claire, and she turned. Claire's future husband stood by the hall doors, and outside the first guests prepared to enter.

He didn't speak, but everything about him reminded her of her promise. Fighting an urge to pull a rude face, Claire hurried off to the seclusion of her room.

Her maids had a tub of hot water ready, and Claire stripped off her working clothes with relief. "Put some rosemary and lavender in the water, Maria."

"Headache?" the maid asked, opening the herb box and taking out some pouches.

"Just from the kitchen heat," Claire lied.

In moments, she was in the warm and fragrant water, and the pain began to melt. Ah, she could get used to this. Normally, she'd bathe in the warm kitchens, but to keep her promise, she'd had the tub hauled up here. Herbed steam, and peace and quiet made a magical combination. As she washed off all traces of her work, she caught a hint of cinnamon, and remembered what Lord Renald had said about spices and violets.

It was not her way to do things grudgingly, or half-heartedly. If she was going to pledge herself to Renald de Lisle, she should do her best to make it work. After all, as she'd reasoned before, none of this was really his fault. The king had killed his brother and seized the throne, leading to the rebellion. That rebellion had killed her father and led to his land being given to another. And, as she'd told Thomas, if a new lord had to be forced upon them, it could have been someone much worse than Renald de Lisle.

So, she was going to accept him without bitterness, and try to make the marriage work. As a symbol of that, she sent Maria for her spice chest, and Prissy to gather some wild violets.

While she waited for their return, Claire stirred the cooling water with her toes, trying to think positively about Renald de Lisle.

So, he'd been a mercenary and tourney fighter. Her life had been so easy, what right did she have to look down on someone who had struggled through thorns to get to where he was? And doubtless he had just been teasing, and had confessed the many men he had killed.

She remembered him speaking of property, wife, and children, and their value to a man such as he. He'd sounded sincere, as if he truly would value and cherish his property and his family. That was good. Very good.

She was startled by a vision then, a vision of Lord Renald, big and dark, with a tiny, blond-haired infant secure in his strong arms. It was nonsense—men didn't usually pay much attention to babies—but it seemed so real that she couldn't entirely resist it. In fact, it grew. Soon he was laughing in the midst of a swarm of happy, healthy children, older ones on his arms, younger around his legs, and an infant on his broad shoulders...

With a dry laugh, Claire shook it away and

sat up to scrub away such nonsense. She'd set herself up for heartbreak if she started to imagine her wolf as a lapdog. She must be strictly practical. Even if he did seem able to turn her weak with a touch…

When the door opened and her mother entered, Claire was glad of distraction. Her mother sat on a stool beside the bath, carefully arranging her rich skirts out of danger of splashing. "This is a special day, Claire."

"I suppose so."

"He will make you a good husband."

Claire suppressed a grimace. It might be true, but her mother had no grounds for her statement.

"Lord Renald is a good man who means well by you," her mother persisted.

Claire glanced up, surprised. "He's spoken to you?"

"But of course."

"I mean, about me."

"Of course he has, Claire. Would he take a woman to wife without a word to her mother?"

"Since it is the king's command…"

"Even so, there are courtesies. I see him as a man who observes the courtesies."

Claire considered that. "Yes, I suppose he is." Courtesies like soothing a nervous young woman in the garden.

She swished the herb bag around in the water, causing the perfume to waft up more strongly. She tried to resist, but in the end she asked, "So. What did he say? About me."

Lady Murielle laughed in relief, which gave Claire ease.

"He told me that he found you beautiful and sweet-natured, and was pleased that in the end you were chosen to be his bride. I did try to tell him that you can be difficult when angered, but he seemed unable to imagine it."

Claire knew she was blushing. "What else?"

"He assured me that he would be a good and tender husband, and I believe him."

"Tender? I'm not sure he knows what tender is." And yet, that vision of him with children would not be denied. Where had it come from if it was entirely false?

"He's a different kind of man from your father, Claire," said Lady Murielle. "Hard for you to judge. I know the type, though, because my father and brother were like that. Such men value courage and action, and guard their honor. Sometimes they stamp and roar, but they do little harm unless attacked or truly angered."

"Like stallions or bulls."

"But with more brain. Do try not to anger him, Claire. Honey will always work better than vinegar."

Claire wasn't sure she could always be honey-sweet, but her mother's hands were twisting with anxiety. She smiled. "I will try, Mother."

Lady Murielle patted her shoulder approvingly, and said, "Good girl." However, then she turned a surprising pink. "I suppose I should speak to you about other things... Though this is only the betrothal, Claire, I should perhaps speak to you about marital duties..."

Claire slid down in the water, embarrassed. "Like the duty to keep his clothes in good repair?"

Her mother laughed and shook her head. "That, too, of course, but... You do not fear the marriage bed?"

Claire went back to swishing the herb bag, remembering the way she'd felt in his arms, the way she felt just from a touch, or the brushing of his body against hers. She didn't fear those feelings, but she wasn't ready to welcome them yet, either.

"It will be some time until the wedding."

"You have set the date?"

"No." She looked up at her mother. "But he will wait. Won't he?"

"Perhaps the king will want a speedy wedding, too. It's unusual to have a long delay."

Claire lay there, really facing for the first time that today would lead to the bed. She wasn't ignorant of the facts. She'd have to let him touch her as he wished. She'd have to let him enter her and tear her maidenhead. She'd have to let him plant his seed, so that they could have babies. She'd have to let him repeat the act whenever he wanted, within the rules of the Church.

Lent, Advent, and Holy Days were likely to be a welcome respite.

She could accept all that. It was the other. The dazedness that made her feel so weak, so vulnerable, so needy...

Clearly there was more to it than the basics. Perhaps her mother was about to explain. "Very well, Mother, get it over with. Tell me all."

Lady Murielle limped through a description that embarrassed Claire as much as it seemed to embarrass her mother, without adding to her knowledge.

"But what am I supposed to *do*?" she asked at the end.

"Nothing. That's the good thing. You don't have to do anything but what he tells you."

For some reason that didn't seem quite right to Claire but she accepted it and climbed out of the bath. One thing was sure. Whatever needed to be done, Renald de Lisle knew about it.

"You always were such a sensible girl," said her mother, though it almost sounded like a complaint. But she added briskly, "And he's a very lucky man to have such a treasure. But, oh, your hair!"

Claire rubbed at it with a cloth. "Sensible," she remarked, with a wry smile, and was rewarded by a chuckle. "You have to admit, Mother, it's easier to dry."

Prissy and Maria burst back in then, chattering with excitement about the guests, the rich clothes, the fine horses, and the feast already being spread in the hall. Claire let them comb her hair, sprinkle her with perfume, and dress her in a clean shift. Then she went to peep out of the window.

As the maids said, everything was abustle down below. A steady stream of guests was arriving, and it was as well they'd prepared a handsome feast. It looked as if just about everyone from the area had come. People called greetings, strange servants hurried backward and forward, and a mass of extra dogs and horses got in everyone's way. The horses, harness bells jingling, were being led out to wait for their masters in the fields.

"Come away from the window, Claire," said her mother. "You should finish dressing. It must be nearly time."

Claire saw her friend Margret ride in with her husband Alaine and their retainers. If only she could have a few moments with Margret, she was sure she could sort out the truth of the marriage bed. She'd promised though. She'd promised to stay in seclusion until the ceremony.

Time enough later. This was just the betrothal. With her father so recently dead, she could surely put off the wedding for weeks, perhaps even for a month or two.

Comforted by that, she let the maids dress her in her finest kirtle, woven in shades of cream and pink, and in a heavy silk tunic banded with gold and pearls. Lady Murielle cinched a jeweled girdle around her hips.

"You look so pretty, Claire," said her mother, kissing her, then taking her place in the hall.

"It's a crying shame about your hair, though, lady," said Prissy. "With it hanging to your hips as it should, you'd be an angel."

Claire sighed for her sacrificed hair, and peered into her silver mirror to try to see how she looked. The metal couldn't show the detail that the eye could, but it told her she had a mass of curls sticking out all around. She tried to press it down, but it did no good.

How long would it take to grow? Years.

She put the mirror down. Vanity was a sin, but she wished custom did not dictate that a bride wear her hair loose and uncovered. A veil would be a disguise of sorts.

Someone knocked at the door.

Despite her best intentions, panic hit. "Is it time? Already!"

Maria opened the door a crack. After some quiet conversation, she turned, smiling, to offer Claire a circlet of forget-me-nots, roses, and delicate violets.

"How lovely!" Claire said, taking it. "Just like the May Queen's crown. Where does it come from?"

"From your husband, lady," said the bright-eyed maid. "Message says as it's a custom of his land for a lady to wear flowers and a veil to her betrothal."

Touching a delicate pink rose, Claire suddenly doubted it. But that would mean that Lord Renald had invented the custom to give her an excuse to wear something to disguise her short hair. Would he even think of such a thing?

Then she understood, but still she smiled. His motive was doubtless selfish—he didn't want her to look reluctant on such a sensitive occasion—but the result was very welcome. The chaplet wouldn't hide her hair, but it would soften the effect.

She raised the flowers to enjoy the perfume, and to enjoy a sense of being in harmony with her future husband, even if it was just in practical ways. For their own reasons, both of them wanted this affair to progress comfortably and without ill-feelings. There were worse foundations for a marriage.

"Maria," she ordered, "my silk veil."

Her father had purchased the sheer head-cloth for her just the year before, and tears stung that he wasn't here to see her today. She forced them away. Tears would destroy comfort.

Prissy arranged the veil over her hair, so the rippling front rested above her brows. Then Maria carefully set the chaplet on top. "Don't want to snag this silk, lady."

"Certainly not." Claire hardly dared move her head. "It's a bit heavy, but that should help it hold. How does it look?"

The maid's faces told her, but they said it, too. "Beautiful, lady."

"Perfect."

"Like one of the fairy folk."

Claire peered into the mirror again, but it didn't show much more than before. She suspected that she still looked a freak, but she'd let the flattery ease her.

As carefully as if she carried a bowl of raw eggs on her head, she went to the window to look out again. Stragglers still arrived, but it must be close to time.

At another knock she turned. That chill panic touched her again, but not as fiercely. She really did think she could make this forced union work.

Maria answered. "They're ready, lady."

Remembering that she was going to be

positive, Claire unlocked her spice chest and took out a pinch of cinnamon to dust down inside her tunic. Then she ruffled a little cardamom and ginger into her hair. Last, she seized a handful of violets, bruised them between her palms, then rubbed her hands around her neck.

There, that was symbolic of her intent to honor the vows she was about to make, to be a good wife to Renald de Lisle. Slowly because of the flowered circlet he had sent to her, she walked out of the room to embrace her future.

The chaplet and veil would certainly ensure that she moved with dignity today, for she feared to snag the delicate silk. Raising her skirts, she stepped carefully down the stairs. The sound of music and chatter grew louder by the moment, swelling when she turned at the bottom of the stairs and walked around the screens into the main body of the hall.

Deep inside she'd worried about seeing condemnation in her neighbors' eyes, of seeing echoes of Thomas's anger. But everyone smiled. The smiles were a little muted, but that was to be expected when her father's death cast a shadow over the day.

She saw bright interest, too, and was sure events at Summerbourne were the talk of the county. There was also surprise, but that was probably because of her strange headdress and the short hair.

One smile wavered. Perhaps Eudo the Sheriff was crushed by her father's death, for he was an emotional man. Despite the fact that Claire placed much of the blame on him for her father's actions, she sent him a calming smile, then faced her destiny.

Lord Renald dominated the center of the hall, of course. His clerk stood on one side, and Bishop Geoffrey on his other, both men a head shorter and half his size. The bishop's presence was an honor and reminded her, if she needed it, that this marriage was the king's will.

Her godfather, the Earl of Salisbury, was here too, standing tall, thin, and haughty by her mother in her father's place. Claire was pleased that her mother had a man to support her at this time.

She walked forward, fixing her gaze on her husband-to-be, trying to consciously accept him as he truly was— warrior, champion, king's man, but reasonable and even kind sometimes. Her mind was distracted, however, and she realized it was because of the earl's expression.

Anger?

No, not quite that.

Condemnation, perhaps. Or disapproval. Or just resentment. But of course. He'd been one of the rebels. He doubtless wasn't happy to see her and Summerbourne passing into the hands of one of Henry's men. He might even have been pressured by the king to come and give support to this wedding.

It was the sudden narrowing of Lord Renald's eyes that made her realize she had halted, frozen in the middle of the crowded hall.

The slightest glance showed smiles dimming as everyone watched her with interest and speculation. She looked back at Lord Renald, astonished that he seemed to think she might back out at this point. She walked briskly forward.

His frown eased. "You look most beautiful, my lady."

"Thank you, my lord." She could say something similar about him. Thus far she had seen him in mail and ordinary clothes, but today his tunic was of richly woven red cloth, embroidered in black and gold by a master hand, and he wore heavy gold in bracelets and buckle. He looked every inch the mighty lord.

She felt a twinge of something close to guilt, for if Felice had seen him like this she would have snapped him up. That was nonsense, though. Heaven knows, she had done her best to match him with her aunt.

As she moved to her mother's side, she glanced at her brother, standing stiffly behind Lord Renald. Thomas was in his best blue tunic, his hair a clean froth of gold. Though he was still a youth, his calm presence was an important part of reassuring all their neighbors, and here he was, calm.

Perhaps Lady Agnes's tart words had made him see sense. She hoped he wasn't cowed by threats of violence from de Lisle.

She tried a smile at him, but he looked through her. With a sigh, she put that aside for now. Once this matter was settled she'd do something for her brother and he'd know she had his best interests at heart. One step at a time.

Her mother gave her an anxious smile and squeezed her hand. Claire tried her best to look calm and content, and squeezed back. She dropped a curtsy to her godfather and turned to face her dark destiny.

She started. Lord Renald was wearing what she thought of as his warrior mien. His alert eyes scanned the room, as if he expected trouble and was ready to face it. If he'd been wearing his sword, she'd think him ready to draw it and kill. She glanced around, seeking the danger, but only saw her friends and neighbors, watching, smiling.

"We are gathered together," said the bishop, "to witness the vows..."

Claire hastily paid attention, as the bishop read the betrothal document aloud so all should know its provisions, and be able to bear witness to them later, even if the document was lost. Claire paid attention in case any detail had been altered, but she didn't expect that kind of trickery.

It was all as before. She was given three holdings by her husband-to-be. They would be her security during marriage, and her dower if she became a widow. They came from her father's property rather than her husband's—except that her father's property was now his.

Her mother and grandmother were confirmed in their dower properties, and Felice and Amice in their portions. There was no mention of Thomas. Claire glanced once at him, but she couldn't even be sure he was listening. In this situation no one would expect Thomas to receive property, yet when all the provisions were so generous, it was a shame there was nothing for him.

If this marriage were harmonious, his sister's loving husband would be expected to assist him. Uneasily, she realized that he would be, in a sense, a hostage for her good behavior, and she for his. She wondered if he'd been told that, and if it explained his meek behavior.

Oh, but this was not how she'd ever wanted to promise herself to a man!

It was time for the vows, however. Her mother and godfather put her hand in that of Renald de Lisle. The bishop sprinkled them both with holy water, praying that God stand witness to their promises. Then a monk held out a crucifix to her as the bishop recited the question, asking if she wished to accept the arrangements and pledge herself to Renald de Lisle.

She had no choice. Hand on cross, Claire said, "I wish it."

The cross was presented to Lord Renald, and the same question asked. His voice was deep and steady as he said, "I wish it."

He then turned to her and slid a ring onto the third finger of her right hand.

The bishop clasped their right hands tightly together. "So you are bound. May God be your guide in your life together."

The room shook with a hearty, "Amen."

The forceful physical link, the unfamiliar ring digging into both their flesh, seemed a true symbol of this match.

Tears prickled as she signed the document. She fought them. She would *not* cry today. She even managed a slight smile as she watched her betrothed make his mark, even though it reminded her again how different he was from her father.

She wouldn't dwell on that. Few laymen were learned as her father was. Most fighting men could not read or write at all. Such skills were considered a weakness, a sign that a man had wasted time best spent in hardening his body and learning ways to kill.

He turned to her and took her hand again, but this time with his left, and gently, and turned her to the company to declare, "Our troth is plighted!"

Cheers shook the beams, and made the hangings billow. The men pushed forward to sign or put their mark on the document. The women clustered to congratulate them.

And to comment on her hair. "Such a shame!"

And the veil, "Such fine material!"

And the flowers, "So pretty. So unusual."

Enveloped in familiar faces, Claire did cry a little then, but they were happy tears. It felt so good to be among smiling faces, and with people who were not forcing her into things. Anyway, it was done. She was committed for life, and this was her betrothal day. She might never have another.

It was time for happiness and feasting, and she would make it so.

# Chapter 12

The men had dragged Renald away, and Claire was grateful. With the women she could relax, especially as they plied her with wine. It was part of the custom to make the newly betrothed giddy.

The man as well as the woman. At laughter and cheers, Claire looked over to see Renald draining a huge horn of ale. At least, she hoped it was ale, the amount he was swallowing in one long, gulping draft. Finally, when she was beginning to fear he might drown, he pulled the horn from his lips and tipped it triumphantly to show it was empty. Sweet Mary, it must have held a quart! The men around him roared their approval.

Grinning, he caught her eye on him, and his expression softened to a smile, but still was more joyous than she had ever seen on him. She couldn't help but smile back.

He picked up his goblet from a table, and raised it to her across the room. She reached for her own to return the salute, but then sunlight flashed on gold and jewel. Frozen, Claire realized he held her father's cup, the king's gift!

"Claire?" asked Lady Huguette, sitting beside her. "Is something the matter?"

"No." Claire forced a smile, seized her own goblet, and toasted him in turn. Something must have shown, however, for Renald's eyes narrowed.

No one else seemed to notice. Everyone laughed and cheered their byplay, with clapping hands and stamping feet. Some men shouted ribald comments. Women giggled. Claire smiled as brilliantly as possible, then turned back into the comfort of the friendly, bawdy women.

He couldn't have known that cup symbolized his master's betrayal, and like everything here, it belonged to Renald. But she wished he hadn't chosen to use it.

"Quite the man you've found yourself, Claire," said one matron, licking raspberry juice off her fingers. "What a chest on him!"

"And doubtless well-built in other parts," said another, winking.

"Now, how would I know?" Claire countered, nibbling one of the sweetmeats she'd worked so hard to bake. "Yet."

The women chuckled. "Let's hope he knows what to do with his size," said old Lady Huguette, nudging Claire with a bony elbow.

Margret winked. "If he doesn't, you just send him to me, Claire, and I'll teach him!"

Everyone laughed, but Claire said, "Touch my man, Margret, and I'll rip your hair out by the roots."

Everyone laughed at that, too, because it was all part of a game, a ritual that moved a woman from maid to bride. Even for a sacrificial bride, there was enormous comfort in it.

These women, young to old, had all gone before her and survived. They formed a community she was about to join. The wives met whenever they could, sharing stories and wisdom, and always ready to help. She remembered her grandmother talking of ways of dealing with cruel men. It was true. The women had their ways.

They had their ways of handling death and sorrow, too. Though Lady Agnes stayed in her padded chair, friends around, Claire's mother had retreated from the celebrations. Various women slipped in and out of her room, making sure she had company and solace.

At last Margret slipped into a place beside Claire, hand on her swelling abdomen. "You look sad, Claire. Your father, I suppose."

Claire hadn't realized that her smile had faded. At least with Margret, she didn't have to pretend too much. "I can't be entirely happy yet."

"No one would expect you to." Margret picked a stuffed mushroom off a platter. "But he's surely a saint in heaven now."

"Yes, I think so." His own particular heaven, where he's free to explore the universe. "How's the babe? Are you sick again?"

"Every morning." Margret sighed, but happily went on to describe all her symptoms.

This was part of the ritual too, this passing on of knowledge. Soon Claire might be swelling with her husband's child, might feel the changes, retch on an empty stomach. Despite the retching, it was another benefit of marriage. She loved children, and would delight in some of her own.

She risked a glance across at her betrothed, looking as much part of the men as she was of the women, despite his being a stranger here. He was fitting in. It was going to work.

Would he use his big hands to rub her aching back as Margret said her Alaine rubbed hers? Remembering their time in the garden, she knew he would. The frost of her resistance melted yet more. In so many ways he was a good man, merely shadowed by the way he had come here.

She tried to think how she would have seen him if he'd come here as a stranger, without the burden of her father's body. He'd still have disturbed her with his size, with the fact that he was a warrior, but she thought she might have come to like him.

As, perhaps, she had.

He was handsome. She'd known it, but now she truly recognized that he was a very good-looking man, especially merry. His dark eyes were remarkably fine when crinkled with laughter. His movements were graceful. He managed his big body with the kind of grace that comes of health and strength.

No wonder the women around her were making salty comments and envying her possession of him. She'd never expected that. She'd thought that if anything they'd all feel sorry for her. Now she could see that her destiny did not inspire pity.

She continued to watch, secretly, noting the ease with which he moved among the men and the approval he left behind. Such a man—a warrior, a champion, a favorite of the king—could try to lord it over everyone, be too loud, too overbearing, too arrogant. Renald de Lisle, however, was fitting into her community like a foot into a well-worn shoe.

It was disconcerting, but she didn't really object. She just felt as if a giant had picked up the hall and tilted it.

It was probably just the drink.

A blow on the knee pulled her attention down, where she found Margret's two-year-old daughter demanding a cuddle. Glad to settle on a simpler thing, Claire hoisted her onto her lap. "Having a good time, Ouisa?"

The brown haired moppet nodded, then pointed at Claire's flower wreath. "Pretty."

"Yes, isn't it? Lord Renald made it for me. I'll have him make one for you next time you visit."

That was pleasant, too, the idea of Margret, Alaine, and Ouisa visiting Summerbourne for a leisurely time with Claire and her husband. Clearly the child thought it pleasant, too, for she threw back her head and screamed, "Lordenald!" at the top of her lusty lungs.

Claire laughed and hushed her. Margret exclaimed, "Ouisa, behave yourself."

But Renald came over. "My lady called?" he said, holding out his hands. Claire tensed, thinking Ouisa would shrink away, but the girl practically launched herself at him.

"She's a dreadful flirt," said Margret. "And acquisitive. Beware, my lord, she'll have the bullion off your garment before she's done."

And indeed, Ouisa was picking at the embroidery around his sleeve.

"Any beautiful lady deserves gold." He twisted off a bracelet and gave it to the little girl.

"Mine?" Ouisa asked.

Claire had feared that, and wondered what he'd do.

"No. But you can borrow it for a moment or two." He smiled at Margret and complimented her on her child.

As the two of them chatted, and as Ouisa inspected the glittering bracelet inside and out, Claire absorbed a picture too close to her silly dreams for comfort. Against all odds, Renald de Lisle—war-wolf and blooded sword—might be a good father. Why that should seem so threatening, she wasn't sure.

Ouisa tried to balance the bracelet on her head like a crown and he moved a hand to prop it there without a break in what he was saying. Then she pulled the gold band down again and hung it on her tiny arm, rocking it. A moment later, she looked up at him, frowning. "Pee-pee," she said.

"Oh dear." Margret rose with a laugh. "You'd best give her to me, my lord, unless you want your finery spoiled."

He put the little girl in her mother's arms, but said, "I need my bracelet back now, Lady Ouisa. Will you put it on my wrist for me?"

Ouisa contemplated wrist and gold for a moment, then tried to connect the two by brute force. It must have hurt, but he simply maneuvered so he could help and twisted into it again.

"Thank you, fair maid." Gallantly, he kissed the girl's plump hand. Smiling—Claire could say doting—Margret hurried off with her, Ouisa watching him all the time over her mother's shoulder.

"You like children."

He turned to her, brows raised. "You object?"

Claire blushed for the sharp edge to her comment. She hadn't meant it. It was just that the giant had rocked the hall again.

"Of course not, my lord. I am pleased that the father of my children will be kind to them."

He looked at her and one brow twitched, and she knew it had come out less graciously than she'd meant. Before she could amend it, he said, "I prefer girls to boys. Little boys are monsters."

As if to prove the point, a young voice yelled, "Lord Renald! Come on!"

His lips twitched. "Alas, I seem to have promised to show a bunch of them a trick with some stones and reeds." He bowed to kiss her hand, and murmured, "Give me lots of little girls, my bride."

Red-faced, Claire watched him join a tangle of eagerly waiting lads even younger than Thomas. Some had the glow of hero-worship in their eyes and it was hardly surprising.

Claire realized she was following him with her eyes as Ouisa had done, and hastily turned back to the women, to find them all watching her with warm, knowing smiles.

The giant was rocking the hall like a boat. She'd come down to make a sacrifice, and now she didn't really know what she was doing apart from getting drunk. Though she knew it wasn't all the wine's fault, she put down her goblet half-full.

A long blast from the horn shook the room,

announcing the meal. Relieved to be getting on with things, Claire stood, a tug on her hair reminding her to be careful because of the wreath. She touched it to make sure it was straight, then went to where Renald waited to lead her to their two chairs at the center of the high table.

Slightly tussled from his time with the boys, he looked younger. Not at all like a hard-bitten warrior. In fact, there was a glow to him that seemed to leap the room and surge into her. The giant turned the whole world upside down.

He moved swiftly to her, taking her hands. "Are you all right?"

"Of course!" But Claire had to hold on to his hands as if he were her only chance of keeping balance. "It's the wine."

She knew it wasn't though. She was falling in love with her husband-to-be, and it staggered her. It was too new, too raw. This wasn't what she had expected of this day.

He led her to her chair and seated her. "Some food will help."

She doubted it.

His raised hand brought Thomas for the hand washing. Claire thought her brother seemed a little more relaxed. Many of the younger guests were friends of his, and with Renald being so admired, perhaps Thomas was warming, too.

She prayed for it. That would be one thing less to worry her to death.

Surely it was no bad thing to love her husband. And yet, it made her feel strange. Precarious. As if she teetered on a slippery rock in the middle of a raging river.

Around the hall, everyone was settling into places and the racket was simmering down into conversation. The music could finally be heard. When her brother had finished attending to their washing, Renald said, "Thank you, Thomas. Now, you may go and enjoy the feast with your friends."

Claire could see a faint desire to glower fight with genuine pleasure within her brother. Pleasure won. "Thank you, my lord!" And he was off to a far corner of the hall where the younger guests were doubtless up to all kinds of mischief.

"Thank you," Claire said, even though it made the rock wobble.

"I've let Josce off his duties, too." He turned to her. "It gives me an excuse to serve you myself." It was the sort of thing a newly betrothed man was supposed to say, but Claire wished he wouldn't. Not now. She was trying so hard to keep her balance.

The servants entered with platters of food, and Claire focused on the practical, both keeping an eye out for problems, and looking forward to soaking up some of the wine with food.

When a suckling pig lying whole on a bed of cress was placed before her, however, she said, "Oh, poor piglet!"

Renald immediately gestured the dish away, but she grabbed his arm. "I would like some, my lord."

Then she froze, seared by the feel of his skin

beneath her hand. Rich muscles crisp with dark hair stung her palm, made her head swim. She carefully took her hand away. "You might as well know the worst, my lord," she said lightly, taking a swig of wine before realizing that wasn't wise. "I lack a sensitive soul, and I love suckling pig."

His dark eyes crinkled. "If that is the worst, then I am a very fortunate man." He selected a piece of the tender meat and put it to her lips. "Let not their sacrifice be in vain."

She took it, blushing, heated in strange places. When she licked away cherry sauce, even having to use a finger to scoop a drip from her chin, his eyes seemed to watch everything she did.

The rock trembled beneath her feet and she knew she couldn't stay out of the torrent for long.

As custom dictated, she chose a piece and fed it to him, aware without looking that everyone was watching. Watching as he caught her wrist and held her there so he could lick sauce from her fingers. Only she could know, however, that he let his teeth catch her for a moment. Only she could know the effect that had.

Then she realized from the look in his eyes that he knew.

The moment passed. He waved the delicacy on to other guests, and served her and himself with chicken. Claire settled to eating as the safest option available to her. If this was love, if it wasn't wine-madness, then she'd settle to it. It would become more comfortable in time. Less aching. Less dizzying.

She chatted to the earl, who was seated on her other side, grateful for calmer waters, even if he did seem rather sour about this whole event. It was nothing he said. Just his expression.

A flash from her left made her glance over to where Renald was raising his cup to drink. It was that goblet again.

He caught her eye. "My lady, what distresses you?" Abruptly, he was in warrior mode again, seeking out danger.

"The cup. It was my father's."

He glanced at the goblet with a frown. "Everything here was. Why does this bother you?"

Fearing his anger, she still told the truth. "It was a gift from the king."

"Ah. And it hurts to see me using it?"

"Perhaps because it's never been used. It arrived after... after King Henry seized the throne."

"Was chosen king," he corrected coolly.

She bit her lip. She'd not intended to stir that pot. "My father never used it. He kept it as ornament."

After a moment, Renald picked up her silver cup and replaced it with the gold and jeweled one. "It is yours. A betrothal gift. Do with it as you wish."

Am I allowed to crush it, she wondered, or throw it into the forge? She wouldn't do that anyway. She, like her father, was incapable of destroying a piece of art. Tracing the inscription, she said, "Thank you."

"What does it say?"

*"To the lord of paradise from the king of angels."*

His brows rose. "A strange message."

"Henry Beauclerk always called Summerbourne a little bit of heaven, a paradise on earth."

"I can understand that," he said, eyes warm upon her. "But the king of angels?"

She smiled, though she knew it carried sadness. "It was a joke between them. They were friends, you know. Once."

"Yes," he said, quite gently. "I know. So, what was this joke?"

She traced the golden rim. "Do you know the story of Pope Gregory and the English slaves?"

A server came by and Renald placed honeyed rabbit before her. "Tell me."

She realized she'd hardly touched the chicken and made herself eat. "Pope Gregory saw some slaves in Rome. This was hundreds of years ago, when the Romans kept slaves. He was much struck by their beauty, being unused to such fair skin—"

"And golden hair," he said, admiring hers. "And eyes," he added, looking into hers, "blue as the summer sky. I can imagine just how he felt."

Claire had to work to swallow a mouthful of meat. "So"—she managed to go on—"Pope Gregory said, 'What people are these?' And the slave-dealer replied, "Angles." But the pope said, *'Non Angli sed angeli.'* Not Angles, but angels. So my father teased Prince Henry that he wanted to be the king of angels—"

She broke off, reminded of what Henry

Beauclerk had done to become the king of angels, and that he'd done nothing to help the lord of paradise. She hadn't wanted anything to do with her father's death to shadow this day, and yet it seemed it could not be avoided.

She saw Renald frown, but not at her. He was frowning at the Earl of Salisbury.

"Salisbury suggested that I use it," he said.

Claire glanced at her godfather, who was talking to her mother on his other side. "He would know of it. I'd think he'd also know—"

"That it isn't a comfortable thing. Interesting, isn't it?"

Something in the air, a dark danger, made her try to explain. "He was one of the leaders of the recent rebellion."

"I know."

She supposed he would. And she supposed it wasn't the best thing to remind a king's man about.

He shrugged and the frown changed to a smile. "We will not speak of rebellion today—rebellion of any kind." He looked into her eyes. "I command you, my lady, feed me."

Claire stared, suddenly breathless. "And if I refuse, my lord?"

"I shall be forced to punish you."

She cocked her head, strangely unafraid. "How?"

"With kisses."

She giggled. She heard herself. It was definitely a giggle. "Kisses, my lord? For some women that would be enticement to riotous behavior."

"Indeed?" His hand curled slowly, shiveringly, hot and rough around her neck. "And you, my lady? Are you rebellious?"

The wine answered, not her. "Riotously so."

She was slammed against his body and kissed. No teasing kiss this, but one of fire. Here, before everyone in the hall, her mouth learned his heat, his taste, and her body felt his intense fire.

Dimly Claire heard drums. After a moment, mouth still in spicy capture, she realized it was the guests pounding the tables and stamping the floor. As the kiss went on, they began to whoop, laugh, scream...

Or was that just the clamor in her dizzy head? She might struggle if she had a bone left in her body.

Might...

Her arms were around him, her whole self entangled with him and his clever, demanding, conquering mouth.

He released her slowly, lingeringly, dark eyes passionate now, passionate and possessive. "Well, you riotous wench, are you subdued? Will you feed me?"

The hall fell silent, listening. Challenged in turn, Claire spoke for their audience. "That depends where your hunger lies, my lord."

"Oh-ho-ho!" everyone shouted in unison.

"And if it's not in my stomach, lady?"

"Then you'll have to wait for the wedding." The women cheered.

"And when will that be?"

Claire looked around the grinning hall, enjoying herself splendidly. "Oh, I think a year or so."

Laughs from the women, groans from the men.

He seized her hand and kissed her fingers, each separate one. "Have pity, sweet lady. I'll starve to death."

Playing for her audience, Claire looked him over. "You could lose some fat, I think."

He smiled into her eyes. "Starve me that way, Claire, and I might lose it where you'll least approve."

The hall rocked with laughter, hoots, and applause.

"Oh indeed," Claire retorted. "Withers away if unused, does it? Might save a maiden many tears!" The women cheered again.

"More likely make her weep with frustration." Applause from the men.

He kissed her hand again, deep in the palm. "Wed me sooner, Claire, and avoid the risk."

She pretended to consider the matter, grinning at her grinning friends. "A six-month, then."

"In the middle of winter? Have pity on our neighbors."

"Aye, Claire!" someone shouted. "And not in harvest time, either. We don't want to miss this bedding!"

"A month, then," Claire said, suddenly aware that she'd been teased into a commitment she hadn't thought to make so soon.

She thought that was it, but he said, "A

month? It hardly seems worth sending everyone home for just a month."

"When, then?"

He grinned and she knew she'd fallen into a trap. "Tomorrow."

The hall fell silent, watching, grinning.

He released her hand, and gestured around. "Here are all our good friends. Here is feast enough for two days. Why delay?"

Genuinely shocked, she whispered, "My father—"

"That is past," he said softly. "The wheel has turned. Why not, Claire? Once it is done we can look to the future, to restoring peace and order here in Summerbourne."

Claire's head buzzed, from the kiss, from the wine, and from a spell he was weaving around her. It was hard to think. But he was right, wasn't he? What point was there in delay?

"Why not, Claire?" he repeated, laying a hand on her shoulder, fingers playing gently against her neck, eyes holding hers.

The whole hall waited, as if every breath were held...

"Why not?" she meekly echoed.

Before she could retract her half-thought words, he surged to his feet. "My friends, my fair lady has no desire to risk any lessening of my person. We marry tomorrow!"

Laughing cheers roared through the room, making Claire's cheeks flare with heat. He sat and pulled her to him for a kiss as hot and thorough as the first. A flaming promise for the morrow's night.

Lingering against her stinging lips, he said, "It's better this way, Claire. Trust me on that. You will be happy if it is at all in my power to make you so." Then he spoke clearly to the attentive hall. "Lady Claire will not regret this day. I swear it by my sword."

It was not unlike the betrothal vows and the marriage vows, but somehow the words said here, plainly before all her neighbors, carried more power. A kind of peace settled on Claire. He was right. It was better to get on with it and move into the future.

"And a vow on such a sword is mighty indeed."

Focusing her unsteady eyes, Claire saw that the earl had risen and raised his cup. "A toast to the famous dark sword, and to a marriage surely made in paradise."

Everyone raised their cups and drank, though Claire could tell that many of them were as confused as she.

"Dark sword... ?" she queried.

"Have you not heard of it?" asked the earl, sitting again. "Lord Renald's sword is made of German steel of a peculiarly dark hue. The only light thing about it is a stone in the hilt. A stone from Christ's tomb in Jerusalem."

Claire turned to Renald with new reverence. "You were on crusade, my lord?"

"Alas, no." Perhaps that was why he seemed suddenly sober and angry, to be forced to deny it. "The stone is a gift from a crusader."

"And a gift from the king," said the earl.

"Such a holy relic." Claire was truly awed. So few had traveled to the Holy Land, and the precious objects they brought back were prized. "You must have done some mighty service for this crusader to be so rewarded."

"The sword was from the king," Renald said shortly.

"Then you must have done some mighty service for the king." When he said nothing, she realized with surprise that he might be modest. Perhaps it was a code among this sort of man, not to boast of their achievements.

It was unexpected, but she approved. "I admire your modesty, my lord. But surely it is a wife's duty to celebrate her husband's feats."

"There are no feats."

She had to hide a smile. How could he expect to hide such a bright light under a bushel? "You cannot expect anyone to believe that, my lord. Not of a king's champion. Your men boast of your achievements. I will have them tell me—"

"Yes, tell us, Lord Renald. Tell us of your achievements."

The earl had leaned forward to interrupt. Claire looked between the two men. Was she imagining that they were eyeing each other like angry dogs? Her wine-fuzzed eyes were not completely reliable.

Before her befuddled mind could even try to sort things out, Renald said to her, "The crusader gave the stone to the king, and Henry had it put into a sword as a reward to me. That's all."

"But what did you do to deserve it?"

"Nothing at all glorious."

She shook her head. "I'll find out and have a minstrel make a song about it."

"You won't find anything I have done worthy of a ballad, Claire." He seized the jug before them. "May I pour you more wine?"

More wine and her eyes would cross, but she could spot an attempt to change the subject. "I would like to see it."

"The wine?"

"Your sword! And the stone from Jerusalem."

He poured her wine anyway and pressed the jeweled cup into her hand. "Some other time. Swords are not fitting at a feast."

"A holy relic is. It would bless our vows."

"No."

She blinked at him. That commanding *no* again, but disarmingly this time it was stirred by modesty not anger.

The earl, listening but ignored, suddenly spoke, his voice raised so others would hear. "I'm sure all here would be honored to see the sword, Lord Renald. Rumor says it can cut through the hardest wood. Perhaps even metal itself."

Now other men were paying attention. "Cut through metal?"

" 'Tisn't possible."

Word rippled around the room. "A stone from Christ's tomb!"

"Cuts through iron."

The hall began to swell with demands to see this wonder.

Abruptly, face set, Renald commanded Josce to bring the sword. When the squire

223

returned, Renald took it one-handed, and laid it—almost dropped it—in Claire's lap.

It was heavy. Heavy, hard, and dark. As her betrothed now was. Claire realized that she'd been wrong. He might be modest about his deeds, but at this moment he was very, very angry.

It was too late to retreat, so dry mouthed she studied the gift she'd demanded. She had never been this close to a sword before, and she didn't like it. He was right. An instrument of death had no place at a feast, especially such a one as this.

Scabbards were usually decorative, painted, and sometimes banded with metal and set with precious stones. This one was black leather over wood. The only decoration came from small silver studs and carved medallions of jet.

It made her think of hell, or of a moonless midnight.

"Well?" he asked.

She knew he could read her expression. "It looks deadly."

"What use is a sword that does not kill?"

She swallowed, for the question applied to him as well as his weapon. He didn't sow, he didn't reap. He didn't create music or art. He just trained to kill and did so when called upon.

She concentrated on the hilt—part of the instrument of death, but shaped like a cross and set with the only bit of color about the thing—a sandy stone. The holy relic that sanctified this dark instrument of death.

Killing infidels was a saintly act, or so the Church said.

Could killing, therefore, sometimes be good? Someone had to execute criminals. And kill the human wolves who preyed on peaceful people.

The stone sat in a cup of fine black ironwork for protection. She put her fingertip through the cold metal to touch it. "Has it performed any miracles?"

"Not to my knowledge."

"But it might. Being from Christ's tomb."

She raised the sword and kissed the stone, praying for the health and welfare of all in Summerbourne, and for her marriage, that, despite all the odds, it be good. At times it seemed that might truly need a miracle. "You are blessed to have this, my lord."

"Then perhaps we should send it around the room. Josce!"

The squire stepped forward and Claire put both hands under the sword to lift it to him.

Then gasped.

Blood smeared her palm!

## Chapter 13

Lord Renald snatched the sword from her. "You've cut yourself?"

Claire rubbed her palm and found no wound at all. "No."

He had stood and was already sliding the sword out of the scabbard, revealing a crimson trace on the blade and around the join to the hilt.

"Josce?"

The squire blanched. "I just brought it from your room, my lord."

Lord Renald touched the blood. "Not fresh, but not old either." Watched by the now silent hall, he drew the sword clear. Lit by torch and candle, the blade stayed dark, light only rippling on the surface like fire on a deep, dark pond.

A pond streaked with blood.

"When did you last kill, my lord?" Claire whispered.

"Too long ago for this. And Josce would be flayed if he'd left my sword in this state."

Claire seized her goblet and drained it. Of course he hadn't killed recently. Not since coming to Summerbourne. But now she was sharply reminded of what he was.

A true blooded sword. It was as if heaven shouted it! Was she wicked to fall in love with such a man?

He shoved the blade back in the scabbard. "Some strange joke, perhaps." He flashed a cold look at the earl, and Claire remembered who had pushed to have the sword brought out. Why, though, would such a powerful man indulge in such a petty trick? Just because he objected to this marriage?

He thrust the sword at his squire. "Clean it. Then bring it back so all who wish can see it." He then sat, calling for water. When it came, he cleaned Claire's hand himself. "I'm sorry for that, my lady. Such matters should not come to trouble you."

"We can't live a lie. A wife must share in her husband's life."

He kissed her clean palm. "I will keep you as joyous as Summerbourne deserves."

"But you will still ride out to kill."

He tossed the bloodstained cloth on the floor and let her go. "It is my duty if called."

"I know that. But—"

Before she could say anything else, he placed a honeyed plum to her lips. She had to take a bite, but he could not silence her mind. She'd been happy. She'd been surrendering to love. But now her dizzy feelings and the gaiety all around seemed like froth, froth on a swamp of violence and death.

She glanced at the earl. He'd been fined heavily for his part in the rebellion, but he still had his life and his lands. His children still had their birthright. What right had he to stir the dark waters beneath her happy day?

Renald turned her face back to him, eyes searching hers. "Don't frown, fair lady." He kissed her gently on her forehead, where she must be creased by troubles. "Paradise should know only smiles, and angels never frown."

Claire let him tease her out of the dark. She was tired, *tired*, of thinking and fretting. When he drew her in for another overwhelming kiss, she surrendered. When he finished, everyone applauded again, and Claire suspected they were as happy as she to put blood and swords behind them.

Then someone called, "The dance! Let's have the dance!" and the musicians started up the Holly Berry, the traditional bridal dance.

Claire was supposed to lead the maidens in the dance, but she wondered if she was able after the wine she'd drunk. Ah well, no one expected the happy couple to be entirely steady on their feet.

When she stood, the world had a slight buzz of unreality, but Claire decided she could walk and talk without embarrassing herself. A tug at her scalp reminded her of her chaplet and veil, and she carefully began to take it off.

Lord Renald rose and helped her, hands mysterious against her head. She remembered to thank him for the chaplet.

"It becomes you," he said, smile warm and comforting.

She smiled back then walked into the center space, gesturing to the maidens to join her. Soon, so soon, she would no longer be a maiden. Soon she would be intimate with him.

It was a strange thought, full of mysterious music.

Ordinary music called, however, and so Claire led the maidens in their dance, turning her attention, as they all did, to her chosen man.

Claire liked the dance, but she'd never before performed it for a significant man. Stamping her foot at him, raising her skirt, flashing challenging looks, seemed to start something inside her. Or set something free. Something fiery that she saw reflected in his dark, dangerous eyes.

He was leaning back in his chair, big hand lax around his goblet, but his eyes stayed fixed on her. Intent. Hot, even. It dried her mouth, that heat, but seemed to drive her to yet wilder movements in the dance.

Then, as she spun, she caught the eye of another man. Lambert of Vayne—young and handsome—was leaning forward, grinning most appreciatively at her.

With purely wicked intent, she danced for him for a while, swaying her hips, flashing her leg, her true attention all on the dark man at the high table.

When she turned fully back to her betrothed, he was still lounging, but now his hand gripped tight around his goblet, and his eyes warned. Instead of making her cautious, that sent a flicker of excitement down her nerves.

What would he do if she really flirted with other men?

For some mad reason she wanted that danger, hungered for it.

She desperately wished she had her long hair loose and free to swing like a whip to torment and defy her dark wolf even more.

When the dance whirled to a stop, she staggered, clutching on to similarly gasping, dizzy friends, joining in the wild, delighted laughter. Then he appeared at her side and cinched her to him, support and capture.

"You are a bold wench," he murmured, kissing her sweaty neck. But then he nipped her sharply.

Even as she squeaked, she knew it was playful chastisement.

She stared up at him, suddenly wishing *this* was her wedding night.

"Ah, Claire, if you dance as hotly in the marriage bed, I will be a very happy man."

"Isn't it the groom's place to make the bride dance?"

His smile was slow, lazy, and blistering. "I will certainly do my best. Now," he said, steering her back to her seat, and gently settling her veil and chaplet back on her head, "sit, my bride, and watch as I perform for you."

He called for the sword dance and most of the younger men leaped forward to take part, keen to show off before the women.

They didn't use swords—though Claire had heard that at one time they used to. As the music began, a beat more than a tune, they clashed short staves with one another. It was a simulation of a sword fight but with a rhythm that became music.

Turning, stamping, beating stick against stick, the men eyed their chosen women.

His eyes were for her alone.

She'd not seen this dance very often for her father hadn't liked it. She'd tended to think it vulgar, and she'd hated the aura of violence it created. But now, something had changed. Now, seeing the ease of Renald's movements, his fluid grace, she recognized a thing of dangerous beauty.

Pure skill. Without any experience of swordplay, she could see that Renald's command was greater than any other man's. Like everyone, she began to clap along with the beat of the dance, but she clapped just for him, feeling the beat thrum through her body.

Then the pattern turned him to face Lambert. Perhaps the local man made a challenge of it. Or perhaps Renald did, itched by her play.

Suddenly the movements seemed less rhythmical, more threatening. The clapping died away. Like ripples in water, the other men drew back into a circle, beating their sticks against the floor as the two in the middle made a contest of it.

Renald and Lambert kept to the rhythm after a fashion, but they also tried to overcome each other's guard. Lambert was hopelessly outmatched. Even Claire could see that. He trained for war, but only as duty. He was no match for a king's champion, a man whose life was battle.

Watching Renald toy with his opponent, Claire remembered him speaking of a skilled fighter in control of a match. It was here before her. He just blocked Lambert's moves, making occasional attacks so mild as to be easily countered. Clearly, he could prolong it, use it, end it at will.

Suddenly, chillingly, Claire imagined her father facing such a man, helpless before unerring death. After all, Lambert was younger, fitter, and much more able at swordplay than her father, but he was drastically outmatched.

She grasped her goblet with shaking hands, praying for the macabre dance to end. Of course her father's death had been nothing like this. It had doubtless been in some muddled skirmish somewhere and he'd not even seen the blade that killed him.

But *End it*, she thought desperately, stick-music pounding in her brain. *Kill him now. Stop toying with him!*

She gulped wine, fighting madness. They fought with wooden sticks. No one was going to be killed. No one would even get hurt. It was a dance.

A *dance*.

She saw Renald flash her a glance and frown. A moment later the rhythm returned. Smoothly, under his control, it blended with the beat of the other men's sticks and the musician's drum. Renald looked untested by it all, but Lambert gasped, the sweat running. Whoever had started the contest, Lambert was relieved to take the escape offered.

The other men picked it up and wound into the end.

It was well done. Claire admitted that. She was doubtless reacting stupidly to a mere entertainment. But as soon as the dance ended, before Renald could return to her, she slipped out of the hall into the cooler, fragrant evening to try to untangle her tormented mind.

The sun had sunk, giving a pearly glow to the scene which soothed her rattled nerves.

At a footstep behind, she turned, braced for his displeasure.

But it wasn't Renald, it was the Earl of Salisbury.

"My lord."

"Claire." He was a tall, rather thin man, but with a sinewy strength, not the thinness of frailty. "Strange indeed to see such warlike entertainments at Summerbourne."

"It was only a dance, my lord."

"Indeed. But a dance of death."

"They were in no danger." She wished he would go away.

"Certainly de Lisle was not."

"Neither of them were, fighting with sticks."

"Men like de Lisle can kill with sticks. Or with bare hands." What, by heaven, was his point? If he wished to argue against this union, he was far too late.

He was studying her, as if seeking the answer to a puzzle. "You must welcome a happy day after sorrow."

His tone made her protest. "I had little choice, my lord. I am simply making the best of it."

"You show great fortitude, then."

Then she understood. No wonder he sounded disbelieving. Her wanton display earlier, and her apparent eagerness to marry tomorrow must make her seem a horribly callous daughter. She moved a little farther from the hall, hoping he wouldn't follow. But when he spoke, he was close behind. "Your father was not a supporter of Henry Beauclerk as king."

She turned with a sigh. "The whole world knows that, my lord."

"Yet you rush to marry one of Henry's closest supporters?"

She spread her hand. "What would you have me do, my lord? The king has given Lord Renald our property, and commanded him to marry here. Are we to make matters worse by refusing?"

His jaw tightened. "Perhaps I am dismayed by your enthusiasm, Lady Claire."

Her cheeks were hot with shame, but she would not cower. "You would have preferred that I drag through this day weeping?"

"Yes, I think I would."

"Well, that is not my way."

"When I saw you kissing that sword—"

"Ah, the sword! The sword you smeared blood on, my lord?"

He stiffened. "I? Why accuse me?"

"Because you asked that it be brought out. Insisted on it, in fact."

"I had my reasons." He seemed to frown even more deeply.

"And what of the cup, my lord? What point was there in encouraging Lord Renald to use a cup that could only remind me of unpleasant matters?"

"Claire, I thought you must know, but—"

"Claire?"

Claire turned and hurried to Renald's side, feeling only sharp relief. She didn't care if he was angry that she'd fled the hall. She just wanted to escape accusations and disapproval, to return to being a happy bride. She had no choice in all this. Unless she was to sacrifice her whole family, she had no choice.

Renald glanced between her and the earl, but then smiled and took her hand. "It is hot in the hall, isn't it? Would you care to walk in the gardens, my lady?"

"That would be delightful." She dropped a curtsy to the earl. "Thank you for your advice, my lord."

She thought Salisbury might continue what he had been saying, but after a moment he turned on his heel and stalked off.

As the din of the raucous hall faded, Renald said, "Advice?"

A thrush trilled in a nearby bush, balm to her lingering distress, and the slight breeze cooled her wine-hot cheeks. "He thought I should have avoided marrying you, and if I could not, I should have dragged myself through the day wailing."

"Thank God you have not." He kissed her hand, studying her. "In the hall. You seemed upset."

She could not really express her irrational unease, so she said, "You were shaming Lambert."

"He looked too fondly on you."

So it had been deliberate. "Will you always attack men who look fondly on me?"

"Would you rather I did not?"

After a moment, she accepted that the answer was no. Something in his hot possession of her sang to a wicked part of herself. It *was* wicked, though. "I do not wish to be the cause of any man's death."

"Then I will not punish unless you command it." A smile flickered. "One advantage of being who and what I am is that I need only frown. As you need only frown at me."

"My lord, I doubt it." Yet deep inside, his words settled like a warm comforting flame in a place that had once been cold with fear.

"Don't doubt. Don't doubt your power over me, Claire of Paradise."

He wove his fingers with hers and led her—unsteady as she was—into the garden, down misty, shadowy paths. How different now from the evening before, when every nerve had been on the alert. Now she was soft with warm security, even if tingling with spicy hopes.

He paused beneath one of the pear trees that grew against the wall. Leaves and branches blocked the fading light, creating mysterious shadows. He led her to a bench set deep in the shade. She knew she was going to be kissed again, and unlike last night, her heart danced with anticipation.

But he did not immediately take her into his arms. "I spoke honestly in the hall, Claire. I do intend and hope to make you happy."

"And I you, my lord." The words were more than formal courtesy. Happiness, that had once seemed gone forever, now hovered within their grasp.

"I know my nature bothers you. I'm a warrior. That is my life and my nature. I must train for war. And train my men."

"In Summerbourne?" Claire hoped her dismay hadn't marked her voice. She controlled herself and added, "Could it perhaps be outside the walls, my lord?"

"Most of the time. I, too, would keep Paradise untainted." He smiled and looked around. "Perhaps this is the Garden of Eden. I've never known a place with such a halo of peace within it."

"An Eden without snakes, thank goodness," Claire said, "except the occasional harmless little adder."

"Heaven on Earth."

She tried to see the familiar garden with his eyes. It had always been part of her life—the shape of its beds, the cool of the stone paths, the seasonal glories of leaf and flower, providing food, healing, and balm for the soul.

"I suppose you've never had a garden of your own."

"Nor access to many. They are generally a ladies' domain. Except for the lord, lusty men would definitely be seen as snakes."

"Surprising then, my lord, that you've seen any."

He grinned at her joke, and she studied the garden further, seeking to see what he saw.

It was just a garden, wasn't it, and not really at its best in this fading light. Flowers clouded in mottled shades of gray and white above dense shadows of bush and leaf. Yet she and Renald sat surrounded by scents and music. Insect-hum filled the air, bass note to the busy chorus of birds. Flowers, herbs, and good healthy greenery spiced every breath.

She was suddenly, fiercely grateful that she would never have to leave. And that was because of this man. She turned to him, and dared to put her hands to his face. Then she kissed him gently on the lips in gratitude.

He accepted it, suddenly still. "And what was that for?"

"Is a bride not allowed to kiss her husband's lips?"

"Indeed she is. And the husband is very grateful. But it seemed a kiss of thanks."

"I am thankful to be here, and to be staying here."

He raised her chin and kissed her back, as gently. "Then we are both blessed. Remind me never to eat an apple again. I have no wish to be thrown out of Eden."

She thought that now he would kiss her properly, but he relaxed and looked around. "Is all this your work?"

Ah, well. It would come in time, and she shouldn't be greedy. "Not at all. I work here, but the garden is old and passed on from lady to lady." She smiled ruefully. "You might as well know more of my faults. Not only do I lack a sensitive soul, I'm too impulsive to be a good gardener, and too much the dreamer. I don't like to plan years ahead, and I forget to water the new plants."

His eyes crinkled. "Somehow, I might have guessed. But an impulsive dreamer sounds charming, too. What plant is that with the purple flowers?"

"Foxglove."

"You grow gloves for foxes?"

She smiled. How precious to have the gift of humor back. "When you get old and your heart falters, you may be glad of it."

His smile faded. "Perhaps I'd rather not grow old. What use is an old wolf?"

Claire wanted to protest, but she knew what he meant. She'd seen old warriors, weakened by age, gnarled by joint disease, frail with a wheezing sickness, reduced almost to beggary once their one asset—their strength—was gone.

Already, however, the thought of his distant death was painful. As his wife, it would be her task to keep him healthy, and now he had property he was protected from the worst.

He asked about other plants and she answered, pointing out the most interesting and describing their uses. His voice, she realized, was deep, relaxed, and comfortable, in harmony with the surrounding peace and the evening shadows.

He clearly knew little about gardens, however, this man whose trade was to damage, not to nurture or heal.

No. She would not think of that.

A robin flew down to the turned earth quite close to their feet and trilled a song.

"Letting us know that it owns this patch of ground," she said. "Ordering us to dig to make its hunt for worms easier."

"Lazy bird. Work for your dinner, sirrah."

As if it understood, the robin stopped its song and cocked its head at them. Then it hopped along. It soon found a worm, tugged it out, and flew off with it.

"More death." Claire sighed. "Why do we not care about the fate of worms?"

"Perhaps because they'll eat us in the end."

Then he stiffened, clearly realizing his words were unfortunate. She touched his hand. "We cannot avoid all mention of death, my lord."

He took her hand in his. "You are a pearl without price, my lady Claire. May I request a boon?"

Without any wariness, she said, "Of course."

"I would have you call me by my name. Renald."

Claire realized that over the past hours she had begun to think of him that way, and so she smiled and said, "Certainly, Renald."

He drew her gently into his arms, and lowered his head to kiss her, gentle again at first, a mere brushing of lips against lips. Then his hand slid into the back of her hair, rough and warm against her nape and scalp, shaping her to him. He kissed her then as he had in the hall, but here in the private dark, it was softer, sweeter, and more deeply intimate than she could ever have imagined.

Every sense heightened, Claire delighted even in the slight roughness of his stubble. And by the stars he was solid. She was half over mighty thighs, her hands clutching broad, broad shoulders hard as wood, hot as hearthstones...

And she liked it!

She, who had once thought she could never like a fighting man, was stirred in a secret part of herself by the dark power beneath her small, soft hands.

His mouth eased free of hers at last, but the strength of his body still encompassed her as their breath mingled. She drifted her hands across the breadth of his shoulders and over the heavy curves to his arms. A startling vision seared her, a vision of him naked to her questing touch, of herself in pale conquest, as beneath, he darkly surrendered.

As if he knew, he pulled her suddenly

against him, tight against his chest, cradled her there, his chin nestled in her hair. She knew his strength, knew she could not escape, and yet she did not feel confined. She felt, for a brief moment like a child in a safe place—one where death was just a fable, and where the sun shined every day.

His chest rose and fell with his breaths, and she began to breathe in rhythm with him. Her own spicy aroma blended with his—sweat, wool, horse. She remembered writing that to Felice. Something about him not smelling foul, but somewhat of horse and sweat. At the time it had seemed a problem to be explained away. Now, however, it was just him.

She found that she had closed her eyes and was taking deep breaths, savoring him as she might enjoy a flower, a spice, or bread fresh from the oven.

Her mouth was watering slightly as if she were at a table loaded with tasty dishes. But beneath the sweet anticipation, something lurked like a stone in the shoe or a thorn on the chair.

What?

The earl's last words. *I thought you had to know.*

Why did they bother her so?

Because they echoed something.

Felice's words at the convent gate! *Wait till you find out...*

If Felice could be dismissed, the earl could not. But what could both of them know that was still secret from everyone at Summerbourne?

He shifted to look at her. Too late she knew that doubts could be sensed.

"What troubles you, Claire? Is it something Salisbury said?"

"No. Not really." But before she slid into complete surrender with this man she had to try to chase away these pricking doubts. "Mother Winifred said you were a murderer. Have you ever killed?"

He moved slightly to look at her. "I am a warrior."

"I mean, outside of battle."

"No. Or yes, in tourney."

"That is wrong, isn't it?"

"Most people don't think so. And both deaths were accidents. We try not to kill in friendly fights." He was still studying her as if she puzzled him. "I've killed any number of brigands and rogues in my time."

But that wasn't murder. That was righteous execution. So much for Mother Winifred.

The sword. The earl had seemed obsessed by his holy blade. "Why did the king give you that sword?"

"For honorable service. I swear it on my soul."

It wasn't a direct answer and she sensed a slight distance over it, but she had to believe such an oath. His slight change in manner, however, made her seek to know more. "It was black. I didn't think swords were black."

"It's just dark, Claire. Something to do with the forging. Don't fret about it." His big hand rubbed her back down low, soothing her. Stirring her. Distracting her.

"You must excuse my nervousness about such things, Renald. I am unused to violence."

He kissed her brow. "It is a blessed state, and I will try to preserve your peace. I vow it."

Only one thorn remained. "The earl..."

"Is a rebel," he said, sealing her lips with his finger. "Claire, he cannot like this marriage. Don't let him distress you."

Her shadowy doubts became mist, and she wafted them away. Enough of it. She knew this man by now. "You will give up killing now?" Looking up, she caught his grimace.

"I'm a warrior," he said again. "If called upon by the king, I must fight."

"I understand that. I mean tourneys."

"I could be called upon to represent the king in a tourney." His fingers played in her hair. "But tourneys are not held in England. The sensible kings here think they waste too many lives."

She smiled. "So you will not have to fight like that again. I'm glad."

His gentle torment across the back of her neck made her smile even more, but then his hand stilled. "I'll doubtless damn myself with this, Claire, but I do enjoy it."

She pushed away to stare. "Enjoy *killing*?"

He held her. "No, never that. But I enjoy fighting. In a tourney, we fight to overcome and win ransoms. Killing is not in the plan." He shrugged, but with a glint of humor in his eyes. "It tends to put a cloud over the event."

"How can you *joke* about such a thing?"

Humor fled, but something in his expression made her feel foolish. Was it foolish not to want people to play at violence? Not to want anyone to risk their life for fun?

"Now that I'm a baron with estates to care for," he said, "I'll have less time for games. Unless we're attacked, I'll likely do little but mop up brigands. I assume you won't mind me dispatching a few of them now and then."

Stung by his wry tone, she muttered, "I suppose not."

He stroked her lips, coaxing a smile. "I must keep up my training, though, Claire, or what use will I be—to you or to the king?"

"I understand. I'm sorry if I seem foolish. This is all so different..."

"And I seem like a snake within paradise," he said. "But I'm not, Claire. I want to keep this place whole as much as you do."

She believed him, and obeyed his teasing by parting her lips for his finger. She welcomed the rough taste, flicking her tongue around it. She didn't resist when he slid it deep into her mouth and out again, again and again, even though she knew what he was doing, and felt the response in another part of her body.

Tomorrow.

At that thought, she tightened her teeth and lips around him, growing almost faint at the look in his eyes.

Then he captured her lips with his mouth and sealed her to him all along his body, pulling her to straddle him. She ached and pressed closer, feeling him hard between her thighs, separated only by layers of clothes. Frustrating layers of clothes.

For the first time she understood why some foolish maidens did not wait...

At long, long last, he drew back, sucking in a deep, unsteady breath, rubbing his head against hers. "Spices again. Delicious lady."

"You can't still be hungry..."

"Not hungry. Famished." He bit quite sharply at her neck.

Claire squeaked and scrambled away, but she was laughing. Laughing for the first time in so long.

He lounged there, looking tussled, younger, lighter and unbearably tempting. And he knew it. He grinned.

A watering bucket caught her eye. Without thinking, she grabbed it and tipped it over him.

After an appalled moment, she ran.

He choked on a curse, half blind, but a sweeping hand caught her skirt. Trying to wrench free, she fell against the bench. Her out-thrust hand stopped the fall, but she sprawled half over the stone.

And screamed.

"Claire?"

She surged back up, her head slamming into his chin.

"Lucifer's horns, Claire—"

But then, sweeping wet hair off his face, he saw what she had seen. In the narrow space behind the bench, carelessly covered by dying weeds, lay a man.

A man who was assuredly dead.

Renald's arms came around her, drawing her safely back. "Hush, love."

Claire stopped the noises she'd hardly been aware of making. "He looks... he looks like my... father!"

He held her tighter. "Is it a relative then?"

She shook her head wildly. "He's *dead*."

He turned her against his wet chest. "Hush, love, hush. He can't hurt you."

The wave of shuddering passed and Claire swallowed. "I'm sorry. I'm not normally such a ninny. I've seen death. But—"

"But it was a shock." He calmly rubbed her back. "It reminded you of the shock of your father's death. I understand. Let me escort you to the hall."

She pulled herself together. "No. I'm over my silliness now. I didn't recognize him. I didn't try. But he must be one of our people."

"Or a servant of one of our guests."

She had completely forgotten the hall full of people. "We still need to see who he is. We can't just leave him there."

He studied her a moment, then nodded. "Very well."

Arm protectively about her, he led her back to the bench where they both peered over. It was dim in the shadows, but the man's ghastly face glimmered up through limp leaves, slack in death. Gritting her teeth, Claire brushed away some weeds, then gasped. "But... It's Ulric, my father's man!"

Renald's hand tightened on her arm.

"I wondered where he was. Why he didn't

return with… with the body. He never left my father's side." She glanced up at Renald's still face. "Did he die in the same engagement?"

He left her, and squeezed closer to sweep away the rest of the flimsy covering. "He's fresher dead than that." Then he slowly raised his hands, hands stained dark.

"Blood?" she whispered.

"Blood."

Remembering a dark and bloody sword, Claire straightened. Then she started to back away.

"Claire, I had nothing to do with this."

She froze, staring at him, trying to sort through panic to truth.

"This blood is fresh," he said steadily, eyes on her. "He must have been killed not long before we came here. Long after you saw the blood on my blade."

That must be true. She rubbed her hands over her face. "I'm sorry. What reason anyway would you have to kill poor Ulric?"

"What reason could anyone?"

She stepped a little closer. "It couldn't have been an accident?"

He rose, wiping his hands on his braies. "I don't see how. Death was fast, I'd judge, and I can find no blade. No, Claire, I'm afraid there is a snake in paradise after all. Murder's been done here tonight."

He looked as deeply concerned as she, and with reason. He spoke of a true snake, one that had stolen the fragile paradise they had found.

247

"We cannot marry tomorrow." She spoke without thinking, but from a deep, troubled instinct.

He came to her. "Because of the death of a servant? Claire, it is announced."

"We can change our minds. People will understand."

"Will they? I don't. You were happy to marry within days of your father's death, but balk when a servant dies? What sense in that?"

None, she thought. "But this happened *here*. Here in Summerbourne!"

"Disturbing, yes." He gathered her into his arms. "But we will find out who did it and set it right. A quarrel perhaps, among the servants."

"But Ulric wasn't even here! I mean, no one knew he was. When did he arrive? Where has he been?"

"Hush." He stroked her. "We will find all this out, and it will prove to be ordinary enough. It does not affect our wedding." He tilted her chin. "Pity me, Claire. I do not want to wait."

And some of the paradise flowed back, along with a lot of the hunger. She didn't want to wait either. It seemed heartless, with poor Ulric lying only feet away, but she wanted to marry this man tomorrow.

"Very well."

He kissed her. "Let's go and put this in the hands of your melancholy sheriff. He's the one most suited to take charge, and it will suit his temperament better than bridals."

She even smiled at his words, since they were so apt. It certainly didn't ease Eudo's mood to be told of a body, but perhaps he was relieved not to have to look festive anymore. Perhaps the earl decided to join him in his inquiries for the same reason.

Margret came over, shaking her head. "A murder. I don't suppose I should have expected your betrothal to go off as usual, should I?"

Claire rolled her eyes. "At least it's hard to imagine anything worse to come."

Renald watched Claire chat with her friend and resisted the urge to move closer, to check what was being said. Lady Margret couldn't know. As far as he could tell, no one here but the earl knew, and he was too cautious of the king's wrath to speak out.

It had been a close thing, however, earlier. Renald had reminded the earl that the king would be displeased if anything happened to prevent this marriage, though he sympathized with the man's dilemma. He couldn't feel harshly toward anyone who cared about Claire.

She was almost within his grasp, though, and he'd let nothing stop him now.

The wedding and the wedding night, and they'd be bound for all eternity.

Thank God that Ulric had never had a chance to speak to her.

# Chapter 14

Claire woke the next morning to her wedding day, nervous, but doubtless only in the way that any bride was nervous. By the time she'd gone to bed the night before nothing had been discovered about Ulric's strange death. She was determined, however, not to let it cloud her day.

She'd rather the culprit had been found, and the matter settled. As far as she knew, all Eudo had discovered was that Ulric had arrived in the middle of the feast, and probably slipped into the hall to eat. No one seemed to know where he'd sat, or who he'd spoken with. No one could imagine who had killed him in the garden.

Eudo seemed to think it would never be solved.

She realized she was half off the bed and squinted sideways to where Margret lay hogging the center, fast asleep. With the crowding in the hall, this big bed couldn't be left with only one. Lady Huguette was snoring quietly on the far side.

It felt nice. As it had been all her life. Three to a bed.

Tonight, however, it would be different.

Two to a bed.

Naked and entwined.

She heard noises outside the window, horses and men shouting. Slipping out of the bed, she hurried to see what was happening. For a moment she thought everyone was leaving! But then she relaxed. The men were going hunting.

A good idea. Fresh air and exercise before another day of feasting, and if they returned with fresh meat, that would be useful, too.

The floor was a tangle of maids, and Prissy stirred and sat up. "Oh, lady. Are you awake?"

"No. I'm sleepwalking."

Prissy chuckled and got up to help her dress. Soon everyone was up, and the day had begun. Renald had made no requests for this day, so Claire felt free to go and help organize the new feast. Thank heavens most of the cooking was done, apart from fresh bread.

All the women were willing to help, too, so soon everything was ready and they could sit and chat, waiting for the men to return so the ceremony could go ahead.

"You seem very calm," said Margret. "I was in a fine state by now."

"I remember. Up and down. Changing gowns. Fretting that Alaine wouldn't arrive."

"At last you don't have to worry about that."

"No." It caused a tiny pang, that this was his home not her father's. But then she remembered the benefit. That she could stay here all her life.

There were other blessings too. Her grandmother was secure here, and her mother almost back to her happy self, comforted by the presence of all her friends and by being free of worry.

She didn't know about Thomas since he'd

gone with the hunt, but she felt sure even he was more at ease.

Truly, she was blessed.

When they heard distant horns, most of the women leaped up to run into the courtyard to watch the men return and to see what they had brought back.

Laughing and triumphant, they rode in, small creatures slung from saddlebows, and a deer across a packhorse. Claire stared at its sad, dead eyes, and for a moment clouds threatened. She drove them away. Enough of folly. She liked venison, too.

Renald swung off his horse and came to sweep her into a hearty, smelly kiss. "Miss me?"

"For a matter of mere hours?" But she had. She realized that now. Summerbourne had seemed empty without him. "I expect you'll be often gone. About the king's business."

"No more often than I have to be, I assure you." He looked around. "Weren't we supposed to be getting married today?"

She wrinkled her nose at him. "Not unless you have a bath."

"I'll go leap in the river immediately."

"Then when you're clean, my lord, I'll be ready." Claire called for her maids and her friends and ran up to her room to change.

She was soon ready to go down to the church, waiting with just her maids to hear that all was ready, when the door swept open without a knock, and in walked her aunts.

Claire's first instinct was panic that Felice had come to try to claim Renald as husband, but she forced a smile. "Felice! Amice! How lovely. Are you home for good?"

"Why not?" Felice dropped her cloak in the middle of the floor. "We heard about the betrothal. Now we're safe, we've come to support you at your wedding."

Claire was sure her aunt had heard about bloody swords and dead bodies, and was hoping for more of the same. She kissed them both anyway. They were like sisters and their presence completed the occasion.

Amice was untangling herself from layers of veils. "The convent is not very nice, really. The beds are hard, and the food rather plain. I'm so pleased we won't have to move there. Oh, Claire, how are you coping?"

"Very well." Claire assisted her. "I'm glad to see you both."

"No wonder." Felice picked up Claire's torn veil and poked a finger through one of the holes. "It looks as if he's already shown his violent nature."

Claire rescued the fragile silk. "Not at all."

"You've kept him sweet? According to his men, he's a terror when angered."

"Then he's slow to anger. Felice, stop this!"

"I'm sure no one could be cruel to Claire," said Amice, but added, "His men did tell terrible stories, Claire. We could hear them." She turned a vivid pink and whispered, "Not only about his rages. About his *lust*."

Claire knew she should silence them both, but a feverish need to know started in her. "Lust?"

"Two or three a night," said Felice.

"And that turned you off?"

Felice flushed. "I've no mind to be ripped open once, never mind thrice!"

"Ripped open?"

"Haven't you found out yet? He's huge. Few women can endure him, but of course, he doesn't care."

"It can't be true."

"His men *boast* of his extraordinary qualities. Of his victim's screams."

"Oh, Claire!" Amice dabbed at her watering eyes. "What are you going to do?"

Though shaken, Claire wouldn't give Felice any satisfaction. "Marry him. I don't believe such nonsense. Now, I'd rather be alone until the wedding."

"Of course," said Felice, but didn't move. "I thought you might be interested in news about Imogen of Carrisford."

"I know about Imogen. She's married to FitzRoger of Cleeve."

"Bastard FitzRoger. A sorry trial for such a sweet and gentle maid."

Claire clapped her hands over her ears. "Felice, I don't want to know!"

"He imprisoned her in his castle."

Claire lowered her useless hands, finally chilled. "Why? What's happened to her?"

"Why? Because she fled his cruelty. And who do you think acted as her jailer?" Before Claire could respond, Felice added, "Renald de Lisle."

When Claire just stood there, Felice added,

"As for what happened to her, I gather she's been allowed some freedom, but only after a whipping." She patted Claire's cheek. "You'd best be a very meek and obedient wife, Claire, and not object to anything your husband demands of you, no matter how painful. Come Amice, we must go below. Claire wants to be alone."

Amice followed her twin, but turned to say, "I'm sure if you're kind and gentle with him..." Felice pulled her on her way.

"Load of spiteful nonsense," said Prissy, coming to fuss with the folds of Claire's gown. "Don't you listen to a word she says, lady."

"It must be true about Imogen," Claire whispered. "Felice couldn't make that up."

"Rumors are funny things, lady," Maria said. "Probably they had a falling out and that's what gossip has made of it."

"After all," Prissy added, "you have to go on what you know about a person. Would you say Lord Renald was a harsh, cruel man?"

Claire began to come out of the dark mist.

"Take that business of three a night, lady," Prissy went on. "Lord Renald's not had a woman while he's been here. I'd have heard."

"But it's only been three days."

"If he were that greedy for it, and that uncaring, he'd have found some of the lusty maids. There's enough been giving him the eye, and that's the truth."

Claire laughed with relief. Talk about snakes in paradise. She'd seen for herself in the dairy how many maids were giving him the eye. And if he were taking up any of the invitations she'd have heard, too, especially if he was leaving them injured.

"After a lifetime, I should know better than to pay attention to Felice."

Prissy patted her shoulder. "It's only natural for you to be nervous, lady. Mind now," she added with a wink, "if you decide you don't want him in your bed, there's plenty that'll take your place!"

Her mother swept in, smiling. "It's time, my dear." She gathered Claire in for a warm kiss. "Oh, I think this is the happiest day of my life. Everything is going to be perfect."

Claire hugged her back, lips unsteady. Yes, astonishingly, everything was going to be perfect.

She took a moment to steady herself, then put on her veil, securing it with a jeweled circlet. Then she went with her mother down to the hall, where her aunts waited to escort her to the church door.

As was the custom, everyone was gathered to witness the vows. Claire took her place before the bishop, and smiled at Renald de Lisle. Firmly, she promised to honor and obey him, and to care for his body and soul. How sweet to be able to say the words honestly.

In turn, he made his vows to her, and moved the betrothal ring from the right hand to her left where it marked her as a married woman. Then he kissed the ring, and smiled. Everyone cheered, but Claire scarcely heard it, lost as she was in the warmth of his eyes.

No, she had never expected this, but it was sweet, deliciously sweet.

And now there were just a few short hours before the night.

They ran to the hall hand in hand, pelted with flowers and seeds, followed by a merry throng. Immediately they were pushed into a dance, a wedding dance just for the two of them, for hunter and hunted. It ended when he caught her, swinging her into his arms and carrying her victorious to her place at the table.

He plied her with morsels of food, but would only allow her watered wine. "I want you to have all your wits about you tonight, my love."

Dizzy without wine, Claire fed him with her own hand, and kissed traces of food from his lips. Acrobats tumbled, men ate fire and swords, and magicians made impossible items appear and disappear, yet she and Renald hardly noticed, so entwined they were in each other.

Once the feast ended, everyone spilled out into the sunshine, out of Summerbourne to the open land beyond to dance on the grass, and to indulge in sporting contests.

A pole had been set up between supports, and boys and men tried to balance their way across it. A prize had been hung over the river and boys rowed down in boats, one of their company balanced on the prow ready to try and seize it. A greasy pig ran screaming around an enclosure, free to anyone who could catch and hold it for a count of twenty.

Barrels of ale stood ready, free to all. Cloths on the grass were piled with all that remained of the feast. Men, women, and children danced all around. Claire danced, too, delighting in the good company of her friends and neighbors, and in her husband.

At first Renald stayed by her side, but then he was dragged into a wrestling match. One of the women called out, "Don't go straining something on a night like tonight!"

He laughed and tossed his opponent easily. Then all the men wanted to drink with him. He looked back at Claire ruefully, but let himself be carried away.

It was only for a little while. The day sped on.

Claire went to sit with some women in the shade of a tree, and talked contentedly about babies, and blisters, and bedstraw. Ordinary stuff. The stuff of life. Then she wandered closer to where Renald and some men were playing a game with a stuffed ball, trying to hit a target. He wasn't very good.

It was endearing to see that he wasn't master of everything.

"A handsome young man."

Claire turned to find Eudo the Sheriff by her side. She was in no mood to talk of murder, but she smiled, putting aside her lingering bitterness with him over her father's death. It wasn't entirely fair to blame Eudo. Lord Clarence had been uneasy about Henry Beauclerk's seizure of the throne from the first. Eudo had doubtless been as shocked as everyone else when her gentle father had put their theoretical discussions into disastrous action.

He talked about books anyway, which was pleasant enough.

"I see your mind is not on scholarly matters today, Claire."

Claire blushed, realizing that she'd been paying more attention to Renald, who was demonstrating something with a borrowed sword. "I'm sorry—"

"No. I'm sorry for going on about such dry stuff when you have other matters on your mind. He seems a good man of his sort. I'm glad to see some happiness coming out of this sad business."

"By the way," he added, "I found some people who saw Ulric at the feast, but he kept to himself."

Claire frowned over that. "How strange. You'd think he'd at least let us know he was home." And then she could have spoken with him. Heard of her father's last days.

"It doubtless didn't seem the right moment. After all, he couldn't have expected his death."

"How true." It reminded her that no one knows the hour of their death, and therefore they should take joy in the moment. She was about to go to Renald to take joy in her own lovely moment, when a man-at-arms hurried over to kneel before Eudo. "Beg pardon, my lord sheriff, but I thought you'd want to know."

"Yes? Know what?"

"We found Ulric's pack, my lord. In a corner of the hall by the stairs. Or at least, we think that's what it is." He held out a battered leather bag.

"Indeed it is," Claire said, reaching for it, a teary smile starting just to see something connected with her father. "He carried my father's personal possessions in—"

Eudo grasped it before she could.

"Eudo! It should go to my mother."

The sheriff hefted it as if judging its weight. "I must look inside first, Claire, to see if it casts light upon his death."

"How—"

But he'd already hunkered down to tip out some undergarments, a spare pair of shoes, some small coins, and a book. Her father always carried a book.

No, not a book!

Claire bent to seize it.

Her hand and Eudo's met on the boards that bound the loose sheets of parchment. "It is my father's journal," she explained, heart racing. "It can have nothing to do with Ulric. He couldn't read." She curled her fingers over the edge and looked him in the eye. "It is precious to me and my family."

His eyes shifted, though his hand lingered almost as if he would fight her for it. "His daily record, telling of every little thing? I remember it. I really should—"

"No." With amazement, Claire heard herself use Renald's absolute tone.

And Eudo let go.

Claire rose, clutching the journal to her chest. "It is very special. You must see that. His last words and thoughts."

And presumably, she suddenly realized, the true explanation of how he came to die. At last she would know, and in her father's own words.

Eudo was staring at it as if he valued it as much as she, as if he might fight to get it back. "You're foolish. It might contain something of importance."

"Only—"

"I insist—"

"No!" She stood and stepped back, out of reach. "The first person to hear these words must be my mother!"

She fled before he could protest further. What did he think she would do? Destroy it?

She found her mother in the Summerbourne garden with two friends. Claire went straight to her and put the journal in her hand. "It's Father's. Ulric had it."

"His record of his journey?" Her mother traced the plain wooden boards which were tied around the pieces of parchment. "What good can it have to say?"

Claire hadn't expected that reaction. "You know Father. He'd make a good story of it."

"Of defeat and death?"

Claire snatched the book back. "I'm sorry—"

"No." Lady Murielle found a smile. "Why don't you read us a little from the beginning."

Her mother was right. The book could only sadden them, and she didn't want that today. But she untied the boards, and uncovered the first loose sheet. She ached and smiled to see her father's blotchy scribble again. He had always been too impatient about putting down his thoughts to make neat letters. It had been Claire's pleasure to transcribe his words into neat script.

"If it's too hard for you, Claire, don't bother," said her mother. "After all, it is your wedding day."

Claire swallowed, shook her head, and began to interpret the familiar squiggles, though it wasn't easy in the fading light. *"The grace of... of summer touched our hero's simple home, bringing—oh—joy to his heart..."* She paused. "This seems more a story than a journal."

"A new story," her mother said, lightening. "That is indeed something to treasure. Go on."

"*...bringing joy to his heart, but sorrow too, for he knew his—*something*—venture would take him far away, so far that he might never find... the pick? No, path, back to those he loved, to those who loved him more than he deserved. But resolute, and making a final prayer, the Brave Child Sebastian—*Oh."

"Oh," echoed her mother. "Another telling of that one. Well, it's a fine story, but we all know it pretty well by heart."

Claire fought a wave of poignant loss, loss of that record of her father's last days in his own words. Now, with Ulric gone as well, she would never really know. Unable to trust her voice, she closed the boards and tied the strings. "We can enjoy it another time, Mother. I'll put it with the other books."

"Yes, dear. Do that. And get back to enjoying your bridal day!"

Biting her lip against tears, Claire hurried away—and collided with a solid chest.

"What?" she snapped at Renald. "What now? Why are you always *following* me?"

"How can I resist, my love?" He steered her away from the interested audience, arm firm around her, then halted. "What has upset you, Claire?"

"Nothing."

"I doubt that."

"Then nothing of importance."

She tried to push away, but he held her close. "It's important to you, and therefore to me. The book?"

"In a way."

He separated them a little and looked at the bound parchment. "What is it?"

After a moment, she sighed. "It's Father's. Ulric had it. I thought it was his journal, the record he kept of everyday events. But it's just a retelling of one of his stories."

"Isn't that of value?"

"I suppose so. It's the only time he tried to write one down." She fiddled with the leather thongs that bound the boards. "We know them all by heart, though, and can pass them on ourselves. I would much rather have had his experiences, his thoughts, on his last journey."

He drew her back into his arms. "I understand."

And Claire found there was comfort in a big,

warm body when a person was feeling lost and sad. What a treasure to have such a refuge whenever life dealt a blow.

Then he lowered his head and captured her lips for a kiss that spoke not of passion, but of caring and comfort. Of healing. It turned however, as it must, into something spicier.

When he broke the kiss and looked down at her, his eyes were deep and dark. "My wife."

"Yes. Please."

He laughed almost shakily. "Soon. It has to be nearly time for the women to lead you to the bed. Then the men will bring me to you." His lips twitched. "Someone once seems to have thought the couple might lose their way."

He took her hand, and she willingly twined her fingers with his. "I think it goes back to Roman times."

Connected by more than hands, they wandered back toward the hall. "Couples lost their way back then?"

"No, but the husband would pretend to capture the wife, to carry her back to his home. Her menfolk would try to protect her, while his fought them off."

He glanced down at her. "Perhaps it wasn't always pretense. Brides are still seized by violence today."

"Heiresses." She realized there was one lingering thorn, a tiny one, but still pricking at her happiness. "Was that how your friend FitzRoger captured Imogen of Carrisford?"

His brows rose. "Not at all. She went to him for aid."

"But did she want to marry him?"

"She went willingly to the church door."

It was evasive, but she was sure it was true as far as it went. Probably Imogen had been pressured much as she had.

"I heard that he beat her, and kept her prisoner. With you as guard."

"Did you hear that she knocked him unconscious?"

*"Imogen?"* Claire stopped to stare. She remembered the girl as pretty, charming, and with no thought more serious than the cut of her gown.

"Imogen. The gentle Flower of the West. It's treason, you know, to attack a husband, especially one who's liege-bound to the king."

Claire crossed herself. "What has become of her?"

"It's too complex a story to get into now. But trust me on this—Imogen is safe in Carrisford, and not unhappy with her fate. I hope soon to take you to visit there. You can ask her yourself."

She studied him and decided he was being completely honest. "But Lord FitzRoger is a fearsome warrior."

"As am I. Are you unhappy with your fate?"

And she had to say, "No."

He raised her chin. "We both had to fight to survive, Claire, to climb from the depths into which fate plunged us. We have both done things we regret. Perhaps one day our souls will be called to pay. But neither of us has ever killed pointlessly, nor hurt anyone merely for amusement."

"For *amusement*?"

He touched her cheek. "Ah, Claire. You live a blessed life here, but there are wolves outside the door."

"And in." The words slipped through her lips before she could stop them.

He didn't take offense. In fact, he might have smiled. "But I'm a tame wolf, conquered by a maiden fair."

"Oh no," she said, blushing at the look in his eyes. "Whatever you are, my lord, you are not tame."

"True. What use is a wolf—even a wolf tamed to the hearth—without fangs?"

"It would be a safer wolf."

But then he snared her, looking down into her eyes. "Do you want that kind of safety, wife?"

After a moment, challenged for the truth, Claire whispered, "No."

He kissed her again—a searing promise of dangerous flames to come. Releasing her lips, he pushed her into the cacophonous hall. "Go. Find someone to drag us to our bed."

## Chapter 15

Claire staggered in on trembling legs. A glance behind showed the sun had almost set, touching the world with gold, scarlet, and black that mirrored the startling heat swirling inside her.

Oh yes. The dangerous bed...

She was holding something. When she looked down she saw her father's book. She'd promised to put it with the other books, but she couldn't go into the solar now—into their wedding chamber—without breaking custom. She had to wait to be led there. She was supposed to look reluctant, not keen.

She saw Thomas and grasped a chance to cool herself down. She went to show him the book. He was no more enthusiastic than her mother had been, though for different reasons. He just didn't like books. In fact, he was keen to get back to his friends who were all playing a game with pebbles.

She held him back. "Are you less angry at me now?"

He looked down and grimaced. "I see that it isn't your fault. And he can't help the way things happened."

Claire said a grateful prayer. "And I will never stop loving you, Thomas."

He squirmed a bit at that, but then looked up, eyes anxious. "I don't want to leave here, Claire."

She sighed at that, but could only be honest. "I wish I could promise that you'll never have to, love, but that's not true. I'll do my best for you. That's all I can say."

"Josce says it's best to go. That I'll like the king's household."

Claire sent a blessing to the squire. "Was Josce in the king's household?"

A lad cried, "Thomas, it's your turn! Come on!"

Her brother stepped away. "Yes. Josce is all right." With that high praise, he ran back to his game.

Claire turned away, smiling. "All right" meant that Josce had been elevated to a level only slightly below God. Her brother was moving forward. He wasn't happy yet, and the changes must still hurt—probably always would a little—but he was healing.

So. It was time.

Margret would be the one to drag her to her bed. Claire looked around the crowded hall, seeking her friend. Then she realized that Margret might be trying to find her, and returned to her seat at the high table, where she'd be expected to be. She saw Renald across the hall, and he raised his brows as if asking why the delay.

She sipped some wine to steady herself. *Come on, Margret!*

Then, as she scanned the hall, the sheriff swooped the book from in front of her, stepping out of reach before she could snatch it back.

"Eudo!"

He was untying it with urgent fingers. "Your lady mother has clearly done with it for now."

"There's nothing in there."

He paused. "The pages are blank?"

"No. But it is not Father's journal. It appears that this time he didn't keep one. Instead he wrote down one of his stories. The Brave Child Sebastian."

He continued with the business of opening

the boards then looked at the first sheet, frowning. "This is an atrocious script."

"Father never took time to write neatly."

He moved closer to a window, grimacing as he tried to make it out. Then he flipped to the end. Claire wanted to protest at that. She didn't want him reading parts she hadn't read, but it was already done.

Clearly he found nothing startling. He tidied the sheets and bound up the book. "As you say, Claire. Nothing. But it will be something to treasure."

She took it and retied the strings just to establish that it was hers, hers and her family's. "I will transcribe it into a fair script. Perhaps you would like to read it then."

"But of course. Clarence was a dear friend."

As he walked away, however, Claire had the impression that he was suddenly carefree. She contemplated the book, wondering what Eudo had thought it might contain.

He had read the last page. She didn't think that had any significance, but she opened the book again. The writing was quite neat here, as if her father had had time and a flat surface.

*And so the Brave Child stood over the corpse of his mighty foe, triumphant by the power of the Lord God. But tears trickled from the hero's eyes. Tears of sorrow that he had been forced to kill, and to kill such a man.*

She read the words again. The story had never ended like that before. Sebastian had never wept over the dead tyrant—

The book was snatched again. "Oh no you

don't," said Margret. "Brides don't get lost in books on their wedding night. And they aren't supposed to frown, either."

"Margret! Be careful with that."

With a grin, her friend gave it back. "What is it, anyway?"

Claire explained, admitting to her disappointment that it was a story, not a record of the rebellion.

"Well you know," said Margret, picking up a lingering sweetmeat and nibbling it, "your father had never fought before, or not since he was a young man. When Alaine has to put on armor, he can get in an odd mood. Sometimes he comes home jubilant—it's strange what men like. But sometimes there's a look in his eye... Perhaps your father saw a different side to heroes."

Claire stared at her friend, surprised by the insight. "That would explain why he wanted to write a new version. To weave in what he'd learned of fighting." She traced the cover of the book. "It makes this even more precious, to see how Father was changed by his experiences." She began to untie the strings.

Margret grabbed it again. "Oh no you don't! Not tonight."

Claire tried to get it back and in the laughing tussle, some pages fluttered to the floor. They were scooped up by the Earl of Salisbury.

"Fair ladies fighting over a book," he said as he returned them to Claire. "It must be a very interesting tome."

She tidied it, making sure to put the errant pages in the right place. "It is a special one, my lord. My father's last writings."

"His journal?"

She glanced up at him. "You know of that?"

"As we gathered to support Duke Robert, I saw him write in it every day. It must contain interesting comments on that sorry affair."

Did he, too, look worried? Would he also want to snatch it away?

Claire firmly retied the strings. "Interesting, yes, my lord. But not a journal. For some reason he decided to write down his favorite story, that of the Brave Child Sebastian."

"Ah, I remember him spinning it one night. A rather foolish tale." He frowned at the book. "Where did it come from?"

"It was in Ulric's pack. It held nothing else of interest."

"And the book cannot shed light on Ulric's murder. That's a strange puzzle, and one that will probably never be solved. Sheriff Eudo also lost a manservant not many months back with the killers never found."

"It can't be that uncommon, my lord."

"Uncommon enough. Most murders are obvious crimes, rising out of moments of hasty anger or fear. But in the sheriff's case, he was set upon by brigands who escaped back into the wild lands. A lesson to him not to ride out without proper escort."

She couldn't imagine why he was talking of such matters, but didn't much care. Darkness had settled, and Margret had slipped away to gather the other young matrons. Her fate loomed deliciously close.

Claire looked across the hall to see her husband down on his haunches with the boys, rolling a knucklebone. Thomas was laughing.

"Ulric must have known how your father died."

Claire looked back to the earl. "Yes, he never left his side." She sighed, despite the major part of her that just longed for the marriage bed. "I wish I had heard his tale."

"I'm sure you would have found it most enlightening."

Claire blinked at his strange tone. "Enlightening?" Where was Margret?

"Lord Renald brought your father here, I understand. In mail, as he died."

"My lord, this is no time for such talk! I am trying to be joyous on my wedding day."

"I see you are eager for the bed." After a moment he added, "Some of us are cowards."

She stared at him, wondering why he thought that of her, but Margret was coming, thank the Virgin, leading a group of noisy, laughing young women.

The earl glanced at them and she thought she heard him sigh. "I will pray for you, Claire." He suddenly leaned forward, bringing his face close to hers, forcing her to pay attention. "Before you revel in your marriage bed, Claire, think more on *death*. Think about your father. About mail, and swords."

She watched him walk away, wondering if

drink had scrambled his wits. Think on death. Now? Clearly he did wish she would weep and wail through her wedding. As if she didn't know that her father had never wanted her to marry a man so fond of his mail and sword. But by venturing into the world of mail and swords, her father had brought all this about. She was just trying to put things back together again.

When the women surrounded her, she let them drive away all memory of the earl's words, and surrendered to laughing excitement.

In moments she was being dragged to the solar, pretending nervous unwillingness. Not having to entirely pretend. Despite desire, the marriage bed was a pit of the unknown, and there were those stories of screaming victims...

Nonsense. Snake stories.

Before she was dragged around the screen to the solar door, she looked back and saw Renald had risen to his feet to watch. It was as if flames of desire licked out from him to sear her.

He took a step forward as if to follow, and three men grabbed him to hold him back. Perhaps it was just part of the act, but somehow, she didn't think so. The power of his desire shocked her. But it thrilled her, too.

Then she was in her bridal chamber, rich with the perfume of flowers and herbs. Scarlet rose petals scattered the coverlet and floor along with other blossoms of every hue.

Busy hands undressed her but then someone said, "By the crown, Claire. Without your hair, you're indecent!"

"Into the bed, I think," said Margret. Claire was happy to get under the perfumed covers and pull them up to her chin. Once again, her rash act of cutting her hair returned to plague her.

Margret touched the ends. "I don't know how you could."

"It seemed like a good idea at the time."

"Typical."

Claire wriggled, swallowing nervously. "Rose petals on the sheets feel quite strange."

"But smell pretty." Margret scattered some grains of wheat for fertility. She also tucked some herbs under the pillow.

"There, that should ensure a merry night and a babe in a nine-month."

"It certainly worked for you. At least," Claire added, blushing, "the second part."

"And the first," said Margret with a wink.

"The first time? It was good the first time?"

"It got better, but yes," said Margret, "it was good the first time."

Claire glanced at the other ladies, who were standing by the door listening for the men. She had time for a quick question. "Margret," she whispered, "is there anything I should know? Things I should do? Other than just lie there."

The men were coming, laughing and singing.

Margret turned a little pink. "Oh. Well, tell him when you like things. Or when you don't."

"He won't mind?"

"Alaine doesn't."

Now they were hammering on the door, while

the laughing young women held it shut. "Anything else?"

"Don't be afraid to touch him. Anywhere."
The door began to inch open. "When you feel
like it, you could put your mouth to him."

"Mouth? To him?"

"You know. Kiss it. Suck it. Drives them
wild."

Claire stared at her friend. "Are you teasing me?"

"No! I swear it." The door was heaved
inward.

"Suck it," Claire repeated as the men burst
in.

"Not right away!" Margret cautioned in a
whisper. "I know you. He'll think you're
overbold!"

Most of the men were three-parts drunk,
but they had Renald held tight in their midst
as if he had, indeed, lost the way and had to
be dragged to her. He freed himself easily and
gazed at her. Her toes curled and breath suddenly became precious.

"Hey, don't we get to see the bride?" one
of the men demanded.

"No." Renald was already stripping, not taking his eyes off her. "Only I do." Naked, he
turned to them. "Anyone want to fight me over
it?"

Claire was not surprised when the men
laughingly backed away. Nor by the saucy comments of the women. She knew Renald was
a big, strong man. Only now did she see that
every inch was hard muscle—shoulders, back,
buttocks, legs. When he turned back to her,

her mouth was so dry she could neither speak nor swallow.

Vaguely, she was aware of people leaving. Mostly, she was aware only of him walking toward the bed. His front was as awe-inspiring as his back, and his male member jutted urgently.

It did seem rather big. Amazingly big.

As fluid returned to her mouth she swallowed. "Don't hurt me. Please."

He stopped, then sat on the bed. "Of course not, Claire. What's frightened you?"

"You're big."

His lips twitched. "Not that big, I assure you. I won't hurt you."

"My maidenhead?"

He shrugged. "Perhaps a little, then. But with good fortune, it won't go too hard." He slid easily under the sheets and gathered her into his arms. "Better?"

After a startled moment, Claire found that everything was better. Being up against his hot, hard body was a miraculous sensation that melted fears. She slid a leg over his, wrapped an arm around his broad chest, and worked her head into a comfortable dip.

"I was just being silly."

His hand traced her back, which was even more wonderful than his teasing of her nape had been. "I won't crush you. But if you like, you can be on top."

"On top?" But he was already moving her so she lay fully on top of him. It was like lying on sun-warmed smooth rock. His erection, however, lodged hard between her thighs, reminding her of certain problems.

"By big," she said, knowing she was turning red but determined to get this out in the open, "I meant your... your manhood."

It felt as if it was growing even bigger. Was that possible? Just how big could it grow?

"Felice..." she said, wriggling slightly. "In your camp, Felice heard your men. Talking about your size. Down there. That you... that you damage women."

He closed his eyes and muttered, "Lucifer..." and something that might have been, "Hoist, indeed." Then he looked into her eyes. "Claire, I swear to you, I have never damaged any woman that way. I'm not so big, and I do take care. Can I show you?"

She nodded, even though she suddenly felt painfully shy.

He eased her off him, flipping the bedclothes back so they were both uncovered, exploring her with his eyes. "So pale. So sweetly curved." Then he ran his hand over her hip, up her belly, to caress a breast. "You feel like silk. My rough hand might snag silk, but it won't hurt you."

At the slight abrasion of his touch on places never touched before, breath became scarce again. Claire put a tentative hand on his hard chest, feeling the heat and the silk of his own skin, but tracing the roughness of scars here and there. As her senses swam in his teasing touch, she counted and cherished her wolf's marks.

Once his size, his strength, had frightened her. Once scars of battle might have disgusted her. But now everything about him stirred only heat, and a feverish, aching hunger deep inside.

She suddenly grasped his wandering hand and looked at the calluses there. "I do accept what you are," she said, kissing the hard ridge that crossed his palm. "I accept the sword."

A look almost of pain crossed his face. "Ah, Claire. Sweetheart..." he murmured, and he kissed her, deeply, drowningly, seemingly with every inch of his hot body. Against her mouth he whispered, "I wish I were a better man for you, my wife. But I will be the best I can."

Then he lowered his lips to her breast.

As Renald tasted her skin, relished the rough texture of her small, untried nipple, a shiver of ecstasy passed through him, swelling him to the point of pain. But he could deal with that. Almost, however, she'd broken him with that trusting kiss to the hand that had killed her father.

He would put that out of his mind, however, and control his own need. He must. The news couldn't be delayed much longer. This was his last chance, his last chance to forge Claire to him in the heat of desire so that she could never break free, not even when the truth came out.

He heard her catch her breath, felt her sudden tension and summoned all his skills. He could read a woman—read her breathing, her subtle movements—as skillfully as Claire could read a book. He would use his skills to enslave her.

Doubts slammed him. Teasing her with his tongue, seeking what she liked the best, he fought them.

There was no other way.

No choice.

*You could tell her,* whispered conscience. *You could tell her now, rather than binding her to you and waiting for the news to break. To break her.*

He rubbed his hard palm over her other breast. Heard her whisper, "Renald!" Felt her touch his hand as if to stop him, then stroke him, delicately, hesitantly.

Ah, Claire. Beautiful Claire. Responsive Claire with skin like silk and courage like fire.

*We're married. It's already too late. But I can give her this.*

*You're not giving. You're taking.*

He silenced his inner voices, raising his head to look at her, at her smiling, wondering face. She was already flushed. Already close to ready. She was going to be a wonderful lover.

A finger in her folds found hot wetness waiting for him. Her eyes widened a little at his touch, but her smile grew and she parted her thighs in eager welcome.

"Not yet," he told her, stroking. "Not quite yet. With the best will, the first time is rarely perfect for a woman. Let me show you the good part first."

He used his hand and the music of her body, and skills learned with too many women, to sweep her into pleasure, into more than pleasure. Blocking all thought of his own urgent desire, he stroked and teased the response he wanted until her body told him she was her the end.

She was silent. Some women were. He didn't mind. Her face still spoke for her with frowns and gasps, and her body danced its message with her writhing hips. He drew it out, teased it out along a long, thin line of aching pleasure until she opened her eyes to plead, mutely, dazedly.

Triumphant, he released her, bringing the cry he'd worked for, the convulsion of ecstasy, the sobbing breaths as sweet as any tourney prize. He gave her his lips and received the violent kiss of total satisfaction.

What she thought was total satisfaction.

For now.

Her lids fluttered open and she laughed, dewy with sweat and rosy pink. "I didn't know... Not like that." Then she turned red at what she'd admitted.

He grinned. "Now you know why two is better than one."

"But we haven't... Have we?"

"No. But we will. Take a moment."

"Why wait?"

"Because I want to."

She looked at his erection. "Do I believe that?"

He chuckled with pleasure at her frankness. "Yes, my cock wants you now. But my head wants a whole new dance."

"Why?" She reached for him and he seized her wrist.

"Don't." His body was asking the same question. Why? It had seemed a good idea a moment ago.

But he needed to be careful when he took her.

In control. A control that was slipping.

He clenched his teeth and thought of icy water instead of dewy, rosy skin, the sweet-spicy perfume of her body, and the hot cream just waiting...

"Margret said men like to have it touched, kissed. Sucked even."

His body bucked its need.

"Is it as hot as it looks?"

Before he could seize control, before he could stop her again, she clasped him, stroked him—

His body convulsed in white-hot relief. His seed shot free. After a few groaning moments of sheer ecstasy, fury bit.

At himself for weakness.

At her for impulsiveness.

For wanton disobedience!

He rolled away to sit on the side of the bed, head sunk in hands. Eventually, he had to turn back. She was sitting cross-legged among crushed crimson petals, looking as if a barrel of ale had exploded in front of her. Which was probably close enough.

"I'm sorry," she said, wide-eyed. "Did that hurt?"

"Only in the nicest way. But I was trying to save it for you." At least she wasn't in shock.

281

He went to get a damp cloth to clean himself, and brought another to her. She was already wiping some splashes off herself with a corner of the sheet.

"Are you upset by that?" he asked carefully as he offered her the cloth. Claire of Summerbourne was not the most predictable woman.

"No." But she looked worried. "Is that it, though? Can we not... ?"

"Look at me and answer yourself."

She looked and blushed. "I'm glad. I want to become your wife tonight."

He laughed for relief and in simple delight at the jewel she was. "You will, Claire. Have no fear."

"No fear," she echoed and smiled so sweetly it could break his heart. "And to think that earlier I was afraid of you. Of it."

He hadn't really thought he had a breakable heart yet now there was a pain in his chest that could only come from that. "But having seen how easily it's conquered..." he teased, fighting, God help him, not to weep.

From habit he picked up his scabbarded sword from beside the bed, checking that it hadn't been splattered. When he glanced at her, she was staring at it.

"I always sleep with it by my hand, Claire."

"It is a holy blade. It will bless us." But she frowned.

"I'm sorry. I'll put it out of sight." Remembering the previous night, he slid the blade out a little to be sure there were no more tricks. It glinted dark and clean so he pushed it back and put it down a little farther back in a less obvious place, trying to come to terms with this new world. The world in which he loved Claire of Summerbourne. Claire—his wife, the woman he was tricking and deceiving because soon, very soon, she would have reason to hate him.

He'd snared and held and tricked and teased simply because he wanted her, and what he wanted he fought to have. What was the difference between wanting and love? He didn't know except that there was, and it changed everything.

Just maybe, if he'd loved her sooner, he would have found the strength to let her go.

But the wheel had turned. There was nothing now but to go forward and pray. He turned to consider the sheet, whether it was too soiled for her comfort, and found her still frowning. "Claire, it would be foolish to keep my sword too far away. What if we were attacked in the night?"

"Why would we be?" she asked, but vaguely. "Someone said it cuts through metal. Through mail."

Something in her tone, in the severity of her frown sent a splinter of icy dread into him. By all the saints, not yet. Not now. He put one knee on the bed and reached for her. "Let's not talk of swords now, sweetheart."

"Do most swords not?"

"Claire. We have better subjects—"

She slid from his reaching hand. "Do they not?"

He let his hand fall. "No. Most swords cannot cut through metal."

"But there must be other swords like that."

"Of course." He didn't try again to touch her.

"Then why was everyone so awestruck by it?"

"It contains the stone from Jerusalem." He made himself meet her panicked, questioning eyes.

"They were even more astonished that it could cut through mail." Her eyes fixed on him as if begging for something. "How many swords in England can do that?"

He knew then, and it settled like stone in his gut. He wished he could lie for her—for himself—but that was one step he would not take. "Just that one as best I know."

She moved back a little farther. "My father was killed in chain mail. By a sword to the heart. The links were cut through." She inched to the very edge of the bed. "Did that sword kill my father?"

After a moment she whispered, "Did *you*— No, it cannot be!"

The lie floated seductively to his lips. A temptation worthy of the snake in Eden. He could not be sure that he stopped it for honor's sake, or simply because the news would come. Such a lie could not hold.

Pale and frantic, she scrambled backward off the bed. "Oh, Jesu, of course you did! Why else were you given his property, one of his women for bride?"

"Claire—"

"Why else were you given that sword! A reward... No." She stared at him. "You had the sword before. Mail is supposed to protect from swords. You *cheated*." She came around the bed in fierce attack. "You *murdered* him!"

He backed away, hands raised. "Claire, listen to me—"

"How could you?" She seized the sword in both hands. "How could you bring this here? How could you face us with his blood on your hands? How *could* you... !"

When she seized the hilt as if she'd draw the weapon, he ripped it from her and tossed it to the far side of the bed.

She whirled to follow it and Renald saw what she saw—stained sheets, the blood of crushed roses, and the black-scabbarded blade. The room reeked of sex and roses, with a mismatched underlay of herbs and spices.

He wasn't surprised when she bent to vomit.

He stood frozen. For once in his life, he had no idea how to handle a woman, especially this woman, the one he wanted to guard against all harshness forever. He'd always known he was forcing her to grasp a vicious blade and now the wound was clear.

His own blood ran.

There was nothing else he could have done. Just as there'd been nothing he could have done to save her father.

*You could have told her the truth.*

*You could have let her escape.*

It was, God help them both, too late for that.

# Chapter 16

The retching stopped and Claire wiped her face on a clean corner of the sheet. The earl's words had started this. Think about your father, and mail, and swords, before you revel in the marriage bed. The earl hadn't wanted her to marry Renald, hadn't wanted her happy about it, because he'd known what a sin it was.

She had married her father's killer! Not just a man who had killed him in the heat of battle, but one who had used a cheating weapon. A murderer.

Why, in God's name, hadn't the earl spoken directly? Why hadn't he stopped her before this?

A sound made her twitch around to face her husband—her enemy—but he was simply pulling on his braies.

"I will have the marriage annulled," she said.

"No."

"You can't stop me!"

He was cold granite again. "Of course I can."

"You will rape me?" Despite the quiver inside she raised her chin. "Why did I think otherwise? Everything else you've said to me has been a lie."

"Everything I've said to you has been the truth. Just not the whole truth. I will never rape you."

She scrambled for her shift and pulled it on, pulled her kirtle over it, and her tunic. She wished she had a thick cloak to gather around herself for protection. "Then I will free myself of this marriage."

"And fling your family into poverty?"

She turned. "You would do that?"

"Why not if you will not give me what I want?"

"How can you want a wife who hates you?"

"Only believe that I do."

"A wife whose body you can never take without rape."

His features were set like stone but his eyes betrayed him.

She remembered him earlier, laughing.

She remembered, with a bitter sense of loss, the tender way he had guided her into her womanly pleasure, the burning spiraling wonder of it all.

The tragedy here, she feared, was that he did indeed want her, and even more than want.

She closed her eyes briefly before speaking. "Renald, I know it must have been in battle. I don't really blame you. You can't have set out to kill him. But you must see I cannot—"

"It was not in battle, Claire. Or not as you mean it. And I did set out to kill him. It was a court battle. One on one."

She stared. "A court battle?"

"Where a man proves his cause—"

"I know what a court battle is! How could my father have ended up in something like that?"

"By challenging the king's right to the throne."

Claire shook her head as if she could throw off the macabre picture. "And you were the king's champion. You and he. What kind of contest was that?"

"None at all."

She put her hands to her head, trying desperately to make sense of a shattered world. "And that sword! It wasn't enough that you're younger, bigger, stronger. That you've trained and trained from the day you were weaned. You had a sword that could cut through mail. You set out to kill him!"

She waited for denial. For excuses.

But he said, "Yes. He had to die."

She backed away until a wall stopped her, and covered her face with her hands. Sweet Mary mild, why had this been put before her? When she'd accused him of murder, it had been a wild word. She'd been sure it had been a true battle death, not really anyone's fault.

But it *had* been murder. Her father had been forced into a one-on-one fight with an opponent he could never defeat.

When she looked at Renald again, he was pulling on his tunic. It was over his head.

She ran for the door. She was through it and around the screen before he caught her in an iron-hard embrace.

The celebrating crowd fell slowly silent.

And in those moments, he whispered, "Don't say a word, or your family will suffer."

Still, the accusation swelled inside her. *This man cold-bloodedly killed my father, and by treachery even. I renounce him.* But his threat,

288

reinforced by his iron hold, held her silent for the crucial moments.

"My friends"—he spoke to the startled gathering, easing his arm so it must seem more like an embrace—"in my hurry to claim my bride, I overlooked her deep grief for her father."

Claire twitched and his hold on her tightened ruthlessly.

"Though she has tried to be a dutiful wife, her grief comes between us and pleasure this night. Therefore, we have decided to delay our consummation. As the Church recommends, we have taken a vow of celibacy for the first month of our marriage. We offer it up for the good of Lord Clarence's soul."

"My father is already in heaven," Claire said, but it was muffled against his chest.

"Perhaps," he said softly. "Accept this, Claire. At least it gives you a month to think before you destroy everything."

Tight with resistance, she was kept there as a murmur of surprise ran through the room. She thought she heard approval. It was true that the priests preached the holiness of such restraint within marriage, but few found the strength to embrace it.

It disgusted her that he cloak his villainy in sanctity, but she could see that it gave a reprieve. She didn't have to decide everything now while her mind was splintered by horror. She had a month to find a way out of this marriage, a way that would not ruin her family.

"You can let me go," she murmured. "I am ready to play my part."

When he cautiously eased his hold she looked him in the eye. "I, too, do not lie, my lord."

Then she turned to meet her friends, to meet their commiseration and admiration.

She saw Thomas looking bewildered and realized she'd have to tell him the truth soon. Sweet Mary mild, what would he do?

And how would her mother and grandmother feel to know they'd welcomed Lord Clarence's murderer? Perhaps, she thought bitterly, her mother would only care that Thomas was threatened again.

When would she have to tell them?

Then she realized that the story would break whether she spoke out or not. She saw the Earl of Salisbury, watching somberly, and glared at him. Why hadn't he told her sooner?

Then she remembered his words about cowards. He hadn't been talking about her, but about himself. He'd wanted to tell her, but hesitated to thwart the king's plan. So he'd hinted. And he'd caused that horrible sword to be brought out bloodstained, hoping for some revelation.

If Renald de Lisle had a soul, he'd have faltered then.

She shed anger with the earl. He'd kept silent to protect himself and his family. She was keeping silent for the same reason.

But it would come out. She hugged that thought to herself. Even if she kept silent, at any moment a traveler or tinker would bring the story of Lord Clarence's death to Summerbourne.

Then, as her friends surrounded her, cossetting her with comfort, she remembered Ulric.

"Such a shame, but right," said Margret.

"A lovely gesture," agreed Lady Huguette, moist-eyed.

"A good man to agree to such a course," added Lady Katherine, the biggest gossip in the country. What an event this must be for her.

Claire let the words wash over her as she absorbed the fact that Renald had indeed had a motive to kill Ulric. He'd killed him so his news wouldn't ruin the betrothal and wedding.

She began to weep. She couldn't help it. She let Margret help her back into the solar. "There, there. Hush, love. Better for sure not to start out your marriage bed with tears."

She fell silent and Claire wiped tears to look. The damp and disordered bed with a black sword lying among crimson rose petals suggested a very strange tale.

Margret stripped off the sheets without comment, however, scattering petals on the ground but putting the sword aside carefully on a chest. The smell of roses haunted the room, along with that other one. Claire feared she'd never find roses sweet again.

"Quite some sacrifice," Margret remarked.

"Not really."

"Well, if I'm any judge, he'll be gnawing the

walls before a month's up. He's been eating you with his eyes all day. Are you sure you're being fair to him?"

"Fair!" But Claire had to remind herself that Margret didn't know. None of them did, except the earl.

Margret patted her shoulder. "There, there, love. I'll send your maids to you."

Prissy and Maria hurried in and remade the bed without comment. There'd be speculation, though, about what exactly had happened here. Let them all wonder.

Claire watched Maria move the big sword so she could get sheets out of the chest and wished she could throw it out of the window. Throw it into the forge, even, to be melted down. That dark thing had pierced her father's heart, driven by the cold hand of Renald de Lisle.

She realized then that all his possessions were here. His chests. His bags. His mail on its hanger. This was his room. Would he expect to *sleep* here?

With her?

Her possessions had been brought down from the maidens' bedchamber. As he had promised, her father's book chests sat against a wall. She went and touched them, seeking comfort.

"Oh, Father, what now?"

Though full of wisdom, the books were silent.

"Do you wish to undress again, lady?" Prissy asked.

She couldn't stay huddled in layers of

clothing forever, so she let them strip her, but kept her shift. If he came, at least he wouldn't find her naked.

What would the guests expect from a celibate couple? That they sleep together to make the sacrifice more meaningful? Or that they sleep apart to show that they were keeping their word? Though the priests preached the holiness of a time of restraint after marriage, Claire had never known anyone to actually embrace the notion.

Embrace.

She hugged herself. She had enjoyed his company, enjoyed his embraces. Yes, she'd even reveled in the passion he'd given her.

It wasn't her fault that she'd not known who he was, but still she felt deeply soiled.

"Are you all right, lady?" asked Maria, fussing around her. "Do you need anything? Some poppy juice to help you sleep?"

"No."

"Do you want us to stay with you?"

"No. You can go."

Alone, she wandered the room, not knowing what to do. She remembered the miller's daughter, who counted stones. Poor Aldreth had lost her husband to an accident. Then a year later, her two small children had been taken by a fever. She'd weathered the first loss, but after she'd buried her little ones she'd started to count stones. She'd never stopped.

Claire could understand now. She could see the pleasure in simply counting stones.

With a sigh she looked around the solar. It had been her parents' room, full of happy memories. Briefly it had been a pleasure-bower. Now it was ruined by the man who had stolen her father and all joy. The man who—curse him—had woven strings into her heart so that she couldn't quite tear free.

That sword offended her! She pulled a scarf out of one of her chests and dropped it over the black weapon.

Someone knocked on the door. Renald? No. If he came, he wouldn't knock. She opened it to find Josce there, looking wary and curious.

"By your leave, lady, Lord Renald asks that I bring his sword to the office where he will sleep as usual."

Claire couldn't find words, so she simply stood back.

The squire hurried in, then stopped, looking around.

"It's under that cloth over there."

He gave her an odd look then uncovered the weapon. He retreated with it as if expecting some sort of attack, and she closed the door after him.

Renald's mail still stood on its hanger, like his ghostly presence. Square, strong, cold, it was symbol of all that he was—a man who couldn't endure to be without his weapon. A man who killed on order, and who would cheat if his master ordered it.

Why was her heart breaking over a cold-hearted wolf?

She was standing staring at his loathsome armor when her mother burst in. "Claire? What foolishness have you fallen into now?"

Claire tried to find the words to tell the truth, but her courage failed. "It was just Father," she muttered.

Her mother gathered her tight into her arms. "Oh, my poor child. You can seem so strong that I forget... Of course it is too soon, and how good of Lord Renald to respect your grief."

Claire winced, hating her own cowardice.

"And a month is not so long," said Lady Murielle, patting her shoulder. "It will give you time to get to know one another, which is no bad thing. And by then the wound of your father's death will have healed."

Claire sighed. It was no good. She could not live a lie. "He killed Father."

"What?"

Claire moved out of her mother's arms. "Renald de Lisle, king's champion, killed Father in a court battle. With that dark sword. Which was given him by the king so they could be sure of victory. Don't look at me like that. He admitted it all! It wasn't enough that he's a decade younger and twice as strong, they made sure of things by arming him with a sword that cuts through mail like thread."

Lady Murielle sat down on the bed. "Lord Renald killed Clarence?"

"Yes."

"But *why*?" her mother wailed.

Claire hadn't really asked that, but the answer was obvious. "To reward another hungry follower. Bastard FitzRoger got poor Imogen and Carrisford, and now his friend has me and Summerbourne. I'm sure other men will come to untimely deaths."

Her mother covered her mouth with a trembling hand. "No. No, it can't be!"

"And Ulric," said Claire, pursuing her thoughts. "He hasn't admitted it yet, but he killed Ulric. I thought he had no motive, but he had."

"Ulric was no threat to anyone. Claire, it's all fancy—"

"No it isn't! Ulric would have been there when Father died. He was bringing the full story. Renald knew that once I heard the truth I wouldn't take the wedding vows. So he killed him."

Her mother stared up at her, lips unsteady. "Are you *sure*, Claire?"

Claire flung out a hand. "Summon him. He'll admit it. He doesn't seem to care. He just wanted to be sure of the wedding. Now he has it and Summerbourne, he doesn't... doesn't *care*." Her brittle calm began to crack and she mirrored her mother's gesture of horror and covered her mouth. "Jesu. I have to break this marriage, Mother."

Lady Murielle seemed numb with shock. "I can hardly believe..."

Claire began to pace. "He says he'll throw us all out if I do. But I must." She fell to her knees at her mother's side. "You see that, don't you? I *must*. I can't lie with my father's killer."

Her mother reached a trembling hand to touch her cheek. "I don't know, Claire. I don't know. One-on-one... Oh, poor Clarence. Poor dear Clarence..."

She began to shake all over and Claire scrambled up to gather her into her arms. "Mother! Don't—"

But Lady Murielle began to wail. Claire screamed for the maids.

Servants and friends came running, potions were sent for, and Lady Murielle was tucked, staring and trembling, into the big bed. Everyone assumed that she, too, had suddenly been overwhelmed by grief, and her mother's occasional gabbled words didn't reveal the truth.

The soothing draft took hold, and soon Claire's mother lay in a peaceful stupor. Her two maidservants settled on pallets on the floor alongside Prissy and Maria. The guests drifted away and soon sounds from the hall faded. The celebration, such as it had been, was over.

Her wedding day was done.

Alone, Claire wondered what would happen if she fell apart. But it wasn't her nature even though it might be a relief. She needed someone, though, someone to hold her. Someone to advise her.

She wrapped a cloak around herself and slipped out in search of her grandmother. Lady Agnes had a small chamber on this floor, but as soon as Claire pushed open the door she heard a mixture of snuffles and snores. Of course, nearly all the rooms were crammed with extra guests and they were all asleep.

Only one place beckoned. No one in this world stood ready to help her, but perhaps she could find ease from the next. She left the hall and headed for the graveyard.

Rounding the corner of the wooden church she jerked to a halt. By her father's grave, a man stood, head bowed, hands resting on the hilt of an unsheathed sword whose point was set in the ground.

For a shocked moment she thought he was about to pierce the grave with it, to try to kill her poor father all over again. But then she recognized the traditional stance of the mourning warrior. He mourned her father?

No.

What then?

She could not say, and her mind would not try. She simply hated him the more for being where she wanted to be.

She prayed from a distance, hoping he would leave. When he didn't—didn't so much as move—fatigue defeated her and she trudged back wearily to the solar, tears running down her cheeks.

They were tears of grief—for her father, for her life, and for something briefly glimpsed now shattered forever. But they were also tears of fear and bitter loneliness. She'd once thought she stood exposed and lonely in a marketplace, but she hadn't known abandonment until now.

Back in the solar, in the room that still held the ghostly smells of the wedding bower, she found that some of her mother's sleeping draft remained. She drained it, grimly anxious for oblivion. As she lay beside her mother, waiting for it to take effect, she prayed again to her father for help.

How could she break free of this marriage?

How could she make the murderer pay? How could she do both and not bring further disaster on her family?

She didn't pray for help for her other pain, however. She deserved her foolishly broken heart.

## *Chapter 17*

The next morning, the poppy juice and general misery made it hard for Claire to drag herself out of bed. The weather had turned, too. Not to rain, but to a dull heaviness. Her mother and the maids had gone, leaving her alone.

She sat by the window, watching servants prepare for journeys home. She listened to their chatter, wondering what people were saying about the strange events. Had news of Renald's deed broken? All she heard, however, was gossip about the vow of chastity.

"Right noble of him, I'd say," said one man who was cleaning out a horse's hooves.

"And of her." The maid had a bundle on her hip, but was in no hurry to get on with her errand. "If I had a chance of Lord Renald in my bed, I'd not put it off!"

"You never put nothing off, Rilla."

"Oh, I don't know. I might put me shift off for you, Eddy."

Around the other side of the hall a woman shrieked, "Rilla! Where are you, you lazy slut?"

The woman hurried off with a wink at the

grinning groom, and Claire envied the servants their simple lives. What would Rilla do if Eddy killed her father? She had no idea. They weren't even Summerbourne servants. Probably they had codes as powerful as noble ones, though Rilla was less likely to be forced into marrying her father's killer.

Even that wasn't sure. On all levels of society property was crucial and often bound by marriage. Generally, though, if a killer was known he was punished.

No one would punish Henry Beauclerk for killing his brother, however, or for arranging the death of Clarence of Summerbourne. No one would punish the man who had used a cheating sword.

It wasn't right. She could perhaps ignore the death of a king, for that did not touch her closely, but she could not ignore the death of her father and her father's innocent man.

In fact, she would find a way to prove that Renald killed Ulric. That was murder, and even a lord could be executed for murder. Henry Beauclerk had made much of the way he was upholding the laws of the land. Let him uphold that one!

"Lady?" That was Prissy, sounding unusually subdued.

"Yes?" Claire said without turning.

"Lord Renald requests that you join him to bid farewell to the guests."

Claire stiffened, tempted to refuse, but she'd choose her battles more carefully than that. She dressed plainly, however. Not in drab and ashes, but not in finery either.

He waited among the bustle of the hall, and with merely a "Good morrow, lady," led her to stand with him by the doors. One glance had shown that he looked as terrible as she felt.

So he should, with the burdens his conscience bore, but her foolish heart wavered. Could she really seek his death?

Perhaps it need not be as bad as that. Perhaps his guilt could be used to make the king agree to an annulment, and to return this property to her brother.

Yes, that was better. Weaker, she knew. But better.

The guests bustled by, checking that they had all their possessions and calling good wishes on the union. Claire noted that word couldn't have broken yet about how her father had died. Her neighbors took warm adieus of his killer, welcoming him into the county. Some even congratulated her for her great good fortune in finding such a husband.

Standing by his side, smiling with her lips, Claire asked, "Why did the earl not tell everyone of your crime?"

"I have committed no crime, lady."

"O blessed soul!" she taunted while waving Margret on her way. "How few can make such a claim of innocence."

"You have committed crimes?"

"I married you."

He turned to her, brows raised. "You already have a husband? Thank heaven we did not take our pleasure any farther."

"It was a crime against heaven, not earthly laws!"

"You think heaven condones bigamy?"

She kept forgetting that he wasn't stupid. Lacking an answer, she turned to wave again as Margret and her husband rode through the gate. "I can't think why the earl kept your secret."

"Salisbury knows his fate hangs in the balance. I merely reminded him that the king would be displeased by any further disruption of this wedding. He already knew it."

"Another coward."

"Is it cowardly to fear the king's displeasure? He can strip a man and all his family of everything, including life."

Then the king can strip you of Summerbourne, she thought. "So," she asked, smile tight around gritted teeth, "how did my gentle father so displease the king?"

"By accusing him of fratricide."

She spun to face him. "Of which he is guilty."

"Be silent!"

"You are so afraid of the truth?"

"I am charged with your welfare. I will not see you, too, destroyed by this."

He waved at the last departing group, smiling. Then he grasped her arm and dragged her into the hall, across to the solar. People stared, but no one moved to stop him.

He was, after all, her lord and master, her husband.

When the door banged shut, she rubbed her

arm. "Chastity too much for you already, my lord?"

He seized her shoulders and thumped her down on the bed, but sitting. "Listen to me. I understand your grief and anger. But nothing is ever simple, good or evil, black or white." Suddenly he went down on one knee, seizing her hands. "Claire, no one will be served by another martyrdom."

She snatched her hands free. "There *is* such a thing as good or evil. It suits you to argue otherwise because you have been the very hand of evil!"

"In a court battle, does not God speak?"

Her mind slammed up against that and recoiled. "In a true court battle, perhaps. Not when a man such as you is sent out against a man like my father. A man like you armed with a special sword."

"And what of the Brave Child Sebastian?"

She leaned back, wishing she could escape farther, to the other side of the room. The other side of the world. "What do you know of that?"

"It is a well-known tale. But it is also what your father wrote in that book."

"How do you know?"

"Lord Eudo spoke of it so I had Brother Nils read parts to me."

She spoke from between clenched teeth. "I suppose I have no right to ask that you not read my father's private writings."

"No. No right at all."

She did move then, scrambling away from

him over the bed and off the far side, mainly so he wouldn't see her tears.

He rose. "Why the anger? Anyone would think those writings contain secrets."

"They are my father's last words. I'm surprised you didn't destroy them as you destroyed him!"

"Claire, you have cause to be angry with me, but don't be childish."

She whirled to face him. "Is it childish to hate my father's murderer?"

After a moment he said, "No, but it is childish not to look beneath the surface of things. I'd think a riddler's daughter would know that. The court battle was a legal process. Think of it like that. Your father was found guilty and died."

"Found guilty by a false king! Killed by his lackey."

A muscle twitched by his tight jaw. "Claire—"

"The king killed his brother," she persisted. "The rebels were *right* to say he is unfit to rule. Therefore, that court battle could *not* have shown the hand of God."

"What an interesting twist in logic."

She swept on, finding wild relief in spilling out all her bitter hurt. "You're tricksters, you and the king both! Don't think I don't understand the games you've played. You claimed to give us free choice, but then had your men tell frightening stories to scare my aunts away."

"To that, I confess."

"There is no custom of the Franks that the bride stays apart."

"Customs have to start somewhere."

"And you are a thief."

"A thief?" Those brows rose, but now, with his cold impassivity, it looked insulting.

"Was it not the action of a sneak thief to woo me? You knew how I would feel when I discovered the truth."

"And what did I steal?"

My heart, she thought, but slammed that door shut. "My trust."

He nodded. "Then I am sorry for it. But if I had told the truth you would not have married me."

"Precisely!"

"One of you had to."

"It could have been Felice if you'd not frightened her off."

"I doubt it. I don't think she would ever have given herself as willing sacrifice."

He was a cryptic script again and worse, she was weakening. Even knowing what he was, something about him sapped her power to hate. "Are you saying that you would have married Felice if she'd been willing?"

He rubbed his lips with his knuckle, studying her. "Yes. But once I knew you, Claire, I wanted you, and I confess, I did my best to win you."

"By tricks."

"By whatever means came to hand." He looked at her, dark eyes somber. "Remember. I fight to win."

Suddenly, he shook his head. "Everything is too raw today. We have a month." He gestured at the solar. "This room is yours. I pledge my soul that I will not disturb you here. At least for a month."

"And after a month?"

"We need more space in the office," he added, ignoring her question. "I'll have your writing desk brought in here."

He was right about one thing. It was all too raw today. She could scarcely think, never mind make true decisions. She wished she could mark him, however. She wished she could reach his soul, and write on it all her pain, betrayal, and grief.

Then she remembered her purpose was not to mark him but destroy him. She was going to prove him guilty of Ulric's murder, and use it to put everything right. Despite a shredded heart, she clung to that. That was now her reason to exist.

All she said was, "Thank you, my lord."

"Is there anything else you require?"

"Just your absence."

He left without a word.

Outside the room, Renald took a deep breath, holding himself still, holding every emotion in check.

He would not howl or beg.

With God's sweet grace, he would not try to win Claire by force. That would surely lose her for all time.

Her anger was justified, but surely in time it must ease. In time, with God's grace, he would be able to woo her again, be able to talk to her about what had happened and explain how it had come about.

Perhaps.

Some wounds were too deep to heal.

Slowly, he raised his hands to his face, the hands that had for a little while touched hers.

No cinnamon today, no violets. But perhaps the faintest ghost of her, of the laughing maiden who had lain with him in joyous harmony.

A ghost of paradise.

In moments, someone knocked on the door and Claire let in two men struggling with her wooden desk and bench. At her direction, they set them close to the window where the light was good.

She fussed with the desk after they'd left, comforted a little by something from the past, something from better days.

Days that they could have again if she was clever and resolute. Days as meaningful as dust.

The men returned, one carrying her box of inks and cases of brushes and pens, the other her folder of parchment and vellum.

She knew she should start on her plan, start finding proof of Renald's guilt, but she didn't want to take the first step toward the end. Instead, she took out the story of the Brave Child.

It was weak, she knew, but reality encircled her like a gnarled woodland full of fanged beasts, a place of destruction, of utter loneliness. She'd rather be here with pictures, with stories whose plots always turned out as they should.

And this was Thomas's happy tale. Once she had… once the matter of Ulric was sorted out, everything here would belong to her brother, as it should. She sat at her desk and smoothed out the half-finished page, but realized then that she hadn't told Thomas the truth.

She half rose, but then sat again. It could wait. No one knew but her. She'd take just a little time.

Her hands shook, though, and were strangely cold. She rubbed them together. As she did so, she smiled sadly to see that she'd finally drawn the cow's face right. But then she saw the blots in the margin. She picked up a sharp knife, ready to scrape down to clean parchment, but then she put the knife aside.

Let them stay. Let the blemishes record forever how her life had been ruined on the day that Renald de Lisle arrived at Summerbourne.

And it would be ruined, she knew, even when she'd put things right. Her heart would stay broken forever.

She stirred her ink and picked up a pen, waiting for the steadiness that always came through this work. But when she tried to trim the pen, she almost cut herself. She put down pen and knife, and wiped her palms on her skirt, knowing it was hopeless.

Renald de Lisle had left her no refuge at all.

Swallowing tears, she bound the work up again and returned it to the chest. She had to move her father's book to settle the larger one, and she stroked it tenderly. She knew her father. He'd doubtless written the last entry just before going out to death, making sure the story was finished. She truly had read his last words.

She wished again that he'd not chosen to write a story. If only she had her father's thoughts about the rebellion, perhaps she could make more sense of it all. Suddenly she wondered if it was both jumbled together. Her father had often leaped from one subject to another.

She untied the boards with clumsy fingers, and flipped eagerly through the pages, but eventually she had to accept that it was all the same. It was the story of Sebastian, though with some new elements. Sebastian seemed to have met some people on a lengthy journey to Count Tancred's, whereas in the old version that part was brief.

But then she was caught by a word.

Salisbury.

Traditionally, the story of Sebastian took place abroad. Had her father put it in England this time? Making out the surrounding words, however, she realized the reference was to the Earl of Salisbury. The passage she was reading was about an evening at a manor called Ickworth and discussion there about the rights of Sebastian's cause.

No, of the rebel's cause!

There *were* real events mixed in with the story! Excited, she sat to study the pages.

*And some wavered, but Sebastian, innocent though he was of worldly matters, rose to exhort them to hold to their course. He wove a story of an ancient king who seized a throne through guile and sin, and thus brought horror on his land.*

The sheet slipped to the ground. This wasn't a retelling of the Brave Child Sebastian. This was her father's account of the rebellion, with himself cast as the child! She covered her mouth with her hand. He *had* seen himself as the Brave Child, right from the very beginning. Perhaps he'd even believed the myth—that God would strengthen his arm.

Her hand shook as she stooped to pick up the fallen page. What did this all make of the end of his story?

She flipped to the last page, to the words she had read before. *And so the Brave Child stood over the corpse of his mighty foe, triumphant by the power of the Lord God. Tears trickled from the hero's eyes, tears of sorrow that he had been forced to kill, and to kill such a man.*

A tear splashed onto the page, and she hastily mopped it. Her father had written the end, anticipating the sadness of killing Renald de Lisle by the power of God. He truly had believed in the fable. He'd been childlike in so many ways.

*Such a man.* She read the words again. So, he *had* met Renald before the end. Would he have written of it? She flipped back through the pages, and eventually found it.

*Hoping to weaken him with kindness, the tyrant gave the child rich lodgings and fine foods. He tempted his affections with gentle company and his mind with scholarly delights, thinking to remind him of the joys of this world. The*

310

*child did not fear to lose them unless it be God's will, but he would not weaken for such earthly temptations.*

*Count Tancred himself came to him in his fairest form, beguiling him with true warmth, tormenting him with false logic disguised by embroideries of fact. The Brave Child almost weakened, but by God's will he stayed resolute.*

*Then they found the sharpest weapon. They sent his opponent to him. Sebastian discovered that he would not fight the tyrant, but his substitute, a comely man with youth still in his merry soul.*

Merry soul, Claire thought. Even when she had been most under Renald de Lisle's spell, she would not have described him in those terms. But then she remembered him at ease with their neighbors, chatting with Ouisa in his arms, and she wondered.

Yes, then, briefly, he had been merry...

She returned to the writing.

*Sebastian came to see the test God put upon him. His true trial was not to face a tyrant and strike him down. Instead, he must kill a man he might have liked, a mere tool of wrong, so as to bring a friend to the awareness of his own evil.*

*He wept and prayed, but the cup could not be taken from him.*

Claire, too, wiped tears. "A man he might have liked." She closed the book, too shaken to read more. Her father had still considered the king his friend. He had seen the good in Renald, as she knew he must. Still, he had stuck to his course. He had done what he knew to be right.

And that must be her guide. Even though

311

a part of her heart clung foolishly to dreams, she must pursue the honorable course. She must punish the murderer and rescue her family.

Rebelliously, she thought that God's ways were extremely difficult to comprehend. Bad people should be clearly bad. They should lack all virtue and charm. And the least He could do was keep His pact with His people and let good triumph over evil!

Then she crossed herself and begged pardon for such impertinent thoughts. The ways of God, they were always told, were beyond human understanding.

As she secured the book again she absorbed the fact that Renald had indeed spoken the truth on one thing. He and the king had done their best to persuade her father out of his course.

They'd still killed him.

She must never forget that.

She must not hide from the cruel reality of what had happened.

She tried to imagine it.

Her father had been kept in the Tower. She'd never been to London, but she imagined the White Tower as big, heavy, and of cold stone. He'd been a prisoner, even if in luxury.

He, a gentle soul, had been forced out in mail to fight a warrior twice his size and vastly more skilled. Her father had doubtless been like Lambert in the sword dance, sweating and gasping as he tried to match the unmatchable.

She flinched from it, but she made herself envision Renald, graceful in his mastery of his dreadful sword, playing with her father as he'd played with Lambert, then moving in at his leisure for the kill. Moving in to drive that dark, deceitful sword through mail and into her father's loving heart.

She wept, but clung to the sickening image as her own mail, as protection against her weak and foolish heart.

Renald had gone out that day to kill. He'd admitted it. To kill as cold-bloodedly as a cowherd slaughtering beef. He claimed to take no joy in killing and probably spoke the truth. The cowherd took no pleasure in slaughter, either.

Ignoring conscience, ignoring justice, he'd killed a weaker man on his master's command, and pretended—still pretended—that it was the will of God. No honorable woman could ever reconcile herself to that.

Desperate for advice and comfort, she went in search of her mother. She found Lady Murielle in her small chamber, sitting by a window, ominously still.

"How are you, Mother?"

Lady Murielle sighed. "It's a sad situation, but we'll put him off."

"Put who off?"

"Why, de Lisle!" Her mother grasped Claire's wrist. "You mustn't marry him! Not now. I've seen how you look at him, but you mustn't marry your father's murderer!"

Claire looked wildly to one of the women who hurried forward to soothe her lady. Soon Lady Murielle was staring out of the window again.

Claire moved away, rubbing at her wrist, still red and white from the fierce pressure. "Has she been like this since she woke?"

"Pretty well, lady. In a fret over you, that you not say your vows."

Claire crossed herself. "Sweet Saviour aid her."

The woman made the sign of the cross, too. "He will, lady, never fear. I'm sure with rest she'll soon be herself."

Claire prayed for it, but remembered the miller's daughter who counted stones.

What now? She'd come here in hope of advice, perhaps even of a shoulder to cry on. All she'd found was more burdens. More reason to destroy Renald.

She returned to the solar, finding Prissy there darning her silk veil. "Leave it," Claire said sharply.

"But, lady—"

"Leave it! It's better ruined."

Prissy put the veil down and eased out of the room, almost as if she expected a blow.

Claire pressed her hands to her face. She mustn't do that. She mustn't take her hurt out on the innocent. Renald was the only one who deserved to suffer.

She needed some sort of occupation, one that wouldn't stir emotions, but she didn't want to go around the manor. She might bump into Renald anywhere and she wasn't ready yet. She wasn't strong enough yet.

She'd try again to find ease in her writing. She took out another stack of parchment bound in boards, one very like her father's.

It was her own record book. She didn't record day-to-day events, for her days never seemed interesting, but her father had encouraged her to start recording customs of the manor, things like charms, and recipes for food and healing.

She wasn't sure there was much point to it, for everyone knew these things, but she'd continue.

She flipped through the loose sheets to a clean one, but suddenly realized that, whatever else they might be, her days were no longer uninteresting. Could she write of recent events? She could try. Perhaps somewhere within she might find something to help pin down Renald's guilt.

She dipped her pen and began at the beginning, when the sound of a horn announced people approaching through a storm...

She had reached her betrothal when the door banged open and Felice stalked in. "Well really, Claire! You are the lady of the manor now, or had you conveniently forgotten?"

Claire sighed and wiped off her pen.

She hadn't found anything to help in her plan, but writing of events had been healing in a way.

Felice came over and flicked the corner of a piece of parchment. "You can't spend your days on such foolery anymore."

Claire pulled it out of harm's way. "Is your music foolery?"

"My music entertains others."

"Perhaps my writings will entertain others."

"When so few can read them? It would be

more to the point if you told stories as Clarence used to."

"But I have no gift for that."

"Then do something useful. Murielle is completely out of her wits, you know."

Claire stood. "It's just shock."

"If you choose to think so. Anyway, she can wait. We need to know how much of the feasting food should be given to the poor, and how much kept for the hall."

"Ask Renald. It's his property."

When Felice's brows rose, Claire knew that snarl had been unwise. She had to remember that at the moment, everyone thought they were in harmony, and just under vow of chastity for a month. Until she decided what to do, she'd best pretend that was true.

She bound up her work. "I'm sorry. I took a sleeping draft and it's given me a headache. But I'll see to the food. Perhaps you could check how many fowl and other animals we have left. We may have to buy more next market day."

"Giving me orders now, are you?"

"As you pointed out, I am the Lady of Summerbourne."

Felice's lips tightened, but she snapped, "As my lady commands!" and stalked off. Unkind though it was, Claire couldn't help thinking that if Renald had ended up married to Felice he'd have been halfway to just punishment.

As she walked to the door, a glint drew her attention to the golden cup once more sitting on its shelf. The king's cup, given to her father by Henry Beauclerk not long after he'd become king. A gift of friendship, and of gratitude for pleasant times here in the place he'd called paradise.

## Chapter 18

In the pantry, Claire assessed the quantity and quality of leftover food and divided it. There wasn't any cherried pork left but that didn't surprise her. Thomas alone would have eaten it all if given the chance.

That reminded her of her brother. She couldn't put it off any longer. As yet, no one seemed to know the truth but herself, her mother, and de Lisle, and her mother was making no sense. At any moment, however, the news could break and Thomas mustn't learn of it that way.

She asked where her brother was.

"He's with Lord Renald, lady," a servant said. When she turned toward the office, he added, "I think they're outside the walls practicing swordwork and such."

Of course, thought Claire. What else?

She heard the noise before she passed through the gates—bangs, clangs, and coarse voices. Even a sharp cry. It sounded like her brother! She broke into a run.

She crossed the bridge and saw a battle going on. After a moment it resolved into Renald and his men playing at slaughter, one-on-one. Some wielded quarterstaffs, some fought with bare hands, some with sword and shield. They'd brought a huge tree trunk from the woods and set it upright in the ground, and a man was hacking at it with a sword, chips flying.

Practicing to hack at men.

To kill men.

*Efficiently.*

That conversation came back to her, the one on the first day when Renald had spoken about killing efficiently. She pressed her hand to her mouth. Oh, curse him for being what he was!

Where was Thomas? In the seething mass of fighting men she couldn't find him.

Where?

Where? She glimpsed blond curls.

He was fighting de Lisle!

Frozen, Claire's first thought was that if she could capture the moment she would have the perfect illustration of Brave Sebastian and Count Tancred. Then, a heartbeat later, she raced forward to stop the unequal fight.

An arm cinched her, swinging her off her feet. "Nay, lady!" Josce gasped. "You'll more likely cause damage by interfering."

Claire struggled helplessly, then froze, watching. "But... But Thomas has a real sword!"

"Of course."

"He'll get hurt! Or hurt someone."

"Lord Renald will keep him safe, lady. Never fear."

She fought again to get free. "Lord Renald killed our father! Why not complete the job? Let me *go*!"

He warily obeyed, but it was clear he would not permit her to interfere.

"I note Thomas's sword is smaller," she said bitterly, arms crossed tightly in front of her. "Does Lord Renald ever fight fair?"

"Have a care, lady," he said softly. "Thomas could never control a full-sized sword. He has a better chance of injuring with that one."

"But little enough." Now she had calmed a little, Claire could see that Thomas was in no immediate danger. It was like the sword dance again, with Renald clearly in control.

Even so, she asked, "He won't be hurt?"

Josce shrugged. "Not seriously."

Her heart raced again. Lose a finger or two, or the proper use of his legs? Renald's mighty sword could smash bone like kindling.

She twitched to interfere but knew, with sick frustration, that she would not be allowed to. Instead, she fixed her eyes on the unequal contest as if her gaze could keep her brother safe.

Thomas's slashing sword could hardly reach Renald, but it was real. The man caught each blow on shield or sword and as he did, wood chipped and sparks flew. Renald didn't attack. In fact, he seemed to be talking all the time.

Aware of being shadowed by Josce, Claire crept closer until she could hear her husband's even-breathed voice. "You can win a battle by wearing down your opponent, Thomas, but I doubt that will work in this case."

"I'll find a way to kill you!"

"Perhaps. One day."

Thomas paused—mouth set, eyes blazing, chest heaving.

Claire knew then that he'd heard the truth and she began to pray, rapidly, earnestly, for his safety.

Her brother slashed a few more times in what was clearly blind frustration, only to halt again. Then he pointed his sword like a spear and charged, screaming with frustrated rage.

Claire cried out, too, and knew to her shame that some of her alarm was for the man. Renald jumped back, a flicker of surprise on his face but deflecting the sword with his own. Then, as if part of the same movement, he knocked the sword from Thomas's hand before the lad tumbled to the grass.

He stepped back, sword point to the ground. Thomas just sat there, sobbing for breath, head down.

Claire took the chance to run forward. "What are you doing to him?" she demanded as she hugged her brother. "Trying to kill him, too?"

"He's trying to kill me."

Thomas shrugged her off and scrambled to his feet. "He killed Father."

"I know."

"It's my duty to kill him!"

Claire closed her eyes briefly. "Thomas, you know you can't. Yet. Wait a few years. Vengeance has no limits."

Thomas stood there, sucking in breaths, jaw thrust out. At times, he could be as unreasonable as Felice.

Claire rose to her feet, too, and looked at

her husband as she spoke. "If you want to make him pay, Thomas, let him train you in the skills you'll use one day to kill him."

Renald's brows rose. "I thought you didn't approve of men of violence, my lady."

"Life forces unpleasantness upon us, my lord."

He looked away, as if the distant coppice had suddenly become of interest. "A truth indeed. Thomas, go to Harry and work at the quarterstaff. But first," he said, looking back as the lad moved away, "clean your sword."

Thomas glared at him, but picked up his sword and carefully dried it with a cloth before sliding it into a scabbard lying on the ground. Then he stomped off toward a middle-aged man-at-arms.

"Where did that sword come from?" Claire demanded.

"I had the blacksmith shorten and lighten one for him." Renald was cleaning his own blade—an ordinary one, not the dark sword that had killed her father. "No one seemed to have provided a practice weapon for him before."

She folded her arms again, shielding herself. "Summerbourne has never been a place of violence."

"Yet even your father trained once. It is a man's duty." He looked up. "Did you want something, Claire?"

He was acting as if nothing lay between them! No, not nothing. But not the monstrous deed that changed everything.

"I came looking for Thomas," she said, trying to decide just how she should behave. "I wasn't sure he knew."

"Your mother told him."

And in the worst possible way, Claire was sure. She should have done it herself instead of hiding away like a coward. She watched the quarterstaff bout, wincing whenever her brother was rapped.

"He's my concern now," Renald said, "and I will care for him." When she turned to protest, he added, "I won't let you or him kill me."

"How pleasant to be omnipotent." But her secret curled inside. There were more ways to destroy than by the sword.

"It is hardly meaningful to be able to best a child." He pushed his blade into a plain scabbard.

"But who can defeat you?" she demanded. "What courage does it take to fight, when to you all men are children?"

"That isn't true. And anyway, don't you believe that God will support the side of justice?"

"Not anymore." She looked away in time to see Thomas tripped by his opponent's staff. "He's hurt!"

It was de Lisle who stopped her this time, arm tight around her waist. "God's wounds, Claire, he'll come to no serious harm. You've cosseted him half to death."

She pulled free and turned on him. "You don't understand love, do you? You don't understand it at all! I suppose I should be sorry for you, torn from your family so young, forced into cruel ways. But not when you bring those ways here."

He seized her shoulders, holding her so she had to face him. "Love doesn't wrap people in silk." Roughly, he turned her. "Look at him! He's not your baby brother anymore. He's nearly as tall as you and doubtless stronger. One day, failing me, he could be your shield against the world, shield for you and your family. He must be strong and skilled."

She swallowed tears, and fought a burning awareness of his hard hands on her. "He was meant for the Church."

"Then he should have been there. Instead, he was left to drift because your father couldn't face the truth."

She whirled on him. "Don't you dare—!"

"Of course I dare. Your father was a good and kind man who brought great joy to the world. But as a brother and father he was disastrous. Your aunts should have been suitably married before now. It's not surprising Felice is bitter."

"She was *born* bitter!"

"How do you know? You weren't alive at the time. You should have been settled with a good man, particularly when he planned such a risky course."

Claire opened her mouth but was overridden. "And Thomas should either have been in a monastery or training for war. He shouldn't have been running wild. You lived an illusion here, pretending that the big, cold world didn't exist. The least your father could have done was not invite it in the gates."

She stepped closer, almost breathless with fury. "You clearly cannot understand the demands of a sound conscience."

"I understand it very well."

She laughed. "You killed my father and feel not one qualm. What sort of conscience is that? I'll make you feel it, though." She'd not intended to spit this out, but she couldn't help herself. "You killed Ulric to hide your guilt from me. I might not be able to make you pay for killing my father, but killing Ulric was base murder and I intend to prove it."

He stood before her, impervious as granite. "You cannot prove a falsehood."

"I don't need to."

She turned and walked away but once inside the walls and out of his sight, Claire sagged. How could he attack her father like that, seeking to destroy his memory as he'd destroyed his body? Defense, she decided. The more he could convince himself that Lord Clarence had not been a good man, the easier he could live with having killed him.

Well, as she'd said, she doubted she could make him pay for that, not with king and church supporting his deed. She'd destroy him instead with Ulric's death.

How though? Just how did someone prove a secret murder? Eudo and the earl had already looked into the matter and found nothing.

Remembering her father's belief in recording details, she found the wax tablets she used for notes. In the kitchen, she wiped off old scribbles with a hot knife, wishing it was as easy to wipe away her lingering reluctance to destroy Renald de Lisle.

Like a snake through grass, she remembered a peaceful time in the garden, teasing about foxgloves, laughing over a robin...

While, she reminded herself, just behind them lay the body of the man he had foully murdered.

"Right," she said to herself. "Where to start?"

At the beginning, she supposed. Stylus in hand, she went in search of the guards on duty the night that Ulric had returned home. One of them was in the guard hut, repairing some piece of leather equipment. "I was on the walk, lady," he said, pushing a thick needle through the skin. "Osric was manning the portal gate and spoke to him. He's up on duty now."

Claire climbed the steep ladder to the wooden walk along the inside of the palisade. Up high, the wind was brisk and rather pleasant, for the day was heavily hot. Claire paused to look over the countryside, spread like a woven cloth before them. How peaceful and fruitful it was—except for the clash and bang of warlike training just below.

She turned her back on that and walked over to the guard.

The man bowed. "Lady Claire?"

"You spoke to Ulric when he arrived the other night?"

"Aye, lady. I was down at the gate that night."

Stylus poised, Claire asked, "What exactly did he say?"

The man screwed up his face. "Very little as I remember, lady. It was a bit of a start, him turning up like that. I think I said something like, 'Ulric! Where've you been, man? We thought you dead.' "

"And what did he say to that?"

He thought some more then nodded. "He said something about being left for dead."

Claire dug the words into the wax. "Someone had attacked him?"

"Dunno, lady."

"Did he seem wounded?"

"Nay. Dead weary, and probably with sore feet, but not wounded."

Claire smoothed out the bit about an attack. "Where did he go when he passed through the gates?"

"He just sort of stood there, lady, as if he didn't know rightly where to go. But Ralph—he always has an ear out for anything happening—he popped out of the guardhouse to tell him there was a feast going on, and plenty to eat and drink in the hall. Ulric looked right surprised."

"Surprised?" She made another note.

The man looked away uneasily. "Well, lady, he surely knew about Lord Clarence's death..."

"Oh, I see. So, what did Ulric do then?'

The guard dug deeper into his memory. "I think he said, 'They're celebrating the lord's death?' Something like that. I said, 'Not the death, the betrothal. Lady Claire's marrying the new lord, this Renald de Lisle that the king sent here.' "

"And what did he say to that?" Claire could imagine what a shock it must have been.

The man shook his head. "Nothing, lady. He just stared at us, then turned and tramped off toward the hall."

Claire made a few more notes then looked out over the countryside again, thinking. She was assuming that Ulric had known about de Lisle, but maybe he'd been separated from her father before the end. It was hard to imagine. Ulric had been fiercely attached to Lord Clarence.

But why then hadn't he stormed into the hall to denounce the murderer? He must have hated Renald de Lisle as much as she did.

As much as she should.

A change in sound drew her attention down, down to the military training below. The mixed noises had stopped, leaving only a rhythmic one almost like music, like a drum.

Stripped to the waist, Renald de Lisle was disintegrating the tree trunk. Massive muscles flexed in his back as he hacked—front-stroke, back-stroke, down-stroke and up—with his dark sword. Light on his feet, he circled the tree in a macabre dance, each strike fatal if the target had been a man.

As in the sword dance at their betrothal, Claire was snared by a terrible beauty in these deadly skills.

At last he stopped, leaving some wood for the others, but not much, and turned, flipping back hair obviously soaked with sweat. Sucking in breaths, he looked up and froze, seeing her there. Abruptly, he turned and drove the sword to quiver deep in the heart of the wood.

Claire turned and fled down the narrow ladder to solid ground, shuddering from a gesture she could not begin to understand.

It took time to steady herself, to pull back from horror, but then she regained her purpose, and with even greater intensity. She needed to destroy Renald de Lisle before he destroyed her.

Reading over her notes, she didn't feel much farther forward. It was perhaps strange that Ulric hadn't rushed in to protest the union, but he'd always been taciturn and slow to act.

Ulric must have been a lad of about Thomas's age when he'd been made servant to the baby Clarence. Despite the age difference and lifelong attachment, he'd never tried to meddle in her father's decisions. He'd certainly said nothing about Lord Clarence's plans to join the rebels, simply packed the bags and had the armor polished.

He'd been a faithful servant, though, and his death must be avenged. So, where could she look next? He must have spoken to someone.

She inquired in the kitchens. A couple of people remembered him being at the back of the hall near the doors, but neither recalled who he sat with. Coming in late, he'd likely ended up among some minor servants of one of the guests. And the guests and their servants had all left.

Claire made her way through Summerbourne asking her question, asking also for any information about Ulric's movements on that night.

She was emerging from the bakehouse, her tablets softened from the heat but unmarked by anything useful, when she saw Renald walking toward her. He wore fresh garments, and though his hair was wet she suspected it was from well water now rather than sweat. He looked both cool and cold.

"I understand you are making inquiries about Ulric."

"Are you going to forbid me?"

"No. But I insist on accompanying you."

She closed her tablets with a snap. "I see. Thus preventing me from finding out the truth."

"Thus preventing us from both asking the same questions of the same people. Since I didn't kill Ulric, I'm as keen as you to uncover the truth." He hooked a thumb in his wide leather belt. "I understand your purpose, Claire. Now understand mine. I intend that eventually we will find some amity in this marriage, but that will be difficult if you believe me a sneak murderer."

"*Amity!* Even if you could prove you didn't kill Ulric, you've admitted killing my father."

"Yes."

She stared, but when he said nothing more—not an excuse, an explanation, or a plea for forgiveness—she turned and headed for the next shed. "No one but you had reason to kill poor Ulric."

"No?" He matched her step for step and she couldn't stop him. "What about Lady Agnes? She seemed set upon our marriage and might not have wanted anything to prevent it."

"Gran?" She stopped to face him. "You're moon-mad! She can't rise out of a chair without agony."

"She was lady here once and must know people who would do her will. She indirectly threatened to have me killed."

"Why would my grandmother have Ulric killed? Even if she knew what he would say, she only had to keep him quiet until after the betrothal."

Those dark brows rose. "An excellent point. I suggest you write it down for later consideration."

"Why?"

"It'll come to you. Now, tell me what else you've found out."

She thought of refusing, but there wasn't any point. She tucked the stylus into the loop designed to hold it. "Nothing. A few people saw him in the hall, where he ate a little and drank rather more. Those I've found so far were all serving, so they'd no time to ask about his journey. No one seems to remember who sat beside him, or anyone in particular he spoke to."

"Where did he sit?"

"At the rear of the hall. Very close to the doors. He came late, so he took the closest space." She realized his tone had been rather strange. "Why?"

A silenced stretched, and he seemed almost dazed.

"Are you all right?"

Still staring at nothing, he said, "An older man with grizzled blond hair and a big nose—"

"What about him?"

"Do you know such a man?"

"Why?" If someone else had fallen into madness, she was going to succumb herself.

It was as if he didn't hear. "And I think... a wench with rather bulbous eyes and flushed cheeks."

"That sounds like Dora from the dye house. But what... ?"

He shook himself and turned to her with a shrug. "I have a gift of sorts. I remember pictures. I can remember some of the hall during that meal, and I think I remember Ulric sitting between those people."

"But you didn't know him."

"I saw him in your father's service."

Of course he had, but it was like icy water down the spine. "Don't you hesitate to speak of it?"

"Why should I?"

She tried to chip his soul. "My father wrote about your visit to him in the Tower."

"Wrote? Where?" He sounded surprised, but not at all guilt-struck. If only she could believe that he truly suffered guilt, perhaps she could begin to forgive him, but she was beginning to doubt that he had a soul at all.

She turned to walk away, but he caught her arm. "Wrote where?"

It wasn't worth fighting over. "In his journal. That book's not a retelling of the story of the Brave Child. He tells the story of the rebellion with himself as Sebastian."

"I thought so." He released her, but his face was set in anger. "He planned all along to bring matters to a court battle."

It took her a moment to understand him. "Are you *daring* to suggest that my father planned his own death?"

He gave a short, bitter laugh. "Oh no. He had more faith in God than you. He believed he could win."

"And so he would if not for that sword!"

"Don't be foolish."

*"Foolish!"* Claire realized she'd screamed it at him, and saw some servants turn to stare. She sucked in a breath and said, "My father was a good and righteous man—"

"—who was seriously astray in his vision of right and wrong."

Claire hadn't realized that rage could make a person dumb. When she regained her voice, she said, "My father was never astray except when he misjudged a false friend."

She stalked away but he said, "Don't you want to find out who killed Ulric?"

She wanted to attack him. Like Thomas, she wanted a weapon and a chance to hurt him. The only weapon she had, however, was the truth about Ulric's death.

If he'd been telling the truth about recalling pictures, then he might have identified people who had spoken to Ulric. She couldn't give him the chance to get to them first—to either frighten them into silence, or ensure their silence by yet another murder.

"Right," she said, whirling back. "Dora will be in the dye house. It's outside Summerbourne, down near the river." She headed toward the gates, not looking to see if he followed.

"So," he asked, close behind her, "what did your father write about me?"

Horror stopped her, turned her to face him. "What kind of monster are you? Do you have a soul at all?"

"All men have a soul. I can ask Nils to read it to me."

She didn't want him or his clerk touching that book. She said the thing she hoped would hurt the most. "He liked you."

"You could take that as paternal guidance."

"You have the sensitivity of that log you destroyed. He expected to weep over your body!"

"Claire, I did weep over his body."

And, like a blow, she saw that it was true. Those tired, bloodshot eyes he'd brought to Summerbourne were from weeping over his deed.

"But you still killed him," she said.

"But I still killed him."

And there it lay between them like iron, like rock, cold and unbreachable.

"Then may God forgive you, for I cannot."

They walked in silence down toward the river, side by side, but eternally divided.

The dye house and the tanning sheds were located out here to be close to water, but also because no one wanted the stink too close. As the smell hit, Claire hesitated.

He put a hand on her arm. "Why not let me go in and ask this woman to come out to you?"

She twitched away. "And give you chance to scare her into silence? No, thank you."

He had to stoop to go through the low door into the pungent rooms full of vats and steam. Colored cloth and yarn festooned from hooks in rafters and walls. Huge vats simmered, and colored puddles muddied the earth floor. Going through the door, Claire wrinkled her nose at the stink of sour urine. The local men were encouraged to donate to a vat there as often as possible. It was needed in the dyeing process.

She spotted Dora working over a boiling vat, sleeves rolled up, skirt kirtled high as she poked cloth under the seething blue liquid.

"Dora!"

The woman looked up, pushing damp tendrils of brown hair back off a red face stained with blue. "Lady?"

"I need to speak to you. Find someone to take your job and come outside."

The chief dye woman was coming over anyway, and so Claire left her to manage and drew the young woman outside into the cooler, fresher air.

"Yes, lady?" asked Dora, looking nervously

between Claire and de Lisle, though the nervousness could simply be an effect of her protruding pale eyes.

"You're not in trouble," Claire assured her. "We're just trying to find out what Ulric, my father's man, did on the night he died. We think perhaps he sat with you at the meal."

"Oh, aye, he did, lady. Though only for a while. He came in late, and then I had to go and lend a hand in the kitchens."

Claire tried not to show her excitement. It might make the woman more nervous. "Did he speak to you?"

Dora frowned as if this were a difficult question. "He said a greeting as he sat down."

"Did you know he'd just arrived?"

"I suppose. He carried a staff and pack."

Claire wanted to shake information out of the woman, but only patience would work. "You know he was my father's personal servant?"'

"Aye, lady."

"Weren't you curious? Because of Lord Clarence's death."

The big eyes remained blank. "Nay, lady. I was watching the tumblers. Right clever, they were."

Claire shared an exasperated look with Renald, then quickly looked back at the servant. He was the enemy.

"So, all the time he was sitting there, he didn't say anything more?"

Dora idly scratched beneath an ample breast. "He told me to shut up."

"To shut up?" Claire couldn't help but

look at her husband again, and surprised twitching lips.

A murderer shouldn't have an infectious smile. He really shouldn't.

"I was only being friendly, lady. Talking about the tricks. Asking if he'd seen the like. And he told me to shut up."

"So he wasn't talking to anyone at all?" Even though she knew Ulric was taciturn, Claire felt that in a properly run universe he would have said a bit more before dying.

As if picking up her thought, Dora offered, "He might have said a bit more to Sigfrith."

"Sigfrith?"

"He were on his other side."

Claire paused halfway through incising the name. "Sigfrith from the stables?"

"Aye, lady."

Claire completed the name. "Thank you, Dora. You'd best get back to your work."

But Renald spoke. "Hold a moment, Dora. Did you notice anyone else speak to Ulric while you sat beside him?"

The woman frowned, which had the alarming impression of pushing her eyes farther out. "I do think some folk paused behind to speak. But they didn't stop. Why would they with him not wanting to chat?"

"You don't remember who these people were, or what any of them said?"

"I were watching the entertainers, lord." She pondered a bit more, and seemed to find scratching helped the process. "I think I remember someone... Someone said something like, 'Ulric. I thought you dead.' Yes. That jogged my memory, like. About who he was. And the lord's death. It made me sad for a moment..."

"But you have no idea who any of these people were?"

She looked between them, rubbing red and blue hands on gray skirt. "Nay, lord. Lady."

He nodded and thanked her, then drew Claire away. "Let's hope this Sigfrith can help us more. I assume he's the man with grizzled blond hair and a big nose."

"Yes."

"You seemed startled by his name."

He was too perceptive by far, but she wasn't going to tell him Sigfrith was a relative of sorts. That would only give him more excuse to try to foist his crime on her grandmother.

She was beginning, however, to wonder about that herself. She'd never seen any sign of connection between Lady Agnes and the man, but if her grandmother wanted a hired killer, she might turn to a foster brother.

It must be nonsense.

Gran?

Try as she might, however, Claire could not swear that ordering a murder was entirely beyond Lady Agnes.

She reminded herself fiercely that *Renald* was the murderer. He had the motive. She simply had to prove it.

"We'd best go to the stables," she said, setting off toward the gates. "I don't suppose your pictures show who stopped to speak to Ulric?"

"I have no control over what lingers and what fades."

"But then, you wouldn't tell me if you did."

He stopped her with a hand in her girdle. "Claire, if I killed him, these matters have no importance. If I didn't, I want you to have the information that will clear me."

She turned to him. "No importance? I'm not thinking you wielded the blade. I doubt you had time. But you only had to order one of your men to do it. I assume they kill on order as you do. So, what if Sigfrith remembers that one of your men stopped to talk to Ulric?"

"Let's go and ask him," he said shortly and led the way at a brisk pace.

## Chapter 19

Since learning about Sigfrith, Claire had noticed the man more, and even detected a faint resemblance to her father. She'd never spoken to him, however, other than about stable matters.

They found him in a stall, cleaning a horse's hooves.

"Lord Renald. Lady Claire."

"Sigfrith," Claire said, "we hoped you might be able to tell us something about poor Ulric."

He kept his head down to his task. "Ulric? Him as died?"

"You sat with him during his last meal."

He glanced up then, in the wary way of one who expects trouble. "So? He came in late and sat there, lady. What of it?"

"We wondered what he said to you."

"Nothing."

Claire shared a glance with Renald, before remembering that this guilty reaction wasn't good for her case.

"Not even, 'Good evening'?" asked Renald. "Stand and face us."

Claire thought for a moment that the groom would ignore the cold command and shivered for him. But then he let the hoof fall and rose. He even bowed. "Aye, well, lord, maybe he said that."

"And did you say good evening back to him?"

"Aye, I suppose I did, lord. I can't remember."

Claire wondered if Sigfrith had always been this sullen and resentful. Or was it now a sign of guilt?

"And did he say anything else?" Renald asked patiently. "About the tumblers, for example. Or about Dora, who was chattering about the tumblers?"

The man frowned, but more thoughtfully than angrily. "Aye, lord, he did at that. Called her a chattering besom, which is true. But Ulric was never much of a one for speech."

"You knew him well?" Claire asked.

He turned his blue eyes on her, eyes very like her father's. "'Course I did, lady. We were of an age, and lived here all our lives." There was an unmistakable edge in the comment and Claire worried again for his skin.

"But since you knew him so well," Renald asked, "didn't you say an extra word or two? Ask him about his journey, perhaps? Or comment on Lord Clarence's death?"

Sigfrith looked as if he were weighing chancy options, but in the end he said, "I suppose we spoke a little. I think I said as I'd wondered where he'd been. And I did ask what happened to Lord Clarence's horse. 'Twere a good one."

Claire looked at Renald. "What did happen to Aidan?"

His dark eyes flashed a command. "Later. So," he said to Sigfrith, "what did he say to that?"

"That it were none of my business. Which wasn't true. Stables are my business."

"Did he say anything about how Lord Clarence died, or about my betrothal to Lady Claire?"

The question clearly surprised the man. "Nay, lord."

"Nothing?" Claire asked. "My betrothal must have been of interest to him."

"Can't say about that, lady. He made no mention of either."

She'd think he had to be lying except that she couldn't see why. Even if he'd killed Ulric, for his own purposes or those of her grandmother, why not admit that Ulric talked of such pressing events?

Renald killed Ulric, she reminded herself. Renald, or one of his men.

Renald picked up the questions. "A number of people stopped by to talk to him. Do you remember any of them?"

Sigfrith shrugged. "Big Gregory. He's married to Ulric's sister. Offered him sympathy, as I remember. Lord Eudo said much the same. And Britha—you know Britha, lord—asked if he wanted comfort."

Claire jotted down the names, distracted by wondering if that *you know Britha, lord* meant that Renald knew generous Britha in a biblical sense.

She tried to pretend she didn't care.

She asked, "And those are the only people you remember speaking to Ulric at the table that night?"

"And the lord's squire, Josce."

Claire's stylus froze, mid-mark, and she glanced up at Renald. He showed nothing, but that—as she was beginning to realize—said a lot.

"Did you hear what Squire Josce said to Ulric?" she asked.

Like, meet me in the garden...

But Josce? Fresh-faced Josce with the freckles and the big smile? What was a squire to do if ordered to kill, however? The same as his master. Obey.

"Nay, lady," said Sigfrith. "The young man spoke quietly. Privately like." Sigfrith's sly look showed that he knew he'd started trouble and was glad of it. She'd have to think more about his place here.

She finished her note, thanked the groom,

and walked out into the sunshine. Once out of earshot, she faced Renald de Lisle. "Well, my lord?"

His jaw was tight, twitching with anger, but not at her. "Well, we had better go and speak to Josce."

He strode off so quickly, she had to hurry to catch up. "Are you still claiming innocence?"

"I still *am* innocent. As Josce will be able to make clear."

"Don't try to lay all the guilt at his door! He's only a youth."

"I'll lay the exact amount of guilt he deserves." His fist clenched. Claire seized his arm with both hands. He stopped, but turned on her so sharply she feared for her skin.

After a shocking moment, the searing danger was leashed. "What?"

Claire had to force out her voice. "If Josce killed him," she made herself say, "it was by *your* orders."

He simply turned and strode off toward the hall. Almost faint, Claire ran after, fearing there'd be blood spilled soon. Would he kill his squire to hide his guilt?

Josce was laughing with a group of young men, but Renald's sharp command brought him at a run, freckles already dark against suddenly pale skin.

"Yes, lord? Is something the matter?"

"What were you doing talking to Ulric, Lord Clarence's man, on the night he died?"

Instead of innocent confusion, guilty red flooded the young man's face so that his freckles entirely disappeared. Feeling nauseous, Claire waited for confession, tempted to silence him somehow.

The squire licked his lips. "I just... just wanted to say sorry."

"Sorry!"

Renald sounded as astonished as Claire felt. Sorry? For a murder not yet committed? If not, for what?

Josce looked at Claire, almost as if asking for intercession. Then he faced his lord again. "You wouldn't let him travel home with Lord Clarence, my lord. It pretty well broke his heart. I know he would have wanted to be at the burial."

Renald had his thumb tucked in his belt again, and one finger tapped against the studded leather. His jaw still twitched. He was still in a rage, though she couldn't see why. Was a kind heart a sin to such a man?

"In his pack," Renald said, "he had two shillings and some pennies."

To Claire's astonishment, Josce—except for the freckles—turned snow white. "I gave him the money," he whispered.

Renald's hand closed around his belt and Josce began to visibly tremble. Claire looked between them, lost.

"Tomorrow, you return to your father," said Renald flatly. "On foot. Though I'll send some men to make sure you get there."

Josce's lips quivered. "Yes, lord."

"You understand why?"

The young man's Adam's apple bobbed. "Yes, my lord."

Renald nodded. "Get out of my sight. Spend the night in the church and pray."

Claire thought Josce would argue or beg, but he turned and walked off, looking as if he'd like to run.

What had just happened? Josce had offended by giving Ulric a few shillings? "What? What's wrong with—"

"I trust you're satisfied that he didn't murder the man." Renald's eyes were flat as stones.

Claire tried to believe that Josce had killed Ulric at Renald's command, but after this scene she couldn't. "Maybe. But then... But why? You didn't want Ulric to have any money? Did you hope to starve him to death?"

"We left him enough food for a week or more." He turned and walked away, but then swung back. "No more secrets. I didn't want Ulric here to tell the tale until everything was settled, so I made sure he'd have a slow journey home. If Josce hadn't betrayed me, he would not have been here until it was all done."

"Betrayed? I wouldn't say—"

A slash of his hand silenced her. "Speak no more of it."

Her mouth dried. He was at the very limit of a ferocious rage. Over Josce? Or over something the young man might confess?

She made herself speak. "So you wanted to keep Ulric away, and when he turned up, you had him killed."

"By Lucifer's horns, if I'd wanted him dead, I'd have killed him in London!" He suddenly rubbed a hand over his face. "My word on this, Claire." He looked straight into her eyes. "On my soul and my hope of heaven, I did not kill Ulric. I did not order him killed. I did not condone his killing. I would never do something like that. As you pointed out in the case of your grandmother, it was unnecessary. I couldn't keep the secret forever. And to kill for such base ends would be murder. I value my immortal soul more even than I value Summerbourne. And you."

He stalked off to the hall and Claire tucked away her stylus, badly shaken. Not least by that *And you.*

Was it possible for him to have a true regard for her and yet to have killed her father?

Indeed it was.

That, put simply, was tragedy.

She recognized it because it sat as black misery within herself. She admitted the truth clearly for the first time. Deeply and forever, she loved her father's murderer.

Numb with that, she headed for the peace and comfort of the garden, to the healing herbs, trying to think things through. Since the horrifying revelation in the wedding bower, she'd not been able to think logically about her situation. Now, walking the aromatic paths, she tried.

Renald was a man of war, a very blooded sword, but her heart believed that he was honorable for his sort. She knew that when he could be he was kind. However, she also knew that Summerbourne was a prize he valued. Landless from a young age, he had hungered for land of his own, for a place where he could build a family, a dynasty.

And that explained his part in her father's death. When ordered by the king to kill, the temptation had been too great and he had obeyed in order to win what he so dearly wanted. Because her father was a rebel, the world would not think that deed wrong, but she must.

Perhaps Renald had persuaded himself that her father's death had been an act of justice, or even an act of God, but that was not true. The king had had no reason to kill Clarence of Summerbourne, not when he left so many other men untouched.

He must have wanted to be rid of a thorn in his conscience, and seen that he could reward a faithful follower. He had achieved both by forcing a man untrained for war to fight a champion.

That injustice made it murder, murder grown from guilt and greed. To make it worse, Renald had killed again in an even more cowardly way to prevent the news from blocking his marriage.

She stopped dead then, however, remembering the point about her grandmother.

*Neither* of them had needed to kill poor Ulric. The news he carried wasn't secret. It just hadn't yet arrived.

Even if Renald had seen Ulric arrive, and had wanted to hide the truth until after the wedding, he could have had his men quietly seize the man and tuck him away. It would be the sensible thing to do, and she knew well by now that Renald was not a stupid man.

Claire slumped down on a bench.

All he'd ever needed to do was delay the news.

As he had by slowing Ulric's journey.

As he had by watching her and by keeping her out of the way in case one of the guests carried news or rumor.

As he had by threatening the earl.

Therefore, unless there was some other, unsuspected motive, Renald would not have killed Ulric or have had him killed!

Her surge of relief was heartbreaking, for the main problem remained. He had still killed her father, and that could never change.

And, she realized with shock, that took away her one hope of getting free of this marriage without destroying her family!

What now?

She hadn't the slightest idea.

After a dazed time, she decided she had to do something or go mad, so she dug up some special plants and carried them to the grave-yard. There, she carefully transplanted them around her father's grave—marigold, gillyflower, and joy-of-the-ground.

She remembered to draw water to give the transplants a good drink. She'd plant a crab apple near the grave to keep away evil, and chervil, fennel, and waybroad against dark spirits. Though she knew her father was gone, was dancing joyous in another life, she'd keep to the old ways and guard his grave.

She paused, bucket in hand, back to the old dilemma. She could only do that as wife to Renald de Lisle.

"Claire?"

She started and turned to find her brother beside her, solemn but unexpectedly steady, despite an angry bruise on his temple.

"Quarterstaff?" she asked, determined not to make a fuss.

"I was slow to duck." He didn't seem to hold a grudge about it. "Claire, should we hate Lord Renald?"

She wasn't ready for this subject, but she knew what it was like not to have anyone to talk to. She drew him over to a bench. "In the eyes of the world, Lord Renald did nothing wrong. But he killed our father. It has to change the way we feel about him."

He sat there, slumped arms on knees. "I hated him when I first found out. Now I don't know. But I think I should."

It so nearly mirrored Claire's feelings that she just shrugged.

"Josce said—earlier—that the things you like someone for don't change."

"But other things can smother them."

He looked up, pushing a curl out of his eyes. "I told him I hated him. Told Lord Renald. That I wanted to kill him. So we fought."

So, that was what she had witnessed.

"I prayed to God I'd be like the Brave Child Sebastian. But nothing happened." His shoulders drooped more. "I'll be stronger one day."

Claire put a hand on his shoulder, eyes

stinging. "Ah dearest, don't. Don't cling to hate."

"But you hate him. I saw you arguing with him."

"Arguing isn't hate."

"You don't hate him?" He looked at her. "So are you going to stay married to him?"

Hope rang in it. Hope she hated to crush. "No, love. I can't do that."

"Why not?"

"Because he killed Father."

"It wasn't his fault."

Oh, Thomas. She didn't know if it was a longing for security, or a genuine liking for Renald de Lisle, but he was fighting to change her mind, and she wished she could let him.

"No one else thinks Father's death was wrong," he protested. "In ordeal by battle, God speaks."

She bit her lip. She wanted to ask if he could truly think their father wrong about the king, but she hesitated to plant treason in his mind. "It can't have been fair. Not Lord Renald against Father."

"It's to the death, you know. If Father had won, Lord Renald would have died."

She'd known, but she hadn't really thought about it. She suppressed a shiver. "He was never in any danger. Unlike Father. Thomas, have you thought? No one else ended up in a court battle. Not Lambert. Not Salisbury. Not even the evil de Bellême!"

"Are you saying it was all a ruse?" He looked so totally bewildered that she knew she should have held her tongue.

"You're not to speak of this to anyone," she said, looking him straight in the eyes. "It's dangerous. Do you understand?"

"Yes, but—"

"I'm going to try to find a way out that will let us live our lives in decency. But we can't stay here. Not after what happened. You do see that."

He sighed. "I suppose so. But what sort of way? What will we do?"

She put it into words for the first time. "I'm going to seek an annulment."

"And then what? Won't that mean we'll be poor?"

She sighed. "Perhaps Mother's family will take us in."

It wasn't much comfort, and she wasn't surprised when he paled. "Go to France!"

"It's better than nothing. But for now, we have to go on as usual. Don't you have work to do?"

"No. Josce's in the church. Crying. Did he not know what Lord Renald did?"

"It's not that." Claire looked over to the wood and thatch church wondering if she could do anything to help.

"He was supposed to be showing me how to clean mail. So I went to the hall and asked Lord Renald, and he said to do as I wished." That clearly struck him as unusual enough to be worrying.

It showed Claire how much Josce's act had upset Renald. Was there one happy soul in Summerbourne today? "Then you're free for a while," she said. "Why not go and find some friends."

A few days ago, he'd have run off joyfully, glad of freedom. Now, he hesitated, then wandered off deep in thought. Claire could have wept for all the changes that reflected.

Could she just discard her scruples, and make everyone's lives simpler? No. It would not even work. If she lay in the bed with Renald with her father's death still between them, she could imagine nothing but evil coming from it.

She contemplated the silent walls of the nearby church. Josce had faced a choice between following his conscience and obeying his lord's command. As she did. As her father had. As Renald had.

Only Renald had chosen obedience.

Those who refused, suffered.

Sent home horseless would carry deep shame. She knew Josce would rather be whipped to the bone. Depending on the nature of his father, he might end up whipped to the bone as well. It would be hard to find him another lord to serve.

She was tugged by the need to intervene, to avoid another tragedy, yet held back by her desire to avoid her husband. She particularly didn't want to ask him for any favor.

Why should she care, anyway, about a war-monger-in-training?

She checked on the weaving and made sure the empty grain bins were being scoured as thoroughly as they should be. She spoke to the bee master about honey and the war-rener about rabbits. She went out—though there was no need—to make sure the fishpond weirs were handling the flow of water well. She even allowed herself some time watching the fat golden carp gliding through the water.

It did no good. She couldn't escape the call. With a sigh, she returned to the manor, to confront her husband, her enemy, and to argue for clemency.

He was not in the solar, so she went to the office, where she found him with Brother Nils and Peter the Woodsman.

"Yes, my lady?" Renald's expression was unwelcoming and the atmosphere in the small room hung like icicles.

Claire fought against a pressing instinct to flee. "I wish to speak with you, my lord. Privately."

"I'm busy at the moment. I will come to you when I can."

Two weeks from now? "It is urgent, my lord."

His lips tightened, but then he said, "Brother Nils, take Peter with you and check the true state of the coppice wood."

Both the clerk and the woodsman seemed grateful to escape.

"Yes?"

He was sitting on a bench beside the window, broad and dark against a bright tapestry.

"I want to talk to you about Josce."

"No."

This time she would not let that flat no stand. "Yes."

He stared at her. "You are a very foolish woman."

Tremors were starting, but she made herself ignore them. "I am doing what I have to do. As my father did. As Josce did."

"Hardly. You are only breaking an oath in the most marginal sense. For which you should be grateful."

Claire took a deep breath. "I wish you to mitigate Josce's punishment."

"Did he seek you out to ask for this?"

"No! As far as I know, he has obeyed you and is in the church."

"As well for him. I would be within my rights to whip him before sending him home. As you see," he added, "I am already being merciful."

She didn't trust her legs, so sat on a small stool by the unlit brazier. "Renald," she said, deliberately using his name, "please cloak your anger and listen."

He shook his head, but spoke more gently. "You are a woman, Claire, with a woman's soft heart and strange sense of right and wrong. Josce understands that what he did was unforgivable."

"He did not follow your order. Are your orders always right?"

"They are always to be obeyed. As I obey the orders of my liege."

Like orders to kill. "Orders aren't always right," she said, and she wasn't entirely talking about Josce anymore.

"Then the blame rests on the one with authority."

"Even before heaven?"

"Even before heaven."

Was that his excuse, his salvation? That the lord took on the sins of his vassals following his orders, just as the husband took on the sins of his wife?

She wanted to ask if he felt that made murder right, but she remembered that she'd come here to plead for Josce. "Forgiveness is at the heart of our faith, Renald. Can you not forgive?"

"Perhaps I have. But I cannot have one so close who does not obey my word."

"So you would do whatever your king commands?" She spoke without thinking, for she could answer herself. Her father's death was answer. Of course he would. Angrily, she threw at him, "Would you kill me if he ordered it?"

His gaze fixed on her, completely blank. "No," he said at last. "But I would expect my death from it."

"Please," she said, knowing tears were swelling in her eyes. "You are supposed to be *teaching* not destroying. Is there no other way you can handle this?"

"I thought you didn't want violence in Summerbourne."

Claire shuddered, hoping she was right about Josce's wishes. "I'm not a fool. Sometimes punishment is necessary."

Suddenly he rose and stalked over to open the door, to order a man to go to the church and command Squire Josce to attend him.

Here, thought Claire, swallowing. Renald

was going to make her witness the punishment, knowing it would be punishment to her, too.

He sat again on the bench and they waited in silence.

## Chapter 20

With a knock, Josce came in, pale and with reddened eyes. "My lord?"

Renald jabbed a finger at the floor in front of him. "Kneel."

Clearly startled, Josce obeyed.

"My gentle wife has begged clemency for you. No, you can thank her later, if you're still inclined. As she pointed out, I'm not infallible. Nor is any man. What then, do we do if we think our lord's commands are wrong?"

After a moment, Josce said, "Discuss it with him?"

"With some lords that alone could command your death. Did you discuss Ulric with me?"

"No, my lord."

"Look at me."

Josce raised his bowed head. Claire could only see his back, but throat aching, she suspected he was fighting tears again.

"Why not?" Renald demanded.

Even from the back, Claire could tell Josce swallowed hard. "I didn't think you'd change your mind, my lord."

"And you think me stupid?"

"No, my lord!"

"Therefore I had good reason for my orders. You think me cruel?"

"No, my lord." Josce's voice was dull now, and his head started to bow again.

"You think Ulric could not have made his way home with the provisions we gave him?"

"He's an old man... No, my lord."

"Look up. Face me. Why then, did you think yourself so much wiser and kinder than I?"

Claire swallowed tears at having to watch this mental flaying. How she'd bear the physical punishment that would surely follow, she did not know.

"Well?" Renald prompted.

Josce's back straightened. "I see now that I was wrong, my lord. I sincerely beg your pardon and accept your punishment."

"Do you have choice?"

"No, my lord!"

Renald leaned back against the wall. "My wife thinks I should whip you and keep you in my service. What do you say to that?"

Claire saw the shudder that ran through the young man. Pleas for mercy fought at her lips, but she kept them back. She had done the most she could.

"I would rather you thrash me than dismiss me, my lord."

Renald studied him, expression shielded. Then he straightened and held out his hands. "Put your hands in mine."

Hesitantly, the young man obeyed.

"You are going to swear your oath to me again. You are going to think about each word, and only say them if you mean them. Do you understand?"

Josce nodded. "Yes, my lord." Claire thought he trembled, and wondered if he might, at this point, refuse. But he spoke steadily. "I, Josce of Gillingford, son of Ralph of Gillingford, do swear to honor and serve my lord, Renald de Lisle, Lord of Summerbourne, to keep his counsel and obey his word."

Renald looked at the young man in silence, then said, "There will be no further punishment. But if you break your oath again, Josce, I will show no mercy. Do you understand?"

"Yes, my lord." The youth's voice wavered.

"Unless we are in desperate straits you may always discuss my orders with me, but ultimately my word is law to you. Yes?"

"Yes, my lord!"

"Now"—and Claire thought she saw a brow quirk—"what would you do if I ordered you to kill the Lady Claire?"

Even the young man's ginger curls and straight back expressed shock. "I... My lord?"

"Well?"

Josce's head slowly sank and tears choked as he said, "I would refuse, my lord. I am clearly not worthy—"

"No." Renald seized his squire's chin and raised it. "That is the right thing, if that is how your conscience speaks. But then you accept your death with dignity."

"I see, my lord... I think."

"Put simply, Josce, in the end our soul is our own, and no man, not even the king, can steal it. But we are ruled by earthly powers as well as spiritual, and sometimes our choices will cost our life. Such a death is not to be feared. It merely takes us to heaven the sooner. Far worse to do evil and live, only to end in hell."

"I see, my lord." Josce's voice was thick with tears as he added, "I am pleased to serve you, my lord, who is unlikely to order me to do evil."

Renald cuffed him. "Even if I do expect you to let a man make his way home penniless. There's another lesson there. Be very careful, lad, to whom you swear allegiance. Now, go and find that rascal Thomas and teach him to clean my mail."

Josce rose, looking slightly unsteady. Claire saw tears on his cheeks and knew she had some escaping her eyes, too.

"I thank you, my lord, for your mercy," the young man said, "and for the lessons I've learned today." Suddenly, he turned and knelt before Claire to kiss her hand. "And I thank you too, lady, from my true heart, for gentling my lord's mind toward me."

Though she was of an age with him, Claire touched his head. "God's blessing on you, Josce. And may you be as wise one day."

The squire flushed, then rose to leave the room, a spring in his step.

"It was your wisdom," said Renald, his feeling shielded.

"I know nothing of oaths and allegiances."

"But something of teaching." He rose and looked out of the window, rubbing the back of his neck. "Josce is my first squire. Before becoming Lord of Summerbourne I was not of a status for it. And growing up as I did, I never had such formal training. You have taught me a useful lesson."

It was dangerous to sit here talking like this. Perilous. She stayed. "Then you learned quickly, my lord, and outstripped your teacher."

He glanced back. "Be careful, Claire, or you'll be thinking me less of an ogre."

"I don't..." But she must.

"Do you still think I killed Ulric?"

She shook her head, grateful for something simple. "No. I see that you had no reason."

"Thank you for that at least."

"But you did kill my father." She placed it like a shield between them.

"Yes." He watched her steadily.

"And you feel no guilt."

"And I feel no guilt."

Hand to mouth, she asked, "Can you not make me see it as you see it? Just now you said a man of honor must choose, even if the choice means his death. How can you not feel guilt when you *chose* to kill my father and win Summerbourne?"

She'd tried to keep all bitterness from her words, but still it rang through. It was hopeless. She rose, but he put out a hand. He did not touch her—he was half a room away—but it made her stop.

"Stay, Claire. Talk to me. Let's try to defeat this together."

"Can we?"

"We can try."

Slowly, she sank back onto the bench.

"Claire, I killed your father. Nothing, God help me, will ever change that. But it was not for Summerbourne, and there was nothing about it to lie darkly on my soul."

She swallowed. Defeat this together. Her life lay in this room, vulnerable as precious glass as they fought an overwhelming foe. "I can't see that," she said. "I can't see how it can mean nothing."

"I didn't say that. It was the most painful thing I have ever done. I will carry its shadow all my days. But I will live despite it, and find joy despite it. It is my own shadow. I won't let it fall on others. Your shadow is your own."

And truly it felt like that. A shadow on all her days. "It would be easy to put it aside." She rubbed at her temple. "I love you…"

She stared up at him. She'd meant the words as simple explanation, only realizing a moment later the weight they carried.

His eyes darkened, but he did not move. "Then why haven't you put it aside?"

"Because it is not so easy," she admitted with a sigh. She looked over at his sword, lying darkly on top of a battered chest, as always, close to his hand. "That sickens me."

He stood and picked it up, holding it in front of him on his palms like an offering. "It is a gift of the king. It carries a holy relic. Would you have me cast it into the forge? It has done no wrong, but if it had, it would only have been as my tool. No blame attaches to a tool."

"*You* are the killer."

"Yes."

She rose. "What good can this do when that can never change!"

"I am a warrior and I fight for what I want. Claire, stay. Stay and fight by my side."

Summoned by his plea, she sat again and tried. "You were the tool of the king," she offered as excuse.

"No. Remember what I said to Josce. I am a tool with mind and soul. Even at Henry's behest, I would not kill if I believed it wrong."

"But—"

"But I killed your father. That is the point that can never change. Never." Abruptly, he switched his hold and drew sword from scabbard, drew it with the ease of familiarity and the grace of honed strength. The blade seemed huge in the small room, and ominously dark.

"Let us have truth," he said implacably, pointing the sword tip at her, so it lay between them like a river of darkness. "I used this sword to kill your father, to sever soul from body. If you cannot accept the sword, you cannot accept me."

Claire stared at it, heart beating like an urgent drum. She wanted to say something, something hopeful, but her tongue stuck silent in her mouth.

Heavy though it must be, the sword never wavered. "I will kill again," he continued. "It is my trade. I will never kill where I think it wrong, but I will kill. If you cannot accept the sword, you cannot accept me."

Claire swallowed and made herself speak. "I accepted the killer. You know I did. It is the one death I cannot live with, and that can never change."

He drove the blade back into the scabbard. He put it on the chest and stayed there, braced on the wall by rigid hands. "You're right. It can never change. And you must accept me, your father's killer. I will not live a lie. That would be worse than no life at all."

He turned sharply to face her. "You think me cold, but I'm no stranger to love, and trust, and laughter. If we are to make anything of this, it cannot be as a sacrifice. You must accept me as I am, without reservation."

"Without reservation? But—"

"But I killed your father. Yes. As long as that lies between us, there is no hope."

She stared at him. "How can it not?"

He sat down again, sat in her father's big chair and she knew it was deliberate. "Listen," he said. "Listen as I tell you why your father died. I don't know if it will help. I fear it won't, but I can't live like this, and neither can you."

Claire couldn't see how it could help either, and she'd long since decided that she didn't want to have the picture too clearly in her mind, but she said, "Tell me, then."

He laced his hands, thinking, then said, "Your father was a traitor to the Crown."

She opened her mouth, and he said, "Don't interrupt. He opposed the right of Henry Beauclerk to be King of England, and that is treason as far as Henry's concerned. Very few died in the rising, and the king had no desire to make matters worse by severe punishment. Your father, like everyone else, was offered the chance to pay his allegiance to Henry and go home burdened with nothing more than a fine."

She frowned over that. "He was offered that, like everyone else?"

"You thought he was given no choice but to face me?"

She nodded. "But then why didn't he—"

"He would not swear the oath."

She remembered, so long ago, talking to Thomas about that. "There must have been many others in that state. Who could swear to the king they believed unrighteous?"

A brow twitched wryly. "Everyone else seems to have had a miraculous change of heart."

"*Everyone* else? My father alone resisted?"

"Apart from those who fled into exile."

"Then why wasn't my father allowed to flee? At least we would still have him!"

He leaned forward slightly. "Because he wouldn't go. He insisted on staying, and on saying that the king had no right to the throne. Friends, churchmen, even the king, all tried to talk him out of his stubborn stance."

She shook her head. "You cannot talk a person out of what is right."

She saw the knuckles of his laced hands whiten. "You're just like him, except that he smiled more in his stubbornness."

Hand to unsteady mouth, she said, "And made up jokes and riddles about it, I suppose."

"Yes."

"But he didn't have to die. Even if the king had kept him in the Tower, what harm could my father do?"

He loosed his hands then, and laughed bitterly. "What harm? He could try to destroy a kingdom singlehanded. The king made a mistake. He had your father brought to a banquet. The king hoped that when he mingled with so many people who were willing to accept the situation—good people, honest people—"

"Cowardly people!" Claire flung at him, fearing that something was coming that would break down all her walls.

"Cowardly people, some of them, yes. Your father was no coward. But among so many, the king hoped that your father would see the error of his ways."

Renald looked away then, doubtless into a past made vivid by his gift. "He kept the company enthralled with stories and riddles. He truly had a precious gift."

"So *why...* ?"

His eyes met hers. "Because he was both clever and resolute, and he had resolved to bring down a false king. At the end of the evening—the merriest evening the court could remember—he faced Henry and demanded his right to put the question of his guilt to ordeal by battle."

Claire stared at him. "He *demanded* it?"

"On my oath. Henry couldn't refuse. He couldn't even try to argue him out of it, because it would look as if he did not believe in the justness of his cause."

"And you were chosen to be his oppo-

364

nent." Claire's heart began to race, as she saw a tiny glow of hope. Her father had demanded it, and Renald, the champion, had been ordered to the task...

"I asked for the honor."

"Asked for it!" She almost shot to her feet and ran, but she made herself stay. If she loved, could she not at least listen? "Why?"

She saw him note her shock, and her restraint. "Claire, you are precious beyond rubies, beyond pearls, beyond breath. I was not, then, the king's champion. FitzRoger was. But he didn't want the task, not least because Imogen was very fond of your father." His lips twitched. "Back then, I did not understand how love could make a man so change his ways."

"Love?" she breathed, thinking of Imogen and her husband. Thinking of her own husband.

"Oh yes. I love you. As I never dreamed a man could love, I love you."

It floated like a sunbeam in the room, but out of reach yet, for both of them.

"So you were given the *task*," she said, not able to keep an edge out of her voice at that word. "But no. You asked for it. Why, if not for gain? Who seeks to kill an innocent man for noble reasons?"

"He was not innocent," he said evenly. "He was a self-confessed rebel."

"But the rebellion was just," she countered.

He closed his eyes and sighed. Then he looked at her again and continued, "FitzRoger irritated an old wound—or that was the story told. Immediately, men were clamoring for the chance to oppose your father in the ordeal, even though it would be to the death. You know that?" he asked.

"Yes. But no one would seriously think themselves at risk fighting my father. It must have seemed an easy path to a reward. A *task*."

"And a way to prove that they were true, ardent supporters of the king. A number of rebels were on their knees pleading for the chance to fight. After all, the king is refusing to give honors and gifts to those he thinks still secretly oppose him."

"Is that all anything comes down to? Honors and gifts? What of right?"

"God would prove the right in the ordeal."

She didn't even try to hide the bitterness this time. "If that was true, my father would be alive. So, how did you come to be chosen for this mighty task?"

He seemed relaxed in the big chair, but she could tell that every part of him was tense. "The king wanted the best."

"And you are the best?"

"After FitzRoger, yes."

"Of course, if God truly spoke through the ordeal, that wouldn't matter."

"You don't believe in the power of God?"

She rose then, restless under her own tangled thoughts. "I believe you all made a pact with the devil!"

"You believe Satan is stronger than God?"

She whirled away. "I don't know what I

believe! Go on with your story. Explain how noble you were to slaughter a man who could hardly wield a sword."

His voice behind her sounded so level, so undisturbed. "The king also wanted the best so as to give your father an easy death."

She turned back. "Is that going to be your excuse? That you killed my father quickly?"

"Not quickly, no. That would have been an insult. But cleanly. Do you know how men usually die in the ordeal by battle?"

"No," she whispered.

"Exhausted and battered to death. Mail stops the blade from piercing, but it cannot stop the bruises, or the broken bones. To surrender is to die anyway, so the combatants stagger on until one can stagger no more. Then, if he has strength left, the victor can pierce the weaker one in the throat and put an end to it."

Claire covered her face with her hands, thinking of her pretty mental pictures of Sebastian and the evil Count Tancred. "And this is your trade?"

"I've never fought in such a contest before, and I hope never to do so again. But I had the skill and strength to strike true, and with that sword, the ability to strike a killing blow through mail."

She faced him. "But if my father had owned such a sword, he could have killed you."

"No!" He shook his head. "No more than Thomas could kill me with that sword. Your father had no idea how to fight, no recent training to give him strength and agility, no stamina even. I had to work hard to make it look like an honorable contest. And that almost led to disaster."

"He almost won?"

He looked at the sword. "I didn't realize the true nature of that blade. I'd tested it, and knew it cut through mail, point or edge, but a blow at his shield cut right through the iron into wood. It jammed there. Your father was clever enough to try to take advantage. But not strong enough."

He turned back to her. "Yes, if your father had been fit and strong, he could have destroyed a nation then. But he wasn't. Why do we practice day after day, week after week from infancy? To gain and maintain strength and skill. It is not something a man can do by will alone!"

Claire bit her lip. "He thought he was Brave Child Sebastian. He thought God would provide."

"So, what do you conclude from the result?"

"That there is no God in this land anymore."

It lay there in the room, shattering glass and drowning sunbeams.

He rose and came to her. "Claire, fight! How can you not see that God spoke? That the ordeal was just."

She retreated before him. "Because you were chosen for your strength. Because you had that sword. If the king had had true faith, he would have fought himself!"

"And both king and father would have suffered grievously."

She was against the wall now, trapped, and he caged her with his strong arms. "Don't you see," she whispered, "it's like the snake in the Garden, whispering how easy it would be. How easy just to accept that right is wrong, that lies are truth..."

He lowered his head and his lips touched the base of her throat. "I have told you the truth."

"As you see it." But instead of pushing at him, of fighting, Claire rolled her head back, opening herself to him.

His lips brushed softly in the sensitive hollow there, making her tremble. "I have no more words," he murmured, "but I am a warrior. I fight."

Up her neck, tongue and lips, scattering thought like feathers in a wind, smothering conscience. To her lips, her parted lips. "If I take you here," he said, breath mingling with hers, "you are conquered."

She felt only lips, heat, desire, and played her lips against his.

"Fight me, Claire," he groaned. "Fight. Make me stop." But his lips captured hers, and his body overwhelmed, and her biting hunger ruled her head.

But not—thank God and pity us—her conscience. Weakly, and from a distance, it made itself heard.

She wrenched her mouth free. "Stop." It was the merest whisper, and her hands against his chest were like a fledgling's wings. "We must not..."

He froze there, still braced rigid against the wall, then he pushed away, put the room between them.

"Fight, Claire," he said again, back to her. "I cannot change the past, so you must try to see the truth. Or God have mercy on us both."

## Chapter 21

She ran then, ran from the room and into the sanctuary of the solar, tears pouring down her face. Paradise danced around, just out of reach, and the snake was her own sense of right and wrong.

No! Not the snake. The snake was the wicked temptation of her love.

Eventually everything settled, sank miserably into a cinder landscape of black and gray. He had told her everything. It broke her heart, but it did not help, because her father's cause had been just. Renald had admitted that the rebels had changed their minds out of fear, not because they suddenly realized that Henry Beauclerk was a good and honest king.

Her father alone had stood for the just cause, and been killed for it. It had to have been an unjust death.

She crossed herself and knelt to pray, begging for strength to resist the tempting snake. Then she rose and seized her wax tablets, to write down ways to escape this situation.

Annulment, she wrote. Essential. Bishop.

Grounds? Non-consummation and possibly deception. She would ask the bishop if there were others. Quivering with memory, she knew she must never be alone with Renald again or, as he'd said, they would be trapped.

But once the marriage was over, what would she and her family do? St. Frideswide's, she dug into the wax. But that was no good for Thomas.

France, she wrote. Her mother's family.

She remembered Renald's account of his childhood. That was not what she wanted for Thomas, and her grandmother could never make the journey.

She bit her lip. There were other relatives, but all in England, all subject to the king.

She looked over her list and scraped away the useless words. What in God's name was she to do?

She remembered writing an account of the past few days. She'd finish it. Perhaps somewhere in there she'd find a key. She looked for her record book, then realized that it wasn't on the desk where she'd left it.

She looked around the room, puzzled, but it was nowhere in sight. She unlocked the chest where she kept her work, and raised the large boards containing her story of the Brave Child Sebastian. Beneath were a number of papers, including her father's journal, but not the one she sought.

She checked the other book chests, but they were locked and contained bound works. It wasn't in her clothes chests. Why would it be?

"Prissy!" She swung open the door. "Maria!"

"Lady?" Prissy leaped up, one of Claire's stockings in hand, darning needle dangling.

"Has anyone other than you been in the solar this morning?"

"Nay, lady, I don't think so."

"Come in here."

Back in the solar, she asked if a thief could have gone into the solar that morning.

"A thief, lady? Something's missing?"

"My record book." Claire began to pointlessly check all the chests again. She ordered Prissy to check behind and under benches and tables, though it was hard to imagine how the book could be there. She even checked under the bed and between the covers. She found a few weary rose petals, but not so much as a sheet of parchment.

"It's not here," said Prissy. "Are you sure—"

"It was here! Why would anyone want to steal it? Books are valuable, but my scribblings on scraps of parchment?" It was really not that important, but in the midst of chaos, this one last loss was throwing her into panic.

"Perhaps someone came through the window, lady."

Claire looked at the opening to the courtyard. "Summerbourne people don't steal." But she'd never thought they'd murder, either. Perhaps it was one of Renald's men, both murderer and thief, snake in the Garden...

"Do you want to tell Lord Eudo, lady? Him being the sheriff."

Claire shook her head. "It's not worth sending so far over a few sheets of parchment."

"But he's still here, lady."

"Lord Eudo? Here?"

"Looking into Ulric's death. Or so he says. Can't say he's done much but eat and drink."

"Then yes. Go and ask him to come and speak to me, Prissy. At the least, I'll have his men's packs searched before he leaves."

But Prissy returned in moments to say, "He rode out not long ago, lady."

"Find me a messenger! I'll ask him to check his men. It's almost funny to think of someone trying to sell my rough notes. But I want them back."

She'd just sent off the message when Felice dragged her out to assess a sick goose. She knew this was unnecessary, but didn't fight it. She had too many other things to worry about.

She didn't know what was wrong with the bird so she ordered it killed and its carcass burned.

She wished all problems were so simply handled.

The book didn't turn up, and over two days of avoiding Renald, no magical solution occurred to Claire. But Eudo returned to Summerbourne, going first to visit Claire's mother.

He emerged shaking his head.

Claire could understand why. Lady Murielle had settled into obsessive mourning, and her vision of Lord Clarence was rapidly becoming worthy of sanctification. Though Claire had loved her father dearly she knew he had not been a saint.

"Poor Murielle," Eudo said. "She is much disturbed."

Claire poured him ale. "We hope with time and rest she will become herself again."

He eyed her. "She seems to forget that your wedding has taken place."

In truth, this was driving Claire distracted, but she said, "It is not uncommon when someone suffers a blow. She'll get better with rest."

"I pray for it." He sipped the ale. "She said some other things. That your father was killed in a court battle. That the opponent was Renald de Lisle."

Claire was strangely tempted to deny it, but she said, "It's true."

"By the cross!" He paled as if he hadn't really believed it. "It can have been little but slaughter."

Renald's account of the battle lingered in her mind like one of his pictures. "Yes."

He put down his cup and took her hand. "Oh, my dear. What a burden this places on you."

She felt tears prick to have an older person giving her support. "It is not easy, no."

"What do you plan to do?"

"I don't know. I think I must seek an annulment. Do you know anything of such matters?"

"Only that you need to apply to the bishop. It has not been consummated... ?"

"We keep our vow. But the king's will must be considered. He ordered the marriage."

"The Church is independent of the king."

She looked at him. "Is it?"

His lips set almost peevishly. "This is unjust! No one could hold you to such a wicked union!"

Claire was wearily reminded that Eudo didn't think clearly, and that his unfocused outrage had set her father off on the path to disaster. He was strong on outrage, but weak on action.

"Perhaps a way will be found," she said vaguely, freeing her hand.

"You have only a month. Less now."

As if she didn't know. "Please, Eudo, let us speak of other matters." She grasped the only thing that came to mind. "Do you have further news of Ulric's death?"

Once she had thought that would be her salvation.

Now, anyway, she knew she might falter rather than send Renald to possible death.

Eudo worked his soft lips for a moment, then said, "Nothing. It must have been an attack of the moment, perhaps out of drink. Such crimes are hard to solve." He drained his ale, and pulled on his gloves. "I actually stopped to reassure you about your book. Of course none of my men had it. I checked their baggage most carefully."

"I thank you for your care. It was silly of me to think it."

"It will have been mislaid somewhere, I'm sure."

"I'm sure you're right." Claire walked him back to his horse, relieved to be seeing him off. "Certainly it's of no value to anyone but me."

He paused, reins already in hand. "Still, you should take better care. I hope you have your father's journal safe. You left the other one out, in sight of the window."

"Oh yes. My father's work is locked in a chest."

"And have you started transcribing it?"

"I don't have the heart just yet."

He made as if to mount, then turned back. "I am on my way to St. Stephen's monastery. Would you like me to take it there? The monks could relieve you of the task."

It was a reasonable suggestion, but Claire shook her head. "Thank you, but no. It is something I need to do for myself."

"You must have little time these days."

"I will find the time. Such work eases me."

She thought he might object again, but instead, he said, "Can I take a letter to the bishop, then, asking about your annulment?"

She hesitated, and realized with despair that she didn't want to truly take that step. "Could you?"

"I have business there. But I cannot delay long."

"It will only take a moment!" She ran back into the manor and wrote a very hasty letter. It was not as elegantly phrased or scribed as she would wish, but the content was clear. She hurried back out and gave it to him before her resolution failed.

"I do regret the state you are all come to," Eudo said, tucking it into his pouch. "I never thought..."

She almost laughed. That could be his epitaph. He never thought, and certainly never saw the consequences of his rash words.

He sighed and kissed her brow. "God bless and guard you, Claire. I will deliver your letter, and hope that it can set you free."

Free. She knew that she would never be free.

Claire watched him ride away, then turned to see Renald watching her.

He must have seen her give Eudo a document, but he hadn't intervened. He was, truly, leaving her to fight the battle for herself. Did he know she was losing?

He'd said he wouldn't rape her, but he'd come close.

No. That hadn't been rape.

When their month was up, he would have the right to her body. Would he claim it? Would she have the strength to resist?

With each passing hour it grew harder, the snake became more persuasive.

Seeking any kind of bulwark for her will, Claire went into the hall to where her grandmother and mother sat together.

Lady Murielle was stitching a seam in one of Lord Clarence's tunics. The trouble was, she kept unraveling them so as to have something to stitch.

Lady Agnes looked more impatient than sympathetic. "Don't know what that Eudo thought he was doing here. Wringing his hands about everything like an old woman."

"Not like any old woman I know."

As her grandmother chuckled, her mother looked up. "Has that man left yet?"

Claire knew she didn't refer to Eudo. "Summerbourne is his now, Mother."

Lady Murielle reached out to seize her wrist. "You mustn't marry him, Claire, not even for Thomas's sake. Promise me you won't. We'll be all right."

Claire patted her hand, fighting tears at hearing the words she'd wanted to hear days ago. Words now so pointless. "I'll do my best."

Her mother let her go, and dabbed at tears. "You're a dutiful daughter, Claire. You know how much I love you, don't you? Now, I must mend this. Clarence will need it come winter."

Claire couldn't stand this. "Father is *dead*, Mother."

Lady Murielle looked up. "I know that. We buried him. In wool. But I must finish this." She went back to stitching the seam.

Lady Agnes shook her head. "Expect no sense from her just now. It's guilt, as much as grief. She pushed you into marrying him and wants to deny it. She's pretending she did her best to protect you."

"You pushed me, too."

"Ah, but I don't suffer any burden from it. If you'll take my advice, you'll stick to the marriage."

This was why Lady Agnes was no counsel. She still played the same tune.

"It would be wrong."

"Wrong." Her grandmother snorted. "It doesn't matter how they die. Battle, ordeal, or an arrow in the woods. They're still dead. It's women's work to keep things going."

378

"Some work is just too hard."

Her grandmother frowned up at her. "What do you find so horrible about him? He's handsome, courteous. Charming when he wants to be. And he looks at you like any woman wants to be looked at."

Snake words. "Perhaps that's just it. If he was unpleasant, I could accept it as a cross to bear. It seems wrong to fall weakly into pleasure."

Lady Agnes shook her head. "You know your trouble? You're eighteen. You'll grow a thicker skin around your conscience soon, but it'll be too late."

Claire couldn't help but laugh, and she leaned down to kiss her grandmother's cheek. "I'm sorry. I'm trying to find a way so you'll be taken care of."

Lady Agnes touched her cheek. "I know you think I'm a wicked, heartless old woman, but don't rush into anything, Claire. You have a month. Time heals."

Claire left, guiltily aware of a letter on its way, and a feeling of having been in this spot before. She remembered. It had been when she'd been planning to escape Summerbourne to persuade Felice to marry the ogre.

Who said the wheel of fate did not run backward?

Claire took part of her grandmother's advice and gave herself a rest from the constant fretting. She had most of a month. Until she heard from the bishop, there was nothing she could do anyway.

Routine summer days, however, did little to make her decisions easier.

Renald was becoming part of Summerbourne. She could no longer quite imagine her home without him and his boisterous men. Even their bawdy songs, loud laughter, and rough play became part of her daily life.

The news that he'd killed Lord Clarence had been a shock, but Summerbourne had recovered quickly. The servants had accepted it as another of those things that happen in life. After all, as one man had said to her, "Lord Renald is clearly a good man, lady."

She knew his acceptance here had been part of his plan. He'd hurried here through a storm so that people would know and like him before they learned the truth. It had worked, but that didn't mean that he wasn't a good man.

She watched him for vices, seeking something she could use to barricade her weakening heart.

She found only virtues. He was considerate of all. He didn't demand unreasonable service. He rarely raised his voice, and never without cause. He'd even kept his promise and apart from the inevitable effect of his presence, he'd preserved Summerbourne as a place of peace. She never saw him in an act of violence. She never saw his armor or his sword.

She assumed he trained his men, but it was done well away from her home.

And yet, without violence or bluster, his nature changed everything, perhaps even for the better. People came to Summerbourne now from far around seeking help with predators—animal or human. Claire had never realized in the past how strange it was that they didn't.

When some unruly knights harassed nearby Sherborn, the townsfolk sent to petition for Renald's help.

He came to tell her of it. "This matter should not take more than a day, my lady."

"You leave now?"

"I must, before more people are abused."

"What will you do?"

"Whatever needs to be done."

She puzzled over that, for he was in wool. Then she realized that he would arm himself out of her sight. Fear stabbed. He went to fight. "Take care, my lord."

He looked at her. "Do you want me to return safe?"

"Of course!"

His hand moved, as if he might reach for her, but then he simply said, "That is our tragedy, isn't it?" He bowed and walked away.

She watched him go without the kiss a man should expect when he went into danger, without any tender farewells. She sent them after him silently, symbol of all that was amiss.

She didn't really think he'd come to harm in such a matter, but she still lived in fear until he and his men returned. She watched secretly from a window as they rode in, and saw how they all bubbled with the excitement of action. Renald glowed in a way she'd never seen before.

Except, perhaps, on their wedding night.

For the first time she realized the truth of his words in the garden—that time so long ago. He truly did enjoy fighting, and she forced him to hide all trace of it.

He came to her later, unarmed and bathed, no hint of violence on him in blood, wound, or glow. "The matter is taken care of, my lady."

"What happened?" she asked resolutely, ready to show that she could at least accept his warlike nature.

"Little enough. It was nothing." And he spoke of minor estate matters before leaving her.

Once, she would have insisted. Now she wasn't sure how.

She heard all about it, of course. The Summerbourne people were mighty proud of their lord, and keen to talk of how brave he'd been, how fearsome, how he'd killed the leader, who'd been an armed man bigger than he, and how the followers had fled or been captured.

"Well?" asked her grandmother at the dinner table, before he came to take his seat. "Is such a man not worth holding to?"

"Yes," said Claire. "If I only knew how."

She spent restless nights chasing her conscience around and around, but she couldn't escape the basic truth. Her father had fought over Henry Beauclerk's seizure of the throne and unfairly lost. Something about that had to be very wrong.

Renald hid his martial exercises so well that Claire would hardly have known at all if not for the scrapes and bruises his men—

including Thomas—sometimes brought to the tables. She noted, but never mentioned them until the day she saw Thomas limping.

He twitched out of her hold. "It's nothing."

"What's nothing?"

"Claire, don't fuss!"

She put her hands on her hips. "Thomas of Summerbourne, like it or not, I'm lady here. The welfare of all is my concern. What injury do you have?"

He eyed her. "Lord Renald said not to bother you—"

"Oh, did he? What?"

"It's just a cut in my foot—"

She grabbed his sleeve and towed him along to her simple room, where all the herbs and ointments were kept. "A cut like that could fester!"

"He'll be angry," he muttered when she pushed him onto a bench.

"I'll tell him it wasn't your fault. Show me."

Pulling a face, he took off shoe and hose, revealing a bandage. When she unwound it, she found a nasty gash just beginning to knit. "Did they put anything on it?"

"No. But it's all right."

She washed off some dirt. "Yes, it is, but more by luck than skill. Who's talking care of wounds, then?"

He shrugged. "Anyone. Lord Renald bandaged this. And told me to wear shoes when walking on rough ground."

She spread a healing salve on a new cloth and bound his foot again. "Come back and let me look at it in a couple of days. And if it starts to hurt—"

"I know. I know. I'll tell you straightaway."

She wanted to hug him and protect him as if he were still a baby. "Take care, Thomas."

He pulled his hose and shoe back on, and limped away. "Remember to tell Lord Renald that I didn't let on!"

Claire put away her medicines thinking that if she truly wanted to protect her brother, all she had to do was surrender to Renald. She could lie to him. Tell him she was easy in her mind.

She shook her head. That was the serpent whispering, offering the juicy apple.

She could at least handle a simple problem. This nonsense about the wounded had to stop.

She found him in the stables. Sigfrith noticed her first, making Renald turn. For a moment, something flashed in his eyes, stinging her like a whip, and she realized she had never sought him out since that time with Josce.

When he came over to her, however, he was calm and controlled. "You wish to speak to me, my lady?"

"What did happen to Aidan?" she asked, reminded of a thread left hanging from long ago.

"Who?"

"My father's horse."

"The king has him." He watched her with painful care. "It was his right and he liked the horse."

Claire could have wept that he thought

she'd be hurt by that. "I was only curious." She wanted to touch him, soothe him. She did not dare.

"You didn't come to ask about Aidan."

"No." She considered how to put it. "My lord, I know I gave the impression that I did not want martial matters in Summerbourne, but you are carrying it to extremes."

"Extremes?"

"Wounds," she said. "I may not want fighting within the walls, but it is my duty to tend to the wounded."

"Thomas," he said, with a quirk of the brows that could break her heart, so familiar it seemed. So long unseen. "Does his foot fester?"

"No, but only by a miracle. And no, he didn't come running to me about it. But then, he can't run with a sore foot, can he? I was bound to notice."

The brows rose. "I'm sorry if I've offended you."

She realized that the distance, the shield between them, was evaporating. It was dangerous—her fast-beating heart told her that—but she would give up her soul, almost, for more moments like this. "Well you have," she said, as steadily as she could. "I expect your wounded men to come to me for treatment."

"And what," he asked softly, "if I am wounded?"

After too many heartbeats, she replied, "Then of course I would treat you. Unless you object."

"On the contrary. You tempt me to be very clumsy with my sword."

Claire's breath caught. "Don't," she said at last, stepping backward, backward. "Don't, Renald. The risks are far too great."

Of course, he didn't come to her wounded, but others did.

Later that day she poulticed a swollen knee that should have been tended to days before. The next day she treated an inflamed and blackened eye. She found out that these more obvious injuries had been hidden from her, kept in a hut in the village instead of brought back to the hall.

After that, she saw a steady stream of wounded. She still didn't think it wise for men to spend their time damaging themselves just in case they might be called upon to fight, but she did her duty and didn't nag.

None of the injuries were on Renald's body, but then one day he did appear in her herb room. A moment after her heart started to race, she saw he was supporting a burly man who kept one leg curled up off the floor.

"Sword cut," he said, lowering the man onto a bench. "Days old."

He helped the man out of his loose braies, exposing a dirty rag over a swollen thigh.

"I thought we had an agreement," Claire said. "Why wasn't he brought to me before?"

"This isn't my doing. He's been hiding it from me, too."

Claire shook her head and unwound the disgusting cloth. She had to soak off the last part because it was stuck to the inflamed, pus-filled wound. "You could lose this leg," she told the middle-aged man. "You could die!"

He hung his head, looking for all the world like an old hound that knew he'd done wrong. Claire took up a knife to lance the wound and saw Renald move closer.

"Don't you trust me to do this right?"

"Completely. But any man foolish enough to let a wound fester could be foolish enough to strike his healer when it hurts."

"Nay, lord," the man protested. "I'd not touch your lovely lady!"

"Then perhaps," said Renald, "you'll feel sprightly enough to try to steal a kiss."

The man chuckled and even winked at Claire, but she saw the sweat on his face, and it wasn't from fever but fear.

She picked up her sharp lancing knife, still warmed by the way Renald said "completely." Something held between them, she realized, running like a sturdy thread and growing stronger day by day. It was an acknowledgment of each other's abilities and a precious resulting trust.

She hoped she could preserve it by saving this leg.

At the first touch of the knife, however, before she'd even cut, the man flinched. Renald stepped forward and held him down. Even then, it was a struggle to make the cuts where she had to.

When it came to cleaning the dirty wound with wine and herbs, it turned into a full, cursing wrestling match. She might have been deafened by the man-at-arm's bellows if Renald hadn't gagged him, and despite Renald's strength, the man managed to kick a bowl of foul water over her.

When she stepped back from the treated, bandaged wound, she was soaked and panting. Her patient, however, was now sheepishly quiet. As soon as Renald released him and gave him a stick, he pulled on his braies, muttered apologies to both of them, and hobbled away.

"Well really!" Claire said, stripping off her soiled tunic and using the clean parts to wipe herself. "Why do you keep such a coward on?"

Renald was rumpled and heated himself. "Rolf's one of the bravest men I know when his blood runs hot in a fight. In cold blood, he can't take any pain at all. I usually keep an eye on him and drag him off to be looked after. I've been distracted..."

At his tone, his look, Claire realized that only her thin summer kirtle covered her body, and it was damp. She clutched her wet tunic to her as a shield, but still his eyes traveled over her. She thought perhaps she could hear his breaths.

It was no good. Hell was worth it. She took one tiny step toward him.

He turned and left with a slam of the door.

She crossed herself. Sweet Mary, protect them both!

This couldn't go on. She dressed hastily in clean clothes, and went to compose another letter to the bishop. It was two weeks since the last, and her month was speeding. This time she wasn't sure how best to send it, so in the end she went to Brother Nils.

The monk seemed quite stricken. "Are you sure, lady?"

"I've less than two weeks to go."

"He's a good man, lady."

"I know. Send my letter."

Nils looked at the rolled parchment, torn, then went to seek his lord. He found Lord Renald up on the palisade, head sunk in hands.

Nils cleared his throat. Instead of snapping back into the lord, the warrior, Renald rose slowly, sucking in a deep breath. "What now?"

Wishing, perhaps, that he'd not come up here, Nils said, "The Lady Claire has asked me to send a letter. To the bishop."

"I see." And he clearly did.

After a while, Nils asked, "Shall I send it, my lord?"

"Yes, of course."

Why won't you fight? Nils wanted to ask. Why won't you use your charms and woo her? He'd watched helplessly as they both moved through Summerbourne like leaves caught in different eddies, spinning close but never touching.

He'd watched as well the way they watched each other. He'd never seen such pain in healthy eyes.

Surely something could be done.

He cleared his throat. "Would you like me to read it to you first, my lord?"

"No." And now the lord and warrior was back. "Send it, Nils, then find the records of that wool factor in Dorchester. You said he might give us a better price."

Firmly put in his place, Nils went with a heavy heart to follow orders.

## Chapter 22

Claire had sent again to the bishop. Now she needed to try to arrange for the security of her family. She rode to St. Frideswide's, thinking ruefully that Renald no longer tried to control her movements.

Sometimes, weakly, she wished he would. Many nights she lay in the big bed and wished he'd come to her, touch her, dizzy and overwhelm her, so she'd be sealed to him forever despite her will. In the dark, mysterious night, she knew she'd never be able to resist.

At the convent, pushing away all memory of her last visit, she asked to speak to the Mother Winifred, and was taken to her office.

"Reverend Mother," Claire said as she took a seat, "I wish to know if you will accept my mother, my grandmother, and my aunts here."

The nun regarded her over her writing table. "Of our charity, we must give refuge, Lady Claire."

"They may have to come without property. What then?"

"Well, there it is a little difficult. Our means are limited, and the needs of the poor are great. We cannot feed idle hands."

"I'm sure they would work, at ladylike occupations."

"We do not have great need of ladylike occupations here."

Claire had expected this. "They could bring a jeweled cup of considerable value."

"Indeed? But would it be theirs to bring? If you are seeking refuge for your family, Lady Claire, you must intend to break your marriage. In that case, if I understand matters aright, you will all own nothing."

"Lord Renald gave me the cup without condition. It is mine. If necessary, he will confirm it."

The nun interlinked her hands on her desk. "A generous man, then. You do not think to hold to your marriage?"

Claire hadn't expected this attitude here. "You called him a murderer."

"As most men are. If a lady seeks to marry, she has little choice."

"Few ladies are called upon to marry their father's murderer."

"True enough. You, too, will come here?"

Claire rose. "No, Reverend Mother. I cannot stay so close. I will seek refuge in France with my mother's family, taking my brother with me, and enter a convent there once he is settled. If my mother and aunts wish to accompany us, I will take them too. But Lady Agnes could never make the journey."

A smile flickered. "Lady Agnes will not wish to be here either, but you may be assured that she will have kindly care with us if needed."

Claire nodded. "Thank you. It is a relief to know that they will have refuge here."

The nun rose, too, tucking her hands neatly in her sleeves. "You are on a hard path, my child. I will pray for you."

Claire was tempted to ask advice, to ask what Mother Winifred thought about a daughter settling to a happy marriage with her father's murderer, with a man who had somehow circumvented God's will in the ordeal.

What was the point? She knew the answer.

Riding back, she told herself that it would be easier once it was over and they need never again meet. For the moment, however, they had no choice.

A barony like Summerbourne was not woman's work or man's. It was a fine meshing of responsibilities in crops, in animals, and in people. Often Claire had to spend the evening going over some matter of administration with Renald and the upper servants. They pored over maps, and she read records aloud as they made decisions for a future she was trying to escape.

Sometimes, as they sat close together in work—close but never touching—she glanced up to find him looking at her.

Hungrily.

A beat of desire would start within her.

Hungrily.

How long could the starving live with a feast and not give in to temptation?

That evening he said, "I hear you have written to the bishop."

She looked at him, but couldn't read him.

"Twice, actually. Eudo took a letter weeks ago."

She saw shock. The sort of shock that comes of a blade in the gut.

"You've received no reply?"

"Not yet. That's why I wrote again."

"And if he gives hope?"

She made herself speak calmly. "Then it will be settled."

"And if he refuses?"

She looked away. She'd tussled with that and still not come up with any solution.

"If he refuses, Claire," he said, "you must ask the king."

She looked back at him, astonished. "Ask him for what?"

"To secure your annulment."

"You think he could do that? Would?"

"Certainly he could. There are grounds enough. And he would because I would add my plea to yours."

Absurdly, it hurt. "You want—"

"No." He even smiled a little. "Never. But there's nothing for us here unless it comes of your free will."

"In the night—" she said, then stopped the words that must not be said.

"I know."

They sat there, side by side. Divided.

The next day, the messenger returned from the bishop. Claire unrolled the parchment, slowly, not sure what she hoped for.

It was refusal.

Against her will, she felt a twisted relief.

"Will you tell me what it says?"

She turned, shocked, for she was in the solar, where he never came. "We shared a marriage bed." She tried to block all thought of that bed so close. "The bishop considers our marriage consummated."

"How very unworldly of him. You could insist on an examination."

She nervously rolled the parchment up again. "He mentions that. He says that as with a proxy wedding, it is the contact of skin that symbolizes the union. Is that true?"

"The king can probably make him take another view. Our month is almost up."

She knew that, knew it with the desperation of needing to escape, and the agony of soon losing him.

"I must write to the king, then?"

When he didn't immediately answer, she looked at him.

"We are summoned to court," he said. "I received the message earlier."

"To London? Why?"

"To Carrisford, where the king holds court. He has heard of our vow and wants to preside over the consummation."

She covered her mouth. "What are we going to do?"

"As always, I will obey, and you must, too. But Claire, can you face Henry and not speak treason?"

Bitterness welled up to burn in her throat. "No, and why should I? He killed his brother. He stole the Crown. He used you to kill my father for saying that, and that led to—"

Warrior-fast, he was on her even as she said, "—this," forcing her to her knees despite her struggles.

She looked up, shaken by fear and his burning touch.

"So," he said, "you are frightened at last. It's time you learned the wisdom of fear. Henry Beauclerk is King of England, acclaimed by the lords, anointed by the Church. He has right of life and death over you, over me, over everyone in this land."

"Under the law," she stated, refusing to be entirely cowed.

"Under the law, he can punish you for what you just said. He can lock you up, have you flogged, put out your eyes, cut out your impudent tongue." His hands slid inward to circle her throat. They trembled. "I will not let you take the road your father took."

Within the hot circle of his unsteady grasp, she swallowed, assailed as much by weakening love and pity as by dread. "I cannot bow to him. I cannot. I will stay home."

"To refuse the king's command is treason, too."

She gave a little sob. "Then it seems I am doomed."

He closed his eyes for a moment. "If you will not vow to be meek at court, I will make sure you cannot go."

"You will lock me up?" There was a kind of relief in that. It wouldn't solve their other problems, but perhaps Renald alone could persuade the king...

He released her throat and raised her with gentle hands. "Your people would doubtless set you free."

"Then how?"

He stepped back from her. "A broken leg would do it."

She stared. "People die from broken bones."

"Your chances would be better than if you go to court and challenge Henry to his face."

She had to laugh. "You mean it."

He was far, far from any kind of laughter. "I am trained to do the unthinkable. So?"

She raised a hand to a throat that still tingled. "You expect me to decide this *now*?"

"If we go, we leave at dawn. We can make it in one day."

"Let me see if I have this. I must promise not to challenge Henry Beauclerk's right to the throne?"

"And not to accuse him of murdering your father. Not a promise, a vow." He drew the sword that he'd not waited to put off. More proof of how close to the edge he must be. "A vow on this. On the cross of the hilt, on the stone from Jerusalem."

Claire stared at it. "Or you'll break my leg? How?"

"Do you doubt I can do it?"

Not for a moment, neither the act nor the will.

Claire looked from the stone before her, the simple piece of stone that had come from the Holy Land, to the stony resolve of his face. How could they have come to this point?

Through love. Her love for her father,

which said she could not lie with his murderer. Her love for Renald, that made surrender too sweet to be allowed. His love for her, that would hurt her to save her.

A tangled knot indeed.

He looked so hard and certain, but she knew it was his mask, the one he wore to conceal his deepest feelings. What had it cost him to make such a threat to her? What would it cost to carry it out?

Too much. He'd spoken of the shadow he carried from her father's death. She could not lay another on him.

She put her hand to the stone. "I promise that for the duration of our stay at the king's court, I will not express any doubt about Henry Beauclerk's right to the throne of England, or any grievance about the manner of my father's death."

He closed his eyes. When he opened them, they were moist. Tears? From a wolf?

But he was no wolf. He was a man, and the man she loved. She longed to hold him, to stroke away his pain, but control here hung on a silken thread.

"Thank you," he said, sheathing the sword.

"I still must ask for the annulment."

"You have two days to decide."

"What can change in two days?"

He smiled then, but wryly. "We can always pray for a miracle."

Claire left the room, flexing her bruised shoulders, contemplating his words. Pray. Did a murderer pray? And he took the host on Sundays. Why had she never thought of that?

He *truly* felt no guilt. She'd never really believed that before. Didn't that fact mean something, no matter how twisted his master was?

Perhaps she could build on that in two short days...

"Claire!"

She turned to where her aunts sat.

"Here," said Felice, thrusting something at her. "You are so careless!"

Claire took a book. Then she realized it was her record book.

"Where did you find this?" she demanded, untying the boards and flipping through the pages.

"In the pile of spare wooden trenchers. You probably put it there in a fit of absentmindedness. You have to start paying attention to real life, Claire, though I suppose that's hard when your brain is fixed so hotly between your thighs."

"Oh, Felice..." Amice muttered.

Claire ignored her aunts and checked that all was there. It was, which wasn't surprising. The work had little value to anyone but herself.

"I'm not careless with books, Felice. Doubtless Eudo slipped it there in his last visit."

Felice smirked. "So you have enough wit left to see that. Have you decided why?"

"Probably so he didn't have to admit that one of his men filched it. But thank you for finding it, Felice. My work could have lingered there till the next feast."

"Work," her aunt sniffed. "But if you value it, take care of it."

Claire didn't argue the point. "Apparently the king has summoned us to court at Carrisford."

"Us?" Felice asked, sitting up straighter.

"Renald and me," Claire said, cursing her careless words. "I must ask you to take care of Summerbourne while we are away."

"Why should we," Felice asked petulantly, "while you gallivant around?"

Renald's voice answered, from close behind Claire. "For kindness' sake, Lady Felice. Next time we go to court, it will likely be possible to take you."

"Only if you and Claire are still married." Felice's eyes flickered between them. "Is it settled then? Has she finally decided that a father's death doesn't matter?"

"Felice!"

"You put on airs of being so noble and honest, but in the end you do just what you want, like the rest of us. I suspect you wanted him all along."

"That's not true."

"No? I still have a letter you wrote to me, dwelling on his charms. I remember the way you rubbed against him in front of the convent gates."

"I was trying to persuade you to marry him."

"But you leaped at the chance to marry him yourself, didn't you? Before I truly had a chance to consider!"

Amice was weeping. "And Claire, you know I... I offered..."

Claire opened her mouth to argue, but

realized it was futile. Felice in this mood wouldn't hear reason, and Amice was right. She had offered.

Renald broke the silence. "Delightful though it is to be the bone between salivating... dogs, Claire must arrange for the journey. We start at first light tomorrow. Come, my lady."

Claire was grateful to obey. Once out of hearing, he murmured, "If ever I forget, remind me that you saved me from your aunts."

The hint of humor could break her heart, because Felice's words had jabbed at her hope. She didn't know if she was going to be able to sort it all out in her mind. As he'd said to her once, mere surrender wasn't good enough. She had to fully accept him, as he truly was. Accept the dark, murderous sword.

One solution had arisen, however. "Renald, Felice has clearly changed her mind. If I cannot continue with this marriage, will you take her instead?"

He looked at her. "I love *you.*"

She closed her eyes on the pain of it.

"Perhaps I do deserve penance, though. I am a warrior, Claire, and all along I fought to win. Henry calls Summerbourne a bit of paradise, and that's how I see it. And you are the angel in it. I fell in love with you almost at first sight, but love didn't make me noble. It made me greedy."

"Greedy?"

He put his fingers over her lips. "Hear me out. This is the confessional. Whatever decision you make, I want it to be in full knowledge. Yes, I do have guilt. All along, I did what I had to do to capture you. If I'd been a better man, I would have told you the truth. I would have let you go."

"But you had to marry here and Amice and Felice were in the convent."

He smiled ruefully. "A messenger from Henry would have had them thrown out into my arms. And they fled in the first place because of the lies I had my men tell in their hearing."

Claire knew she should be furious, but she could only think that without his stratagems she would not now be here. If all they ever had was this month, she would not have missed it, pain and all.

"I forgive you. But you're right. You do deserve a penance. If I find I cannot keep our marriage intact, will you take Felice?"

He sighed. "A lifetime penance... But yes, if only to make the choice easier for you. And I even promise to be kind. I have some skill at pleasing women."

"Renald..." But Claire had no idea what to say. She couldn't release the protest that leaped to her lips. This was freedom, wasn't it?

No.

"Which leads to another confession," he said. "I did not give you honest love in the marriage bed."

"I don't understand..."

"I'm not sure you can. But I turned whore that night. I used God's gift as a weapon against an opponent as helpless as a babe."

Claire cocked her head. "Helpless, was I?"

He laughed at that, and she thought that perhaps it was true what the priests said—that confession brought healing. "No, as it turned out, you weren't helpless at all. But my intent was wrong. Don't be swayed in your decision by the pleasure I gave you. Another man will do just as well."

"But you're the only man I love." She knew the words were unwise, but they were honest. She was so adrift, she had no idea what to be anymore but honest.

He touched her then, hands trembling, a light resting of his fingers on her cheeks as he kissed her brow. "God be your guide, then." He stepped away. "I must ask one thing of you, though. If I marry Felice, I will care for all your family, but you must leave here. I'm not trying to make this hard for you, but I could never be fair to her with you in our home."

He entered the study, closing the door firmly between them.

Claire sagged against the post.

So it was settled. She could follow her conscience and perhaps not harm her family at all.

She should, perhaps, feel a little bit more at peace.


## Chapter 23

Urgent organization for a journey provided an escape of sorts. By the time they rode off into the morning mist, Claire hadn't had much time to think over her problems, and she was glad of it. If it were possible, she'd ride away from them entirely—ride into the mist with Renald and never have to think of right and wrong again.

She had visited her mother just before leaving and found her rather better, which in fact was rather worse. It seemed that Felice had gone to protest to Lady Murielle about being left behind. This had pulled Claire's mother out of melancholy and into rage.

Felice seemed to have convinced her that Claire was hot for Renald and intended to consummate the marriage without complaint.

"Unfeeling child!" her mother had screamed at her. "Ungrateful daughter! How can you think of such a man even touching you with his bloodstained hands?"

"Mother, I—"

"I've seen you looking at him. Everyone has."

"No!"

"Drooling over the man who killed your gentle father in cold blood."

And that silenced Claire because it was true.

When her mother's harangue sank to mutters, Claire said, "If I escape the marriage, Felice may take my place. Will you scream at her, too?"

Lady Murielle turned away. "She's not my daughter. Not Clarence's daughter. Anyway, I won't be here. I'm moving to St. Frideswide's. I understand you have promised the king's cup as payment."

Claire thought wryly that she should never

403

have expected Mother Winifred to turn away from that temptation. But it was a solution to part of the problems. Her mother clearly couldn't stay here.

"You can join me there if you wish," her mother added. "If you stay pure. Send Thomas to me."

Claire had kissed her mother's cold cheek and left. She had not sent Thomas. He was coming with them to join Henry's household, and despite the pain of parting, she knew he'd be better off there. As long as he didn't have simmering rebellion inside him. He seemed resigned, but it was so hard to tell.

Renald was now riding beside her in mail and helmet. It had been a shock, she couldn't deny it, to see him like that in the chilly morning, and yet there had been good in it. This was reality, and she still loved. If only the love was possible.

"How's Thomas?" he asked.

She wasn't surprised that he seemed attuned to her thoughts. "If he's upset at all, I think it's that he'll soon be separated from Josce. You've been kind to him."

"I am by nature kind."

And she knew that was true.

"He's a good lad with high spirit," he continued. "He'll do well if he doesn't let his mischievousness take him too far."

"I do worry—"

"Don't. He'll doubtless feel the birch a few times. It will do him no harm. And believe it or not, Henry will have a care for him."

"Out of guilty conscience, I suppose."

But he met her eyes steadily. "No more than I."

He rode off to check the long line of horsemen and pack animals, leaving her shaking her head. The only sense to it seemed to be that she had a completely different view of right and wrong from the rest of the world. Perhaps it was inherited, for the same thing seemed to have sent her father to his death.

Claire wondered if Renald had said anything to Thomas about not opposing the king. He'd feel more than the birch for that. She didn't think her brother was interested in politics, but he could be as impulsive as she. She called him to ride alongside.

"Do you think you'll enjoy court life?"

"I don't know."

"You won't have any problems with serving the king?"

He glanced at her. "Should I?"

"By the rood, no. But after Father—"

"I don't think I'm old enough to understand these things. So I will serve him according to my honor."

Claire smiled, sure she heard an echo of something Renald had said. "Good. I, too, don't intend to stir up trouble." Her vow bound her to that, but with sudden insight, she added, "After all, if any wrong has been done, God will amend it."

Thomas brightened. "Josce said that."

"And it's true. We don't have to make a point of trying to correct such wrongs." Of course one day Thomas would have to choose whether to take his oath of loyalty to the king, but that was years away.

He was chattering now. "Josce says the king has dozens of pages, and they get up to all kinds of things! It'll be fun to have so many boys of my own age and station. And he says I'll have arms and armor fitted to my size for training. And..."

Claire listened, smiling, thanking heaven that this part, at least, might work out well.

Her mother would be content enough in the convent. And, whatever happened, Lady Agnes would have her place in Summerbourne. Felice might end up with exactly the sort of husband she wanted.

She looked to where Renald was riding with some men. The only ones to suffer would be she and him, and all she had to do to avert that was to see that her father's death had been legal and righteous.

She sighed.

Could she hand that over to God, too? It seemed to her that people were supposed to make moral choices.

Most of the time they rode at a walk to spare the horses, so the company chatted and sang. Then one man started to tell a story, and that made Claire think of her father's journal. She'd brought it with her, hoping for a chance to read it, hoping that something in it would cut through the tangled knot of her dilemma. She pulled the book out of her bag and settled to read.

Miles passed, and she was deep in the story when Renald came alongside again. "Your father's book? Can you tell me what he says?"

The calm between them now was heartbreaking. "It's maddening in a way," she said. "I think he was as confused as I am much of the time. He had a low opinion of the rebellion. He thought too many of Duke Robert's supporters were self-serving."

He nodded. "Drawn by promises of powerful positions in the kingdom."

"He detested Robert de Bellême and his brothers."

"Hardly surprising."

His big warhorse put him inches higher than her, so she had to look up. "Is it true de Bellême so abused his poor wife that she died of it?"

"So rumor says."

She sighed. "Father—or rather, the Brave Child Sebastian—struggles with these issues. He even questions the justice of the cause."

"Would to God he'd questioned more."

She couldn't help but say, "Amen. He *was* much troubled by the company he kept. He writes of knowing a tree by the fruit it bears."

Renald shrugged. "As for that, there were doubtless as many rogues on our side." He twisted to look up and down the line. "We'd best stop to rest the horses soon." He rode off to give the orders, leaving Claire exasperated.

Was neither side of *anything* right or wrong?

As they fed and watered the horses, the humans refreshed themselves, too, wandering around to stretch their legs. Claire read as she walked, still seeking a magic message in her father's writings.

Doubtless to counter the "bad fruit," her father listed the good men who supported Duke Robert, including the Earl of Salisbury and Eudo of Peel. Eudo? Claire squinted at it, but that was definitely what it said. Her father must have referred to Eudo's ardent support of the cause.

It seemed many of these men felt uncertain. Though uncertain didn't seem to be quite the term for her father's mind. Troubled, yes, uncertain, no. She came to the passage she'd found earlier, where the Brave Child Sebastian rose before the company to speak eloquently about the justice of their cause, telling the story of the bad king who brought ruin on his land.

She looked around at peaceful, lush countryside. The heavy rain, though miserable at the time, had spurred a burst of new growth. England seemed to be prospering rather than falling into ruin. Was that a sign?

Everyone knew that Henry Beauclerk had promised a return to law and order, and word was that the roads everywhere were already safer. True, some harsh punishments of brigands and outlaws had been necessary, but that was fair in such a cause.

She was pondering links between the placid idyll around her and the king's right to the throne, when one of the horses reared with a shrill whinny. A hoof knocked over a tub of grain, creating a minor chaos of horses, men, and spilled feed.

In every idyll an occasional wasp will fly, she thought with a wry smile.

A sharp cry to her right startled her, as if someone had hurt themselves. She walked around a bush to see if she could help.

And was immediately seized.

A hand over her mouth stopped her cry. A strong arm confined her as she was dragged, kicking and writhing, farther from the camp. The book—the precious book—slipped from her hands and she moaned a special cry at that, fighting even harder.

"Claire?"

At Renald's call she tried desperately to clear her mouth, but she was helpless. When her skirt caught on a branch, it was ripped free as her captor—captors, for there were a number of men about her—desperately dragged her away.

Then Renald bellowed, "To me! To your lady!" and she heard him coming after, crashing through the woods. She struggled as fiercely as she could, doing anything to cause delay.

"Kill her," someone said, low-voiced.

Claire's captor halted. Another man turned to her, drawing a wicked knife. She watched in horror as he stepped forward grinning.

She'd once thought Renald without a soul. Now she knew what it truly meant.

Grin turned to rictus as a thrown blade thudded into his chest. Her captor's hold slackened for a moment and she twisted an arm free, slashing up with her fist. More by luck than skill she caught him in the throat and he went down, choking.

Claire whirled, looking for other dangers. Where was the man who had ordered her killed? The only sign was a crashing as he fled. She spun back to other noises.

Three men were attacking Renald.

His thrown knife had saved her life. Now he fought for his own against sword, ax, and quarterstaff.

His men were coming, calling and crashing, but they were not here yet. The quarterstaff cracked on his leg even as he beat aside the sword and ducked the ax. On his next move, his weakened leg almost gave way.

One sweep of his sword, his special sword, and the quarterstaff was half its length.

Claire ran forward to seize the fallen part. With all her strength, she slammed it against the head of the ax-wielder.

The burly redhead staggered, but didn't go down. Bellowing, he turned on her, mad rage in his eyes. But then he screamed as a sword impaled him. Blood gushed from his mouth as he crumpled at her feet.

Claire stood frozen, but then she realized that Renald must be swordless!

Sweet Mary mild! He dodged a wild thrust from the swordsman, but the jagged quarterstaff jabbed viciously at him. He beat it aside with his fist.

Josce charged from between the trees. He'd be too late. Renald fended off another sword slash with his arm. Thank heavens that sword could not cut through mail!

Claire ran forward and whacked the swordsman hard behind the knees, a childhood trick to bring someone down. As he must, he crumpled. The man with the broken quarterstaff tried to run, so Claire tripped him. To be safe, she slammed her stick on the fallen swordsman's wrist then snatched up his weapon.

Armed with sword and stick, she glared at the men who had dared to threaten her love. "So there!"

When she looked up, she saw Renald's men staring at her, and her lord and master helpless with laughter and exhaustion against a tree. He opened his arms, and without thought she dropped her weapons and ran into them.

"I suppose you think I'm funny," she said, beginning to shake with relief and shock.

He stroked her hair. "I think you're magnificent."

She looked up. "You could have died."

He sobered. "So could you. Next time, woman, keep out of a fight!"

"You were in difficulty. Don't deny it!"

"I was in more difficulty after I lost my sword."

"You should have kept hold of it."

"By the rood, Claire, I had to throw it." But he cradled her face. "My heart stopped. I swear it." Then he kissed her, desperately, tenderly, and she kissed him back.

He'd almost died.

Sweet Mary, he'd almost died. Like a stream of pure water, it washed away all doubt. "Tomorrow, I want to consummate our marriage."

Instead of delirious joy, he sighed. "Though it pains me to say it, you're suffering battle fever, my love."

"Are you saying I'm mad?"

"I'm saying that I can't hold you to anything you say at the moment."

"I'll say the same tomorrow. I can't live without you."

"I pray for it, but I won't hold you to it."

She puffed out a breath. "I could begin to think you don't care."

"Never think that. Never." His hands tightened at her waist. "My heart is yours, Claire, now and through all eternity."

It was what she felt, but it shook her. "If that's true, it would be very unfair to tie Felice to you."

He kissed her forehead and pushed her away. "I hoped you'd see it that way."

She rolled her eyes, yet couldn't help but smile.

His smile faded when he looked at the two men on the ground, guarded by his own soldiers. Josce had retrieved the dark blade and came over, cleaning it. Renald straddled the white-eyed swordsman and put the point of his sword to the man's heaving chest, leaning on it slightly so the eyes widened even farther. "Why did you seize my lady?"

The wild eyes flickered around as if searching frantically for help, but then settled again on the nemesis above. "We were paid, lord. Mercy, lord."

"Mercy? Only in the speed or slowness of your death. Who paid you?"

"A man, lord. Mercy—"

"What man?" Renald leaned on the sword a little more and the man cried out.

"Don't know, lord! Don't know! He gave us gold to upset the horses and seize the lady."

"And to kill her."

"We didn't know nothing about that, lord, until he spoke it!"

"Renald," said Claire, "the man who was holding me got away. And the one who paid."

"A shame, that." Renald looked at the other man, who snarled like a cornered animal. He stepped away and sheathed his sword. "Come, Claire. Let's see if we still have horses."

She let him guide her along, but then paused, looking back. "What will happen to them?"

"They'll die quickly."

"Could we not—"

He forced her on, out of sight. "Not what? Let them free to savage the next group of travelers? Take them to Carrisford for trial? What point in that other than to extend their agony?"

She heard nothing, and when Josce and the men emerged there was nothing to see except, perhaps, that the squire looked a little pale. She suspected he hadn't seen much killing yet. She was very grateful that Thomas had been left with the men guarding the camp.

The horses were all present, fed, and watered. It was only as she went to mount that Claire realized she didn't have the book. She turned to the woods. "I must look for my book."

Renald stopped her. "I'll go."

She shook her head at him. "Dead bodies don't frighten me."

"Live ones should. At least two of your attackers went free."

She'd forgotten. She wasn't used to the idea of someone wanting her dead.

She didn't complain, however, about Renald and three men escorting her back, swords drawn. They followed the path of churned-up ground and broken branches that showed where she'd been taken. She paused to pluck a scrap of her torn skirt off some brambles. "I think I dropped the book here."

The ground was deep in leaf mold, and settled over by fallen leaves and branches. Small plants and bushes captured drifts of them where a brown book could hide. Still, by the time they had to give up, she felt that they'd searched everywhere.

"Perhaps it wasn't here. I can't be sure."

They went farther, the men poking their swords into likely spots. "Brown wooden boards could disappear here," Renald said, kicking aside a rotten tree stump. "I'm sorry, Claire. It's a bitter loss."

"I hope those brigands spend their due time in purgatory. What did they want with me anyway?"

He turned her back toward the camp. "I don't think they knew. The one who paid them? Interesting, isn't it? You aren't an heiress, to be snatched for property."

"And he wanted me dead." She shivered. "It frightens me."

He was looking at the ground near the brambles one last time. "And me. We must press on, or we'll have to stop on the road. I daren't risk traveling at night now." He put an arm around her. "I'll keep you safe, Claire, as long as I have breath in my body."

His strength and skill was a comfort, as was the feel of his once-hated mail. But protecting her had almost cost him his life.

He wasn't immortal or invincible.

She had decided she couldn't turn her back on him, but now she could lose him to this evil.

Who was the danger? Who wanted her dead?

Hours later, when they came in sight of Carrisford Castle, solid and strong with its stone walls and tower, she knew why Renald didn't entirely trust wood. Thick, high stone walls seemed very comforting, when wolves prowled. Passing through gates into a long, easily defended tunnel, she felt she'd be very safe if she could be sure the enemy was outside.

"You'll be safe here," he said, and she could sense his relief.

She spoke her fears. "What if the man who wanted me dead can get in?"

He stared at her. "He was Norman?"

She thought. "I'm not sure. He spoke in English, but— Yes, I think so. Do Normans live in the woods with brigands?"

"Very few. And clearly the man hired them. By the rood, Claire. Do not be alone. Ever."

"Willingly, but I wish I knew who to fear."

She searched through her acquaintance for the villain, pausing on the Earl of Salisbury. He'd been angry at her marriage. Could he be angry enough to try to kill? It seemed impossible, but no other likely name came to mind.

Now she came to think of it, they'd never considered him as a possible murderer of Ulric. She couldn't imagine his motive, but certain sure, if he was at court, she'd avoid him!

One enemy certainly was in Carrisford. Here she would have to face the king, and by her vow she could not show how much she blamed him for her father's death. But here she would consummate her marriage to Renald. Hours of riding had settled her wildness, but not changed her mind. She refused to think anymore about right and wrong. Life was precarious, and she would seize what happiness she could.

On the great square keep three banners flew. One belonged to the Lord of Carrisford, one was the gold lions of the king. The other was stark bars of green and black.

"Whose is the third banner?"

"FitzRoger's. It only flies when he's here. He gave Imogen lordship of Carrisford."

She turned to him. "Lordship?"

"Don't get ideas. Carrisford was hers by right and she struck a hard bargain before she'd wed him."

"*Imogen?*" Claire tried not to sound as surprised as she was. The Flower of the West, Lord

Bernard's pretty, pampered daughter, had struck a hard bargain with Bastard FitzRoger of Cleeve?

Then she saw the lord and lady waiting to greet them and knew that Imogen had changed. She stood differently for one thing, every line proclaiming that she was no longer a girl, but a woman.

And her hair.

Claire suppressed a laugh. They'd make a matched pair. Lady Imogen's famous hair, that had reached to her knees in honey-gold waves, now only brushed her shoulders.

"Did she cut it in protest, too?" she asked Renald.

"What?"

"Her hair."

"Oh. Not at all. She cut one plait to escape. There was nothing for it then but to cut the other."

"Escape?" Claire suddenly remembered that this was not a pretty tale. "Was that before or after he whipped her?"

Renald flashed her a look. "She wasn't escaping FitzRoger. There's no time now. Get Imogen to tell you the whole story."

The moment of horror passed. If Imogen was to tell it, it could not reflect too badly on her husband, because Imogen was no beaten, terrified wife. She was tilting her head to make a comment to the man beside her, smile bright.

So that was the mighty and feared FitzRoger of Cleeve. Claire had expected someone bigger, someone rather like Baldwin of Biggin.

She should have known Renald's confrere would not be of that type.

He stood beside his wife but slightly back, clearly giving her the lordship here. He dominated all the same. He wasn't a monster of a man, but Claire wasn't sure she'd be able to drive any sort of bargain with him.

Something in the way he stood, in the lines of his body and face, said *hard*, said ruthless. He reminded her of the first impression she'd had of Renald—the war-wolf ready to kill. With Bastard FitzRoger, however, she doubted there was a softer, gentler side. She had no trouble believing that he would whip a rebellious wife. She pitied Imogen, even if the young woman did seem to be happy with her fate.

Had Imogen really knocked him out? The man looked as invulnerable as Carrisford's stone tower.

But then, as the horses stopped and Claire waited for Renald to help her down, she remembered how easily her own husband had been thrown into danger. Strong men and good fighters though they doubtless were— perhaps some of the best—they were only flesh and blood, and thus vulnerable.

Even, it would appear, to a determined young woman with a rock. Or a stick. Her blow behind the knees would bring down even FitzRoger if she had chance to use it.

With some surprise she realized what had happened today.

Renald was setting her on the ground. "You look troubled."

"I've just realized that I helped kill."

She expected some kind of debate on the rights and wrongs of it—wanted it—but he simply said, "I'm very glad you did," and led her toward their hosts.

Killing, she thought. All in a day's work.

But he'd said she must accept the sword and now she did. Or at last, she accepted that when her loved ones were threatened, she too could become a wolf.

## Chapter 24

Claire tried to decide whether FitzRoger was a handsome man or not. There was something about his elegant features and dark hair that said yes, but the harsh overlay and a scar or two made him something else.

If Renald was granite, FitzRoger was black marble.

His smile was pleasant enough, however, as he greeted her, and turned startlingly warm when he spoke to Renald. Claire winced at her own misjudgment. Like brothers, she remembered, as she watched them embrace.

Then Imogen pulled Claire in for a greeting kiss. "Is everything all right now? It must have been terrible." She wrapped an arm around Claire's waist and led her up the wooden steps that climbed the outside of the stone keep. "Everyone was upset about your father. And your hair! Isn't it strange? I'm growing mine, of course, but I must admit it's a great deal easier to have so much less of it. The queen is so excited."

"About your hair?" Imogen hadn't changed entirely. She'd always been a chatterbox.

Imogen chuckled. "No! About your wedding! Or your wedding night. She loves weddings. Come and make your curtsy."

In all the turmoil, Claire had forgotten to prepare to face Henry Beauclerk. She was glad to have her vow to Renald to guide her. She curtsied low before the chair upon which the king sat, then raised her head to look at him. On the surface he hadn't changed. Dark hair framed bright eyes in a comely face marked quite distinctly with ruthlessness.

"Lady Claire, we are pleased to see you. Rise, and sit beside me."

Claire obeyed, taking a stool by his chair, as he greeted Renald. "How goes Summerbourne, my lord?"

"Well, sire. May I present Thomas, son of Lord Clarence."

Thomas looked flushed, though whether with excitement or nervousness, Claire couldn't tell. She worried still that he might suddenly turn rash, but he knelt properly.

The king leaned forward to raise his chin. "Young Thomas. You've grown into a fine lad. Will you like being a page in my household?" Claire saw the king's searching look, and knew what he checked for. Rebellion.

Thomas frowned and hesitated, and Claire's heart missed a beat. Then he said, "I don't know, sire. I don't know what to expect."

Henry laughed. "A sensible answer. Do you like horses and hawks? Swordplay and fighting?"

"Oh, yes, sire."

"Then you will like my household as long as you are obedient and work hard." The king crooked a finger and a lad of about Thomas's age hastened forward to kneel.

"Bruno, this is Thomas of Summerbourne. Take care of him."

In moments, Thomas was gone, swallowed up in the king's enormous household. Claire resisted a weak urge to reach out and hold him back.

"I will have a mind to him," said the king, clearly seeing her concern. She looked at him, remembering Renald's words. He probably meant what he said, though she was still sure he must have an uneasy conscience over whatever he'd done to be sure that her father could not win.

"The Summerbourne angels," Henry said, studying her. "I called you two that, you know."

"Yes, sire. As in the story about Pope Gregory."

"Indeed. That was how I felt when I saw you at your father's knee. Such pretty children, and so very English in your looks. I was born in England, you know, and I have an English wife." He patted the hand of his fair-haired queen. "Perhaps our children will be little angels, too."

Before Claire could think what to say, he frowned. "I am not pleased, however, by this new fashion for ladies to chop off their hair."

Claire couldn't help but share a glance with Imogen.

"Nor," said the king, "with a certain boldness we detect among the young women of the kingdom. Lady Imogen, at least, should have learned her lesson."

To Claire's surprise, at this casual reference to her whipping, Imogen just smiled.

Henry shook his head and raised his queen's hand to his lips. "You would both do well to take the example of my sweet wife."

With soft fair hair—properly long—and large, gentle eyes, Queen Matilda did seem sweetly docile. "It is a shame," she said, "that your hair is so short, Lady Claire. But hair at least grows. Poor Imogen is blemished."

Claire hadn't noticed, but now she saw a pale scar down Imogen's cheek. Her mouth went dry. More brutality of her husband's?

Suddenly she wavered with doubts. This was a world as unreal as the pictures she drew on parchment. The king seemed gentle and benign, but everyone knew him to be ruthless. He'd proved it when he'd arranged an old friend's death.

The queen seemed content, but she, too, was a forced bride. The only reason for the union was that she carried the blood of the old royal house of England in her veins.

Imogen seemed to be a happy bride, but she couldn't be, could she, when she'd been beaten and scarred, and had tried to escape. Perhaps she had to pretend for fear of more of the same?

So, what did this say about Thomas's fate, and her own?

"With your leave, sire," said Imogen, "Lady

Claire must be exhausted after such a long journey. May I take her to rest before we eat?"

Claire realized that she must have sat in dazed silence for far too long.

The queen leaned forward to pat her head as if she were a dog. "Of course. We certainly want the bride well rested before tomorrow night."

Claire rose and curtsied, happy to escape.

Tomorrow night. And now doubts were coming back to crush her.

Imogen led Claire and her maids up a wide inner staircase to the upper floor, then through a maze of rooms to a small chamber in a corner of the keep. It could just hold one large, curtained bed and a bench beneath a narrow window. Herbs hung in bags to sweeten the air, however, and the hangings were rich.

"I'm afraid with the king and his court here, we're desperately short of space. If this wasn't going to serve as your wedding bower, you'd be five to a bed like the rest of us."

Claire sat on the bench, suddenly exhausted. "I'm still not sure..."

"No?" Imogen's glance was sharp. Oh yes, she had definitely changed. "The king is set on it."

Was that fear in her voice?

Claire dismissed her maids. "Imogen, what happened between you and your husband?"

Imogen perched on the edge of the bed. "Happened?"

"Your marriage. Was it forced?"

"Not exactly... Oh, do you think I was dragged to the altar screaming? No. I needed a man to protect me, and FitzRoger was an excellent choice."

"So you could have said no?"

Imogen grinned. "No. But by then I didn't really want to."

"You love him?"

"Of course."

"But he whipped you!"

Imogen wriggled back to sit cross-legged on the bed. It was a childish position, but there was nothing naive about her manner. "Who told you that?"

"Isn't it true?"

"Yes and no. I simply wondered what form of the story was out there."

"I was told you knocked him out, and in retaliation he locked you up and whipped you."

"Interesting. And mostly true." She looked astonishingly cheerful about it. "The long story will have to wait, but the short one is that we were imprisoned by Arnulf of Warbrick. De Bellême's brother?"

Claire nodded with a shudder. She'd heard Warbrick was as bad as his monstrous brother.

"It was awful. But when we had him at our mercy, FitzRoger was set upon fighting him to the death. One of these man things. No one else would stop him, so I knocked him out."

Claire blinked at the prosaic words. "You didn't think he'd win? Renald says he never loses."

"Normally, he doesn't. But he was wounded. When we had Warbrick in our power it seemed wrong to give him even the smallest chance. But you know men..." She shrugged.

Claire wasn't sure she did, or not the wolfish sort of men, but she could see that Imogen's interference wouldn't have gone down well. "What happened?"

"Well, after I'd had Warbrick killed—"

"*What?*"

Imogen dismissed that with a wave of her hand. "I simply ordered our men to fill him full of arrows. So, after that, Renald carried me off to Cleeve. That's FitzRoger's castle—"

"Imprisoned you, you mean."

Imogen laughed. "Oh, poor Renald. How can you think it? He just wanted me out of reach of FitzRoger's first rage. It was probably as well, though I wanted to nurse him."

Claire rubbed her head, feeling dizzy. "But then when FitzRoger did recover, he put you on trial and whipped you."

"No. The king put me on trial, pressured by the other barons. *They* really wanted my skin. For some reason," she added with a wicked glint in her eye, "men don't like to hear of a woman knocking out her husband to make him see sense."

Claire couldn't help but laugh. "But surely Lord FitzRoger didn't have to whip you."

"It *is* a grievous offense. Attacking a husband is bad enough, but attacking a vassal of the king is the same as attacking the king himself."

Claire crossed herself. "But even so—"

"But even so, he managed to make it symbolic. Only one stroke, and over my clothes."

She rolled her eyes. "He was *so* angry! He wouldn't have had to do that if I'd taken the oath."

"The oath?"

"Never to do such a thing again. Henry and he had set it up, you see. A way out. But I *would* do it again. Better a whipping than to see him dead. I couldn't take a false oath."

"No. Of course not." Claire stared at a hanging on the far wall. How close this was to her father's case. He hadn't been able to take a false oath, either, but Henry hadn't tried to make the punishment symbolic.

Or rather, she realized with sudden insight, Henry had again come up against someone who wouldn't take the easy way out.

Henry and Renald. Now she understood Renald's anger at her father.

Just as FitzRoger had been angry at his wife for making him whip her, Renald was angry at her father, angry at being forced to be an executioner.

What's more, if Claire had thought to stop her father, stop him physically as Imogen had stopped her husband, all this might never have happened.

Imogen slid to her feet. "I've chattered too much and tired you even more. I'll send your ladies."

"No." Claire put out a hand to stop her. "It's only that your story makes me think. About my father." She wasn't ready to pursue her interrupted thoughts openly, so she addressed another. "I love Renald, but I'm still uneasy in my mind about the fact that he killed my father."

"As I would be. But it was a court battle."

"But such an unequal one!"

"Before God, that doesn't matter."

Claire searched Imogen for a trace of doubt. "Do you believe that?"

"Of course. Don't you?"

"Yes. So I can't see how my father lost."

Claire knew she should keep her counsel, but she had to talk to someone and Imogen seemed to have a sharp insight. She lowered her voice to a whisper. "I still feel that the king murdered his brother, so if God had a hand in that battle, my father should have won."

Imogen pushed a tendril of hair out of her eyes. "But that wasn't what the trial was about."

Claire stared at her. "It wasn't? What then?"

"Your father's treason, and thus the king's right to the throne."

"That's the same thing."

"Not really. It's all to do with elections and consent and things. I don't pay much attention. But would you rather have Duke Robert ruling England through de Bellême and his like?" When Claire didn't answer, Imogen shook her head. "I'm chattering again. I'll call your maids."

Stunned by the new idea, by a light as hopeful as dawn, Claire had to know one more thing. "Stop a moment! How did your cheek get scarred?"

Imogen turned at the door, touching the long

pale line. "Do you think FitzRoger did it? Poor man. Everyone thinks he's harsh, but truly, he isn't. Or not unless he has to be," she added carelessly.

Oh yes, Imogen had changed.

"He'd never willingly hurt me," she continued, without a trace of doubt. "This happened when I was escaping Warbrick's men. I smashed the lanthorn and a jagged piece of the horn cut me." She smiled, still stroking the mark. "I was afraid he'd be disgusted by me. It looked awful when it was healing, and there was my hair as well. But he pointed out all his scars. He's a good man. So's Renald. And Renald's a great deal sweeter."

She disappeared, calling for the maids. Claire stayed on the bed, buffeted by a dozen new thoughts, all of them hopeful.

Renald and FitzRoger were up on the wall—one of the few private places in the crowded castle. Guards patrolled, but they were not many in a time when no danger threatened, and they knew to keep their distance.

Renald gave his friend a brief account of the last few months.

Leaning back against the battlements, FitzRoger asked, "Do you regret taking the task for me?"

"No." After a moment, he added, "I love her."

"Clearly."

"Is it that obvious?"

"Perhaps only to a friend. What worries you?"

Renald grimaced. "Terrifies, more like. I've

428

made her swear an oath, but... She believes that the king had his brother killed—"

"So does most of England."

"But she thinks that means her father's cause was just. Therefore the fight was unfair. She hates everything about it." He told his friend about the betrothal banquet and the sword.

"Salisbury, as you say, trying the indirect route."

"And Claire has made me promise not to act against him over it. He's her godfather."

"It's probably as well. Henry wants things to settle, not be stirred."

"At least that attack on the road may have convinced her that fighting skills are not all evil. But what if her beliefs overwhelm her promise, and she accuses Henry to his face?"

FitzRoger winced. "She's sworn not to?"

"I forced her." Renald pulled a face. "I threatened to break her leg if she didn't."

"A bit crude."

"What else was I to do? Refuse the king's 'invitation'? Claim she was ill and lock her up? Even if we could pull off the deception, her people would release her."

"Could you have done it? Injured her?"

"Could you?" Renald countered.

After a thoughtful moment, FitzRoger shrugged. "Yes. Just as Imogen would knock me unconscious again. Love drives us to strange behaviors. And speaking of love..."

Little in his face showed his feelings as Imogen climbed the wooden stairs to join them, holding her veil against the breeze.

"Oh, pest," she said, and pulled off both headcloth and circlet, leaving her cinnamon curls to be tossed by the wind. "Renald, I think you'll be pleased to know that I've told your bride all about my folly and punishment, and blown away some of her fears. She seemed to think poor FitzRoger had split open my face." She went into Renald's arms for a hug and a kiss. "You, however, are looking weighed down by cares, my friend."

"While you are blooming, little flower."

She smiled and went to stand by FitzRoger. "Three months' blooming, though it hardly shows yet."

"Congratulations."

FitzRoger moved a finger to play in her hair and she smiled. Renald watched, wondering if he and Claire could ever achieve the peaceful connection he saw between these two. They'd started in acrimony, but not with a father's death between them.

"I think she'll consummate the marriage tomorrow," he said.

FitzRoger's brows rose. "You don't look particularly happy about it."

"It won't mean much if she still thinks it's wrong." He laughed wryly. "If I'd had any sense, I would have taken her into the bushes and done it when she was exalted by battle fever on the road."

"With a murderer on hand? Highly unwise. Who do you think was behind that?"

"I have no idea. No one has any reason to wish Claire dead. But if they did, an arrow could have done it. Why drag her away?"

"Rape?" asked Imogen, then answered herself. "No, they can't have thought they'd have time. Could they have thought her someone else?"

"I don't see how."

"At least she's safe now."

"Is she? She said the other man, the one who'd paid, sounded Norman. He could come here."

"We'll put guards on her when she's not by your side," said FitzRoger.

"Which will be rarely if I have my say."

"Ah, how sweet to see another man victim to a woman's power."

Imogen elbowed him in the ribs. "And here am I, weak for love."

FitzRoger turned her face to his. "Is that a seductive request, wife?"

Her color flared. "We've been sharing other beds for three nights now—"

"How true. And had scarce a minute to steal during the day. Renald, go away."

"But I have so many matters I wish to discuss," Renald teased.

FitzRoger never stopped smiling into his wife's eyes. "Go, or die."

As Renald left, laughing, he heard her say, "The place is too crowded. We can't—"

He grinned, sure that his friend would find a way. After all, failing all else, the massive walls of Carrisford keep were riddled with secret passageways. He'd check later for cobwebs in their hair.

Claire woke to darkness in a strange room, and it took a moment for her to remember where she was. But *darkness*? An oblong of paler dark showed where the window was, proof that it must be night. She'd lain on the bed to think, and must have fallen asleep. She still had her clothes on.

There were bodies in the bed with her, and she assumed they were her maids. She shook the one closest. "Wake up."

"Wha... ? Oh, lady!"

Claire recognized the voice. "Maria, I need to piss. Where should I go?"

"We have a pot, lady." Maria scrambled out of bed, waking Prissy.

"Do you need anything else, lady?" Prissy asked sleepily.

Claire hated to send her off around the castle in the middle of the night, but she was desperately hungry. "Something to eat and drink," she said as she climbed out of bed to use the pot.

"We have food." Prissy could be heard stumbling over something on the floor. She brought over a wooden box.

Claire opened it and felt inside. "What's here?"

"Only cheese and bread, lady. And we have watered wine." She brought a wooden cup and Claire drank thirstily.

"You can both go back to sleep. I can feed myself."

The maids tumbled back into the bed and in moments she heard their soft sleep-breathing.

A lifetime of sleeping with her aunts had

taught Claire never to leave an empty space or the others would take it over, so she sat on the bed to eat and go over her thoughts.

Perhaps her brain had been working on the situation as she slept, for it all seemed clear to her now. Her father had fought to establish his innocence of treason—which meant that the question became whether Henry was rightful King of England or not. Perhaps if he'd fought on the question of whether the king had killed his brother, he might—by the power of God—have won. The king's right to rule, however, did not hinge on whether he'd killed the former king or not.

Why hadn't she seen that before?

In history, rulers frequently took power by conquest and slaughter.

Claire knew a bit more about laws and the English crown than Imogen did. The king was elected by the great lords. The wishes of the last king were taken into account, and the crown generally went to the oldest legitimate son, but it still had to be ratified by election.

So, did Henry Beauclerk have the right to the throne? He was, as Renald said, acclaimed by the nobles and anointed by the Church.

And Imogen was right. Who would want Robert of Normandy ruling here, particularly when his supporters included such devils as de Bellême?

It was quite possible, therefore, that her father had asked a question—did Henry have the right to the throne of England—to which the answer was yes. Henry had the right because he was the choice of most men, and he was the best suited to bear good fruit.

And thus, her father had died without any need of cheating.

Truly, Claire wished she'd had the vision to see this months ago. Then she might have had the courage to do as Imogen had done and prevent her father by force from taking the path to death. But now, she could throw off her doubts of evildoing. She could never forget that Renald had struck her father's death-blow, but she understood now why he felt no guilt.

At least that riddle was solved.

Perhaps, as Renald had said, life didn't neatly fall into good and bad, virtue and vice. If her father had understood that, if he'd steeped himself more in the confusion of real life, perhaps he wouldn't have died.

Claire sighed, popping the last of the cheese into her mouth. If she'd seen more of real life, perhaps she would have recognized the danger in time to prevent it.

Renald had threatened to injure her so she wouldn't be able to come to court. He'd been willing to hurt her to protect her from even greater danger. She knew she would do the same for him if the case ever arose.

She, like Imogen, would rather give pain and risk punishment than watch the death of anyone she loved.

Nearby, Renald lay sleepless on a straw mattress on the floor of a crowded room, surrounded by the snuffles, snores, and smell of a dozen sleeping men. There was a bit more space than there should have been, however, because FitzRoger was not here.

Clearly having bethought themselves of the secret passageways, the host and hostess had settled in there. What were damp and a few rats when lovers wanted to be together?

As he wanted to be with Claire.

As they would be this time tomorrow, God willing.

He worried, though.

No secrets lay between them now, but his very nature did. Despite the ambush on the road, her rescue, and her own burst of violence, he wondered whether she would always be uneasy with the fact that he must fight and kill.

He didn't revel in violence, but he didn't flinch from it, either. He was good at fighting, he enjoyed the fire of it, and it was all too often necessary to protect the things he valued.

He valued Claire—that was too mild a term for a passion that now ruled his life. If she came to him troubled, however, their love would shatter under the strain.

He'd rather lose her than cause her that sort of pain.

Suddenly, he had an idea of how to test the blade before it struck. He hesitated, because any tested blade could fail, but better now than later. He put his hands under his head and thought the whole thing through.

# Chapter 25

To her surprise, Claire slept again and was awoken by Prissy shaking her. Maria stood behind with a breakfast tray. Claire sat up in daylight, to the sound of a busy castle.

"What hour is it?"

"Gone terce, lady. And you are asked for."

Claire scrambled out of bed, wincing from a headache grown out of too much sleep. "By the king?"

"And the queen. And your husband." Prissy poured warm water into a bowl and Claire began to wash, demanding the clothes she had worn for her wedding. This was, in a way, a second wedding day.

Not too far away, her second wedding night awaited.

"There's to be fighting," Maria said.

"What?" Claire looked to where her maid was peeping out of the long narrow window. "We are attacked?" she asked with sudden panic, even thinking that her mysterious attacker still pursued.

"Nay, lady," Maria said with a laugh. "For fun! For your delayed bridals. They're building a stand. You're to sit there with the king and queen."

Claire picked out the rap of hammers. "For fun," she muttered and went back to washing. Though she'd witnessed the need for wolves to fight off other wolves, and even shown a touch of wolfishness herself, she still did not like the idea of anyone fighting for fun.

She remembered Renald confessing to enjoying it. She remembered his glow when he rode back from killing the brigand knights. She remembered him holding his sword between them and demanding that she accept the sword as well as him.

"Will my husband fight?" she asked, already knowing the answer.

"Oh yes, lady. He's to fight against Lord FitzRoger. Everyone says it's a wonder to see them. Though they do say," she added with a wary look at Claire, "that Lord FitzRoger is better."

"My Lord Renald says the same thing, so it's likely true." Claire didn't relish having to watch a fight. She certainly didn't look forward to watching Renald lose. "At least they should know better than to hurt each other."

She dried herself and dressed, hoping she appeared calmer than she felt. It wasn't the faint chance of injury that upset her. It was that she suspected Renald had set this up deliberately. He was going to show her the full nature of the blooded sword—force her to accept it—before she committed herself.

He deserved to be nibbled to death by fleas. How could he doubt her? Doubting her, how could he force her to this? Tugging a circlet down on her troublesome hair, she fretted. What if she failed? In her heart she still hated the harsher world, hated armor and swords and the calluses men had to put on body and soul to use them.

She was determined to be sensible, and she'd persuaded herself that Renald had not done anything truly wrong in killing her father, but she still worried that she could not wholeheartedly embrace the sword.

"Nibbled to death by eels!" she muttered, startling her maids.

Dressed in her finery, with her veil already slipping, Claire left her room to find Josce awaiting. It gave her a start, reminding her how once he'd guarded her, but then she realized he was her protective guard now, in case her would-be murderer was about.

Angry at that unknown villain, she made her way to the great hall. Hung with banners, and gleaming with precious plate on sideboards all around, Carrisford's hall was full of noise, sweat, and richly dressed bodies. At long tables nobles, ladies, and clerks broke their fast. Servants wove around with jugs and platters. Dogs were everywhere, as were young pages, who were mostly as troublesome as the hounds, and as likely to snitch food. Claire glimpsed Thomas once, weaving through the crowd at a run along with two other boys.

They might be on urgent business, but she feared not. They looked as if they were up to mischief. Instinctively, she moved to follow and control, but then she stopped herself. She must let him go. If he fell into mischief and was corrected, it would do him good.

Summerbourne was lost to him anyway, and he needed to be among men. The past weeks under Renald's firm rule had done wonders for him. He might look like an Angel of Summerbourne, but if he was, he was more like the Archangel Michael, warrior of the heavenly host. It was hardly surprising. He came of warrior blood on both sides of the family.

So did she. She prayed that blood would run in her veins today as she watched her beloved fight.

Where was he?

If she was asked for by husband, king, and queen, she didn't know where to find them. Claire was thinking of seeking the peace of the garden when a page found her and led her to the solar.

This handsome room's walls were hidden by rich hangings, and there was even a woven cloth on the floor. Carrisford was rich. The queen sat by the window attended by a dozen ladies. She beckoned Claire over and demanded a full account of the betrothal and wedding.

Claire skipped the bloody sword but she had to mention the corpse and listen to the details of a fruitless search for a murderer.

"We were all most distressed by your father's death," the queen said at last. "So discourteous of him."

Claire bit back a sharp protest. With her new understanding of the matter, she could understand what the queen meant, but the woman lacked tact.

"Such wonderful stories as Lord Clarence told," Matilda said. "And the riddles. Very clever. Do entertain us with a story, Lady Claire."

Claire stared at her. "Highness, I do not have my father's gift."

The queen frowned. "Surely you can remember some of his work. You must have heard it often."

"Yes, Highness, but I do not have his gift of telling." The frown deepened. "Perhaps I can try to remember some of his riddles."

The royal frown eased. "Yes, do so."

Claire wondered how people lived their days under this kind of tyranny. She searched her memory, however, fearing that the queen must have heard them all. She recollected one she'd made up herself and tried to tell it right. "Sharp to the attack am I, with mighty followers, determined to change all in my wake. None can withstand my mighty thrust, and yet I am gentle as can be, and seek to improve not to destroy. Often I shed blood, but not by my will, and when I have passed my mighty way, I leave the world enhanced behind me. What am I?"

When the ladies looked at one another, pondering, she knew that at least she'd found a novelty for them.

"Sounds like my husband," said one matron with a smile. "He always thinks the world best for his roaring and fighting."

A chuckle ran around the room, threaded with agreements.

"But," said the queen, "Lady Claire said *what* am I, not who. I cannot think of an object so brutal yet kind. Would a conquering army fit? Perhaps the army of my lord husband's father conquering England and leaving it the better?"

Claire couldn't think of anything diplomatic to say to that. Matilda was of the English royal line and Claire thought she should-n't be quite so enthusiastic about the Norman invaders.

"By your leave, Highness," said one older lady, "I doubt any army would claim to be gentle, or to not want to shed blood."

They tossed out suggestions, some clever, some silly.

"A plow."

"A ship."

"A penis!"

"Mighty followers?" someone questioned.

"His balls!" called out one young woman, and everyone laughed.

They all looked at Claire, sure they had it, and she had to admit it fit in many aspects. She was also rather embarrassed at the cheerful bawdiness of them all. "I'm not sure it could be said to enhance the world, my ladies."

"Try telling that to any man," remarked the matron with a twinkle. "So, if we don't have it, Lady Claire, give us a hint."

"This is a ladies' matter—"

She was interrupted by the bold young woman saying, "So is stick and balls!"

"In fact," Claire added quickly, "it is something some of you are engaged in now."

"Not something some of us *wish* we were engaged in, Alida," said the queen, and the younger woman laughed. "So, what are we doing that could fit?"

They all looked around, and then the queen clapped her hands. "It is sewing. No, it is a needle! The needle breaks through cloth and drags the thread—its followers. It does not seek to shed blood, but alas often pierces our fingers. And it does leave the world much enhanced. How very clever."

As everyone echoed the queen's praise, Matilda said, "Do ask another one, Lady Claire."

Hoping her inner sigh was not obvious, Claire found another. And another. And another. When the king came in and interrupted, she could have fallen at his feet and kissed his boots.

Of course, the queen immediately told him her favorites of the riddles—which she tangled so that the meaning was much too clear. After some time of this, he came to Claire. "I thank you for amusing the queen so well, Lady Claire."

"They were mostly my father's riddles, sire, and I fear I do not tell them as well as he." Despite everything, she could not keep a hint of bitterness from her voice. She still couldn't believe that this powerful man could not have turned fate.

"Truly, he had a gift." The king seemed unaware of her tone. "He said he planned to write down his stories and riddles. Was any of that done?"

"My father had little patience for fine script, sire. I was writing them for him. I had only just begun the work."

"Continue it before they slip from your memory, and before children take up your time. I would like to see such a book."

It was almost a royal command, and Claire took it as such even though his manner distressed her. He clearly had no feelings about her father at all.

"What of your father's journal?" the king asked. "He always had writing materials with him. At the end, he often wrote." He must have seen something in her face, for he added, "Do you expect me not to speak of it, as if I had an uneasy conscience?"

It was a direct challenge and carried a warning. The king was commanding her to accept his right. Yesterday it might have pushed her into disaster despite her vow to Renald. Today she could say, "It upsets me, sire, as is only natural. But not through any fault of yours. It was a death, and a death I would have prevented if I could."

"As would I," said the king shortly. "So, what happened to his book? I would like to read what he made of that sorry rebellion."

She had to tell him of its loss.

Another royal frown. "You cannot have searched well enough! I will have the location from Lord Renald and send out more men. And you should be more careful with something so precious."

This so closely echoed Felice, that Claire smiled.

"You laugh?" he asked sharply.

"No, sire." Claire struggled for an acceptable explanation. "Or yes, but only because everyone is always saying that of me. It is a sad failing. I lost my own book at Summerbourne not long ago. And someone chided me for leaving it by a window..." She trailed off, seeking to pin down who that had been.

Felice? She didn't think so, yet it seemed important that she remember...

"Lady Claire!" The king's voice was sharp and Claire found herself helped to a bench by the king's own hand. She blinked up at him. "Have I so distressed you that you turn faint?"

Now the queen was there, fussing, and all her ladies were gathering. "No, sire. I apologize. I must still be tired from the journey."

"And doubtless the queen has demanded too many riddles. I come to escort the queen to witness the contests. I hope you are not too weak to attend, for you are to have a place of honor."

It was virtually a command, so Claire said, "Not at all, sire," and rose to take his hand. He gave the other to the queen and led them both out.

At least during the progress to the stand Claire had some opportunity to think, for the queen chattered all the way.

Who had accused her of being careless with a book? And why did she feel it was important? She couldn't really be accused of carelessness with her father's book, except in bringing it on the journey at all.

Claire found herself seated at the queen's right hand and victim of Matilda's inane chatter. She thanked heaven she was not a lady of the court, obliged to put up with this day after day.

However, Claire became truly interested in the sport. Horse riding and archery had a kind of beauty, and quarterstaff fighting was rather like the sword dance. Though she knew a stone from a slingshot could kill, she couldn't see the target practice as unpleasant.

She definitely enjoyed watching the young men doing acrobatics in their chain mail to show their strength and agility. When she spotted Josce among them, she cheered him on.

But when the events turned to swordplay, sadness assailed her. These men were all so well-honed. She couldn't forget that her father had left his books and his rabbit-fur rug to challenge their world.

Assailed by the clang and grunt of it, she began to shake. This was all leading up to Renald fighting, and she had to be ready to accept it. She couldn't fail. She *couldn't*! Yet already she was shaken by a panicky reaction she couldn't control.

By the time he and FitzRoger came out to fight, she wished he'd be nibbled to death by ferrets. Then, perhaps, he'd know how she felt.

They walked into the open space prepared for them, two men of iron. Despite their different builds, they were alike in one thing— the ease with which they moved within their armor. Like fish in water or birds in the air, they were in their natural metier, and beautiful.

The stand was crowded with nobles, and many of the court had joined the castle folk in the rough circle within which the two men would fight. Children sat at the front, eager for the entertainment. No one wanted to miss this treat, to miss seeing prime predators in action.

Try as she might, Claire couldn't avoid seeing Renald as the dark warrior who had come to claim Summerbourne. Mail covered him to the knee, belted at the waist. His coif was up, his helmet laced. He was ready to kill.

But then, with a start, she realized he was different, and not only because she knew him now, and loved him. Today, he was relaxed and completely unwary. He smiled as he chatted to his opponent, then laughed at something FitzRoger said, teeth white.

FitzRoger was dressed exactly the same, though no one could mistake one man for the other. In mail, Renald looked solid, massive, like the warhorse she had once likened him to. FitzRoger was much leaner, and his mail seemed to flow over him, making him like a gray wolf on the prowl.

Claire's panic twisted into other ways as she recognized the danger in this man. He was better than Renald, by Renald's cheerful admission. If this were a true fight, he would win and Renald would die.

Already, she didn't want to see this.

"Are you all right, Lady Claire?" The queen's voice seemed to come from a distance, but Claire made herself turn and smile.

"Oh yes, Highness."

"You seem a little pale. Perhaps it's the heat. Wine!" she commanded sharply, and Claire found herself clutching a goblet. The wine shivered in echo of her trembling hands.

She raised the cup and managed to drink without spilling, and the strong wine did steady her. In fact, her spurt of terror seemed ridiculous now, with the two combatants chatting to the king. But then she became fretful in a more practical way. They were just like Thomas and his friends, laughing about taking risks. True, they were armored and their swords were blunted, but as she'd always been telling her brother, accidents could happen.

Then the king said, "At it, my friends, and fight well."

Renald turned to her and held out his hand. She put hers in it, hoping it didn't feel chill and unsteady. Perhaps it did, for his smile faded. "Alas," he said, kissing her fingers, "I can't promise to win for your glory, my dear wife. I can only promise to fight my best."

She tightened her fingers over his. "Just be careful. Be safe."

"But safe is boring!" He grinned and kissed her hand again. "Wish me well."

She raised their joined hands and kissed his fingers. "Of course I do." She remembered when he'd left Summerbourne to fight, left without a blessing. "God go with you," she said.

Perhaps he remembered, too, for his eyes turned deep for a moment before he turned to walk into the center.

FitzRoger kissed Imogen on the lips then joined his friend. Imogen smiled reassuringly. "Don't worry. They've done this lots of times."

Claire really wasn't worried about their safety. She was worried she would react in the wrong way, causing Renald to refuse to complete the marriage. He was capable of that kind of sacrifice.

Very well, then. She was a wolf's bride. She would act the part.

Each man slipped his long shield onto his left arm, and took his sword in his right. No special swords today, for these were blunt. Supposedly safe. They could still break bones, and—as she had pointed out to him—a man could die of a broken bone.

He'd said the same of court battles. That often the fight was won by battering blows.

She wanted to cross herself and pray.

The squires moved back out of the way, and Claire tried desperately to relax. She could not afford to show fear!

Within moments, her hands gripped one another.

If they fought for show, it was to show violence!

The first blows had not been fierce, but now the clang of metal on metal shrieked the ferocity of their attack. They held nothing back. Sweeping sword blows crashed and Claire could *feel* the impact against the blocking shield. She saw the jolt of it, the dents and splinters, saw how impossible it would be to halt. One slip and a sword would burst flesh and bone.

From time to time, both men staggered under the brute force of a blow caught slightly amiss. It didn't seem to halt them for a moment. She saw Renald grin.

Not grimace with effect. *Grin!*

Nibbled to death by rabid dogs while rolling in nettles and stung by wasps...

Sliding out the other side of panic, Claire saw the wildness was an illusion, that control was almost absolute. She could even appreciate, with horrified fascination, something very like the sword dance.

Both men moved in balance, knees flexed, rooted to the earth. The fiercest blows only rocked them. They anticipated and reacted almost perfectly. From years of experience, they probably knew just what the other would do.

However, it wasn't a dance. Both were alert for the smallest mistake, anything that might give the victory.

Oh yes, show fight or not, they both fought to win.

She began to think they were too well-balanced, and that they'd dance themselves into exhaustion. Then FitzRoger made a different kind of move, and almost succeeded in knocking Renald's sword out of his hand. In a wild recover, Renald's shield clipped the edge of his friend's helmet, knocking the man to his knees.

Everyone gasped.

Renald thrust at his friend's throat. FitzRoger could not block it! Surrounded by gasps and a few screams, Claire covered her eyes, but peeped.

Instead of trying to block, FitzRoger gave into the fall and rolled flat, coming to his feet like a cat just out of sword's reach. Amazingly, both men laughed and took a moment to recover as the crowd cheered its approval of the moment.

Show fight or not, everyone was caught up in it. Claire realized some of the nearby men were wagering. FitzRoger was the clear favorite.

A page offered her more wine, and she gulped it greedily.

"An interesting move, that," said the king. "Clearly needs work, though."

"Lord FitzRoger will have a sore head," said the queen. "They must both be growing tired. Should you perhaps stop it, my lord? We don't want the groom too tired for his night's bout."

Claire's face heated, but she hoped fervently that the king would agree. Her nerves wouldn't take much more of this.

The king didn't speak, however, and the fight continued.

That was when Claire saw everything change. FitzRoger took control.

It reminded her again of the sword dance, of the way Renald had mastered Lambert of Vayne. It was only a subtle change at first— Renald had to work harder to match the strokes. She thought perhaps it was something in the angle of attack, and the rhythm. Whatever it was, Renald could only cope. He could no longer make an attacking move.

She realized she was leaning forward, hands over mouth, praying for a miracle that would give Renald a chance. It wasn't fear anymore. It was a kind of battle fever.

She wanted her man to win.

It wasn't to be. FitzRoger somehow put Renald off balance, and beat his sword wide with his shield. At the same moment, he knocked aside Renald's shield enough to threaten his heart with his blade.

Renald threw out his arms in surrender.

The gasp this time was followed by a beat of silence on the stand. Then the common people began to cheer, tossing hats into the air, and chatter started all around her.

Claire noted, however, that the king's hands were clenched tight on the arms of his chair. Had there really been danger there?

Behind her, Claire heard someone say, "That move. But—"

It was almost as if he'd been silenced.

Perhaps it had been improper, if they had rules to their deadly games. Claire was more interested in watching Renald, wanting to be sure that he wasn't hurt.

He and FitzRoger seemed completely relaxed. They unlaced helmets and tossed them to waiting attendants. As they strolled back to the stand, they pushed back coifs to let the breeze cool sweat-damp hair. They were chatting, doubtless going over the fight in detail, as if it had all been the greatest fun.

Which it probably had been.

For them.

"A strange end, that," said the queen, nibbling on an almond. "It wouldn't be a killing blow, that, to the chest."

"Unless the sword could go through mail," said the king.

"But they can't, can they?"

Claire's breath caught. Of course. No wonder people were surprised that a threatened strike at the chest had been seen as deadly, but some—including the king—had recognized the meaning. If FitzRoger had been wielding Renald's dark blade, the thrust could have been deadly.

That last move had been a reenactment of the blow that had killed her father.

Claire couldn't think of a nibbling awful enough.

She was sure that fight—the end of it, at least—had followed the pattern of her father's death fight. Renald was making her face what he was, and what he had done. He had played the part of her father, while FitzRoger had been the executioner. The difference in skill level was not as great, but as Renald had no real chance of defeating FitzRoger, it had been the same in the end.

If she wanted to, she could put her father in Renald's place. She could see him fighting at first in some sort of control, then how in the end he'd been outmatched and Renald had moved in for the kill.

The quick, the skillful, kill.

Renald and FitzRoger were before the king now. Henry's hands had relaxed, but he didn't look pleased. "I trust you have made your point, Lord Renald."

"I hope so, sire."

"I think you could have had him when he went down."

"Perhaps. In your cause, sire, I would have pursued."

"Make sure you do. And you, FitzRoger, that move was not yet ready for combat."

"How better to perfect it, sire, than to try it against a good opponent? I may need it one day in your service."

"But why bother," asked the queen, "when God will decide?"

Claire saw a flicker of communication between the men which probably translated into, "Women!"

The king said, "But my dear, just as I expect my men to train to be fit to do my will, so God expects the same of us all. Should we tax Him to use inferior tools?"

"God is omnipotent, Henry."

"But prefers that His people on earth make suitable attempts to take care of themselves. Come, my dear. No more theology. See, they are setting up for more archery." He turned back to the combatants. "Go rest, my friends, and have your muscles eased. You, especially, Lord Renald, should not exhaust yourself."

Claire knew she'd turned red again, and when Imogen slipped into the seat beside her, she grimaced at her.

"Isn't it strange how everyone talks about it?" Imogen asked. "I'm quite glad to have had a quick and stark wedding."

"I had a feast with all my family and friends. It was lovely, until I found out the truth."

Imogen squeezed her hand. "Are you feeling better about it? If not, we can probably arrange something—"

"Renald," Claire interrupted, glaring at

her departing husband. "He put you up to this, didn't he?"

"He doesn't want you to feel forced."

"Hence the macabre sword fight! I could hit him over the head with a rock, and not for his good, either."

Imogen giggled. "Clearly you love him madly."

Claire had to laugh. "Clearly I do. But I want no more of his *fairness*, thank you. My nerves can't take it. I wish I could speak to him now and tell him I've resolved it in my mind."

"I don't think you can follow him to the bath."

"It's tempting, believe me. I'd like to settle this before we move to other things."

"Bed-play." Imogen's eyes twinkled.

Claire eyed her. She wasn't a friend like Margret, but she was a young woman not long married. After a quick glance around, she asked, "Do you like it?"

"Bed-play? Yes indeed. Are you nervous?"

"A little." She couldn't speak of her first wedding night, but she said, "I don't really know what to do."

"Don't worry. Renald does." She rose. "The queen's leaving."

Matilda turned to them. "My lord husband wishes to hunt," she said. "We poor ladies will be left to our own devices. Lady Imogen, you may play for us."

Claire looked for a chance to slip off to speak to Renald, but found none. A queen's court, she was discovering, left as little freedom as a convent. She soon learned anyway, that he and FitzRoger had been dragged out of their baths to join the hunting party. She certainly hoped her husband was as robust as he seemed.

At least with Imogen and some others commanded to perform, Claire didn't have to amuse. She could think at last about books left by windows. Who had said that, and why was it important... ?

The music was excellent, however, and her mind too giddy with thoughts of the night. Instead of logical analysis, she drifted through the long afternoon in spicy dreams.

## Chapter 26

The men returned raucous and triumphant, the king bursting into the solar still stained with blood and dirt. The blushing queen dismissed everyone, and Claire emerged to find mayhem. The castle was already in frenzied preparation for the evening banquet and now muddy dogs were everywhere along with muddy men wanting wine, food, and baths. The hunt had brought back three deer and numerous small animals, all needing to be attended to by servants already rushed off their feet.

She prayed to heaven that the court never visited Summerbourne.

She tried to find Renald, but soon gave up. They'd be seated together for the feast and perhaps she could talk to him then. She saw Thomas hurrying by, and snagged his tunic. "How are you?"

"Well. Stop fussing, Claire!"

"I'm used to fussing. It'll take a while to break the habit."

He grinned. "You can fuss over Lord Renald instead. Did you see the fight? Wasn't it exciting?"

"It certainly was."

He puffed out his chest. "I'm going to be as good as Lord FitzRoger one of these days."

Claire made herself smile. "I'm sure you will be."

"I've got to go, Claire. If I tarry, I'll get another whipping."

"Whipping!" She reached out to grip his tunic again.

He twitched free. "Oh, not a bad one. And it was worth it. We—" A male voice bellowed his name. "I have to go!" And he was off, clearly driven more by pride in his mission than fear.

Claire went to tidy herself for the evening then returned to the hall. She kept an eye open for Renald simply because she missed him, but it wasn't until the horn sounded for the meal that he appeared. She suspected he'd bathed again. He entered the hall with a group of men, all clean and glowing from the day of action. He smiled for her alone, however, and came over to lead her to the high table for the meal.

"Our wedding banquet," he said as he seated her.

"Again," she remarked.

"And fresh. Not leftovers."

She looked at him, startled, and he shook his head. "I'm not clever enough to say something like that on purpose. No leftovers?"

"None," she said with a smile, but realized this wasn't the place for a long, thoughtful discussion. "I'll explain it all later."

He raised her hand and kissed it. "I'm pleased. But I don't think I'll be in the mood for talk. Later."

He pressed his teeth into the base of her thumb, and her heart started an urgent beat.

They washed their hands, then a server presented some sort of fish. Renald chose some for their trencher. Claire looked at the rich food without appetite. That kind of appetite. "I wish..."

"I know. But we have to wait."

"Why?"

"Custom, remember?" He raised a morsel of fish to her lips and she took it. It was eel, highly seasoned with spices.

"I wonder if it's painful to be nibbled to death by eels?"

His brows rose. "You know someone that happened to?"

"No, but someone narrowly avoided the fate."

He shook his head, clearly recognizing nonsense.

Claire grinned and chose food from the next platter, one of meat. They playfully fed each other through endless courses as they waited for their night. When she fed him a honey cake, however, he captured her hand and slowly licked her fingers clean. "Honey, ginger, cinnamon—"

"Don't," she breathed. "We must have ages still to wait, and I can't bear it—"

"It's surprising what a person can bear."

"I want to drag you to our room. Now."

"I'd resist. Waiting enhances pleasure."

"We've waited a whole month."

"True enough." He took her hand and carried it down beneath the tablecloths to brush over his thigh to his erection, long and hard.

"Are you sure you want to wait?" Wickedly, she rubbed it, delighting in his caught breath, his look almost of agony. When he seized her hand, it hurt.

She bit her lip. She'd forgotten last time. "You started it," she hissed.

"Perhaps I should start something else."

While raising his goblet with his left hand and sipping from it, his right hand released hers and slid between her thighs. He worked a looseness in her skirt so he could press against her.

For a moment she thought of resisting, but then she relaxed. She even spread her thighs, daring him with her eyes, knowing he couldn't go far with this here at the high table. The long cloths covered their legs, but waist up they were exposed to everyone's interested gaze.

His lips twitched a warning. He turned the goblet toward her, presenting it to her lips even as his other hand moved, bringing the tingle of desire, causing her to suddenly shift in her seat. She hastily steadied the goblet with her right hand and sipped, hoping one movement hid the other.

Then she felt him slowly pulling up her skirt, felt his fingers brush her bare thigh. She gulped from the goblet again, trying not to show the way her breathing had changed, fearing her cheeks must be turning red. Surely someone would begin to notice what was going on.

Did he not care?

When she looked at him, his smile widened. He took back the goblet and sipped, then kissed her with winewet lips.

At least the music and chatter drowned her moan.

His hand stilled.

Her first instinct was to protest.

One hand tormentingly still, he put the goblet down and picked up a piece of the meat. He fed it to her, teasing her lips until she took it, until her mouth was full. She felt almost as if he stroked with his other hand, yet it did not move.

As she chewed then swallowed the tender beef, he teased her lips with his fingers, inviting her to lick them, then suck them. Aware at every moment of his other, still fingers, she drew him into her mouth to deliberately savor him with her tongue. Surely he must be suffering as much as she!

Clearly not. Almost breathless, she tried to squirm free of his hand. It was impossible. She wished desperately he'd either do something—lewd though it would be—or leave her in peace. She seized a spoon and fed him a mouthful of herbed barley, then one of stewed cress.

He swallowed. "You think I need nourishment, wife?"

"I'm afraid you might have lost some fat in important places."

"If anything, I'm growing. Feel me and see."

"I can imagine."

"Then imagine me deep inside you, big and hot."

She stared, hit by desire so strong she could almost feel him there, or feel where he should be.

Her spoon tilted, spilling greens on the white cloth. "Please—"

"Wait."

"Wait! It'll be ages yet." She slid her own hand beneath the cloth to try to move his, smiling at him all the time. Of course, he was too strong, but he leaned to kiss her, saying, "Wait. Just a little while."

"There'll be entertainments before they let us go," she said fretfully. "You're a tyrant."

"Remember our first wedding night? I still want you to feel the pleasure before the pain, but when we're alone, I won't be able to wait."

"Then what—"

"Ah, the tumblers. Good."

Indeed, the formal entertainment had begun with a troop of tumblers cartwheeling into the center space. They were extremely clever, and Claire could almost have been fascinated if not for the fingers between her thighs that occasionally flickered in a cruel tease but never moved enough.

What had he been talking about? The pleasure? Here? He *couldn't*.

She heard herself moan, and hastily drowned it in a whole goblet of wine. When the ewerer refilled it, Renald said, "Feed me wine, wife. I find myself engaged elsewhere."

" 'Twould serve you right if I poured it over you."

"I might find the cooling welcome."

"If you're heated, it is your fault! If we must wait—"

"You wouldn't want to miss the man who juggles with fire."

She stared at him. "I couldn't care less about the man who juggles with fire."

"I think you'll change your mind. Wine, wife. I thirst."

With a playful scowl, she raised the goblet to his lips, tilting it so he had to drink every drop. Then, trying to break his control, she leaned to lick a lingering drop from his lips.

She found that by changing the angle of her body, she could press against his tormenting hand, so she leaned closer. Remembering past occasions, she nibbled at his neck, his ear...

"Matilda, only look how impatient our lovers are for the night," said the king, who sat on Renald's other side. Claire realized with horror that she'd climbed half over Renald in a public place!

"Indeed we are, sire," he said, with apparent calm while stopping her from moving too far away. "A month is a long wait."

461

"But a holy one," said the queen. "It will bring you great blessings. And we can't rush things." She shook a finger at them both. "A little patience here will be good for your souls, as well as whetting your earthly appetites. Anyway, I'm sure Lady Claire won't want to miss the man who juggles with fire. It is wonderfully clever."

"Very true, Highness," said Renald. "In fact, Claire is wild with waiting. Aren't you, love?" His fingers moved, almost depriving Claire of words, but she managed to agree.

"Trust me," Renald murmured. "You *really* don't want to miss Abdul. Ah, here he is."

"I've seen fire jugglers before."

"But Abdul is so good the king keeps him in his personal train."

"Even so—"

He silenced her with a kiss. "Watch. I promise you. You'll never forget it."

"After this, can we go?"

"Yes. I think after this we'll be ready."

The fire juggler was a black man, which added a certain drama. Claire had only seen one Moor before, and in ordinary circumstances she'd want to talk to him of his homeland. At the moment, she simply wanted him to perform, finish, and leave.

He began with fire-eating, quenching fire with his mouth, or gushing out flames like a dragon. He was good, but not good enough to take Claire's mind off Renald's passive hand and her own unquenched fires.

Then Renald's hand began to move.

Claire gasped, welcoming the touch she

ached for, but horrified when they were the focus of so many eyes. Certainly most people were fascinated by the performance, but not everyone.

She tightened her thighs. He *couldn't*!

Then the hall plunged into darkness. As women shrieked and men gasped, Claire realized servants were holding up large boards to cover the windows. In the deep gloom, Abdul's flaming torches spun wild patterns, driven by the juggler's clever hands.

Clever hands.

Renald's clever hand moved against her, then slid right into her. "Stop!" She clutched at the goblet for all she was worth.

"No one can see," he whispered. "No one can hear. Surrender."

The musicians had started a wild, raucous melody to go with the fire, a strident Moorish tune with a harsh drumbeat underneath. It seemed to bounce off the stone walls and up through the floorboards into her thrumming body.

Renald's hand quickened in tempo. In sudden panic, Claire tried to close her thighs, but his leg came over hers, trapping her open as the drumbeat quickened and the torches whirled impossibly fast, dazzling her eyes.

He shifted hands, his right curling around to hold her, to tease her breast. His lips breathed heat on her sensitive neck.

Clutching the edge of the table, Claire pressed back, but not to escape. She no longer cared, even, if the whole world watched. She closed her eyes, and the whirling lights shone red, while music pounded to her soul.

She fought it. A trace of inhibition made her fight. She could not win against such an opponent, but the struggle drove her mad and madder. Like a babe at the breast, she sought his mouth, and drowned in his kiss as she spun into a void of dark silence.

It was only slowly that she realized that the void was real. Somehow the juggler had quenched all his torches at once, and the music had died, creating that dramatic moment.

No, that hadn't been all that had created the moment.

As the servants took away their shields and the last of the sun flooded red into the room, Claire straightened in her seat, closing her trembling legs. Renald slid his hand free and, hot eyes on her, raised it to his lips to kiss it.

Loud applause and cries of approval buffeted her, crazily as if everyone applauded her orgasmic moment.

The king tossed a heavy, clinking purse to the grinning black man. "Well done, indeed! Your skills improve with each performance."

The juggler bowed low. "You give me chance to perfect my art, sire."

The queen leaned forward to speak to Claire. "There, you see. You wouldn't have wanted to miss that, would you?"

Claire couldn't help a weak laugh. "No, Highness. I wouldn't have wanted to miss that, strange though it was."

"Strange?" queried the king. "You have not seen fire jugglers before?"

"Not quite like that, sire."

"I suppose not," he said, with the pride of a patron. "He is remarkably clever."

"Indeed, sire," said Claire, looking at Renald.

"A precious gift."

"How true, sire." She bit her lip and struggled for control. Renald was looking strained.

"I am constantly amazed at what that man can do," the queen remarked. "Such clever hands."

Claire couldn't speak for fear of the giggles.

"Result of years of practice, I suppose," said Renald.

She kicked him under the table. "Perhaps I would like to practice such skills. It would be interesting to create such excitement. Almost ecstasy, wouldn't you say?"

"Now, now, Lady Claire," said the queen, "a gentle lady shouldn't play with fire."

Claire slipped a hand under the table to tease the long bulge there. "Oh, but Highness, I suspect my Lord Renald might quite enjoy a wife who liked to play with fire. Especially with clever hands."

"He might at that," murmured Renald, who looked as if he was fighting private battles.

"My dear," the king said to the queen, "I think it's time to get these two into their bed before abstinence turns their wits." He was straight-faced, but his expression suggested that he had guessed some of their byplay.

"So soon?" said the queen. "But we have a very clever riddler to perform. I'm sure—"

"I'm sure a lady of Summerbourne knows all the good riddles, and would much rather explore other puzzles. Is that not true, Lady Claire?"

She gave him a smile of genuine gratitude. "Very true, sire. Am I to go up to my room with the ladies?" Suddenly she hated the idea of parting from Renald, even for a moment.

As if he guessed, Renald stood and swept her into his arms. "With Your Graces' permission, this is not a true wedding night and I would take my wife and retire."

Claire saw that the queen might have protested, but the king laid a hand over hers. "It is as Renald says, my dear. But we can't do without ceremony entirely. Ho!" he called. "Music for the abstinent couple!"

So the musicians started up a merry march, and soon the whole hall was clapping to time, and laughing. Pelted with raucous advice, Renald carried Claire across the hall and up the wide stone steps. She just hid her face against his chest, desire swelling in her all afresh.

In the room he tossed her on the petal-strewn bed and started to strip off his clothes. After a startled moment, Claire struggled out of her own. As she emerged from her shift, he came down on her for a kiss so wild that it took a moment to realize that he was settling between her thighs.

At last.

At last.

She struggled free of his mouth. "I wanted to say—"

466

He covered her mouth with his hand. "Not now." Watching her, holding himself up off her, he slid inside.

He *was* big, and she felt herself stretching, filling. She remembered Margret saying to tell him how he was doing. She didn't really think Renald needed words, but she mumbled. When he took away his hand, she said, "It feels good."

He laughed, but said, "I'm not hurting you?"

She shook her head. His face fascinated her, tense, yet composed, focused on their slow joining. As she was. She itched and hungered down there, and he was satisfying her. Slowly.

She knew it was costing him to be so slow, but that he did it out of love.

It was a strange sensation, and she moved slightly, trying to adjust. He closed his eyes and sucked in a breath.

She remembered last time and made herself stay still. She didn't want another disaster.

"Still all right?" he asked tightly.

She nodded, then realized he still had his eyes shut. "Yes." Her voice squeaked.

"Push your breasts up."

When she eagerly obeyed, he curled down to suck first at one, then at the other. So much for staying still. Her hips went up. He went deep. Pain cut.

She couldn't stop a cry.

"Pray," he said, "that you are lightly made," and thrust to settle deep within.

"Thank God," he gasped.

"God should indeed be thanked," she said,

stunned to be full of him, and with so little discomfort. "How wonderful a gift, to possess a man this way."

He laughed again, shaking with it as he moved, sliding in and out wetly. It was like but unlike what he had done before. Nothing like anything she'd ever done to herself.

She struggled desperately to stay still, though every muscle in her body screamed to dance.

The heat of his big body heated her. The smell drove her wild. "Can I move?" she gasped, even though she was anyway. She couldn't help it.

"Hell, yes." He put his hands beneath her to help. She didn't need it. She danced in the bed with him to a wild private music, loving the sound, the feel, the slamming of their well-matched bodies.

"I'm glad it's not dark," she gasped, buffeted by the power of his thrusts, wrapped around his hot, hard flesh.

He didn't answer except with a teeth-gritted groan that clearly had nothing to do with her words.

Feeling the whirlpool suck at her, Claire laughed for joy and bit him. She dug her nails into his buttocks as if—impossibly—she could urge him deeper, harder, faster.

More.

More.

More!

Perhaps she shouted it. As she clutched herself around his whole magnificent, rigid body, his groan rumbled through her. No, she couldn't have shouted. Her mouth was full of his shoulder. He collapsed down, rolling and carrying her with him on her side. She had to let go with legs and teeth, but she kept her arms tight around him.

His lips met hers and she tried to eat him. Or that's what it felt like. She wanted to. They were plastered together by sweat, she twined around him any way she could, he binding her to him with strong arms.

By all the saints and angels, marriage was a wonderful thing.

At last, at last, the kiss diminished, the grasping eased, and they relaxed into a softer embrace, but still entwined, still loving with lingering hands.

"All right?" he asked as he had so long ago. He brushed hair out of her eyes, and studied her—but without great doubt.

She stretched, watching him with wonderful, wicked possession. "I'm not sure. I think we'll have to try again."

He fell to laughing, rolling onto his back, pulling her to sprawl over him. She'd never seen him laugh like this before, but it was the true Renald. She knew it.

"Oh, definitely," he gasped. "Perhaps we'll have to hire our own fire juggler, too."

She trailed her hand over his chest. "You mean we can't have so much fun without?"

He kissed her lightly. "We'll just have to be inventive."

Claire moved slightly off him, the better to appreciate the beauty of his powerful body. "I come from inventive stock." She looked at a particular part of his powerful body. "Will it always explode if I touch it?"

"Only if I'm a fool, and try to use God's gift for base ends." He took her hand and brought it to his new erection. "I long for your touch, Claire."

She stroked him, fascinated by every flicker of expression on his face.

He covered her hand. "Let me show you how to make fire."

"I think I know." She escaped and slid down in the bed. "I want to practice fire-eating instead."

Bright sunlight didn't really incline them to leave their bed, exhausted as they were from little sleep and much exercise. Still, as they lay there, idly, lovingly playing with one another's bodies, they mentioned the vague possibility of rising to face the world. And also, a bit more urgently, the thought of eating at some point in the future.

Still, contented exhaustion and physical delight pinned them down.

Finally, Claire realized that she'd never told Renald her thoughts about her father and she went over them for him. "So I see now why you don't feel guilt. I still think Henry killed his brother, but he's probably the best king."

"Yes." He rolled to his side, head propped on hand. "It's not an easy subject. I'd have given my right hand to save your father if I could. He was a good man. A blessing on the earth."

"And yet perhaps he should have been a monk not a baron."

"No. For then he'd not have made his angels."

She touched his face. "It's troubling, isn't it? If he'd not joined the rebellion—if he'd not forced the duel—I would not have you."

"We might have met. Surely we would have known."

Tears threatened at the thought of having Renald and her father both, but Claire fought them away. "I'm sorry he made you kill him."

He didn't brush it off, but kissed her. "Thank you. I confess, I harbored anger, even hatred, for him over that. I thought he intended to die to put point on his cause, and had forced me to be his instrument. That would have been a dark sin. I see now that he really thought he would win."

"If he'd stuck the fight on the issue of whether the king killed his brother, could he have won?"

"Faith says he could. It wouldn't have happened. Such an ordeal would have rested on the king's guilt, and the king would have had to fight. If your father had come even close to that, he'd have died in his room in the Tower."

"Sweet angels," Claire whispered. "The king is not a good man."

"What is good? A king must sometimes be ruthless. It all rests in the end between him and God."

"But," she couldn't resist asking, "what would you have done if the battle *had* been on the subject of regicide? Would you still have fought?"

She realized while speaking that she worried about this, worried about him being the champion of a less-than-perfect king.

He just shook his head. "Claire, don't borrow trouble. Such battles are extremely rare." He looked around. "If we were to call, do you think someone would come with food and drink?"

She decided to let it go. "We could eat each other," she said, putting her fingers to his lips.

He nibbled them, but said, "We've done that. I don't think it can work as permanent sustenance. You don't want me to lose weight, do you?"

But Claire had been struck by another thought. She pushed herself into a sitting position, looking around. "Where's your sword?"

After a moment, he reached and pulled it out from behind the bed. "It's not a matter of trust," he said in response to her unspoken protest. "I just don't take unnecessary risks."

She put her hand on it. "Renald de Lisle, I accept the sword. I don't entirely like it or what it stands for. I'm going to die a little every time you fight, be it tourney or battle. But I accept it. And anyway, it has a holy relic in it." She touched the stone and blessed herself.

Then she took hold of the scabbard to stand the weapon upright against the wall, looming darkly over their marriage bed.

"It is strange," she said, sitting back to study it, "that a weapon look like a cross."

"Don't make another riddle of it." He pulled her to him, but one-handed he retrieved the sword and laid it on the bed before he slid into her. "I don't want it falling on our heads, love."

"I accept the sword," said Claire, and held tight to the black scabbard as his fleshy blade took her to ecstasy.

"By St. Amand," he muttered as they lay together afterward, still stickily joined. "I hope the king doesn't want me out riding today."

She giggled. "Are you sore, too?"

"Only in the most delightful way. But don't tempt me any more, wench."

"Me?" she protested as they wriggled apart. "What do I do?"

"Wriggle. Giggle. Smile. Breath..." He groaned and rolled out of bed to open the door and bellow for food and drink. "What hour do you think it is?" he asked, stretching.

"Perhaps as late as sext." Claire decided that admiring his body was hazardous to her stinging flesh and went to peer out of the long window. "The castle looks in full bustle."

He came up behind her, leaning against her, big, warm, and hard. Her breath caught. "It's a pity we're sore."

He kissed her neck. "We have our lives, love. Keep this position in mind. You might like it. I hear people coming."

Claire hastily slid beneath the covers again. Renald just wrapped a cloth around his waist as Maria, Prissy, and Josce hurried in with platters of food and jugs of ale.

They'd have hovered to see if they could be of further use, but Renald sent them away and he and Claire settled to a long, lazy, and much appreciated meal. They might have slipped into a nap if Josce hadn't returned, announcing rather nervously that they were wanted below.

"Why?" Renald made no attempt to get out of bed.

"The Lady Felice has arrived from Summerbourne and demands to speak to you both."

"Felice!" Claire almost leaped out of bed but decided to spare the squire's blushes. "It must be Mother."

Renald waved Josce away and they both got up and began to wash and dress, Claire in a fever because she feared something terrible had happened.

Renald stopped her and straightened her clothes. "Whatever has happened, happened some time ago. Don't fly into a panic."

"But—"

"This is your Aunt Felice, remember? The one who wanted to come to court."

Claire laughed and calmed. "Oh, of course." After a moment, she added, "Perhaps I'd better see her alone."

"I won't fight you for the honor. But since she's here, I'll see if I can think of any men who might suit her."

She kissed him. "And who'll take Amice as well. Try for someone big and important."

"I thought she fled to escape big."

"You frightened her off with stories of being *too* big!"

"And now, alas, by being able to walk, my bride will announce to the world that I'm a pitifully endowed sort of man."

Claire pushed him and he obligingly collapsed back onto their bed, an interested light in his eye. She shook her head and hurried out to see what excuse Felice had found to rush here to the king's court.

## Chapter 27

"Where's Renald?" Felice demanded. She was pacing in a corner of the crowded hall looking genuinely unaware of the interest of those around. Perhaps she did bring serious news.

"I can summon him if we need him. What's amiss?"

Felice looked around. "I don't want to speak here. Isn't there a private place?"

"Carrisford's bursting. There's a church against the bailey walls. That might be more peaceful."

Felice nodded, so Claire led the way, more concerned by the moment. What could be so troubling that Felice did not want anyone to overhear? Claire had the dreadful fear that it would be something else to do with Renald.

She'd swear on her immortal soul that they now had honesty between them. But what if they didn't?

The small thatched church was cool, dim, and empty.

"So," Claire asked. "What?"

"You think I've made an excuse," Felice accused. "You always think the worst of me."

"Please, Felice. Just tell me what's happened."

Her aunt sniffed. "Nothing's *happened*. I only thought to try to save your life."

"Save my life?"

"There, see. You don't believe me!"

"Yes, yes I do!" There was a stone bench against a wall beneath a narrow window. Claire drew her aunt over to it and sat. "Did you hear that I was attacked on the road?"

"Of course I did. Lord Renald sent half the escort back. That's why I came."

"And you think you know who was behind it?"

"Eudo the Sheriff," said Felice smugly.

"*Eudo!* What possible reason—"

"See! I knew you wouldn't believe me. Renald would have."

"I don't know why you think that." Claire smothered the urge to bicker. "Felice, I'm sorry, but you must admit that it's shocking. Tell me why. You've never been given to wild fancies."

"All right." But Felice still sulked. "Not long after you left to come here, Eudo arrived, saying he wanted to ask more questions about Ulric's death. I doubted that. I saw no evidence all along that he was really trying to find the killer. Well, of course not. He killed Ulric."

"Eudo!" But Claire managed to make it sound astonished rather than disbelieving.

"To hide his involvement in the rebellion."

Claire closed her eyes then opened them again. "Felice, can we start at the beginning?"

Her aunt cocked her head and frowned over it. "No, not really. I have to tell this as it came to me. First, Eudo turning up like that. I wondered what he was up to so I kept an eye on him. As I thought, he hardly spoke to anyone about the murder. But he did try to sneak into the solar a couple of times."

"Why would he do that?"

"Really, Claire. I think your husband has humped the brains right out of you! He wanted Clarence's book."

"Eudo!" And now it was a gasp of recognition. "Of course. *He* was the one who mentioned my leaving a book by the window. He knew because he'd seen it there. In fact, he'd stolen it, but it turned out to be my record book."

"Quite. And he went to the trouble to bring it back. He must be fond of you."

She managed to make that slightly salacious. Claire just said, "He respects books. Fondness didn't stop him attacking me on the road to get Father's book. But why want me dead?"

Felice shrugged. "I think he's beyond reason with fear."

"Because," said Claire, hardly listening, "he saw me reading it and feared I knew whatever it contained."

"What it contained, I assume, was that he, like Clarence, supported Duke Robert."

"I only saw an oblique mention. It was hardly incriminating. And even so—"

"Better safe than sorry."

Claire shook her head. "I can't believe Eudo would want me murdered just in case I'd read something. After all, most of the rebels have been let off lightly."

"Clarence died."

"But only because he insisted on the court battle. At worst, Eudo would have been fined. After all, as best I can tell he didn't join the rebels. He only talked about it a lot."

"Ah," said Felice, "but he killed Ulric. Everyone knows King Henry has pledged to uphold the law. If that crime came out, at the least Eudo would cease to be sheriff—the king's representative in legal matters."

"So why kill Ulric?"

"Because of being sheriff. The king has refused to let rebels administer the law. Eudo's proud of his rank. Proud that it's passed through his family for generations. He couldn't risk losing that. He must have thought it so easy. A servant alone in the garden. But then of course you wouldn't let it lie."

"Ulric turned up," Claire said, "and Eudo panicked. But he wasn't part of the rebellion. We'd have known."

"I think it must have been like this. Clarence rode out with only Ulric in attendance, and he'd arranged to meet Eudo. They were supposed to join Duke Robert's forces together. Eudo must have kept the rendezvous."

"With his own man!" Claire covered her

mouth with her hand. "He died, too." Chilled by this sequence of deaths, Claire rose to pace, thinking it through.

"Eudo talked a lot about supporting Duke Robert," she said, "but he never expected Father to put it into action. No one did. When Father proposed joining the rebellion, Eudo must have been horrified. But he went along with it because he didn't want to look a coward. But, when the day came, he changed his mind."

"Probably tried to talk Clarence out of it," Felice said. "Talk is his main weapon."

"Not anymore." Claire shivered at the memory of that voice whispering, *Kill her*.

"He doubtless thought he'd succeed. Who'd think Clarence would stick to a violent course?"

"But in the end," said Claire, "Eudo turned back. I wonder when he began to fear that ride had been treasonous?"

"Not, at least, until after Duke Robert fled, leaving Henry in full power."

"When we heard that rebels were being fined and removed from offices, Eudo must have been on needles waiting for Father to reveal his part. And then Father died. No one knew. He was safe."

"Until Ulric appeared."

"Angels! Sigfrith *said* Eudo was one of the people who'd spoken to Ulric. That must have been when he arranged to meet him. Once Ulric was dead, he must have thought he was really safe. Until the book turned up. No wonder he was so desperate to read it." She looked at Felice. "But how can we prove any of this?"

"If we bring this to the king, he'll order Eudo put to the ordeal. That will prove his guilt."

Claire shuddered. Ordeal again. Hot iron, cold water, or battle.

With hot iron, the accused had to hold a red-hot iron rod. If at three days the wound had not festered, then God showed that he was innocent. By cold water, the accused was bound and lowered into water. If the water rejected him, if he floated, his guilt was proved. If he sank he was hauled out, proven innocent.

She prayed that Eudo be put to the more merciful cold water.

Surely he wouldn't demand the third option, ordeal by battle. Though fit and trained, Eudo was not really a warlike man.

He had the right, however, to demand to fight his accuser, or his accuser's champion and he might feel his dignity demanded it. In that case, who but Renald would be put to oppose him? He'd said he prayed never to have to fight that way again.

And what if they were wrong?

Renald would die.

"Well?" asked Felice. "Do you not agree?"

"What if we're wrong? What if he's innocent?"

"Then his burn will quickly heal, or he'll sink."

"We could face penalties for false accusation. We could be put to the ordeal ourselves."

Felice frowned at that, but said, "Not when we have so many good reasons for our suspicions."

Claire had to tell the truth. "If it's put to the ordeal, then I think Eudo will demand ordeal by battle. If we're wrong, his opponent will die."

"But we're *not* wrong," said Felice, who was always sure of herself, even when she was totally wrong.

"We'll have to think more about it. After all, Eudo isn't here."

"Oh, but he is." Felice smirked. "I asked his escort. He was only too pleased of an excuse to come and grovel before the man he has so often denounced as unfit to rule."

Claire wanted to scream. She fixed her gaze on the altar, on the flickering candle that showed Christ was present in the form of the host. *Please dear Lord, guide me, so that what I do now be for the good of all. And do not let my path lead to harm for my husband.*

She had choices. She and Felice could go to Eudo and tell him all they knew, and all they suspected. She could make sure that he understood that they wouldn't reveal his crimes unless he sinned again. He was not at heart a bad man, only a coward who had sinned through panic. She remembered his grief over her father's death, and over her own fate. Both had surely been genuine.

That still hadn't stopped him trying to kill her.

Like a rabid dog, he really wasn't safe to leave unchecked.

She could kill him herself. She wasn't sure how, but she knew she could do it to protect Renald. That, however, would be murder, no matter how justified she felt. She would have usurped God's role in dispensing justice.

Heavily she realized that the only right thing to do was to make their accusations public and let justice take its course. It would be put before God through battle, and then, heaven help them if they were wrong.

She turned to where Felice was waiting, idly buffing her nails on her skirt, seemingly without concern. And yet she had come here. True, she'd doubtless wanted to be at court, and wanted to puff off her own cleverness. But she probably truly had wanted to keep Claire safe.

Claire was learning many things, one being that people were never saints or devils, but a complex blend of virtue and weakness.

She wished Eudo *were* evil, someone who clearly should be wiped off the earth. Instead he was a generally decent man who had lost his way and now must die.

For this purpose, it would be good if Renald were pure wolf, able to kill without qualm. But he had a soul, in many ways a gentle one, and killing pained him, particularly the cold-blooded, judicial kind.

She remembered thinking that she would protect the ones she loved, but she saw no option here for hitting anyone over the head with a rock.

"Well?" asked Felice. "I know you have to think everything through ten times over, Claire, but really."

"We had best tell Renald."

"And then, I assume, we will have to explain it all to the king." She rose, smiling, complacently sure that the King of England would be impressed by her courage and beauty.

Touched by the rising sun, the stands held only grim-faced men—and Claire and Felice. As accusers, they were obliged to be here. At the hearing before the king, Renald had tried to assume the role of accuser, but the king had disagreed. No penalty would hover over the Summerbourne ladies, since their story was clearly not based on malice, but every man had the right to face his accusers at all times.

Felice seemed to be quite looking forward to the fight.

Claire's eyes were hot from weeping. The tears were mostly for Eudo, who had clung to his claim of innocence, but who had struggled desperately not to face any kind of ordeal. It had not been a pretty scene.

Renald had turned somber. She didn't blame him. She knew he would hate what he had to do, and could only pray that he wouldn't hate her for it. She would have liked to comfort and receive comfort from him, but she hadn't seen him since late the day before. An ordeal was a holy rite. The participants must fast, pray, and take the host before asking God to stand in judgment.

Her heart ached at the thought of how Renald had first come to Summerbourne. After a night of fasting, and a tragic duel, he'd made a long, storm-pounded journey to face the family of the man he'd killed. Why had she seen only harshness then? Why had she not seen the anguish?

Her heart ached even more with worry. What if they were wrong? What if Eudo was innocent?

She'd put that to Renald in the last words they'd spoken. "What if he's innocent?"

"He's not. His guilt hangs around him like a stink."

"We can't be sure. I'll die if I've sent you to your death."

He'd held her close, even laughing. "Claire, if you don't have faith in me, have faith in God. He will not kill an innocent man in a holy rite."

His faith shamed her. She sat in the stands, praying for the same certainty.

She was hating this in simple terms, too. It had been bad enough watching a show fight. She did not want to witness a fight to the death. Anyone's death.

She was shaking by the time the men walked out into the open space. FitzRoger had taken the seat beside her, and he put a steadying hand over hers. She wished she could cuddle into him like a child, but she must keep her dignity for Renald's sake.

Men-at-arms stood around to form the rough circle. By the king's order, no casual spectators were permitted at this trial.

Renald was all wolf. Why had she forced him to this?

But no. Eudo had forced this battle by maintaining his innocence. A plea of guilty might even have led to the mercy of exile, but he'd clung to innocence with the blank desperation of a drowning man.

He was pale now, his eyes flickering as if seeking some escape. She ached for him, and for his family. But mostly she ached for what opposing such fear would mean to Renald. It would be like slaughtering the Michaelmas goose, without honor or dignity.

Unless, of course, they were wrong and God strengthened Eudo's arm.

Once the men stood before the king, the crier stepped forward. "Hear ye, hear ye! Eudo, Lord Sheriff of Dorsetshire, sworn to uphold the king's peace and law, stands here accused of the murder of his man, Gregory, and of one Ulric of Summerbourne, and of the attempted murder of the Lady Claire of Summerbourne, and of brigandry on the king's highway. Eudo, Sheriff of Dorsetshire, how plead you?"

"Not guilty." But it came out hoarse.

"Who stands to support this accusation?"

"I, Lord Renald of Summerbourne," said Renald firmly. "I claim the right both as Lord of Summerbourne and thus protector of the man Ulric, and as husband of Claire of Summerbourne, my right worthy lady."

"Do you both call upon God," the crier demanded, "to use your bodies to prove justice and right?"

"I do!"

"I do!" But Eudo sounded merely hopeless. Surely, thought Claire, that was proof of his guilt.

*Merciful Christ, let it be over quickly.*

A priest came forward and gave both men a cross to kiss, then sprinkled them with holy water, chanting a blessing. Then the priest anointed them both with holy oil. Eudo began to shake.

When the priest stepped back, the crier announced, "May God show the truth of your cause!" and the king raised his hand.

The two men drew their swords and turned to face one another. For a long moment, nothing happened. Then Eudo slowly sagged to his knees, sword and shield sinking to the ground as if too heavy to be borne.

Was it surrender, or a plea for mercy? There could be no mercy at this point.

Renald swung his mighty sword and beheaded him.

Just like that.

Claire stared at the dismembered body, at the spreading pool of blood, then realized Renald had given his sword to Josce for cleaning and was coming to kneel before the king. FitzRoger had her hand tight in his. She suspected it was to stop her from flinging herself weeping into her husband's arms.

The king raised Renald and kissed him. "We thank you for your service in defense of justice in our realm." Then he turned and left, his great lords following. FitzRoger raised Claire and led her to Renald, who was pushing back his coif and looking remarkably unaffected.

"I definitely must get myself one of those swords," said FitzRoger, passing Claire over.

"I'll escort the Lady Felice back to the keep. Walter of Daventry, you suggested?"

"He's big and in the king's favor. He has children from his first marriage, but only girls. Felice would have the chance to provide the heir. And he's fair but won't put up with nonsense."

When FitzRoger had left with Felice, Renald wrapped a mailed arm around Claire and they followed. "I'm sorry you had to witness that, love."

She was shaking, but tried to match his tone. "At least it was quick."

"As I said once, I'm good at killing."

"Don't!" But then she looked up at him. "You really don't mind, do you?"

He grimaced. "Should I pretend otherwise? I'd have honesty between us. Killing your father was wrenching, but Eudo was no loss to the earth. Such a string of venal crimes sickens me."

Something was bothering her. "Did he admit guilt at the end? Should he not have been offered mercy?"

"Claire, once into the ordeal, the only legal mercy would have been maiming and the loss of all his rights. There's justice in that, but no kindness."

Claire looked back to where Eudo's men were taking away his body. She crossed herself. "God have mercy on his soul."

"Amen." He stopped to look at her. "It's a long day's journey back to Summerbourne, wife, but I'd like to make it. I want to be there, with you, in peace and harmony."

"Oh yes, please!" She pulled a face. "For one thing, the queen's demanding more riddles!"

Summerbourne sat placidly under an opalescent evening sky, thatch dry after days of sun, work over for the day. All the same, people swarmed out to welcome their lord and lady home.

The great gates stood open as they generally did, and so Claire, Renald, and their escort rode in to the dusty bailey, into a milling throng of animals and people.

Lady Agnes was sitting outside enjoying the evening air. Her sharp eyes studied them, and then she smiled. Claire slid off her horse and went over. "Yes, everything has worked out well, Gran."

"Thought it would. What of Felice, then?"

"She's staying for a few days. We have hopes of a certain Lord Walter of Daventry, a mighty man of middle age and lusty appetites."

"I see. And Thomas?"

"Sniffled a bit at parting, but seems to be having a wonderful time. In between beatings."

Lady Agnes chuckled. "And what happened to Eudo the Sheriff?"

Claire told her the story, and her grandmother nodded. "Right and proper. So, with your mother at St. Frideswide's, and Amice doubtless soon to join Felice, you've just me cluttering up the place."

Claire leaned down to kiss her. "What would I do without you, Gran? This is your home, and you'll always have your place by the hearth."

She looked around and saw Renald over by the pigsties. She joined him in watching a litter of piglets chase around squealing. "I hope they won't have to meet their fate so soon."

He turned to wink. "Perhaps I like suckling pig."

"Perhaps, my lord, you can be contented by merely suckling."

His brows rose. "Such sacrifice just for pigs?"

She hooked a finger over his big belt and pulled him to her. "Who said anything about sacrifice?"

He captured her hand and freed himself. "Wife, I think it's time we established some decorum in Summerbourne. We will wait until nightfall. There must be plenty of work to be done after our absence, especially with Felice away for days."

"Oh, very well." Claire looked around. "Let's see. I believe I was intending to show you the middens..."

"Ah. On the other hand"—he took her hand and drew her toward the manor house—"I suddenly see the virtues of a very early night."

# Author's Note

The medieval mind was firm about justice. To them, God's plan was for a peaceful world free of sin, and it was the duty of all God's people to make it so. Wrongdoing required both reparation and punishment. Reparation was usually a payment of money to victims and their families, or to the king. Punishment was often designed to deter others, but to leave the sinner alive and able to repent. Hence the tendency to chop off hands, feet, and/or genitals.

In a time when everyone knew everybody around them, catching criminals wasn't a high art except in the rare case when a crime was committed by an outsider. For this reason, strangers were regarded with deep suspicion, and crimes of stealth, no matter who committed them, were punished most severely. "Murder" was reserved for a crime of stealth, and was punished more severely than a mere killing in a fight or feud.

However, sometimes guilt wasn't clear, and in these cases ordeal was used to settle the matter. Ordeal was by means of hot iron, cold water, or battle, and was a strict ritual administered by the Church. In fact, it almost became a sacrament along with baptism, marriage, and extreme unction.

In ordeal by hot iron, the accused person had to grasp a red-hot rod and carry it a fixed distance. The burn was then bound and inspected in three days. If it was healing, God had shown that the person was innocent.

If it had begun to fester, then the person was guilty.

Rather preferable, perhaps, was ordeal by cold water. The accused was tied up and lowered into the water on a rope. If he sank, he was innocent. (No, he wasn't left to drown, but hauled out still able to celebrate.) If he floated, he was guilty and dragged off for punishment.

Ordeal by battle was much rarer, but it wasn't reserved for nobles and knights. It was most often used when two people accused each other of crimes, or as a kind of civil prosecution when the law wasn't clear. (This lingered as the duel, and in fact was still a possible judicial solution until 1819.)

In ordeal by battle, or a court battle, the men fought to the death, no holds barred. The weapon was usually a stick, and it soon became a wrestling, gouging, stomping brawl. However, there are instances of more knightly duels with swords, and that is what I have shown in this book.

As with the Brave Child Sebastian, there were stories of duels between children and mighty warriors, and actual cases where a weak man defeated a strong. It was even possible for a woman to challenge a man, in which case the man was buried up to his waist in the ground as a handicap.

I recently attended a lecture on the risks of ordeal, and I'd like to share some of the points with you because I found them fascinating. Margaret Kerr, a barrister, has studied records of ordeals and found that remarkably few went against the accused. She speculates that ordeal was often used by the Church as a way of providing mercy in harsh times.

Certainly William Rufus—the king before Henry Beauclerk—was not at all pleased when fifty men accused of breaking the Forest Laws were put to the ordeal of hot iron and all passed. In fact, his reaction to this was to decide that God was too easily persuaded to mercy by prayer. Since a king was much tougher minded, in future he would decide who was guilty and who was innocent.

Perhaps this was another reason for that wayward arrow in the New Forest!

The low rate of conviction led Ms. Kerr to investigate the techniques of hot iron and cold water. (Ordeal by battle doesn't enter into this, because one of the two must lose.)

She found that today, severe burns often don't fester by three days, and can even look healed. The accused would only fail this test if the iron was too cool and gave only a second-degree burn.

Ordeal by cold water is even more interesting. You may have noticed that earlier I referred to people being tested by cold water as male. That's because this test was never done on women until the much later witch-hunting period. Men generally have a much lower ratio of body fat than women, and in modern studies it has been shown that a bound man rarely floats in cold water unless he's notably fat.

(Want to bet that those witch-hunters had

this all figured out? Let's talk about the persecution of women sometime.)

A guilt factor can enter in, of course. With hot iron, moisture on the skin might make a difference, so a guilty person's clammy hands might be disastrous.

With water, a fit man can float if he has a lot of air in his lungs. Guilt might lead to panic, which might lead to sucking in extra air. In one case, an abbot was implicated in a crime and set to undergo the ordeal by cold water. He repeatedly checked himself out in a big tub of water to be sure he would sink. Every time, he did.

Come the day, however, he floated. Presumably, panic caused him to suck in breath. Was his panic caused by guilt, and by his belief that God knew his secrets? We'll never know.

His panic is understandable, however, because he *chose* the ordeal. Anyone always had the option of confession, and the civil powers preferred this. The Church also approved, since it was the step to repentance and salvation. Therefore, the penalties for those who underwent an ordeal and failed were harsher than for those who confessed.

There are a few interesting records of ordeal by cold water that describe the accused being trussed up with their knees to their chest. At first glance, this might seem harsher, but in fact it's a sign that someone really wanted them to get off. It's much more difficult to float like that, and almost impossible to take a deep breath of air.

So how does this finagling mesh with the medieval interest in justice?

Then as now, there was a sense of right and wrong that overrode the actual laws. If people didn't see the crimes as wrong—as with violations of the Forest Laws—ordeal could get around the king's laws.

In addition, however, ordeal was doubtless often used in an honest sense—requesting God to clarify an uncertain case so that reparation and punishment could wipe the evil from the community.

For many reasons, however, ordeal fell into disrepute. (Interestingly, one of the objections was religious. Some theologians thought it wrong for anyone to demand a service of God, as those undergoing ordeal did in demanding that God be their judge.) The jury system had always been around, and in 1215 ordeal by hot iron or cold water was forbidden by the Pope and judgment by one's peers became the norm.

As I said earlier, however, this didn't affect trial by battle.

I hope you enjoyed this story. If you missed it, the story of Imogen and FitzRoger is told in *Dark Champion*, published by Avon Books in 1993. He appears briefly in another novel, *The Shattered Rose* (Zebra, 1996) and the hero of that book is the crusader who brought back that stone from Jerusalem.

I write historical romances set in three periods: the early medieval, the Georgian around 1760, and the Regency. My next novel from Topaz is set in 1814 and involves a plain, prosaic heroine; an eccentric, enigmatic earl; and a magical Irish statue that grants wishes—but always with a sting in the tail. Look for it on the shelves the end of this year.

And speaking of magic, I hope you found a special collection called *Faery Magic*, out in January 1998. All the stories are set in the Regency, but in places where the real world intersects with the dark world of Faery. My story is called "The Lord of Elphindale." Yes, I know I said that story would be in a 1996 collection, but this time there's no mistake.

Romance novels have a magic of their own, bringing love, light, and laughter into the world. Romance readers are wonderful people who believe in looking for solutions and working with others. Never let anyone denigrate romance books or readers and get away with it.

I am always pleased to hear from readers. Please write c/o my agent, Alice Harron Orr, 305 Madison Ave #1166, New York, NY 10165. I appreciate a SASE to help with the cost of a reply.

Or e-mail me at wp823@freenet.victoria.bc.ca

My web page is at WWW.sff.net/people/jobeverley.